By Roopa Farooki

Bitter Sweets
Corner Shop
The Way Things Look To Me
Half Life
The Flying Man

THE Flying MAN

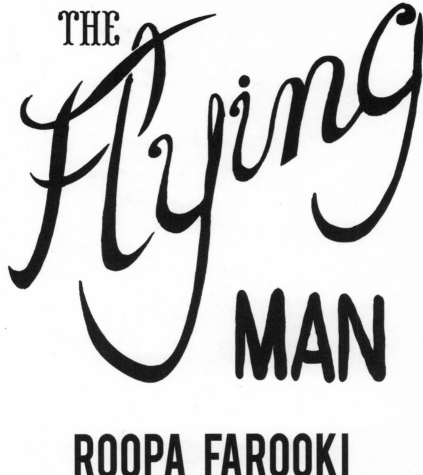

THE Flying MAN

ROOPA FAROOKI

headline
review

First published in 2012
by HEADLINE REVIEW
An imprint of HEADLINE PUBLISHING GROUP

1

Cataloguing in Publication Data is available from the British Library

ISBN 978 0 7553 8338 2 (Hardback)
ISBN 978 0 7553 8339 9 (Trade paperback)

Typeset in Sabon by Avon DataSet Ltd,
Bidford-on-Avon, Warwickshire

Printed and bound in Great Britain by
Clays Ltd, St Ives plc

Headline's policy is to use papers that are natural, renewable and
recyclable products and made from wood grown in sustainable forests.
The logging and manufacturing processes are expected to conform
to the environmental regulations of the country of origin.

HEADLINE PUBLISHING GROUP
An Hachette UK Company
338 Euston Road
London NW1 3BH

www.headline.co.uk
www.hachette.co.uk

For my children, Jaan, Zaki, Zarena and Alia,
with all my love

He'd fly through the air with the greatest of ease,
That daring young man on the flying trapeze.

George Leybourne, 'Champagne Charlie'

When, in disgrace with fortune and men's eyes,
I all alone beweep my outcast state
And trouble deaf heaven with my bootless cries
And look upon myself and curse my fate . . .

Yet in these thoughts myself almost despising,
Haply I think on thee . . .
   For thy sweet love remember'd such wealth brings
   That then I scorn to change my state with kings.

extract from William Shakespeare, Sonnet XXIX

Biarritz, France – 2012 – Showtime

HE'S WRITING A LETTER HE NEVER INTENDS TO POST, BUT
which he knows will one day be found. It might be in his jacket
pocket or in his suitcase, or maybe here just moments from now
(why not?) on the vinyl-surfaced bureau of the cheap hotel, once
his pills finally stop working, once that whirling gang of his old-
man maladies finally catch up with him and drag him down,
jackals tearing into their prey on the ground. After he's found
lying there, twitching and helpless, the letter will be discovered,
carefully unfolded, and it will answer all their questions,
that motley crew of the casually abandoned, the tearful and
indifferent, the largely harmless and charmless. (He pities them,
now, in the ambiguous way one would pity a slow, defective
child that you know deserves affection more than pity, in the
way that one would pity the brave and brittle smiles of
the parents of that same child who must offer the affection, the
protection, that the world does not.) His unfortunate tribe. His

Family and Friends. This humble letter, on hotel stationery, is misleadingly dated the day after tomorrow – he can't help himself, little deceits such as these remind him that for the moment, at least, he is alive, and this deceit in particular promises that he will still be alive in two days' time. He has always made his promises for the day after tomorrow; after all, tomorrow comes too quickly to fob off whoever is after him – his former business associates, his latest wife, his children, his creditors, his doctors, Death – but the day after tomorrow is neither so close that he has to make plans to actually do what he promised, nor so far that people will suspect that he will do nothing at all. This flimsy scrap, scrawled by his ancient hands, gnarled with stiff bones and bulging veins, his paper skin dotted with brown spots and broken by roughly red eczema, his once impetuous and slapdash handwriting now simply scratched and barely legible, may be the most important thing he has ever written. It will bear witness when they finally get him – when they beat him up and slap him down, those yobs in the shadows of an alley – it will say what he no longer can, and pay his final debts. It may even provide salvation of sorts, and ensure his immortal legacy – in this world, if not the next.

He realises, as he struggles to read back what he has written, that it is getting dark, that the streets outside are silent apart from the occasional lonely car, and the dog barking in the distance. That he is an old man beginning to write the letter of his life in the failing light, in the quiet dignity of the bare room, where plastic wallpaper peels up from the painted skirting in scrolls. A timeless pose, something to be brushed on paper, preserved in paint. An image of quiet dignity himself. He is suddenly furious with his preposterous posturing – he is no firefighter trapped in a burning building, calling out to his wife that he loves her, he is no family man on a crashing commercial jet bidding a tearful farewell to toothy kids called Sport and Scout, he is no military hero telling his men it was an honour to serve with them amidst the sound of sniper fire – he despises his pretension, rejects the inevitable pity they will feel for him when they find him. Perhaps he should abandon the letter, or just leave the hotel to trace it out in the coarse moonlit sand the full length of the Biarritz Grande Plage, and then sit back on a wrought-iron bench and watch the waves swarm in to lick over it like flies on a wound, blurring the lines and finally lifting it away into the Atlantic.

'That's the trouble with pity. You can give it out, but you can't take it yourself,' says a voice, amused rather than adversarial. He knows that the voice is his, that it must be, one way or another; he is alone in the room. He supposes that it is the voice of his dementia, his swansong into senility, his chirping cricket of a conscience. It is a voice that comes from somewhere deeper than his conscious mind. From his hollow chips of bone. From his smears of stubbornly clinging marrow. From his doubtful soul. He hears it so often, these days, that it has started to irritate the hell out of him. He has had enough of posing as the subject of a muted watercolour. He flicks the switch, and drowns the cell-like solemnity of the room in a flood of harsh electric light, the furniture suddenly orange and lurid green, as bright and sinister as a clown at a children's party. The silence is still unnerving, it leaves too much blank space for the voice to fill, and so he flicks on the TV as well, bolted high on the ceiling where it can't be stolen or spat upon, and fills the air with canned laughter instead. It's an American comedy – one of those generic, successful ones with a fat husband and skinny wife – expertly dubbed into French. He had hoped for an inoffensive quiz show, he has recently developed a mild addiction for the French version of *Who Wants to Be a Millionaire?*, but his disappointment passes. After all, the skinny wife is quite attractive, even with her nasal whine, and the persistence of the laughter is curiously compelling; after writing a few more lines, he lets his pen roll aside, and sits on the bed to watch. Looking up gives him a crick in the neck, and he is soon forced to ease back into a more comfortable position, leaning against the plastic padding of the headboard, his feet up on the bed, still in his newly polished shoes. The bedspread is bobbled, and orange and green as well. That fat man won't live too long, thinks Maqil, watching the skinny wife reward his various witty insights with meatloaf and doughnuts; the man shovels the food in with a gusto that seems as much to do with appetite as acting. How many takes of the scene before this one that made the final cut? How many plates of meatloaf and doughnuts did the actor digest? He'll be dead in his fifties, Maqil reflects drily. He'll certainly die before his skinny screen wife, even if she has cigarettes for supper and a coke habit. He might even die before me; he considers this last possibility with a certain satisfaction.

This cheerful train of thought reminds him of something he told his son a little while ago – an unremarkable young man who swapped his school uniform for a banker's suit in his teens, and has never changed since. Harmless and charmless. His son is married to a pious American girl whose parents are from the Punjab, and has recently become a father himself. He has a safe job, a solid house of brick, a wife and a child; his life is conventional, respectable, deplorable. Perhaps Zamir is aware of his father's poor opinion – he seems to be in permanent mourning for something, with that dry-cleaned charcoal suit and that dry-cleaned sober expression; he travels in black limos from the Charles de Gaulle and Orly airports for business in Paris, and makes a point of seeking out his father when he's in town, and arranging to meet him to serve up his concern over aperitifs. Sometimes Maqil is vain enough to think that his son doesn't have meetings in Paris at all; that Zamir simply turns up

4

to check up on him, because he still cares, and isn't brave enough to admit it. He had told his son, he had boasted even, Everyone Thinks I'm Dying, But I'm not Dead Yet! Zamir had sipped his coffee rather nervously (he no longer drank; he had rediscovered his Muslim roots since his marriage), but hadn't commented, which had annoyed Maqil into listing all those he had outlived – those younger and healthier than he, those who had never been chased down by debt or angry pike-bearing villagers, those who weren't being systematically choked by the creeping vines of heart disease, high blood pressure and everything else. 'What about Akbar? Do you see him much?' Zamir finally asked, mentioning Maqil's old friend from the sixties who had moved back to Paris some years ago, a flamboyant Egyptian queer who had once insisted on entertaining Zamir and his wife in one of the greasiest Chinese restaurants in his arrondissement, fondly telling Maqil's daughter-in-law that the duck was to die for. 'I'm sure someone has,' she had muttered under her breath to her husband, looking around with obvious disapproval at the grubby walls, discoloration blooming with mould on the rising damp, and for some reason Maqil was insulted by her lack of manners, even though he had been thinking exactly the same thing himself. When she just bobbed her head as the waiter dumped the steaming baskets on their table, acknowledging the service with the barest of condescending smiles, Maqil snapped at her, 'What, you can't say thank you?'

'I nodded, I smiled,' she had said defensively, glancing quickly at Akbar, who was obliviously flirting with the restaurant owner, and then between her husband and her father-in-law, suddenly embarrassed that she had fallen into that subtly offensive group, the moneyed middle class who dress well and perform public charitable acts but who are rude to receptionists and people who work in restaurants. She was pregnant at the time, with Maqil's first and only grandchild, and placed a hand protectively over her bump, as though this provided her with an excuse.

'Nodded and smiled,' he repeated loudly, and then, spurred on by her apparent discomfort, added, 'Who do you think you are, the bloody Queen?' He had said it in French, with calculated malice, knowing that everyone in the restaurant would understand perfectly, apart from her, who would barely understand at all. No wonder his son now made these visits on his own; he probably used work as an excuse to hide them from his wife altogether.

'Akbar died earlier this year,' Maqil finally answered, with a little pride glittering inappropriately in his voice. 'He was almost twenty years younger than me. Twenty years! I could have been his father, but one little heart attack, and pop.'

'I'm very sorry to hear that,' his son said. His tone was much more appropriate, but he sounded polite rather than sorry; in fact, it seemed to Maqil that he was motivated as much by his eagerness to sound polite as by politeness itself. He wondered whether his own death would merit these same words from his family members, with the same banal formality. Sincerity, he supposed, would be too much to ask for.

'Pop!' he repeated, as though the word itself was somehow delightful. He found himself putting on his Chacha Zafri's Punjabi accent in subtle mockery, just to goad a reaction. 'I've had heart attacks all over the world. London, Rome, Hong Kong. And a bypass. Ugly great cut down my chest. I might have joined the zipper club, but I never went pop . . .'

'I remember the heart attack in Rome,' said his son thoughtfully, as though determined to reminisce, as though their roles had been suddenly reversed, and he was the old man at the table, recalling a golden childhood from a simpler age. 'We threw coins in the Trevi Fountain. And I remember the bypass operation, you had that back in London. We went walking with you in Hyde Park afterwards. The daffodils were out.'

'The daffodils...' Maqil repeated despite himself; he remembered them too, impertinently yellow and stiffly upright against the mushy green of the park. He had only ventured to Hyde Park a few times that year; his hay fever had been particularly bad, and had bothered him after the surgery. He began complaining truculently: 'And who was that bullshit bastard who sent all those flowers to the hospital – trying to kill me in my sleep with the bloody pollen? Why didn't he just come in with a pillow and smother me then and there?'

'Those flowers were beautiful,' said his son, 'Amma managed to fill every vase in the flat with them.' Maqil's eyelids flickered briefly as Zamir mentioned his mother; this happened rarely, as they did not discuss her with tacit agreement. Maqil never asked his son how she was doing, as they both knew that no answer would satisfy him; he did not want to think of her alone and unhappy, he certainly didn't want to think of her happy with someone else. In fact, Maqil tried not to think of Samira at all, but there was a guilty pleasure whenever he did, a little like a recovering alcoholic inhaling the dregs of wine left in a stranger's glass at a bar, a sensation as grubby as nostalgia, as delightful as eavesdropping. Samira, a slap in the face, and the love of his life, eloping with him to the mountains, singing with him off-key in the wilderness, casually signing an assumed name with him at the Ritz, and stalking society by his side; Samira, the mother of his children, walking away from him with the click of her smart heels, and never glancing back. She had always known him so well; she had beaten him at his own game. He liked to think that wherever she was, she was trying not to think about him either. 'I don't know who sent them, but it was a lovely gesture, whoever it was,' added Zamir, a touch reproachfully, obviously unaware of his faux pas. There was something rather womanish in the way he said 'beautiful' and 'lovely'; but then there had always been something womanish about his son generally; possibly, it was that telltale propensity of his to care. It was the way he cared as much for *how* something was said as for what was said; as a child, it had been frustratingly easy to reduce him to tears with a careless turn of phrase. Zamir wasn't tearful now, at least, but seemed tired and a little disappointed; finishing his coffee with a long sigh of a sip, he glanced over at his father's empty glass of pastis. 'So, are you ready?' he asked. Maqil ignored him, and carried on as though he hadn't spoken.

'Maybe it'll take a pillow, in the end. Everyone's expecting me to die, everyone thinks I'm going to die any minute now, but I just go on. Living. Outliving. Everyone. Even Akbar. They all say, "Come home, Bhai, Come home, Bhai",' he whined, now imitating his almost-as-elderly sister. ' "Come home to Pakistan, we'll treat you like a king." What they really mean is, come home to die, so you don't inconvenience us by dying abroad and alone. Come home to die, so we don't have to pay the shipping fees for your withered carcass in a wooden box. Come home and die! Everyone thinks I'm dying, but I'm not dead yet!'

'So, are you ready?' his son repeated, looking at his phone. 'My limo's here. You're still sharing my ride to the airport, right?' He looked around the railway-station café, and scribbled across the palm of his hand when he finally caught the eye of the waitress. She brought the bill over, and he pulled his credit card out of his wallet.

'Tch, put that away,' Maqil muttered, suddenly offended. He emptied a shrapnel of coins out of his pocket, and paid the bill himself, with a generous tip. The waitress nodded with approval at this fulfilment of parental duty, but he noticed as he glanced at his son's card that Zamir shut his wallet swiftly, and then put it firmly back in his pocket with a bit too much emphasis.

Someone must have warned him, his sister most likely. Maqil saw his daughter much less often than his son, and she always treated him with politely edged caution – as though he were a guest at a house party suspected of stealing the silverware. It amused Maqil that his children thought he'd go to the trouble of card fraud; it flattered him that they thought he could still learn sixteen digits by glancing at them; the truth was that his memory wasn't what it used to be.

'I'm not ready,' he said eventually. 'There's a problem with my prescriptions, I need them to show the doctors in Pakistan. They're not done as yet.'

'When will they be done?' asked his son. 'I could get a different flight and wait. I could even stay in a hotel tonight and go in the morning – I'd just need to call home, and clear it with work.'

'Day after tomorrow,' Maqil said.

Zamir looked straight at him. 'Day after tomorrow?' he repeated. His clean-shaved face rippled briefly with a wave of disbelief; his mouth twitched unexpectedly with something that could have promised the onset of tears after all, or even rueful amusement. But then his face set back into place, smooth and sinless, with a heavy, familiar sigh. Disappointment, yet again. Maqil wondered how many times he could keep on disappointing his children and get away with it. He'd spent his life getting away with it, and getting away from them. His son was shaking his head, but then he got up and straightened his jacket, before asking quietly, 'I guess you're going back to Biarritz, then? Tonight, on the fast train.' Maqil nodded. He didn't know why his son sounded so reproachful – Zamir must have known that he wasn't really going to the airport with him, that he wasn't going back to Pakistan to die; he must have known the moment he had seen his father turn up at the café without his case. Unless Zamir had simply assumed he had left his luggage

9

at the hotel, so he could skip out without paying the bill. It wouldn't, admittedly, have been the first time.

Maqil held out his hand, with the instinctive politeness he would show to anyone, but his son put his arms around him instead, carefully, as though aware of his fragility, his hollow bird-bones. They had never been much for hugging in the past, but every time they said goodbye these days, his son chose to hug him with ceremonial deliberation, as though it might be the last time. It both touched and exasperated him. 'Not dead yet,' he said. 'Remember.'

'I guess I'll email the folks in Pakistan, and tell them to expect you . . . day after tomorrow.' Zamir said this lightly, shaking his head again, like a careless actor about to break role with a laugh, winking to the audience. But he didn't laugh, he didn't wink; he remained resolutely calm, as though keeping a private vow. Maqil wasn't sure why this illusion was so important to his son, after all that had happened between them; the unconvincing little play they put on at each meeting, that he was a dutiful son hugging his father, that he was an ordinary father behaving as might be expected, paying for drinks, taking prescription medication and planning to go back to his family home in Pakistan. He didn't really understand his son's dogged refusal to acknowledge out loud that he was a corrupt old hobo, dying in debt, in cheap digs in a glamorous seaside resort that was less than glamorous out of season. Who had given him those flowers, all those years ago, the extravagant hand-tied bouquet from Harrods? The flowers that his son remembered, and had thought were beautiful. It was possible that the bouquet hadn't been delivered to his hospital room by his enemies, after all, but the truth was that he disliked acknowledging the existence of friends. Real friends. Stormy-weather, thick-and-thin friends who sent flowers on appropriate occasions and who didn't just hang around when he had money to spare. He had always preferred to buy his friends; it seemed cleaner and more honest than tricking people into messy affection, reeling them into emotional dependence with his charming conversation and apparent interest in their personal concerns; these days, however, conversation was all he had to offer, it was the only bait on his hook, because talk, at least, was cheap. Talk was what he brought with him to the marble-topped café table, sitting with his son in these stilted little interviews, each one slightly shorter than the last. Each one leading inevitably closer to the shortest meeting of all, a hello followed by a final goodbye. Perhaps this is what he wants from him; this is why he maintains the illusion of propriety: Zamir is waiting for a final goodbye, a valediction to expiate all the times his father left him without saying a word. A magic closing line to their story that might illuminate and justify all that has happened before; a door closing on a clean, bright room.

His son walked him to his train, which was already waiting on the platform. It was no coincidence; Maqil had timed their meeting to his convenience. Zamir stood at the barrier, watching him as he made his way down the length of the train to the second-class carriages; aware of his son's gaze, Maqil was suddenly too conscious of his cane, and found himself trying to use it as little as possible. He thought Zamir would have gone by the time he finally climbed the steps to the carriage, an overly helpful middle-aged lady dashing forward to assist him, despite his waved protests; he clearly appeared much more feeble than he felt. But when he turned, he saw that his son was still there, a blurred figure in the distance, his sensible grey overcoat buttoned over his suit jacket, falling to his knees. There was something about the set of his shoulders in the coat, something a little sad, and defeated – perhaps Zamir was thinking the same of him, his ailing father in his once-presentable raincoat. He knew that he had failed his son, in unique and various ways, but now he was suddenly wondering whether his son thought he had failed him in his turn, on this unremarkable afternoon. He had lied, and his son had accepted his lie without criticism or comment; Zamir had failed to argue, failed to strong-arm him into a limo and on to the plane. He had failed to prolong his father's life. Maqil unreasonably resented his son's infuriating acceptance. His dumb acquiescence. It took almost all the fun out of lying in the first place.

Maqil has dozed off briefly; he only realises that the comedy has finished when he hears that voice again: 'You can give it out, but you can't take it yourself.' Sometimes the voice echoes unbidden into a chorus around him. It speaks all the languages that he speaks – although on occasion he thinks it speaks better Spanish than he ever did. He tries not to let it bother him unduly; he knows it is just a symptom, an addition to that tiresome list of diseases and maladies, something to be managed and medicated along with his weak heart and high blood pressure. It is occasionally entertaining, but he still wishes it could just be switched off, like the television, and he could be the man he was before it took him over.

He moves off the bed, awkwardly, as his limbs and back are stiff. He is beginning to feel weighed down by his thin, saggy body; sometimes he supposes that he deserves the sunken face and the flimsy flesh he has ended up with. But sometimes it feels unfair; sometimes, deep inside, he feels every bit as vital as when he was a young man, with a song in his heart, careless and utterly carefree. Leading a life as light as a bird in flight. Cycling through the dry, dusty streets of Lahore, pungent with fruit sellers and the sticky sweetness of ice-cream vendors, walking animatedly through his college halls in New York, through the bone-white light of Cairo, the damp elegance of Paris, the indifferent smartness of London, the humid smog of Hong

Kong, and finally here, the siren song as strong as ever in his triply attacked and once bypassed heart, the song itself unchanged. 'Everything changes, but I have not,' he says out loud, unembarrassed to be addressing himself in the mirror, pleased with the way the words sound. He has declared what he has always suspected, that he is more consistent than Everything, he who has been so often criticised for changing so frequently: his home, his country, his profession, his spouse. His name.

It is finally dark outside, and the night looks soft and welcoming, a velvet glove to slip into. 'Showtime,' he says, to himself, to that persistent but succinct voice that frequently addresses him, and he goes to the small suitcase precariously balanced on the edge of the bureau, and flips open the lid. The case is packed, beautifully. He always keeps it packed, in case he decides to leave on a whim or in a hurry, travelling with a capsule wardrobe that fits as precisely and with as much thought to organisation as a jigsaw; if he ever needs to add something new, he throws something else out. He can pack and find any item he needs in his sleep, in the dark, with angry voices banging on a door, in the precious seconds when an aggressor is occupied with an insult or glancing at their watch or phone; he does this with the indifferent, instinctive skill of a typist letting her fingers click-clack over a keyboard – he doesn't need to think, he doesn't need to look. But tonight, the room is brilliantly lit, and the only urgency is the one he feels inside, telling him to get out on to the damp streets and put on a show, to rejoin life in the way one would wander back into a party that has been carrying on in another room. He pulls out the expensive cashmere blazer that his third wife bought him, and a fresh shirt, leaving blazer-shaped and folded-shirt-shaped holes in the interior of the case, waiting for their safe return. He shakes both out – the blazer doesn't crease, so it doesn't matter that the shirt has. The trousers that he is already wearing are smart enough, and appear to have escaped any sauce stains from his lunch, so he doesn't bother to change them. He selects sapphire cufflinks from a small metal box, and combs his thinning hair. He is proud of his hair, still so soft and straight, and still with black among the grey – he lets it grow too long sometimes, because of this small vanity, lets it divide on his collar carelessly and elicits sympathy from young waitresses, who assume he isn't taking care of himself, and take greater care of him themselves, with an extra cup of coffee, or an extra sugar biscuit, gritty and golden as sand, on the side of his saucer. His comfortable jumper is removed, folded, replaced, and he pushes his arms through the sleeves of the shirt, linking the cuffs, putting on the blazer and brushing away an invisible speck of lint and another of dandruff; he feels just as light hearted as a woman preparing for a date with lipstick and heels. He feels just as much glittering-eyed anticipation. In his trouser pocket, the pile of notes is fastened with a fat gold clip. Tonight he might double, triple his money, or lose it all. The truth is, he doesn't mind which – it's playing the game he loves. The game won't really be lost until he stops, and he never intends to. He is a man, after all, of few vices: he drinks in moderation, he doesn't smoke except the occasional cigar out of sociable politeness, he has been faithful to each wife, and uniquely faithless in a way that has nothing to do with personal intimacy and everything to do with personal integrity. He is a man with just one vice, in fact, one true calling; he is a man with one true love.

He leaves the room, leaves the hotel, and walks to the casino, his limbs less stiff with every step, his cane less necessary and more of an accessory with every increasingly flamboyant tap. He is eighty-one, and he is eighteen, and he has refused a comfortable ride to the airport because he is not going home to Pakistan to die. Not tonight, not tomorrow, and not the day after. He is living, rudely living, and at this moment, in this drizzle-softened starless night, he loves life, and he loves himself so much that no else needs to. He will enter the casino and be greeted with respect, by his current name, and be welcomed with the warm sincerity reserved for the big spenders. He will order dinner, and be charming, and unfailingly cordial to the people who work in the restaurant. He will go to the tables in the windowless rooms where night never turns to day, and he will play, play, play until a small crowd gathers around him, stunned by his insouciance, his audacity, his disease. That daring young man on the flying trapeze. It's showtime. It's playtime. He will not think about Samira, and he will not think about the letter he has started. The letter of his life will wait on the bureau. It is dated the Day After Tomorrow, after all. There is no need, as yet, to scratch it into the moonlit sand. There is no need to finish it tonight.

Lahore, The Punjab – 1931 – Birth

THE TRUTH IS THAT I'M NOT MUCH OF A LETTER-WRITER – I've always been lousy at keeping in touch with people, as any of my wives will delight in telling you, and there's something serious about letters. They can be kept as evidence, filed for posterity, and read again and again. I'm better at destroying the evidence than leaving it behind. But I do like telling stories. Stories are easy, they're just about entertainment. I change the names sometimes, not to protect the innocent, but to let the guilty have a head start. It seems that these days I only have two stories left to tell. His, and mine. The road up, and the road down. So, are you sitting comfortably? More importantly, am I? I suppose it doesn't matter really, where I sit. It's just another café with rattling metal stools, just another hotel with under-stuffed, sweaty-looking upholstery, another pine-scented cab ride from here to there. It's how we Pakistanis of a certain class and age tend to live – in a series of air-conditioned rooms, moving between them in air-conditioned cars; we instinctively hold our breath when leaving the porch for the Merc. We never see the sky if we can help it. So we're all comfortable. You and Me and He. We're ready for a little light entertainment. Well then, let's make a start. Where we start is easy enough – we'll start at the beginning. Once upon a time. A long time ago.

My story begins with my mother, whose name was Maryam. She was a renowned local beauty, privately educated at home, accomplished, and always, I assume, a little resentful of the limits that had been placed upon her. By her sex, by her class, by her religion, by her nationality. She came from a well-off Muslim family in the Punjab. She could not hope to become a doctor or an engineer, like her brothers, she could not hope to be a musician, a writer or a poet, except in frustrated privacy. She could not hope to sing, to perform plays or star in movies, as singers and actresses were classless whores. Her various talents were nurtured by her loving, realistic family, who opened her mind with enthusiastic tutors and free access to novels of genius, and then shut the door with parental firmness. She had only one path in life, one occupation to which to aspire – to be a beloved wife and a loving mother. She knew she was allowed no ambition higher than having children, who might eventually do what she could not.

By the age of fourteen, she had already received several offers. Her parents gave her the illusion of choice, sharing the similarly posed portraits and particular achievements of her suitors with her, indulging her with mischievous gossip about those they had rejected on her behalf, the pocked complexion of one and the alarming stutter of another. When she was sixteen, they let her meet the most eligible who had been presented to them. They chose the boy – barely a boy; he was twenty-one – not because of his own charms, but because of his parents'. Husbands were relatively easy to manage, but in-laws were not;

their prized daughter, the jewel of their family, would be living in the household of her husband's parents, and until they died, she would have to abide by their rules. Her parents were careful to select in-laws who were not so superior that they would look down on their daughter and treat her like a slave, but not so inferior that they would be eaten up with jealousy at having to support an overeducated princess in their home. They found a family just the right side of grateful, with a son they had educated abroad but who would remain in Pakistan. The man and the young girl met, several times, at staged family gatherings; they shared tea, sweets and samosas, but barely managed to look each other in the face. They married without romance; but they did what was expected of them, and more.

When I was born, my father wasn't allowed to attend the birth. My family was sufficiently enlightened to arrange for a hospital birth, the hospital was sufficiently traditional to keep husbands outside; only Maryam's mother and mother-in-law were allowed into the room, painted white, poorly lit, and smelling of damp and disinfectant. Maryam, cosseted at home her entire life, was a physical coward. She screamed and swore and vomited, as contractions churned and shuddered her insides, she pissed and shat on the bed, she wept with the indignity as much as with the pain, and finally, twenty hours later, I emerged, bloody and too tired from our combined labour to manage more than a couple of plaintive shrieks and a lacklustre suckling. The fortune-tellers had predicted a girl, and everyone had been steeling themselves for this – to accept and love a girl. But when they saw I was a boy, they no longer pretended any diplomacy; they were all too delighted to hide their relief. 'My Sonny,' murmured my mother, watching me nuzzle ineffectively at her breast. 'My little son.' At seventeen years old, she had achieved what women of that era dreamt of – a firstborn son. She should have been given a medal on a podium and a marching band. And there I was – a scrap of naked humanity, a surprisingly small morsel of flesh for the enormous bump she had shown off so proudly, with a squashed old-man face, but still loved and adored, simply because I was their son. I had nothing more to do than breathe to be loved. And so I breathed for them. While my grandmothers urged me, and the midwife slapped my buttocks and pinched my cheeks, and my mother held me in her arms, I yelled, albeit weakly. I breathed their love; I inspired it.

Like most perfect moments, this one was short lived, as Maryam's contractions began again. The reason for the surprising smallness of the baby became obvious: there was another baby that had yet to emerge. Hidden behind the first throughout the pregnancy, squashed in a transverse lie, the second baby offered a useless hand, and then a foot, both of which were pushed back while the midwives tried to correct the position. Then the baby offered nothing at all, and was eventually expelled, blue and lifeless, buttocks first, apparently asphyxiated by the long wait in the womb. He was my identical twin, but was so small and shrivelled he might as well have been my shadow. These enlightened days there is a name for the uneven deal struck between my brother and me – twin-to-twin transfusion. I'd been stealing his share of nutrition in the womb, and left him so weak that he couldn't even survive the trauma of being born. A stillborn child wasn't so much a tragedy back then as an occupational hazard of marriage and motherhood; babies were replaceable, and there were far too many in most families anyway. The midwives privately thought it was a good thing that the weak runt had been born dead, as he probably wouldn't have survived the week. They publicly said that Baby Sonny, the firstborn son, was doubly blessed – having taken on his brother's generous spirit, he would live for both of them. The second child – unexpected and dead before birth – was never officially named. He needed to breathe to be loved, and he failed at that first and most basic test. I suppose our mother loved him, in those desperate minutes between learning of his existence and having him die inside her, and perhaps she had a private name for him. But no one else loved the shadow baby, or missed him, apart from me, who had spent nine months wrapped around him, unwittingly menacing my poor twin into a corner of the womb, like a bully in a school yard stealing lunch money; only I, newborn and alone for the first time, noticed the absence of my brother in this strange new world. The absence of a soft little head, flapping limbs like wings, a second beating heart next to mine, as our red and black waterworld was replaced with airy space, and a hard wooden crib lined with colourless silk jersey and cotton, trimmed with Chantilly lace. The stillborn baby was buried, and I suspect it was swift and without ceremony. No one ever got around to telling me about my missing twin – a combination of kindness of intent and disinterest – I didn't find out about him until I was at school, preparing the complicated paperwork for my American university application, when I came across our birth certificates in a box. But I wasn't surprised or even upset; it felt like it was something I had always known anyway, but briefly forgotten, like the lullaby the ayah hummed to me each night when I was restless in my crib, like the taste of mashed coconut with cream and cardamom that I was fed when I was teething.

My father's family had a tradition where each eldest son was named Maqil; and so I was named Maqil, as was my father, as was the first child of each and every uncle. The result of so many Maqils was that no one used this name at all, and the many Maqils went by our family names instead, our pet names, our childhood-nonsense non-Maqil nicknames. In fact, every family member had a formal and an informal name, but unlike in the West, where Elizabeth might be Lizzie, Betsy or Beth, unlike the novels of Dostoevsky, where Alexei might lend itself to Alyosha, there was rarely a connection between the two names. The pet name could not be guessed from the formal name; it had to be known. The names were like secret codes, a set of household keys hung on the matriarch's waist. There was to be no blurring between who was in the family and who was not; the steel cage of pet naming marked the boundary, making sure of the exclusivity of affection. My father's pet name was Ali, a princely name with high meaning but little tangible presence; a pleasingly slight, ubiquitous name, something that could be said quickly enough to be mistaken for a slip of the tongue, a liaison between one word and the next, an alley of little significance. It suited him perfectly. Ali let his wife choose their child's pet name, which remained simply Sonny, the first name she had called me in the moments after the birth; when family members objected to him that this was hardly a name at all, that it was a placeholder, a default, an excuse for not bothering to think of a proper family name, the sort of nickname an uneducated villager might come up with (after all, how many village boys were just called Boy or Son, by those too tired with persistent reproduction and lacking in imagination to think of something more ambitious?), my father just shrugged his shoulders ineffectually, and let them complain.

Ali was a quiet man, and he let his quietness protect him; cross words came at him like a persistent snow, a flurry of white notes, and their discordant music melted against him to nothing. His apparent helplessness regarding his wife's choice, his refusal to stand up like a man and name his surviving son, was a source of concern to his family; bending to his wife for the little things, he would soon bend to her for the bigger things (and was it so little, after all, the nicknaming of a child, when everyone who mattered would never call him Maqil, a name that simply existed for the purpose of birth certificate and government administration and the insignificant colleagues in the civil-service job the boy might one day take up?). What these bigger things were, nobody was quite sure, or else they were too timid to say. The family wondered whether it had been a mistake to marry Ali to someone slightly better than he was, whether their modest ambition had resulted in a devil's pact and they had done him some terrible wrong; that they had attempted to advance their family's status only by means of his own humiliation.

In fact, Ali loved his wife, loved his son, and loved his son's name. There was something archaic in him, some ancient stirring that made him believe that by failing to name his son, he was somehow protecting him. As though the angel of death, that had taken one child from him already, might spare the firstborn son if he remained humbly anonymous, if he couldn't be called out in a crowd. That when the angry mobs came to round them up, they wouldn't stop at the unnamed door. His son was called Son, a name both extended and diminished still further with affection, Sonny. Eventually he agreed with his wife, with the well-meaning intention of smoothing relations for her with the muttering in-laws, to change the English spelling of my name from Sonny to Sunny. This small concession made all the difference; everyone accepted that Sunny was a perfectly appropriate name for such a golden child; beloved, cosseted, cuddled and dandled by the entire household. The name was not without precedent; I already had cousins called Pinky, Rosie and Goldie, Chubby and Chunky, named for obvious reasons. But despite my parents' diplomatic deference, I think that I remained Sonny in their hearts. Sonny the Survivor. The Baby that Breathed.

Ali was aware of his tremendous good fortune; it seemed impossible to him that in a difficult world, recently shaken by war, he should suddenly have so much: the comfort of his minor civil-service position in the Punjab, the respect of British colleagues in pre-Independence India (who correctly interpreted his softly spoken manner as signs of both discretion and deference), an attractive and capable wife, a beautiful child who slept in that extravagantly lace-trimmed crib in their room. He was grateful to his family for having the wealth and wherewithal to arrange his marriage, because he knew that left to his own devices, his natural quietness, his harmlessness, would have blossomed to fill him with a sweet-scented, floral blankness, and he would have remained alone, a quiet, harmless single man. The sort who people would dismiss as a confirmed bachelor, but gossip about privately, debating whether he was too impotent to marry, or really just queer as a kipper. He knew this from his time studying in England; he did not suffer unduly from bigotry, as between the wars the English he met seemed to have other concerns. Besides, Rabindranath Tagore had won the Nobel Prize for Literature, young Chandrasekhara Raman had just won the Nobel Prize for Physics, and it seemed that Indians of a certain class were beginning to be considered interesting rather than offensive, with their exotic names and worthy accomplishments. No one joked about whether he smelled of curry. It was England, after all, and curry was not readily available; he lived on a typical student diet of limp sandwiches, eggs and beans, occasionally supplemented on Sundays with meat and potatoes and two vegetables boiled to death. He was appalled at the way the young Englishmen had to put themselves out to meet women, asking them to cafés, dancing with them on Friday nights. The work they had to put in, the conversations, the choice of clothes, the need to be charming, the ever-present spectre of rejection, and having to start again. He was an insignificant young man, not plain and not pretty, although his solemnity was not unattractive, and he had a smile as luminous as an infant's, because like an infant's it was unexpected and completely sincere. People sometimes felt sorry for him, and the need to take care of him; his race notwithstanding, the sharp-nosed faded-paisley women and red-faced beef-scented men who served him in shops were more polite to him than they needed to be, and called him 'Ducky' or 'Sir'. Even the Northern Irish lady who ran the grocers, who greeted any Southern Irish with a marble-eyed glare and obvious sniffing to indicate the depth of her contempt, simply withdrew to the counter when he shyly entered her premises; she would promptly take down the shoe polish and tooth powder from the shelf on his barely spoken request, and count out his change loudly and deliberately, as one would to a small or slow child. They all seemed to think that a single unkind word would break him. He suspected that they were right to pity him; he knew that he would never achieve anything on his own. He passed his exams, he learned to speak English with a passable accent (although people sometimes strained to hear what he said, and would simply smile vaguely rather than attempt to understand), and he returned gratefully to the Punjab, where his uncle's connections had secured him a job, and his parents' hard negotiations had secured him a wife.

You might think that my father, who fell in love with his wife, would have loved any wife. But in fact the young couple were taken by surprise, by their love, by the discovery of physical intimacy. They were both so shy, so embarrassed by the fact of their bodies, by the fact that bodies existed under the layers of local tailoring and stiff Barhasi silk. On their wedding night, they lay fully dressed on the enormous rose-strewn bed in his father's house, and said almost nothing, as transparent wings of hesitant breath fluttered between them, she so certain that something had to happen soon, he equally certain that he was incapable of doing anything at all. 'Well,' Maryam said eventually, as the silence became too fraught to bear. She said it softly, without accusation, as a question. She said 'Well,' but she really asked, what do we do now?

'Yes?' replied Ali, still looking up at the ceiling, still too uncertain even to turn his head towards her, to look at her profile, her lips polished to cupid points, her eyes lined in kohl, the jewel sparkling on the side of her nose. She didn't reply, and he repeated himself, wondering if she hadn't heard, 'Yes?' It was an apology, she realised, and it was a plea for her to speak, to fill the silence for him. And so she started to speak, hesitantly, about Little Things. The smallest of small talk.

'Well, it's warm tonight,' she said.

'Yes,' he said again, encouraged, encouraging. 'It's warm.'

'The musicians were good, I thought. They played at another wedding, last month. My cousin Deena's wedding.'

'They were, weren't they?' said Ali.

'And the caterers, they were good too . . .' my mother carried on. And like Scheherazade she spoke into the night, her words another blizzard of flakes flurrying towards Ali, carried on her sugar-sweetened breath, but which offered a dampness that moistened his lips, softened his dry throat, and let him speak his own words in response. Maryam, becoming aware of the manner of man to whom she was now married, accepted his few words like something precious, like a gift. In the morning, exhausted by the heat and the words they had shared deep into the night, they woke curled up against each other, still fully dressed, and hurried to put on proper clothes before they were found that way, moving with tacit understanding, like conspirators in a crime.

Ali did not know if the start of their married life was unique, or was the way it happened with every couple who had not married for love (the lewd comments thrown his way by his uncles, and the bustling nosiness of his mother and aunts in their bedroom, made him suspect not). But he knew that their way was the only way it should ever be, the unfurling of a nightly intimacy so gradual, in conversation, and in flesh, it was almost vegetable in its movement, like that of a flower turning towards the sun from a dark place. He felt he knew everything about her before he had so much as touched her hand, tracing a shy finger across the fading henna patterns on her palm. He knew the deep scent of her hair, neatly coiled and oiled for the night, long before he let his lips brush against her braid. By the time he eventually held his wife in his arms, they shared an understanding so deep that no words were necessary, as the silence was soaked with the words that had been spoken already. It was a true marriage. Neither of them had expected to find love in that least romantic and most dutiful of institutions, but they did. They taught each other to love. And if the uncles and the aunts were to gossip about the suspicious cleanliness of the sheets in the early days of marriage, the beatific smiles of the bride and the luminous silence of the groom that gave away nothing, the gossiping was put to rest within the year by the proud announcement of pregnancy.

I was named Sonny by my mother. I was named Sunny by my father. I was named Maqil Karam by my family, and since then I have had many other names, of my own choosing. I was the firstborn son, hatched into a house built on duty and filled with romance, a house that celebrated the living and rejected the dead; perhaps I blamed my parents for this, for providing these hard-soft, sour-sweet virtues in such unpalatable abundance, like ripe mangos falling from the tree and rotting on the ground. Perhaps this is why I valued these virtues so little when I was older. But I do not blame or credit my parents for what I became; I never have, and I never will. I am Sonny the Survivor, and I wasted little time in shrugging off my family's golden legacy, of duty and affection, but I have still carried a small part of my heritage with me, throughout my wayward life. My parents taught me this: that to live is to be celebrated, and to die is to be forgotten, and that it is breath alone that inspires love. And I have never forgotten, that He loved Her. A hard, shining fact, glittering like a crystal shard in the dust, like pearls of teeth set in gums, vulnerable and vicious all at once. This fact remains, it endures; even now my parents' bodies have fallen slack and crumbled into the earth. Even now that my own body has fallen slack and threatens to do the same. Like my parents, I never sought love, but it found me anyway; it got me, and I have never gotten away. So I know that it matters, this memory, when everything else is broken or breaking, when I struggle to breathe in the night, when each weak thud of my heart feels like it might be the last; it has always mattered to me that once upon a time, a long time ago, He loved Her, and that She loved Him back.

Lahore, Pakistan – 1948 – Education

SUNNY WAS BORN TO BE THE HERO OF HIS FAMILY, AND AT sixteen he blazes like a star, perfectly formed, with romantic lips and silky straight hair that ruffles in the wind. He sits at the end of the dark carved table, and makes it seem that he is the one sitting at the head; he lounges on a chair like an idol on an altar for worship, the golden little god of house and home. He walks out of the house to take his final school examinations, shoulders back, and chest out. He is stuffed to bursting with the sense of his own achievement; you could even say that he struts. One of the servants, old Khadim, has already wheeled Sunny's bicycle to the front drive, and is holding it upright for him, swatting away street urchins who have come to admire it, who are taking it in turns to race up to the shiny machine and flick the bell. The colourful swearing that Khadim comes out with every time one of the shabby children succeeds is more memorable and delightful than the metallic *tring-terring* of the bell itself; it as though he is the one they are ringing. Khadim is becoming sweaty and agitated, and stamps his sandals in the dust, his exposed heels as cracked and brown as the leather strapped to his feet, but he beams when the young master approaches, displaying an almost full set of betel-stained teeth. 'Thanks, Uncle,' says Sunny, with the careless familiarity that appals his real uncles and aunts.

'That boy treats servants like equals,' complains Chacha Zafri to Ali as they take tea on the veranda. Chacha Zafri looks down to where Sunny is chatting easily to Khadim, and his hooked nose twitches with ill-concealed irritation. Ali glances politely at his younger brother, but doesn't respond, not even when Chacha Zafri adds aggressively, 'You'll have to watch him, he'll end up one of those bullshit bastard commies.'

'He's going to America to study,' replies Sunny's mother, long used to speaking on behalf of her husband, who smiles at the sound of Maryam's voice and settles back behind *The Pakistan Times*. 'The last thing he'll become is a communist.'

The three of them watch Sunny take his bike and wheel it a few steps towards the gaggle of urchins that Khadim has been holding at bay. Sunny reaches into his pocket, emptying out a shrapnel of shining sweets and dull metal coins; he distributes these to the street children with the swagger of a visiting film star. Khadim disapproves, his lips pursed like an easily scandalised governess, but he still places a palm gently on Sunny's head, like a blessing, before returning to his house duties. Sunny hops nimbly on his bike and starts cycling in wide circles around the drive at the front of the house; the children, ragged, grubby and utterly seduced, run around after him, shouting, 'Bhai Sunny! Sir Sunny! Sunny Sahib!' The tallest calls after him, 'Break a leg, Sunny Bhai!'

'Insolence,' huffs Chacha Zafri. 'Bhai! Sir! Sahib! Who does Sunny think he is? And who was that ragamuffin good-for-nothing telling him to break his leg! We should go beat that child off the street and into the gutter!' He looks around, as though anxious to find someone to get this done, as though to promise that he means business rather than bluster. 'Where's Khadim?'

' "Break a leg" just means "Good luck",' explains Maryam gently. 'Sunny told the children never to say "Good luck" when he goes for an exam. It's from a Western superstition. You tell someone to break a leg when they're going on the stage.'

'That boy's been on the stage his whole life . . .' mutters Chacha Zafri. And at that moment, Sunny turns and winks over his shoulder, grinning broadly, not at the urchins, but at the three adults watching him from the veranda, before riding off up the street, leaving his adoring public behind.

'Insolence,' rages Chacha Zafri again. 'Did you see that! Did you see?' He notices that Ali glances over his paper and exchanges a complicit look with his wife, as though apologising for his younger brother's behaviour. Chacha Zafri puffs up with annoyance like a paratha on a hot plate, preparing to protest in riper language, but on seeing his sister-in-law looking at him with something like sympathy, decides that he doesn't have the energy to be sufficiently bad tempered so soon after breakfast on such a balmy morning; he deflates with a less satisfying, but more acceptable, sigh.

'Yes, Zafri Bhai, I saw,' says Maryam softly, but she is smiling with affection after her son, as is her husband, surreptitiously behind the paper; they are completely charmed by him, they cannot believe that this magnificent creature, this bird of fire winging its way down the street, was made by them.

Sunny is riding though the streets of Lahore, the dry dust settling in the creases of his neatly pressed shorts, on his lovingly starched and scented white shirt. The servants compete to take care of his laundry; like the children in the street, like his

30

parents, they are seduced and charmed by Sunny, utterly and completely, and have been since he was a cooing baby who preferred chatting and gurgling to his audience above nourishment, pulling himself off his anxious mother's breast to beam around the room with innocent appeal. He treats servants with confidence and familiarity, as individuals rather than a group, and they do everything he asks, and everything he doesn't think to ask as well. They cover for him when he slips out at night on his bike, they pretend not to notice when he slips back in; they even wipe away the telltale traces of street mud from his shoes. The maid who cleans his room does not mention the secret hiding place in the wall behind his bed, where a brick has been worked loose, and a small tin box of personal treasures is stored. They feel honoured, dignified by his trust. Sunny loosens his school tie, and rides past the school without even a guilty glance – he has over an hour before his exams. He carries on to a local bookshop, and sees, as he expected, a couple of older boys there.

'Ho!' he shouts out. 'Jamal, Farid, it's time to pay your debts.'

'Well, if it isn't swindling little Maqil Sunny Karam,' mutters Jamal. 'How did you know we'd be here?'

'It's a small town,' says Sunny, and he winks in a passable imitation of a mustachioed Hindi movie star that he has seen. 'And I know everything . . .'

'What debt is he talking about?' interrupts Farid, replacing a book he had been considering on the shelf.

Jamal, aware of the shopkeeper's interest, switches from Punjabi to English. 'The little sneak saw us in the trees outside Mr Shafik's house.'

'I wasn't the one sneaking,' says Sunny, unoffended. 'Although I wondered why Mr Shafik's house? His four daughters are the fattest in town.' He adds conversationally,

'But then I realised, with the fat ones you see a hell of a lot more tit than with the skinny ones. Quantity over quality. A volume discount, hah?'

Despite themselves, Jamal and Farid start laughing. 'So what are you after?' says Farid eventually. 'You're a little young to start blackmailing your friends.'

'I don't have friends,' says Sunny proudly. 'I have colleagues and associates. And it isn't blackmail, it's business.'

'How much?' asks Jamal shortly.

'An hour with your father's Bentley,' says Sunny promptly. 'I know it's waiting for you outside the faculty. Tell your driver to get some tea, and meet me with it at the old factory.'

'You just want a ride?' says Farid, amused; it seems that Sunny is simply a little boy after all.

'Hell, no,' says Sunny, imitating another movie star, a Western one this time. 'I want to learn to drive. When I go to America, I'm going to drive a Cadillac.'

Jamal and Farid look at each other uneasily. 'Abbu would kill us if we let an underaged schoolboy drive his precious car. If the house was on fire, he'd save the car out of the garage before he'd save us.'

Sunny nods with sympathy. 'É, that's too bad.' Speaking in Punjabi once more, he says, 'Maybe Mr Shafik would let me drive *his* car, as a reward for arranging the marriage of his two fattest daughters.' He turns towards the shopkeeper, and adds nonchalantly, 'Once a customer has unwrapped the goods, it's a sale, isn't it, Uncle?'

'That's the rule, Sunny,' agrees the shopkeeper.

'So allow me to be the first to congratulate the two of you on your engagements,' Sunny says with a smile, offering his hand.

'Enough, you little nit,' says Jamal, swiping his own hand to cuff Sunny on the head. Sunny ducks easily, and pushes himself away on his bike, 'The factory,' he calls after them.

As Jamal storms off and Farid trails after him, Sunny sets off in the opposite direction. Suddenly he stops, looks thoughtfully over his shoulder back at the bookshop, and wheels around, gracefully avoiding a rickshaw and an old woman driving a dishevelled goat down the lane. He returns to the shop and calls over to the shopkeeper: 'Ahmad Uncle, have you ever noticed that people look at your books, and then they go to the tea-and-coffee stand and have a drink while they decide what to buy? Your shop makes the tea-and-coffee man a lot of money. You should get a percentage.'

'The landlord gets the percentage from us both,' says the shopkeeper. 'If I started asking for a percentage as well, I wouldn't have a shop left. They'd raise my rent and kick me out when I couldn't pay it.'

'Maybe you should just sell your own tea and coffee. Call the shop "Ahmad's Books and Coffee". With a slogan. Something like "As Easy as ABC". Every student would come.'

'What a stupid idea, Sunny,' says the shopkeeper. 'No one would ever sell coffee in a bookshop. The customers would just spill coffee all over the books. I'd lose stock. It would be the biggest mess you ever saw. For a bright boy, you have some really stupid ideas.'

'I bet you can get books with coffee in America,' says Sunny, shrugging, and rides off again into the dust, like a hero in a Western.

Sunny arrives at the school in time for his examinations, having learned to drive the Bentley – that is, having learned to drive forward, left and right without hitting anything significant – in less than an hour. 'If you screw up these exams, you'll at least get a job as a chauffeur,' Jamal tells him with grudging admiration, as Sunny parks with a noisy, gear-grinding flourish in the shade of a sprawling tree, dotted with fleshy white flowers at various stages of sickly-sweet decay. Sunny signs in, finds his place in the hall, and starts the exams. He completes the paper with quarter of an hour to spare, and spends this time watching a lizard on the far wall that is bathing in a square of light from the high window on the opposite side. The creature seems ancient, a little dragon or dinosaur, something from myth or history; he wonders whether he will ever be ancient himself, whether he will become lizard-like with age, bathing in the sun with shifty, mistrustful eyes. The lizard moves on, chasing a scuttling insect, and disappears into the cracked join between ceiling and wall. Sunny cannot bear the boredom of having nothing to do – he can't even doodle to pass the time as he has only his exam paper on the desk – so his fingers begin to tap agitatedly. The other students look at him, and grunt, 'Tsk' and 'Ouf' and 'Humph' with distracted annoyance, not just at the noise, but at the fact that he has obviously already finished while they are still hurriedly struggling. When the examiner finally allows him to leave, he cycles home, and encouraged by the light breeze that is shifting the dry leaves and dust of the driveway, decides to go to the roof to fly his kites. He likes to fly two at once, setting one swooping high and the other swooping low; he is impossible to beat in the rooftop kite battles that take place in the neighbourhood; he tapes old razor blades to his fighter kites, and effortlessly cuts all his opponents' strings in mid-air. He is just unrolling the string from his first kite when he is distracted by a miserable sniffling, punctuated by deep wet sobs. Leyla, the neighbour's unattractive daughter, is crying on the roof of her house, her feet dangling over the guttering. Sunny can't remember the last time he felt sad enough to cry, and is too curious to ignore her politely. 'What's up, little sister?' he asks, gallant enough to make sure that his interest sounds like concern. He drops the kite, and jumps across from his own roof to join her.

'I'm not going to be able to take my final examinations tomorrow. Amma says that she needs the car to take Dadi to the hospital for her tests, and she won't give me money for a rickshaw. She thinks I'm making a big fuss about nothing, that I'm being selfish because Dadi isn't well, and that girls don't need a school certificate because we just get married.' She blows her nose noisily on the cotton scarf she is wearing over her head against the beating heat of the sun. 'Of course Dadi's not well,' she wails with the injustice of it. 'She's about a hundred! She's ALWAYS not well.'

'You could cycle to the school,' says Sunny, offering a practical solution rather than sympathy. 'Lots of girls cycle, I've seen them.'

'I don't have a bicycle, and I don't know how to ride anyway,' says Leyla helplessly. She howls and blows her nose again, as though she has already decided to be defeated, already accepted that she won't have a school certificate, that she will have a marriage instead; it is as though she has just worked out that wailing and crying is the only choice she has left in life, and so she has decided to do it thoroughly.

'Don't be such a *girl*,' says Sunny impatiently. 'Take mine. I'll teach you to ride it right now.'

'I can't do that,' Leyla says fearfully.

'My four-year-old brother can ride a bike,' says Sunny. 'If you can't be bothered to try, maybe your mother's right.'

'Enough,' says Leyla. 'I'll do it. I'll do it right now.'

Sunny hops back to his own roof, and goes down to wait for her in the driveway. Leyla takes a few undignified falls in the dirt, and her shalwar kameez keeps getting caught in the chain, but despite all this, she learns to ride the bike with basic proficiency – to go forward, left and right, without hitting anything significant. He passes her the bike by the handlebars when the lesson is over, and carelessly tells her to keep it. 'But

35

you love this bike,' says Leyla. She knows that this is true; she always sees Sunny on his bike, charging in and out of his drive like a victorious prince in a fairy tale.

'It's no big deal,' he says. 'I'm leaving town soon.' And he adds, cheekily, as he strolls back into his house, 'Besides, I'm too old for bikes now. I've outgrown it.'

Leyla wheels the bike back to her garden, unable to believe it is hers. (In fact, it isn't; she uses it successfully to go to school for her exams the following day, but when Sunny goes to America, his Chacha Zafri notices that she has the bike and demands it back for Sunny's younger brothers.) She wonders if the extraordinary generosity of his gift might mean that Sunny has some romantic attachment to her, or else some secret knowledge about their future. Whether he might be the marriage that her parents will one day arrange. She wouldn't mind that one little bit. But in fact, the extraordinary generosity, and the casual, thoughtless nature of the giving, all this is just Sunny being Sunny. He isn't attached to his bike after all; he isn't attached to anything. Even as a boy he is conspicuously lacking in baggage. I can tell you for certain, even after all these years have passed, and the bike has long since been handed over to Khadim's grandson (a middle-aged man who keeps it in an oily garage full of other tin junk, with the vague intention of one day stripping it for parts), that Sunny didn't think of his little brothers or his baby sister when he gave it away, didn't once consider that they might need it someday too. And that's because Sunny, this blazing star, this preening bird with his feathers fanned, only thinks of himself. At the age of sixteen, he's already matured into a charming opportunist, but he still has the shameless selfishness of a child.

Sunny might have finished school with soaring grades, and swiftly thereafter achieved an internationally valid driving licence with his ill-gotten driving lessons, but his real education is only just beginning. Everyone reinvents themselves in college, and let loose in the Land of the Free, Sunny is no different. He is renamed for his new world, and in 1950s New York he has begun to mask his past behind wittily appropriate initials. He is known simply as MSK, his polished shoes clicking authoritatively through the campus at Columbia, hair short and sharp, ablaze with ideas for improving the world. So here's MSK ordering small, bitter coffees in Greenwich Village, unravelling the Cold War politics of the Middle East, commenting fearlessly on the Persian oil industry and Stalin's legacy, while his classmates hang on his every word. And here's MSK in the bagel shop blithely informing the Jewish owner that the Germans might have lost the war but are all set to win the peace. There's MSK in Chinatown, in Little Italy, in the polite drawing rooms of Fifth Avenue and the barbed activist meetings of the Upper West Side. The raw-faced young men in sweaters with letters, the ponytailed girls in flared skirts and cardigans are in awe of him; our golden boy has become a tanned young man with superbly white teeth, and an almost electric charge of energy. His presence is enormous, and they are always surprised when he approaches, when he stands up from sitting at a table, at how small he is in real life. As though he were a movie star who really existed on a big screen or in a magazine spread.

MSK is the campus international man of mystery, and the question everyone asks is simply, 'Where is he from?' They puzzle over it, as he knows everyone and is intimate with no one. They piece together clues. His name is Mike, although the girls who harbour romantic intentions towards him prefer to say Mikey, and use it possessively to mark their territory: 'I'll be seeing Mikey at the Bistro tonight.' Or at the gallery, the lecture, the screening of Elia Kazan's *On the Waterfront*. He doesn't offer his surname, and even his signature is MSK and, as a result, easily forged. He doesn't carry ID: 'Everyone knows who

I am . . .' he says with innocent vanity, and with less innocence adds, 'And if they don't, they should.' He pays cash, and keeps a roll of notes in a fat gold clip. He always seems to have money, and he tips lavishly. He has started a fashion for having an abbreviated name that others try and fail to follow.

The one thing that everyone knows for certain is that MSK, or Mike, or Mikey, is not American. His English is so correct that he has to be foreign, and he slips between an Oxbridge and East Coast accent with the ease of moving between foreign languages. He speaks fluent French and German, but that doesn't mean he is European, as after his first degree at Yale he claims to have spent a year in Switzerland. No one else speaks French and German well enough to ascertain whether he might be a native. His skin is tanned enough for people to wonder whether he is South American, but his Spanish is heavily accented and patchy – though knowing Mike as only you and I do, it is possible that he is just putting this on to mislead his admirers.

'He's a Jew from Biarritz,' says Susie Santini to her ponytailed girlfriends. 'That's in France,' she adds helpfully; Susie is the Irish-Italian art student who will finally succeed in seducing him after months of dedicated attention. 'I asked him where his favourite place in the world was, and he started talking about the beach at Biarritz, how there was something special about the way the light hits the sea. He said that you could hold a picture frame up to the ocean and it would create the perfect, living painting. And he must be Jewish; he wouldn't have ham or bacon with his eggs at breakfast.'

'He's an A-rab from Morocco,' says Ted Peterson to the young men with sweaters; Ted is the editor of the student paper that MSK occasionally contributes to. 'He told me that he once had a summer job working for a paper in Marrakesh, and got fired for writing about the corruption in local politics. And A-rabs are Muslims; they don't eat ham or bacon either.'

He's a Middle Eastern prince, he's a Latin American politician's son, he's a member of an Italian 'Family' that rules half of the Bronx, he's the adopted heir to an American retail empire . . .

Maqil Sunny Karam hears the rumours, and smiles. He has the extraordinary gift of being able to talk as much as he wants, without ever giving anything away. He never intended to conceal his nationality, and in fact he did tell people he met when he first arrived in America that he was from Pakistan. But it seemed that no one had heard of Pakistan, that small state carved out of the left and right of India, like ribs lifted from Adam; it was just a word, like that of an obscure village passed in the night, a secondary character in a little-known novel, and so easily forgotten. He introduced himself to fellow students in his first dorm with his real name, but when he said 'Maqil', they inevitably replied, 'Michael? Hey, great to meet you, Mike.' And gradually he began to like the freedom of being Mike, an anonymous man who could be from anywhere. An Anywhere man with his Everywhere accent, freed from family, from nationality, from religion, from every tiresome box or cage that these might imply. The dull chains of familial duty that had once bound him had expanded and thinned away to almost nothing. A wedding ring melted down to a slender sliver of a bangle, a manacle beaten out to a child's hoop – something that was no longer about responsibility or containment, but for decoration, for play. He plays with his heritage; he wears it like a costume when the fancy takes him, he exploits it for exotic or commercial appeal, for the attractive woman working on her dissertation in subcontinental literature, for the small Pakistani fraternity he has stumbled across in the coffee shop opposite the Embassy, who treat him like a long-lost brother, for the Indian owners of Taj Mahal Authentic Savouries and Snacks, whom he has let believe that he is from the Indian side of the Punjab, for the sake of the free food (the proper stuff they share with the staff, made with thick yellow ghee, thin green and red chillis, and the full rainbow of spices, rather than that served in the shop, which is made bland enough to suit the American palate).

Maqil catches his face in the mirror of his tiny student studio, the bed propped up against the wall with a creaking metallic mechanism, and seeing himself briefly as a stranger might, is surprised by his own good looks. He is vain, it is true, but just as much of his vanity is intellectual – he thinks he might be the cleverest man he knows. If he'd been born in America, and was willing to work hard enough, he could be president. He thinks he could even be a genius; he dares to say this out loud on occasion. 'I have nothing to declare but my genius,' is what Oscar Wilde said on coming to America, and was something that he had considered saying too, as he went through customs, but the square jaw of the thug in uniform made him think better of it. He was barely seventeen then, and not yet filled out on American burgers, hoagies and root beers; he is still small, even now, with the type of wiry build that could climb a mountain, run a marathon, but be thrown easily to the ground in a physical fight. Unlike Wilde, his genius doesn't lie in the world of letters, as he lacks the dedication; he has scribbled out some exciting papers and political pieces, some brief plays and briefer poems, but without energy or effort. He is of the firm belief that if something can't be done easily, it's hardly worth doing at all. He knows that he is a dilettante, someone who is good at a little bit of everything, but truly concerned with nothing in particular. He has no idea what he will do when he finally leaves college, having delayed the decision as long as possible by overeducating himself as far as the family funds would allow. His mother writes him long letters, full of discreet ambition for him, and all of them asking him, as gently as she can put it in black and white, 'Sunny, what will you do?' He fails to reply to this specific, sensible question, and instead sends postcards back to the whole family, updating them on his heroic exploits, sharing his various witty insights and, with a little irony, telling them about the New York weather.

He likes the sound of his voice as much as everyone else does, and sometimes talks out loud to himself, to the Anywhere Man in the mirror. There is a medical label for this habit of his, symptomatic as it is of a psychological condition, but it is something he will never mention to the many medical professionals he will see during his life, as it feels perfectly natural to air his views with that handsome fellow who is looking back so expectantly at him. His mirror twin, his missing twin. He addresses them both, as he casually shrugs on a jacket: 'Do you ever worry that if you're from Anywhere, you might be from Nowhere? That if you can do Anything, that means you do Nothing? That you're just getting away with it, day after day, but not getting anywhere at all?'

'Are you talking about finding a calling?' replies the Anywhere Man. 'You sound like your mother.'

'Maybe I should just go back to Pakistan, and start a revolution,' he comments idly, smoothing the jacket, a fine wool blend, over his shoulders.

'You'd do better to prevent one,' comments Anywhere Man. 'Revolutions are a lot of hard work. And you know how we feel about that.'

Maqil is about to discover his calling after all. He and his girlfriend, Susie Santini, are going on a trip to Las Vegas, Nevada. He has always liked gambling: he goes to the races in New York, shivering at the first spring meet in his fashionable but inadequate topcoat; he plays poker in dimly lit back rooms; he has even played chess for money. He can never refuse that golden invitation, 'Care to make it interesting?' He himself has made more benign and dull events interesting than he can remember; he has cleared out his own pockets, and slightly more often those of his acquaintances, but just by a few hundred dollars or so, as they are all students of relatively modest means. But he has never entered a palace of money like this before, an oasis in the desert where cold hard cash pours out from the slots like water; he is Aladdin before the cave, seeking the magic words to a room of treasure. There is a geometric beauty to this sort of gambling that appeals to his Muslim upbringing, the lack of imagery, the red and black of it, the numbers, the odds, the statistics. The messing around with the horses that he has done in the past seems just that, messy – dependent on the whims of the nags, the weather, the idiosyncrasies of the course, the diets of the jockeys, the mud on the ground. Here, the gaming tables are clean, and he is playing himself – the best kind of game there can be. The winning is effortless, the losing just as much so. He forgets that Susie is by his side, and finds himself lost in intricate calculations – the house will always win, but sometimes it has to lose to keep the people in the game. When their game is lost, his will be won. The numbers and odds tick through his mind like loops of punched paper, and as the crowd gathers around him, he begins to get a sense of being on stage. He is a conjuror with a wand, raising oohs and aahs of appreciation from the audience as he flips over his cards, a trapeze artist flying and falling with grace and daring as the stakes get higher and his chips form teetering towers before him. He is putting on a show; he thinks he could do this for ever.

Later, he and Susie find themselves upgraded to a suite in the hotel. When the hotel security delivers the red sack with their winnings, Maqil opens the door with a grin, and, reaching into his pocket (rather than the sack, which might seem rather crass), tips generously with a handshake. 'Thanks, Clarence,' he says, reading the broad-shouldered goon's name tag. 'You go have a great night now. Keep an eye on all those cheating bastards downstairs . . .' He laughs, and the goon laughs too, conspiratorially, as he folds the notes in his hand. Maqil has made a friend, not for life but for the rest of the season. When his luck is down, Clarence will still let him in, and when he has to throw him out, he will do it with a wink, play-acting violence while treating him gently, and then share a cigarette with him out back.

Susie is sitting on the bed and has been watching the exchange with amusement, and a little jealousy, that he is giving some anonymous piece of human meat the same attention and warmth of voice he might use for her. 'For God's sake, Mikey,' she says when Clarence leaves. 'Don't you ever switch it off?'

'Switch what off?' he asks innocently, feeling the weight of the sack, tossing it from one hand to the other.

'Your charm, your ever-loving, don't-you-just-love-me-like-I-love-me, oozing, oily charm,' she complains.

'You say that as though I'm not sincere,' he says with apparent injury, his big brown eyes, straight lashed, growing wide. For a moment Susie feels guilty, as though she has somehow spoilt his game, but then he grins, and throws the bag at her. 'Catch!'

She reaches for it, but misses, and the bag hits the headboard behind her and gushes out notes. 'Jesus, Mike, how much is in there?'

'I don't know, eleven or twelve, maybe.'

'Are you kidding me? Eleven or twelve? Eleven or twelve grand? Eleven or twelve thousand dollars!'

'No, eleven or twelve hundred. I just packed the rest of the bag with paper to make me look good.' He shrugs, and empties out the bag on to the bed, and after the real notes on top, the clipped squares of newspaper float out like printed confetti.

'You're the limit, Mikey,' scolds Susie, delighted by this subterfuge even more than she had been at the thought of the money, delighted at being included in his game. 'You're the living end.'

She leans back on the bed, dramatically, and Maqil realises that he's meant to kiss her. He suddenly feels a bit weary. He likes having a girlfriend; he likes the way it makes him unavailable and interesting to every other woman; he likes the frisson of excitement when he looks at or kisses another woman, the idea that he is misbehaving and might be caught at any moment. He likes having someone thin and attractive like Susie on his arm; he likes going to good restaurants with her, and watching her use the right fork for the starter, and that she is smart and educated enough to have opinions about art and politics. He likes the public life of a couple very much. It's the privacy that bores him a little; here in the hotel bedroom, now that it is just the two of them, there is no show to be put on. It is just him and her, a sack of fake money and a bed groaning with expectation. He wishes, without malice, that she would just disappear, painlessly, and reappear for breakfast. He wants to be alone, to wash his face, brush his teeth, say his evening prayers, and go to sleep with the peaceful innocence of a child. He never thought that he would miss looking for Mecca and saying his prayers. But here she is, his latter-day Eve, holding out an apple, beautiful but in no way tempting. He sighs.

'Is something wrong?' asks Susie, suddenly concerned. If she dislikes his habitual overuse of charm, this sudden slipping of his mask, the disappointed exhalation, is more worrying still. Her confidence falters, and she is feeling guilty again. She wants this man to be charming and happy, and somehow she has made him neither. She says, 'Is something wrong?' while fearing that she's done something wrong, that she is what's wrong in the first place.

Maqil sees her concern, and feels mean. She's played her role for him today, a besotted beauty by his side, and now it's time for him to play his. It's time for him to deliver all he has promised, with the hand-holding, the kissing, the restaurant, the drinks, the glances over the gaming tables. It would be cruel to have led her on, it would be impolite. If the word for a woman treating a man in this way is unpleasant – cocktease, pricktease, a staccato spitting that finishes with a baring of teeth, a mockery of a smile – then the logical word for a man treating a woman this way is unthinkable. He smiles at her, and he sees her visibly relax, her face soften, her mouth drop open gently as she releases the breath she had not even known she was holding, her shoulders falling. 'You're very lovely, you know,' he says. 'You should do that pose for a calendar.'

'Which month?' she asks, a little flirtatiously.

'I would say June, a month for delicious romantic mis-understandings in country gardens with mazes,' he says, joining her on the bed. He takes her hand and kisses it with sober formality as she giggles with delight. He tells himself that she is a lovely girl, really, and there'd be something wrong with him if he couldn't enjoy being with her, enjoy her generously offered body. She is rather too slim and straight, but then he's never been fond of softness, of curves – they imply a weakness, a dependence that is appropriate in mothers and aunts, but less so in lovers – and Susie's ass is practically perfect, as firm as a boy's, almost as good as his own. It's time, he accepts without resentment, now that he is finally an adult, to complete his education. There have to be worse things than making love to a pretty girl out of politeness. The act of love is just an act after all. An easy performance. Another show to put on.

'You know,' he says, as he and Susie start to kiss on the bed, the paper notes rustling beneath them like a blanket of autumn leaves, 'there's a saying back in the old country. A woman for children, a boy for pleasure, but for ecstasy . . .' He pauses dramatically.

'Uh-huh,' breathes Susie encouragingly, amused.

'Get a goat,' he finishes, pulling her into his arms while she starts to laugh.

'Now which old country would this be, exactly?' asks Susie, as he still hasn't told her where he's from. She begins unbuttoning his shirt.

Maqil shrugs and smiles, and helping her slide her dress down over her shoulders, he kisses her short, pretty nose. 'I forget which one,' he says.

Cairo, Egypt – 1965 – Politics

MAQIL APPEARS TO HAVE GROWN UP. HE IS FIRMLY IN HIS thirties, and in the years that have passed since he lost his virginity to Susie Santini, he has fearlessly moved continents, and done what grown-ups tend to do. He has found a Home, a Job and a Wife, but sometimes he wonders if he himself has got lost along the way. Like many lost men, he indulges in prayer. He still prays just twice a day rather than five, because frankly he hasn't the time. He tells himself he prays from habit, rather than belief, that on balance it is smarter to pray than not, to pray a little if not a lot, just in case there is a God after all, benevolent or otherwise. The risk of eternal damnation is small, but that there is a risk at all outweighs the odds. He tells himself that prayer is a matter of insurance, an inexpensive bi-daily payment, a practical decision. It's a matter of statistics, of mathematics, hedging his bets on both black and red. But sometimes, in the middle of a prayer, facing in the direction of

Mecca, he finds himself comforted, and warmed inside by something more than just the resonant river-flow of the words, the firmness of the sentiments, the exquisite nature of the Arabic and his mastery of the long and short vowel sounds it requires. Perhaps, under his brittle armour, he really does believe, and is tainted by belief as much as any capricious crusader of medieval times, as much as any pious patriarch back in Pakistan who would disown the fallen brethren like himself.

He is beginning to suspect that he is a fraud. That he is none of the things he has pretended to be – that he has no genius, that no scrap of his intellect deserves to last beyond his lifetime, that his cleverness is a con just like the many he has pulled for fun and financial profit, and that his famous charm is simply over-the-top flattery, aimed at those too vain or stupid to notice the insincerity. He has been a social drinker and a champagne socialist, a polite fornicator, a compulsive gambler, and in the nicest possible way, a liar and a thief, but it now seems possible, after all his big talk and bigger thoughts, that his good clothes and extravagant gestures were just shiny wrapping, sparkling scraps designed to distract the magpie eye from the truth of the matter. That in fact the package is just like any other, and he is an ordinary man, destined to live an ordinary life. That it has all been a pretence to impress people. A spectacle. A show. And as with any show, from Las Vegas to the Moulin Rouge, the back-stage mechanics are dreary and disappointing – the ageing star with the drinking problem and the sagging gut pulled in with a corset, the dancers with pockmarked skin from too much make-up and perspiration, stripped of their false eyelashes, filing their bitten nails and discussing their abortions.

After all, he thinks, inspecting himself in the mirror after his morning shower, there is something cowardly about it, his inability to make decisions and stick with them. If he looks closely enough, he thinks that he can see the trace of cowardice

48

in his face, in the curve of his upper lip, the fold of his eyelid that sometimes flickers when he blinks. He is always Janus-faced, looking both ways. Living two lives. It is likely that he blames his missing twin for this, as he himself takes responsibility for as little as he can, his own character included. That he blames the absence of that shadowy infant for his desire to take every possible twist and turn around the maze, as though covering all the ground is more important than reaching the goal, the fountain or stone bench at the centre. Maqil seeks neither refreshment nor rest. He wants to be everything; he wants to live everywhere, he wants to stand out, and fit in. The main constant in his life has been his continuing good looks – he still has all his hair, though he had been afraid it would thin dramatically in his thirties, like his father's did – and a fondness for the initial M in his chosen pseudonyms: M for me, myself, mine. He is crafting the story of his own life, and is disappointed that the story is no longer as daring and heroic as it once promised to be. After all, he was the golden first-born son, blazing with ticking energy like a flashy watch, as inexhaustible and ingenious as a clockwork toy – just wind him up, and oh my, see how fast and far he'll fly. He was the future president of a country he wasn't born to. The entrepreneur, the dilettante, the maker of oh-so-much money at so little personal cost . . . the cost of others unaccounted for. Consequences cheerfully ignored. But look at him now; it feels lately that he is just winding down, with nothing to set him going again, no midwife's slap on his buttocks, no urgent need to breathe, no joyous song in his heart. M for me, in a minor key.

Take this chap Mehmet, a character he has designed for himself, like a modern-day avatar in a game; he had picked a good Middle Eastern name, popular in Egypt, because that is where Mehmet works and lives. As far as his colleagues and neighbours are aware, the Middle East is where the man they know as Mehmet is from, and he has let the pale gold of his Punjabi skin – where paleness is almost as good as wealth in achieving social standing, where young ladies bleach their faces to a ghostly greyness – tan to a burnished bronze, which rather flatters him, making him seem both political and princely, a character from *The Thousand and One Nights*. That said, these acquaintances could not say with confidence exactly which part of the region he hails from. He is obviously Western-educated, and they have to assume he is of mixed parentage, a little bit from everywhere; the confusion persists, as there is something about Mehmet that makes a direct question seem either impolite or inappropriate; and when asked by a blundering visitor, he assumes an attitude of both disappointment and forbearance, judging and forgiving with the same expression, giving just the slightest of gestures, a barely-there sideways shake of his head, as though there is something too painful or tragic in his past to put into words. But despite his carefully nurtured air of mystery, there is no doubt that Mehmet, the intriguingly vague Pan–Arab, is utterly conventional. His home isn't a hotel room in a casino, or student digs in the city, or a canvas tent in the desert. He lives in a house, a normal white house in a wealthy suburb, tastefully furnished, with an internal courtyard and a small garden. I have already mentioned that he has a job, and a wife. He has staff, even, a maid and a cook. He is a man of conventional commitments and responsibilities. He is tied down, manacled to his front gate like a protester to the iron railings of Whitehall. There are cuffs tightening around his wrists, his ankles; metal bands constricting his chest and making it difficult for him to breathe.

It wasn't meant to turn out like this – a coward like him when it comes to decisions could certainly not have chosen any of this. He simply let life happen to him, and this is the banal result. It was once an adventure, back in the US during his post-college years – he had become irritated by his former student acquaintances who spoke airily of revolution and civil rights and McCarthy, supported financially by parents in the Hamptons, with calculatedly shabby clothes, but with full bellies and hot and cold running water in their apartments, and laundered towels in their bathrooms. It felt that they hadn't really tasted life, and neither had he. His casual work grifting in the casinos, his occasional employment by casino owners as a player goading the big spenders into spending more, his various short-lived projects that required investment charmed from important men didn't seem daring enough either. He watched the Anglo-French humiliation following the Suez affair with interest; he was back in New York, just a few blocks up from the UN, when officials there announced the ceasefire they had negotiated; it irritated him that he was outside, looking in. He drifted from the safe and sanitised States to the dangerous and murky Middle East – a boat to France, a train through Spain, and a passenger ferry to the north African coast. He took a job as a political correspondent for a national paper, as a way to travel around the region, to seek out and record the fomenting crises. The outside world watched with distant interest, just as he had once done, as revolution pushed aside the monarchy from Iraq, and the French from Algeria, as the American forces were summoned to the Lebanon, and the British bolstered the Jordanians. He was no longer simply watching; he was there. He flattered and irritated officials for information, he was thrown into jail in three different countries, he proved astonishingly good at his job. A promotion to editor for political affairs didn't seem such a bad thing, after he was finally released from jail; he was based in Cairo, and met an elegant Franco-Egyptian PhD who worked at the museum, with the Keeper of Egyptian Antiquities, on classification and dating.

There was something about the way Carine el Sadat said

this, with the sun-kissed Mediterranean accent inherited from her Provençal mother, that made it sound like the most beautiful calling on earth, 'the classification and dating of Egyptian antiquities' something modern and ancient, the unearthing of immortal history in a shifting, fractured world. Her Arabic was beautiful too. He watched her mouth framing her words, her fingertips grazing his sleeve, as she reported on the past, on the ages of myth and magic. He wondered what it would feel like, to be something from antiquity, classified and dated, dusted and stored with her delicate touch, placed in the specific acid-free wrapping, the controlled-humidity environment, receiving the studied care given to precious things. Her soft brown hair smelt of jasmine, and he buried his face in it when he held her in his arms, with the innocent pleasure of a child rolling in clean bedlinen. She had found the house, and suggested that he marry her if he wanted to live with her in it. She wasn't a bold woman, and so the trembling boldness of her proposal touched him. It seemed a clever way to get out of his endless wrangling with the Embassy over his visa – his Pakistani passport constantly calling him back home, saying he could stay in other countries, but just for a bit, just as a visitor. He married her out of consideration – she loved him, wanted to live with him, to share his bed, and it was a time and a place where women had to marry the people they lived and slept with; it wasn't just about good manners, it was obligation. He married her because he had been briefly hypnotised by the lovely agitation of her hands as they flew before her in the café, her dramatic gesticulation emphasising a breakthrough in her work, a rare discovery that would force a reclassification, a re-evaluation of previous dating. He married her because she spoke Arabic exquisitely, with the tender music of a prayer. But he mainly married her because he had got bored of filling out immigration paperwork and living under the constant risk of deportation every time he crossed a national boundary. It bothered him that he hadn't married for love; that he had made a marriage of convenience, not so different from the marriages his brothers and sister had been urged into. Consequences. He supposes that he had ignored these for too long; it seems he is now living with the consequences of his actions after all.

'What's wrong, *cheri*?' asks Carine over breakfast, watching as he gloomily surveys his house, and her, with tangible disappointment from behind his newspaper. He has sipped his strong coffee, but hasn't touched the fruit, the juice, the preserves or even the croissants that Carine orders specially from the bakery for him. Maqil fiddles with food, and seems to live on coffee and air, as though nutrition is some sort of peasant weakness holding him to the soil, the peasant need to eat, earn a living, and find a place to shit. He glances at her as he scribbles something down the margin of the paper, his disappointment subtly shifting to irritation, and she coughs to hide her embarrassment that she asked such an obviously stupid question, like a housewife. She coughs again, as though this might somehow reduce the trace that her words have left in the air, as though coughing is her main business, and the question she asked was something incidental that happened before she got round to it. Of course, coughing is irritating too, and she is suddenly annoyed with herself for being so sensitive, for letting herself be tacitly bullied by the brief eloquence of his expression. She lets him get away with too much; what could be more housewifely than that? She feels a rebellious urge to provoke him, to prod him out of his fog into something cleaner and harder, something like anger, something from the heart instead of his head. She coughs once more, this time to clear her throat, to get his attention, rather than to excuse herself, and asks with a sharp edge to her voice, 'I asked, "What's wrong, *cheri*?" Didn't you hear me?'

'I heard,' says Maqil. 'Isn't it a bit early to be in such a bad mood?' The unfairness of the accusation, the pinpoint accuracy of the jab where it will aggrieve her most, leaves her momentarily silent.

'I'm not the one in a mood,' she eventually says. 'It's not about me.'

'Oh, it's all about you,' he says, casually, a little cruelly.

'I just asked what was wrong, Mehmet,' she mutters, sipping her own coffee. 'You don't seem happy; I was showing concern. There's nothing wrong with that. It's a perfectly ordinary thing to ask someone, and you act as though I'm starting a fight.'

'Perfectly ordinary,' he repeats, looking straight at her. 'That's what is wrong, if you're so keen to know.' He stands up quickly, and pulls part of the tablecloth with him, the movement so uncharacteristically clumsy that she wonders if it was deliberate, the tugging of the Egyptian cotton cloth, the clattering of the cutlery and the small coffee cup as they strike the tiled floor. The ceramic cup in two neatly asymmetric pieces. Well, thinks Carine, that's how easily he would break my heart, so casually that you might think it was an accident, a blameless act. She had fallen in love with him across a table in a small café in the market, over sweetened mint tea in a silver pot, and now here they are, barely a year later, sitting at their own breakfast table, and he has already fallen out of love with her, and isn't even bothering to hide it. And with the clatter of cutlery, the neatly sliced cup, she realises that she has started to fall once again back into the unremarkable life she led before she met him. It is already inevitable. She picks up one of the croissants she bought for him, that she doesn't really want but can't bear to waste, to see it given to the servants or thrown away, and rips it into neat lace, placing small pieces in her mouth as she watches him wave away the maid and tidy up the mess on the floor. As though tidying his own mess in this small instance will make up for the larger mess that he will leave in her life, and refuse to tidy.

'There,' he says, 'all done,' and it seems that he is. He picks up his paper, and walks to the door. It is as though in this age of oil and imperialism, of deal-mongering and *coups d'état*, marriage doesn't matter; it is at best a distraction, at worst an obstruction. He doesn't kiss her goodbye, not even in the absent-minded way that husbands are meant to do, when they are already in another place, their office, their working world, thinking of the jokes they will share with their colleagues, the cruel barbs they will throw to junior incompetents who perform their tasks with insufficient care. He is not even looking her in the face. Carine feels that urge to provoke him again; she wants to ask him, 'Do you love me?' to dare him to deny it, or even, 'Don't you love me?' which expects the denial already. At this moment in time, she wants to be seen, to be noticed, more than she wants to be loved, even.

Instead she simply says, 'Have a good day at work, *cheri*,' playing the role of housewife once more, the perfectly ordinary role. It sounds diplomatic, and sincere. She is unsure if she is doing this cleverly, ironically, as he might do. She suspects that she is simply being weak, gutless. No wonder he has fallen out of love with her.

'I'll try,' he says. 'I suppose all animals have a good day in their cages. What would be the alternative?' He looks straight at her, considering her face. 'I suppose caged animals love their zookeepers, too.' And then he leaves. His attack is personal, and she suddenly wishes he hadn't noticed her after all. She now feels just as caged as him, in her elegant, linen-covered bones. With her long nose and small, bright eyes, she is not pretty, she can see that herself, reflected upside down in the coffee spoon, although her husband seemed to find her beautiful when they first met, which was not so long ago. He had hung on every word she said, studied her lips as closely as though he were reading them, and given her the impression that she was the most important person in the world; but he can do that with almost anyone, she has now learned; in a way, it is an extraordinary gift. She is aware that sooner or later she will simply disappear for him. He won't see her as anything any more, not as a sentimental distraction or obstruction, not even as a zookeeper with the keys to a cage. And he, for practical purposes, will disappear himself. The absences for business will become more common than his presence, the traces of him around their home will be swept away with each increasingly infrequent visit – his shaving brush, his metal box of cufflinks – and eventually he will not return at all, and no one will notice, at least not for a while. They are already scattering, she and he, like dust on the breeze. It will happen soon. It has already begun, with the clattering on the tiled floor, the broken cup, the ordinariness of their morning, and their diffident leave-taking. Diplomacy over intimacy. Their failure to share a goodbye kiss and mean it.

Carine gets up from the table and walks to the door with her firm, decided step; she carries her coffee cup with her, even though it is almost empty. She supposes that she is trying to look casual, the sort of woman who drifts around the house sipping a cup of coffee, and who reclines on scatter cushions while reading magazines. But she cannot change the crispness of her pace, as it is an old habit, and she realises that she must walk even quicker than usual if she is to make it to the front door before he leaves. He is getting in the back of the car just as she steps over their threshold; the driver nods to her politely, but she is too distracted to nod back. She simply asks her husband, 'So, will I see you tonight?'

'Not tonight, there's a meeting I need to cover in the south.'

'So tomorrow, then?'

'If I can. Someone was meant to be taking over, but it seems as though he won't be able to make it.'

'So the day after tomorrow?' she asks, trying to sound careless and unconcerned. She had first been attracted by his studied air of mystery, but now his vagueness, his refusal to offer details, his casual references to 'in the south', 'someone', 'it seems as though . . .' just make her want to scream. She wants to pester him with 'where!', 'who!', 'why!' like a wretched shrew. She resents being put in that frustrating position where she is forced to ask the questions; she resents knowing that she will never actually ask them, to avoid being labelled a nag. What is he hiding anyway? What would be so difficult about saying 'in Dahab', 'Omar Khaleed', 'he's off sick with dysentery'? She thinks, swelling up with all her Arab intransigence and French righteousness (or is it the other way around?), *Ce n'est pas Juste*. It is not Fair.

He surprises her by smiling, and for a moment disloyal to her own brimming emotion, she forgets how she has been wronged along with almost everything else. Something in her melts as she feels suddenly warm and luminous, as though basking in the soft slanted rays of the rising sun. This morning hasn't happened after all, and they are still there, at that café in the market, leaning across the low, round table, their words rippling towards each other like ribbons in the breeze.

'Sure,' he says, careless and unconcerned himself; it seems to her that something in the easy way he says this whispers of affection. Dare him to say he loves me, she thinks, dare him to say he doesn't, because she is suddenly hopeful once more that they still exist for each other, She and He. That there is a future as well as a past. 'The day after tomorrow,' he repeats, and grinning, blows her a kiss. Of course he could not kiss her properly now, even if he wanted to; they are in public, and this is Egypt, and the world is changing around them. He shuts the car door. Her reflection flickers indecisively across the window as the car moves off; it is as though she is watching her own departure rather than his.

Paris – 1969 – Play

IT TURNS OUT THAT SOMETIMES, WHEN HE TAKES ONE STEP forward, he takes a couple of steps back, into an old identity that he had once shed like a snakeskin; it seems that identities are like clothes: they can be washed and worn again, with different accessories. That past selves, like foreign countries, can be revisited when the fancy takes him.

Maqil had always liked France; it was a country he had toured during his long student vacations, in the old days when he was known as MSK or Mike. He went back there as Mehmet, on a brief business trip to cover an important Pan-Arab trade meeting; but he soon discovered that Mehmet Khan, the fearless journalist who had emerged from the dusty sunshine, faded whitewash and pungent, oily scents of Cairo, was out of place in the butterfly-bright dining rooms of Paris, in the brittle metropolis that sparkled with artificial light. Mehmet was too Arab and earnest, too well regarded and self-important, a man with a mission who left his articulate and understanding wife at home while he suffered for his cause, risking jail and persecution just so he could expose small tyrannies and minor corruption, and report on irresolvable regional wars. In Paris, Mehmet's worthiness bored him to tears, and if he had bumped into him at a party, he would have ditched him in seconds, in the time it took to drain a martini and excuse himself back to the bar to order another. When the trade meeting was over, the man known as Mehmet wired his copy back to the office, but he himself never made it home. Mehmet collapsed with the pile of respectable clothes left on the hotel-room floor, he evaporated with the view of the sunrise over the sleeping city from the steps of the Basilique du Sacré-Cœur. Sitting there among loose groups of late-night revellers, students spinning empty bottles of cheap *vin de pays*, long-haired travellers with guitars and hippies passing their joints around in a circle, he realised that he was MSK once more, urbane and devastating, a fixture of the smart salons and the Left Bank cafés. The student activist had given up his causes, and had failed to grow up after all; he would now choose to live a swallow-light life, of all play and no work. He would abandon politics and become a playboy. A Parisian.

He didn't feel too bad about deserting Carine, whom he would later refer to obliquely as 'My First Wife' or, even more succinctly, 'No.1', as he never made a conscious decision to leave her. He never packed a suitcase, wrote a letter, or even made a call. He didn't do anything at all, apart from fail to return. It didn't occur to him – until much later, far too late to make amends – that the casual nature of his departure was its cruellest aspect. Carine would not realise that he had left her for days and weeks, and then worried about him for months. She eventually flew to Paris to find him, and when she did, coming across him at a crowded gathering at the American

Embassy, entertaining a glittering group, holding a cocktail in one hand and a feline Parisian princess with the other, she was too humiliated to consider confronting him. He never even realised that she was there, never noticed the one woman who wasn't dressed for an Embassy party walking out of the elaborate marble-floored room through the swinging double doors. She left the party, left Paris, and on her return to Cairo had him announced as dead to save herself the trouble and further humiliation of divorce. She kept her dignity, she mourned him, honestly, and never spoke badly of the man he had been. She even kept his name, which she had taken in the French tradition, until she remarried a few years later; her second husband was a colleague from the museum, a quiet academic with a clear-as-glass conscience, who dissected the mysteries of past artefacts with her, found beauty in the dust of ancients, and kept all his mystery at work and never at home. A man who paid little attention to the wider world, who noticed and appreciated her many small achievements around the house, gave her children and ate the croissants she ordered.

MSK, or Mike, or Michèl as he is often called in France by the locals, the 'ch' shushed softly to give it an alluring, almost feminine tone to those with an anglophone ear, surprisingly and undeservedly appears to live with an unclouded conscience too. But perhaps his rather cowardly and despicable actions – let's face it, that's what they were – regarding his loyal wife have left some damage in his mighty ego, in his soaring sense of self. For one thing, under the influence of rather too many absinthe-infused cocktails at parties, he speaks to his reflection more often than he used to. He protests too much, admitting out loud that he is not made for a calling, for revolution or counter-revolution, for changing the world. He had tried to be valiant and controversial, and it wasn't the hard work or even the

discomfort of occasional stints in prison that had put him off –
it was the tedium of earning a living. He hated, above all else, to
be bored. He hated being boring even more. Prison was a dull
place, the moral high ground even duller, and both were
populated by people he had no interest in.

'I'm a shallow man,' he tells the mirror, linking his cuffs
with sapphires from the little metal box that travelled with him
from Cairo. 'I don't like causes. I like cocktails and cash and
casinos and cars. I like pretty French girls in pretty French
clothes.'

'Everyone likes French girls,' says the mirror man, yawning a
little. 'There's nothing particularly daring or special about that.
We've been here already, haven't we? Is this all you are, some
lounge lizard in white flares? It doesn't matter whether it's New
York in the Village, or Paris on the Left Bank. It's still the same
old you.' The mirror man, tinged green with the absinthe that
has made him so talkative, suddenly does a mocking imitation
of his mother: 'You need to *be* something, my son. Something
respectable. Make a choice, any choice. You could still be a
doctor, a lawyer, an accountant.'

'So I can take money from sick people, crooked people and
rich people?' Maqil replies, mockingly in kind. 'I take money
from those sorts all the time.'

'Well, not enough, evidently,' says the mirror man. 'We're
broke again, aren't we?'

'It's good to be broke occasionally,' Maqil says out loud,
admiring his tailored shirt and gleaming flares, admiring the
panache with which he wears them. He is still occasionally
surprised at how handsome he is. 'It's good to be hungry and
thirsty occasionally, to feel too cold or too hot.' He smooths his
hand across his hair, dislikes the neatness of the effect, and
shakes it out again. 'It's good to feel a little pain, even,' he says,
as he glances out of his window into the night, and looks down

the four storeys to the cobbled street below, glistening with damp and puddles. He remembers the trip to Niagara he made with Susie Santini, the thundering whiteness of the water, the weight of a river falling into the abyss; he had imagined what it would be like to travel with that white water, not in a barrel, but naked and unprotected, a speck of humanity carried on the flood, as minute and comical as a sperm without a tail. He imagines himself now, quite clearly, heaving open the window, the wooden frame creaking on the frayed rope runners, and sitting on the sill. He watches his other self, his mirrored self, his missing self, as he lifts one leg and then the other over the edge, so his feet are dangling high above the dark street, above the muted sparkle of the crystallised minerals embedded in the tar, like crumbled sugar or glass. He watches himself disappear over the edge without drama, and fly off into the night. He is immortal. He is Superman. He blinks and sees that the other man is still in the mirror, regarding him thoughtfully. 'It's good to be broke,' he repeats. 'To live on the edge, about to fall. It reminds you that you're alive,' he says.

In the casino that night, he picks the blackjack table. His memory has always astonished people, the fact that he can play a game of chess against someone without even looking at the board, that he remembers every card that passes from the deck. He starts to win, and from a modest start of a few thousand francs finds himself at ten thousand francs, thirty thousand, fifty thousand, a hundred thousand. His betting becomes more immoderate, the more he has to lose. Approaching three hundred thousand francs, his dealer is replaced, and he sees the casino manager smile and nod in his direction. The casino needs people like him; they need the occasional big winner to give hope to all the other losers in the place, to keep them at the tables, believing that with the next throw or spin or hand, the beam of luck might find them instead, that they will be the ones spotlit in the room. The casino needs people to believe in the democracy of fortune, something available to all, at one time or another. If there wasn't a big winner like him, if there wasn't a little golden god shining with promise at the table, they would be forced to make one with trickery.

His table is becoming packed with slightly drunken admirers, the men in crumpled evening dress, shining with sweat and rosy with cocktails, the women stiff with ruched taffeta and sprayed hair and heavy eye make-up, all with the sense of something sad about them, something cracked and peeling around the edges. While he, dressed in white with his carefully maintained tan from the Middle East, is as glowing as a dewy-faced bride walking down the aisle. And like a bride, he is the centre of attention; today is his day, tonight is his night. People are surreptitiously touching him, brushing his clothing for good luck. A group of friends come into the casino – Virginie, the same Parisian princess who unwittingly prompted Carine into giving up her husband without a fight, just by leaning on him overfamiliarly at a cocktail party; Virginie's American admirer Brett; and Akbar, a wealthy Egyptian, barely out of his teens, who has allowed himself to become flamboyant since arriving in Paris for his education. The mismatched trio, sweet young things in international ice-cream shades of cream, pink and brown, make their way towards his side, edging out the over-dressed strangers; they don't say much to him, trying to maintain a composed indifference to the game, but cannot stop their eyes widening with wonder at his stacks of chips, at his cheering fans. He feels a certain pride, at the show he is putting on for them all. He should stop now, he really should, while he is ahead; he has earned more in a night than many people earn a year in respectable professions. He should take the money in a bag, book into the George V for the night, and take his friends for a victory dinner. He should, but he can't. He can't leave this excitement and simply walk away; he can't abandon the people staring hungrily at him for more. It would be like rolling away in the middle of making love to make a sandwich instead. The show hasn't finished yet, and no great story ends like this – on a high. He feels, if he is honest, burdened by the obscene amount of money he has won; he feels it dragging him back down into respectability, because such a quantity of cash can't be stuffed casually in his pocket or in his gold money clip. It will make him respectable because it demands to be treated with respect – to be given a bank account, a chequebook, a wife with a budget to care for it. With this money raging in his possession, he'll end up possessed himself, back with a mortgage and a marriage and a middle-class life. A mid-life crisis. He begins to lose, just as dramatically as he has been winning; he loses hand after tragic hand, and the spectators at the table realise his luck has changed and start to drift away. His friends stay by his side, but they aren't good enough friends to tell him to stop. They watch his descent into poverty, obscurity, with the fascination of someone watching a slow-motion car crash. The casino manager is still smiling and nodding in his direction, as though he alone understands why he's doing this.

'Oh Michèl, Michèl,' says Virginie eventually, leaning into him with hopeful familiarity once more. His pile of chips is now a sparse scattering, and it is just her and the two men she has walked in with left standing by this gleaming gambler's side. It is possible that she hopes his disappointment will finally make him vulnerable to her undoubted charms. She adds rainbows of meaning to his name; she could be saying it as a gesture of rueful support, or just as a sorrowful accusation, as one might to a little boy: 'Oh Michèl, Michèl, what have you done? You've broken the jars in the pantry for fun.' As she speaks, he hears someone else say, 'Enough. We're done here, aren't we? Take a bow, Maqil.' The tone is irreverent, dismissive of his loss. It is his own voice, he realises, but no one else has heard. Virginie places a sympathetic hand on his shoulder, but she doesn't look at him as she does this; instead she glances at Akbar and Brett, who nod in tacit agreement with her, across Maqil's bowed profile in the smoky light. They all seem to think that he needs their support at this moment, that he needs their compassion. Akbar clears his throat, wondering what jokey comment he can come up with to help make any of this better. Brett looks at the floor, studying his feet with embarrassment, sure that he can say nothing helpful at all. Maqil ignores them all for a moment, but then looks up with a grin, his white teeth flashing in the gloom against his burnished face. He takes Virginie's hand from his shoulder, and rejects it with a gallant kiss.

'You know, it's not my night,' he says carelessly to them, jumping to his feet with easy grace. 'Let's get some dinner.' He adds, laughing, 'In fact, let's get champagne to celebrate my narrow escape from fame and fortune.'

They realise, after an initial moment of shock, that he means this, that his carelessness and his laugh are sincere. What manner of man is this, thinks Virginie, who can recklessly bet everything, recklessly lose everything, and not even care? She is a little bit in love with this playboy she knows as Michèl, but she makes a private vow never to marry such a man, never to risk having his children. She shifts back from him, just a touch, and offers her hand to Brett, who is so delighted as he takes it that he finds he can speak after all.

'Dinner sounds good, Michèl,' he says simply.

'You know,' Akbar adds with humour, 'we should be in mourning for your money. I think that I'm more sorry for your loss than you are.'

'No need for condolences,' says Maqil briskly. 'If I didn't lose it tonight, I'd have lost it tomorrow. It would have been a millstone until then. It would have been a bore.'

66

He collects his winnings, and winks at the manager, and even tips him as he leaves, a casually placed note in his hand. He has still tripled his money that night, so he has just enough to keep him going for a few days. Tonight, tomorrow, the day after; he doesn't like looking further ahead than that if he can help it. And he had kept the count on the cards; he had seen that the new deck had been tampered with, that certain key cards never showed up, and some showed more than once. He feels a certain admiration for the manager in showing this dishonesty, this daring. It matches his own, in some respects. He'd have bought the man a drink, but given how inappropriate this might be, the tip will have to do.

Later, in his rented room, after staying out for dinner and drinks until the early hours, he is sitting on his bed, regretting the need to sleep. The streets are quiet, and the only signs of activity are from the local bakery on the corner: a yeasty, metallic smell, the occasional clattering of tins, and a scraping of coals on clay, as the dough is prepared for baking before first light. He twists open the sapphire cufflinks, a gift from Carine; he had told her once that her mind was a bowl of sapphires, sparkling with white-blue heat and icy intelligence. 'You're teasing me,' she had said over bitter coffee and almond sweets in the medina, but she hadn't sounded offended. 'You think I'm one of those girls who likes outrageous compliments.'

It turned out that she was one of those girls after all, as after their marriage she had presented him with the sapphires. She liked it when he took the cufflinks with him when he travelled, as it implied he took something of her with him too; she always slipped them into his small valise when she packed it for his trips away. That was why he had them now, when really he should have left them for her. Still, he liked the cufflinks very much, and he had left her almost everything else, the spare suit and the toothbrush in his overnight bag notwithstanding.

Dropping the cufflinks into his metal box, each making a hollow, surprisingly heavy sound, like a penny dropping into a well, he hears a knocking on his door; when he doesn't reply immediately, the knocking becomes a banging. He is still thinking of Carine, with her icy intelligence, and wonders if his past has caught up with him once more. He wonders if she is standing there while he is sitting here, with just a cheaply painted door between them. He gets up without saying a word, but hesitates before opening the door, as he is suddenly a little bit afraid that he will betray himself, that he might be truly glad to see her, bury his face in her thick, jasmine-scented hair, and find himself to be Mehmet once again.

The banging continues, insistently and inconsiderately given the inappropriate hour, loud enough to wake the other residents, and he knows that it couldn't possibly be Carine. He is relieved, and surprised at what a coward he is, after all. He opens the door. 'Sunny?' says his ageing uncle, Chacha Zafri, looking at him in astonishment. 'Sunny, is it you?'

'No one's called me that in years, Uncle,' he says, stepping back, trying not to seem too dismayed.

'I've been searching all over Paris for you. Every bloody five-star hotel. Some concierge with a stick up his ass said that he'd sent your case over here last week.' He looks around at the rented room, and snorts with amusement. 'Shitty little place, this. Are you finally down on your luck?'

Maqil sits on the bed, and indicates the only chair to his uncle, offering him a cigar. Zafri, taken aback at the survival of ordinary etiquette in the slovenly space, accepts the cigar, and the efficiently proffered light. He leans back almost affably in the chair. 'A good smooth smoke,' he says grudgingly. 'So, are you enjoying Paris, Sunny? Is the big city treating you well?'

'I'm treated well everywhere, Uncle,' he says. 'It's almost annoying.' He smiles, and asks, 'So what brings you here?

Business?' He pauses, and adds mischievously, 'Pleasure?'

'Enough of that, you impudent scoundrel,' grunts Zafri. 'I'm here because I have to be. The family sent me.'

'What's happened?' he asks, but he already knows. He supposes he knew the moment he saw his uncle at the door, and was trying to delay the inevitable. He knows what must have happened, but he doesn't know to whom. The faces of his family slide before his eyes: Abbu, Amma, Little Brothers Sadek and Syed, Little Sister Uma. Another game of chance. He places no bets. He looks up, and waits.

'Your father,' Zafri finally affirms. 'A heart attack.' He coughs, as though embarrassed to be giving this news, as though he hasn't already given it dozens of times over. 'We've buried him already, obviously; we couldn't wait to find you.' He pauses, while his nephew takes this in. 'He didn't suffer, Sunny. Don't feel bad for him. Feel bad for your poor mother. She's beside herself. She keeps asking for you. Bring back my Sunny, she says, he has to come back. I need my little Sunny.' He adds with grim satisfaction, 'You know that with your father gone, you're the head of the house, Sunny. Everything belongs to you. It's up to you to divide it up among your brothers, and look after your mother and sister. The house, the lands, the money, it's all yours.'

Sometimes, he thinks, looking at his gloating uncle drawing on the expensive Cuban cigar, when he takes one step forward, he takes a couple of steps back, into an old identity that he had once shed like a snakeskin. One move forward, two moves back. A dance. He hadn't been Sunny, he hadn't been a son, for over twenty years. And yet here he is again. Sunny the Pakistani. A middle-class landowner with a grieving mother and a tribe of siblings to care for. Manacled. An animal in a cage, with a different set of zookeepers. It is probably his own fault, and the man in the mirror catches his eye, shrugs and agrees with him.

Consequences. They would never have found him in Egypt, he thinks, looking at the sapphire cufflinks glinting with a sudden fractured menace in the tin.

Lahore, Pakistan – 1970 – Love

MAQIL HAS ALWAYS ENJOYED THE DRAMA OF SUDDEN departures. A shut door, a shrill screech of tyres, a race to the airport and the next plane out. A fight, a flight, a fall. A superhero leaping away from the apartment ledge. Returning, however, is something of a novelty for him, and he finds it altogether blander; returning feels furtive and apologetic. Quietly tragic rather than boldly dramatic. After Chacha Zafri's visit, he wired his mother that he was returning to Pakistan. That he would leave Paris that very morning. But he didn't make it back for several weeks. He didn't lie; he simply refused to race to the airport and fly. He crept back home to Pakistan under protest, he practically crawled. He bought a cheap car from a fellow tenant in his building, flung his valise in the back, and started to drive.

He supposed at first that the sputtering motor would probably have had enough by the border, that it would grind to a halt in an undignified, overheated mess of metal, and that he would dump it and get a plane after all. But the car kept going, stalling and protesting all the way, and so did he. He spent ten or eleven hours a day on the road, with just himself for company, aside from the spider that stubbornly clung on to his left wing mirror for the first nine hundred miles, anxiously rebuilding its web at the gas stations, while he refuelled and bought sandwiches and soft drinks. He watched it with interest while he was driving, and sometimes with alarm as it waved precariously in the air, hanging on by just a couple of sticky threads; he tried moving it inside the car, but the spider always made its way back to the wing mirror; perhaps, like him, it liked the company of its reflection. More probably it liked the bugs that splatted into the glass. The concern he began to feel for the creature's well-being bothered him, and eventually he picked the spider up by an invisible thread and dropped it unceremoniously in a grass verge. He carried on driving, and felt both relieved and abandoned when he glanced at the wing mirror, at the shabby lace vacated by the spider flickering in the breeze. He let his hair divide over his collar, he grew a rakish moustache and beard that made him look like a medieval aristocrat, or an Indian movie-star villain, depending on his bearing. He let everyone he'd been for the last twenty years melt away in the stifling heat of the car, and left MSK, Mike, Mehmet and Michèl to drift behind him like confetti on the wind, like dollars blowing off the back seat from an open case. He was greeted with suspicion at every border, a lone bearded man with an almost empty car. He bribed officials and carried on. At the Pakistani border, despite looking nothing like his passport, he was greeted like a long-lost brother. 'Back for the fight, hah?' said the officer patrolling the frontier. The East Pakistanis, the inhabitants of that piece of Bengal sliced off the other side of India at Partition, were asserting their own independence from West Pakistan. Both East and West Pakistan were readying themselves for civil war.

'Anything to declare?' he was asked, somewhat glibly given the cigars and the whisky that he had bought on route and left ostentatiously on show for all the officials to help themselves to. He considered saying, 'Nothing but my genius,' just for fun, but decided that it might offend the officer and his customs colleagues; he still didn't think he could best any of them in a physical fight, even the relatively small Punjabi like the one standing before him. He shrugged his shoulders, and handed over a bottle and a wad of notes.

'Welcome, brother,' said the border officer, putting away his loot tidily and then stamping the well-worn passport, so overhandled that the gold embossing on the green leather had faded to grey, with just memories of it glinting with sunlight in the edges. 'Welcome home.'

His mother would have been mortified to know that he had checked into a hotel the night before he came back. An inexpensive hotel, where they did not know his family and would not guess who he was. He washed off the roadside dust in the communal bathroom with exposed, complicated-looking plumbing, all bumps and bones, like an awkward girl sticking her elbows out. He had a roadside shave and trim, sitting with a line of middle-aged men outside the hairdresser's shack with damp towels wound around their throats, while the assistants, small boys who should have been in school but were learning a trade instead, ran to and from the shop with bowls of hot water and soap. He accepted tea from the vendor who served the hairdresser's customers. He accepted a shoe polish from a skinny teenager with a grubby box of brushes and round metal tins, whose infant sister trailed after him dragging a wounded plastic toy on a string. He let all the commerce of the street come to him, while he was seated and scented and wrapped; he might as well have been a king on a throne. It is too easy to be a big man here, he thought, passing loose change to the grateful children on the streets. Bhai Sunny, Sir Sunny, Sunny Sahib. It is too easy to be a good man, too.

And now Maqil stands on a rooftop at dawn, and looks across the town that contains his family home. His wide world telescoped down to this little, unalarming place, where children fight kites with their neighbours, and old women drive goats through the streets, where booksellers are too frightened of their landlords and of the future to sell coffee too. He supposes that this is one small thing in his brave new world that he can correct. It is not so much that he is ashamed of where he has come from – it is really not as simple as that. He just knows that he doesn't belong to this dry-as-dust parochial town; he belongs to the big, wet metropolis – where he can be a big fish in a big, wet pond, or else the scum that rises to the top. It is not shame that has kept him away, but rather guilt that has made him come back; he enjoyed his unfettered life too much, and now his father, a gentle man whom he has largely ignored for the last twenty years, is dead. Now he has to take on a dead man's life as his punishment. He knows he needs to make amends. Consequences, again. He just wishes he could feel less hypo-critical about it – he is watching himself once more, a romantic figure in the white saffron-threaded light, and has to resist giving himself a mocking slow clap. I'm doing what is expected, thinks Maqil, like a good Punjabi boy, even after all these years away. Sincerity, he supposes, really would be too much to hope for.

He thinks it best to arrive early in the morning at the townhouse, so his mother can gather the family and they can get the reunion over with. His mother is tearful and thankful, which he expects. 'My God, Sunny. After all these years, my little Sunny.' And then she slaps him hard around the head, which he does not. 'Did you even think of me, of us, all the time you were gone!' And the rest of the family. God, how they have changed, into even more of themselves. How his brothers have bred and re-created themselves several times over. How his sister has become their mother without even trying, dominating her husband while standing meekly behind him. All resentful of his departure, all resentful of his return.

When he comes down from his old bedroom (surprisingly unchanged, except that the brick he had worked out of the wall for his hiding place has been replaced and re-rendered), he has a sense that they are all putting on a play for him – the doting, reproachful mother, the jealous siblings confused by their desire for his approval – and that when he leaves the room, they relax and congratulate each other on the sincerity and success of their performances, and pass the time until his return doing normal things like reading the paper and playing backgammon. He suspects that he isn't playing his part – the returning prodigal, the black sheep – quite convincingly enough. He needs a bigger theatre to be himself – the family ensemble provides inadequate cast support, the downstairs living room makes for an unremarkable stage. It reminds him of mad Mrs Woolf, a brilliant mind choking on domesticity, driven to suicide in the suburbs by the banal choice of whether to have chicken or beef for dinner. He had believed that he was glamorous and different, a bird of paradise that grew from a pot of grey garden dust, but the mirror no longer reveals a Parisian playboy, simply an ordinary, pleasant-looking man approaching his forties. A bachelor in a beige kameez, unmarried as far as anyone is aware, childless, and therefore a failure. To be pitied as much as any gawky maiden aunt. He is no longer

75

surprised by his good looks, but by how small he now appears in real life.

'What will you do, Sunny?' asks his mother one morning, over breakfast. His brothers have already eaten and left for work; their wives are busying themselves preparing the children for school, wiping faces and shouting at the servants to find their satchels. Amid this bustle, his mother asks out loud the gentle question which she used to write to him so persistently, knowing that no one else will hear. It is a source of concern and mild embarrassment to her that Sunny, her golden, gifted child, is now approaching middle age and still has no occupation; that he still seems to be skipping through life like a barefoot boy in a cartoon, with a slingshot in his back pocket. It doesn't mean anything to her that he has made a lot of money in his life, more than she might have dreamed of; as he has lost it too. Activist and entrepreneur, journalist and gambler – these words mean nothing to her; they are just excuses for someone who does not have a proper calling. Who has not given proper attention to this business of life. Doctor, Lawyer, Accountant are the words she understands.

'I think I'm going to open a club,' he says carelessly. He hasn't given much thought to this; he is just making conversation really. His mother's eyes widen, and he knows that she knows of his gambling habit, that Chacha Zafri has told her everything he learned stalking him through Paris, but that she is too well mannered to acknowledge this.

'A . . . club?' she asks faintly, and he grins and nods mischievously.

'Yes, a club,' he replies. 'A literary club for members to read and debate. Is there any other sort?'

His mother recovers, recognises the mischief, and retorts, 'There are plenty of other sorts, Sunny. Tennis Club, Cricket Club, Golf Club, Music Club, Film Club, Theatre Club, Knitting and Crochet Club, Ladies' Luncheon Club . . .'

'So this will be a Literary Club. I'll get premises and provide books, and members can browse over a coffee, buy or borrow whatever they want to read, and have grand discussions about the future of literature,' he says, his mind racing ahead. He adds confidently, making up his proposal as he speaks, 'I'll have an exhibition space for local artists as well, to draw in a wider crowd. So it will be a Literary Club with Art, Books and Coffee. The ABC Club.' He seems a little too pleased with the catchy name that he has apparently just come up with; his mother looks at him shrewdly, guessing correctly that he only suggested Art so he could have an excuse for the neat abbreviation.

'So you're going to be a Gallery Owner? A Shopkeeper? Or a Librarian?' asks his mother, trying to fit his casual declaration into boxes she can recognise, and write in any official form that requires 'Occupation'. She tries to keep the distaste from her voice, as although none of these are professions of status, they are still better than nothing at all.

'All of the above, I suppose,' says Maqil. 'It'll give me time to write.' His mother's eyes widen again, but this time with delight. 'Sunny, you would be a wonderful writer. You tell such funny stories. An author, though, not a journalist. Journalism isn't respectable.' Maqil smiles, as he supposes that he has done something right at last. He can see his mother having her friends over for tea and fried pastries, and serving mango sprinkled with chilli, and orange slices sprinkled with salt, and saying, 'My Sunny, he's a Writer. He's an Author. He's writing the Great Pakistani Novel.' And when she is questioned about the tricksy subject of his ABC Club, she will dismiss it as an eccentricity, a way of surrounding himself with books and readers to inspire his craft, and the sort of thing that writers of genius should be allowed to indulge in.

The truth is that Maqil can write very well; he likes telling stories, and he really does have lots of amusing stories to tell – he writes as he speaks, quickly, carelessly and with lots of dash and verve. The truth is that for all of this, he is no writer of genius, no more than he was in his college days. He still doesn't have the patience to sit in a room and type. He doesn't even have the patience to learn to type, and stabs away at the modern typewriter he has ordered from Karachi with two fingers, gaining a callus on both for his trouble. He looks at the twin mounds of tough skin on his fingertips with irritation; it proves to him that writing is too much like working with one's hands, just as much as a plumber or electrician or any manual shit-shovelling labourer. It feels too much like *work*. He would have to do a lot of typing to produce a novel of eighty thousand words – at least one hundred and sixty days of typing at five hundred words a day, if he follows the Graham Greene model, and he really can't plan that far in advance or behave that consistently. He likes books, but the truth is that he is no reader, either. When he gets to the point where he can work out what's happening, he confirms his guess by looking at the last few pages, and leaves the book altogether, believing sincerely that he has finished it. With short books he doesn't even get that far – he'll just read the back cover, the first page and the last page, and then quote from it as confidently as a scholar. He can't see why other people *wouldn't* skip to the end. He is unsure of the point of beautiful prose, because it just gets in the way, doesn't it? And although his natural vanity wants to produce the book of his life, something all about him that will be admired, and hold his cleverness up for everyone who might have doubted that he was anything more than style over substance, the same vanity suspects that actually it would be wrong for him to write it. His mirror man agrees: 'You should be written about, you shouldn't be the writer.'

'I should be written about,' he repeats to his reflection, and pushes the typewriter away.

By contrast, the setting up of the ABC Club is hardly like work at all; it is fun, even. He is better on his feet, strolling through town, than he is at a desk; he is better at charming local businesses and officials than sitting alone in a room. He scouts out buildings for rent, and finds an old townhouse in the elegant Gulberg district, just a few streets away from his family home. He buys up old books from the local sellers, and pillages the libraries of his family and friends to make up the loan stock, the name of the donor marked on the front and given free membership for the first month. He gets doctoral students from the university to make up a well-read, polite and poorly paid staff, and sets up an office for himself. He is soon bored with the nuts and bolts, and advertises for a manager, to cover the day-to-day running and set up events. The ABC Club is a success, and soon all the intelligentsia of Lahore are members, and engage in literary and political debates in the comfortable rooms. Maqil looks down on all this from his desk on the first-floor gallery, a benign king on a throne overlooking his court. He stabs away at his typewriter, writing not the great novel that he claims, but glib and irreverent articles for the international press, which he writes for mischief rather than money, and publishes under one of his many pseudonyms, delighting in the fact that his old associates, colleagues and creditors might see his name brazenly in the paper.

'What will you do, Sunny?' asks his mother gently over breakfast, before he sets off for 'work', another day of socialising over coffee. The question now has quite a different meaning. She is no longer asking about the occupation of his days, but the occupation of his evenings, nights and weekends. The lack of a companion in his life. The lack of children. The conspicuous lack of love. Maqil knows from this that she has already made enquiries, and he shudders to think of what she might have turned up for an almost-forty dilettante.

'Nothing,' he says. 'I wouldn't want any woman willing to have me.' He is unembarrassed by this declaration. Love has simply passed him by; he never really found it, and it was never a sufficient enough priority for him to search for it. He is unembarrassed that he has always been happier on his own. Besides, he tried marriage once, tried it with someone elegant and intelligent, and found himself immune to its charms.

Over the next few weeks, he finds himself being introduced to young women at the ABC Club, by family, friends and in-laws, rather too consistently for coincidence. Farhana is a talented singer, you must have so much in common, says his brother, bafflingly, as one thing Maqil emphatically cannot do is sing. Parveen works in the history faculty at the university, says his old crony Jamal, whose pretty wife is every bit as pigeon-plump as the fat daughters of Mr Shafik that he was once caught spying on. Mumtaz is studying medicine, says his sister's husband's mother's cousin, dropping in casually with the embarrassed intern by her side. They are all more pretty than they are plain, and of marriageable age, that is to say, far too young; they are all from good families fallen on hard times, which is why they are being introduced to him rather than to younger, more conventional suitors. He is politer to them than he needs to be, because he feels sorry for them; these prettily accomplished, eligible women all bore him to tears.

And then he sees her from his throne above the Club, unfashionably thin, unfashionably dark skinned, unconventionally dressed in a dramatic burnt-orange sari that makes her glow like a candle in the shadows. She walks to the centre of the room, and looks around, holding herself with astonishing poise, as shimmering as dust suspended in a ray of light. She looks up,

80

and finding him looking back at her, smiles pleasantly and efficiently. 'Mr Karam? I'm Samira Rai. We have an appointment,' she says in English, tinged with a Kerala accent. He is overwhelmed by her, and can't take her all in at once; he doesn't know where to look first, and lets his gaze slip down in inches from the crown of her head: at the thick cloud of hair that she has cut into a smart bob, like a European movie star, at the bright mischief of her eyes, at the whiteness of her teeth against her skin, at the dip between her lower lip and chin. There is no family member, friend or in-law present; no one appears at his elbow to nudge him with a coy introduction. He finds out for himself that Samira is a history of art and European languages graduate who works in public relations. His family, friends and in-laws will all point out to him later that she is of unmarriage-able age, that is to say, far too old, and that she couldn't possibly be considered pretty, with her dusky skin and lack of womanly curves. Looking at her now, it is obvious that she isn't anything as ordinary as pretty. Her collarbones are astonishing, the soft dent between them surprisingly tender.

He sees a future as she walks up the stairs, her head held high and almost regally, her skirts sweeping like a future queen approaching her rightful place, the throne by his side; he sees Samira on the Left Bank, in skinny black sweaters, a beret studded with metal, and extravagant flares; he sees Samira in Monaco, holding court in a casino to a crowd of admirers, dragging on a cigarette and blowing perfect rings; he sees Samira in New York in the winter, dressed in white cashmere and drifting around the museums and galleries, which she already knows by heart. He is astonished at how easy it is, after all these years, to fall in love, every bit of his flesh and blood tumbling towards hers. He had once felt that he was immortal, heroic – a man of steel whom bullets would bounce off, whom knives would bend uselessly against. He is disappointed at how ordinary he is, after all, an ordinary man so easily pierced by a bumbling cherub's arrow, finding love where he wasn't seeking it. The cover of the latest book he has failed to read, *The Fall* by Camus, mocks him openly. He is just as disappointed at his own dumb incapacity: he hasn't yet said a word to this woman (he is, still, stupefied by her); she must think him an idiot for not having opened his mouth, or worse, for opening his mouth and closing it again as he has found nothing at all to say, like a goldfish or a guppy. He hasn't so much as touched her hand. He knows almost nothing about her apart from what he sees – is he really that shallow, to fall in love at first sight? He is watching himself as he watches her approach, and shouts to himself in silent frustration, 'Say something! Say anything at all, you bloody fool. Don't just sit there like the furniture.'

'Can I help you, Miss Rai?' he finally says, and they are both surprised at how bad tempered he sounds – he who is normally so unfailingly polite – as though she has thoughtlessly interrupted him in the middle of something important. Well, hasn't she, he argues, hasn't she just interrupted my life and shown me a whole new world with her at the centre? You bloody fool, he replies sharply back to himself, you stupid, ordinary little man. Did you really say 'Can I help you?' Really? You want to fall sobbing at her feet. You want to sing out loud and dance in the rain. How can you possibly help her? You can barely help yourself.

'I should think so,' she says, still pleasantly, still approaching. She reaches the landing and walks up to him, holding out her hand. 'I've come about the managerial post,' she explains. 'You seem surprised. Your assistants didn't tell you about our appointment?'

So here she is, in front of him, offering her hand. Not in New York, or Cairo, or Paris, but here in the heat and dust of a good residential neighbourhood in Lahore. Defiantly dressed in a politically incorrect south-Indian sari, showing too many inches of smooth-skinned waist, when every other woman in Pakistan would be wearing a more modest and patriotic shalwar kameez. He is still sitting down, he realises; but now he is unsure that his legs would have the power to hold him up. He remembers belatedly that one of the assistants had mentioned yet another interviewee for the managerial post; they had altogether failed to mention that it would be a date with destiny. He is far too scared to take her hand, and does so only when she gives him a slight frown, no doubt wondering what is wrong with him. He shakes her hand tentatively, relieved that there is no spark of electricity, no shock, just a cool and surprisingly dry palm, with nails trimmed short and polished pale pink.

'They told me,' he says, scowling to hide his discomfort. He has a physical pain in his gut, as though he's just been kicked there. He has been told that love hurts, in countless silly songs, but never realised it was true until this moment. 'You know, you're really very late. I've been waiting for you.'

She frowns herself at this declaration, and then replies calmly, 'I wasn't aware of being late. I'm sorry for the inconvenience. How long were you waiting? Would you like to reschedule?'

This flurry of comments and questions from her: how long was he waiting? He doesn't have the nerve to say that it was possibly all his life; she would laugh in his face. And rescheduling would involve her walking away, sweeping down the stairs with the same majesty and air of finality with which she arrived. He realises, with a flash of insight, that he could tell her to leave, to have her walk away, and never reschedule at all. He could keep his life private, keep his heart closed, and live alone and unfettered until he dies; he could shut that door and burn that bridge. But he just isn't strong enough – he's a fraud. He is as weak as every hopeless man before him who has had his head turned by the flash of a neat ankle under a skirt, by the flash of scornful eyes. What fools they all are, really.

'No,' he says briskly, his tone implying that he is too busy and important to reschedule. 'I've waited long enough for you, I'm not waiting any longer.' And so she sits, taking the chair on the other side of the desk, apparently unconcerned by his cross tone. She has such presence, it is as though a pool of music has formed around her, accenting her slightest gesture, as though every surface she touches will become shining and reflective. He guesses that she is taller than him by almost two inches; he wonders if this is why he didn't find himself able to stand up when she approached him. This is the Punjab, not Paris – he cannot ask her back to his place for coffee and liqueurs, and pour out his heart to her all night. He can only speak to her like this, in public, in a workplace, at a social gathering. He is uselessly aware that all his charm has escaped him, and that all she sees is a bad-tempered, possibly tyrannical future employer apparently lacking in basic social skills. He has no idea how to woo; he has never done it before – he has never needed to. Flowers, chocolates, poetry – all these seem ridiculous as the currency of romance: the gardens around the townhouse are bursting with more flowers than a New York florist could provide; chocolates melt in the heat, and a grown woman would surely not appreciate the sort of sticky, childish sweets that do not; and they are already surrounded by poetry, placed on the highest shelves of the Club, as poetry is the least popular category. He panics slightly, as he knows that he should be interviewing her, but the most obvious question, 'Come live with me and be my love,' the most obvious request, 'A jug of wine, a loaf of bread and thou, singing beside me in the wilderness,' both whispering from those forgotten volumes on the top shelf, cannot be repeated out loud.

'So, tell me why you think this job would suit you?' he finally asks. And she nods and proceeds to do just that, telling him about her degrees in art history and Italian, her work in the faculty library, her experience in events management for an international pharmaceutical company, the public-relations work she has taken on for a local literacy charity. She has done everything apart from actually run an Arts, Books and Coffee Club, although she admits, with humour, that she does not know how to make coffee, as she has never had to make her own. He realises, with increasing delight, that he has every excuse to hire her, even though he would have hired her if her only business experience had been tidying the papers in her grandfather's office. He supposes he ought to ask what sort of books she likes, just to be thorough, just to keep her in the chair opposite him for a few moments more.

'So, what are you reading at the moment?' he asks casually.

'A little bit of everything,' she replies. 'I don't really have favourites.'

'What about poetry?' he persists. 'Any favourites there?' It seems that his head is suddenly full of little-read romantic verse; he is afraid that he will start speaking in sonnets and iambic meter, quoting nights of cloudless climes, and intemperate summer days, and dark red love knots and red, red roses, unless someone slaps some sense into him.

'There's a line from Tagore's "Flying Man",' she replies. 'I think I like it because it's about ambition rather than romance. *Land and sea had fallen to his power. All that was left was the sky.*' She looks at him with a half-smile. 'I know it's not very original to quote Tagore. In fact, it's not original to quote anyone at all, quite obviously. I promise not to make a habit of it.' So there it is, a slap in the face. She has only just met him, and she has read his mind.

'I'm so glad you came,' he says, only realising just then that

85

he has said it out loud, as besottedly as the whispered borrowed poetry.

'Well, thank you,' she replies. 'I'm relieved that you think I was worth the wait.'

It occurs to him suddenly that she might be flirting with him, or possibly even attempting to charm him, the way he has charmed so many others. He wonders whether he should test this – perhaps by telling an unfunny joke, and seeing if she laughs, or by voicing an absurd opinion, and seeing if she agrees. He decides to do both. 'You know, there are a lot of bachelors in the Club, so a lady like yourself has to be prepared to put up with their indelicate sense of humour. They have a saying, "A woman for children, a boy for—" '

'I've heard that one already,' she interrupts him. 'Don't feel you have to give me the punchline.'

He looks at her carefully; she is neither shocked nor amused. She is simply waiting for him to make his decision regarding her.

'Will you start tomorrow?' he asks, almost humbly.

'I'm afraid I'm not available quite as soon as that,' she says.

'The day after tomorrow, then,' he suggests, trying to keep his voice calm, trying to avoid an off-putting note of desperation creeping in. He keeps his palms flat on the table, as he is afraid that he'll embarrass himself otherwise, that he'll touch her hand, or brush the forearm that she is now resting lightly on the desk. It seems to him ridiculous and suddenly magnificent that men and women should be drawn to one another in this way – without logic or reason or even self-knowledge – just by this tugging of flesh, a magnetic attraction from iron-soaked blood, in living tissues and aching guts, as ancient and unstoppable as bodies falling together with gravity. She is his highest ambition; all that is left is the sky.

'The day after tomorrow,' she agrees. She looks straight at

him, and holds out her hand again. It is as though she has been the one deciding whether to take him on, instead of the other way around. It is as though they both know that this is true. He takes her hand, without hesitation this time; he is aware of the dryness of her palm, the pink polish on her nails. She smiles.

London – 1973 – Marriage

MAQIL IS RUNNING IN HYDE PARK. HE'S IN AN EXPENSIVE tracksuit purchased by his stylish second wife, his hair (worn long, like every other man in seventies London) flipping in the breeze, and kept off his forehead with a sweatband. Now in his forties, he feels the need to take care of himself a little more; he has lived a butterfly life, as light and bright as wings in flight, but finally this carelessness has taken its toll. His relative indolence, the lack of any conspicuous physical labour, the meals characterised by haste (foie gras scooped straight from the tin, peanut butter eaten from the jar) or extravagance (five-course marathons at clubs and hotels, entertaining friends or being entertained) have not been kind to his figure, and on seeing himself in a mirror with his wife, as they entered a cocktail party, he was aware that he was becoming a fattish man with a skinny wife. A shortish man with a taller wife. An oldish man with a slightly younger wife. Suspiciously close to a sit-com cliché. A joke. He had noticed, with jealousy rather than pride, that her ass was higher and firmer than his; he had not realised how much his vanity about his hair, just slightly receding now, had extended to the rest of him. He had got heartily sick of other men and women at society functions looking appraisingly at his wife, and then nodding with approval at him, as though thinking that he had done well for himself, rather than the other way around. He is a man of shallow gods and trivial desires, and he has decided to spend twenty minutes running in the park for the state of his once perfect little tush. To get the plums back in his buns. He's not committed to running every day – just when he feels like it – and the truth is, he's always been good at it. He's proud of how easily he runs, of how little he sweats, as though the object of running should be ease and the lack of sweat, rather than the other way around. He still sticks to that self-imposed rule – if he's not good at what he does straight away, he stops doing it. None of this try, try again. He congratulates himself, once more, on the amount of time this little directive has saved him in his life. Although his wife (his second wife, his sultry and sports-car-sleek No. 2) will point out, with exasperation and wit, 'Well, what are you saving all this time *for*, exactly?' as it seems that he does nothing at all, except more of the same. And his answer, as always, is 'Just for fun.' Because ultimately what else is there in life? What's the point of anything, if not for fun?

And this is fun, now, running around the Serpentine, ducks quacking and swans hissing in his wake, while nannies in prim hose walk Silver Cross prams, and tourists conspicuous by their too-bright clothes take photographs of each other, and couples with identically long hair and jeans neck under the trees and merge so much with each other that you can't tell which is the woman and which is the man, or whether they're both men or both women after all. And why not? This is the life he loves, this is a town that loves him. Life, London, Love. This is a magnificent April morning, shimmering grass that feels so clean underfoot that it squeaks, air that feels so pure that it pings like a wine glass. This is a once-handsome man regaining the perfect butt he deserves so he can compete with his wife. There is something delicious about the lightness of his concerns. His brief return to Pakistan, the couple of years spent weighed down by family and responsibility, by filial duty to a dead father, has evaporated like morning dew on the early roses in the park. Love has not been the cage with a keeper he had once feared – as it turns out, he loves someone, and she has set him free.

He is guiltless about his departure from Pakistan, as this time he had not abandoned his family, but had rather been – to all intents and purposes – abandoned. He had finally crossed the line that had got him kicked out of the family home, and warned away by his relatives – in turns furious and tearful with his treachery – he was told never to darken their door again. It had honestly never occurred to him that his family would be so vehemently opposed to his marriage. He had supposed, and indeed intended, to irritate them mildly with the hasty nature of it – the casual elopement that was barely an elopement, just an afternoon off work, and in fact Samira had insisted on returning to the office afterwards, to finalise some paperwork and finish arrangements for a new artist's exhibition. They had then spent a few days in the mountains, before he returned to tell the family. Samira had not been looking forward to the prospect of joining him in his family home; it turned out that they had never needed to, as his family refused to recognise the validity of the marriage; they refused to recognise her as his wife. Of course, she had an unmentionable family background – she was from a Hindu family who had converted to Christianity, as some sort of whim on the part of her eccentric father, a conscientious objector to the caste system, who had refused to arrange marriages for any of his children, and who had overeducated his daughter to be practically unmarriageable anyway. Of course she was a 'career girl' and of an unthinkable age (thirty, at the very least), with a height to look men squarely in the eye rather than simpering up through her eyelashes. And then there was her wonderfully dark skin – which made him think of Belgian chocolate, and Italian espresso, but which was compared less charitably by his family to low-class, low-caste mud. When his mother had first met Samira, as the new manager of his little enterprise, she had commented at dinner that the girl (she was hardly a girl, but his mother had no desire to refer to her as a lady) was probably part Negro, with her polished-wood skin, her thick hair, and the impertinent nose that was flared rather than hooked. Perhaps she had hoped that this little comment would be enough to damn any fledgling romance, forgetting that for Maqil, calling someone black was simply a matter of fact, much like eye colour or height; he didn't even register until afterwards that she had intended to be insulting. His melting-pot education and frequent travels meant that he was conspicuously lacking in racism, although he made an exception for the Germans, not because of the last world war, but simply because as a nation they seemed strangely immune to his charms. It annoyed him most because he spoke near-perfect German, the result of his time spent studying in Switzerland; he wondered if they disliked the Swiss cheese and milk chocolate flavour to his accent, the cuckoo clock ticking in his diphthongs. It seemed a rare failure on his part, that for all his hard-earned language skills he had never yet successfully grifted, hustled or bankrupted a German. He should have gone to Rome and learnt Italian instead; his espresso-skinned Samira spoke charmingly accented Italian with a passion that complemented her operatic temperament.

He supposed that Samira's religion, career, age, height and

colour would have bothered his family, but that they might still have put up with it, had it not been for the small matter of the war. Samira's family, although long settled in Kerala, were originally from the Indian side of Bengal, and as soon as East Pakistan announced independence as Bangladesh, she became, to the eyes of his family, a traitor. An infiltrator. A spy. The fact that he continued to employ her was bad enough – to become a traitor by marriage was unforgivable. Even more unforgivable were his comments regarding the atrocities that had been reported, committed by the West Pakistan army in the nascent state of Bangladesh. He published these in the international press alongside his usual glib articles; the family blamed Samira's subversive influence. In fact, Samira had nothing to do with it – she had no interest in politics, and was too smart to court controversy. To be honest, he didn't do it from any worthy political motivation, either; he just did what he wanted, and said what he thought, without particularly caring what others might say, both of the opinion, and of himself. He sometimes wonders if this is what persuaded Samira to marry him: the fact that he simply lacked some fundamental sense of self-preservation. Perhaps she – unmarried at thirty-at-the-very-least, and full of herself, with good reason – believed that she could protect him when he failed to do so. Perhaps – and this thought amuses him so much that he breaks into a snorted laugh in mid-run – she wanted, and still wants, to *save* him. He suspects that he is way past saving, especially from himself.

He remembers sitting at his desk above the Club, watching her work downstairs. Samira would start the morning with her clipboard in hand, briefing the assistants on the business of the day. He would see her greeting all the new members she had brought in, with the ads she placed on local radio, and the publicity she had put up at the multinationals; she chatted with them easily, made introductions, offered coffee from the steaming percolator. (The graduate staff were the ones who made and poured the coffee; Samira charmingly refused to be anyone's coffee wallah.) He saw Westerners from the pharmaceutical firm she used to work for come in to talk to her, and stand too close to her for his liking, admiring her too obviously. The nervous blond fellow from Sweden who was clearly in love with her, too tongue-tied to make much sense when he spoke to her, discouraged by her professional courtesy. The dark crew-cut Canadian with the confident swagger who talked to her as bluntly as though she were a man, calling her 'Sam' in a familiar tone, and offering her cigarettes, which she accepted graciously. 'So, Sam, what's he like, that mad old superior of yours?' the dark crew-cut asked too loudly one day, just making idly irreverent conversation, not realising that her boss was within earshot. Maqil had fumed with frustration behind the bookshelves where he had been browsing through new stock; it seemed that she had not only failed to notice his charms, she had even been making him out to be a figure of fun to her former colleagues, a cranky caricature, an anecdote to share.

Samira had glanced around quickly at this comment, and on catching Maqil's eye, completely failed to look abashed at being found out. She gave him a conspiratorial smile instead, a smile that practically winked with mischief, and then turned her attention back to her friend. She exhaled a perfect smoke ring, and the way the young man's face flickered into yearning as she did this made Maqil realise that the confidence and swagger were just for show, and that the dark crew-cut was in love with her too. He suddenly felt sorry for the boy, he felt a kinship; they were brothers in arms, both fighting for the same lost cause. 'My mad old superior?' she repeated thoughtfully, inhaling and blowing another smoke ring. 'Well, he's a little mad, far too old, and I'm not altogether convinced that he's my superior,' she said. Maqil felt the dewy kinship evaporate as quickly as it had settled; damn you, he seethed in the direction of his rival, this is war.

'Really,' laughed the dark crew-cut, relieved at being taken for a confidant.

'Really,' she said, and she leant towards him, as though about to tell a secret. 'But you know, I think I might marry him anyway.'

When the young man had left, defeated, Maqil had gone to her. 'Well, sir,' she said impishly. 'Can I help you?'

'I hope so,' he replied, 'because I can barely help myself.' He reached out and touched her for the first time since those mannish handshakes at her interview; her sari blouse was sleeveless, and he held her by her cool forearms, his fingertips sliding down from elbow to wrist to hold her soft, dry hands, breathing in her smoky coffee scent. She smiled again, she practically grinned, her teeth very white against her perfectly painted lips, her lips very red against her dark skin. She looked like she was about to laugh out loud, at the daring of it all, as she moved forward, very slightly, and brushed her cheek against his, with greater intimacy than a kiss or an embrace. The bustle of the Club receded around them, everything toppled down like cardboard cutouts and fell flat, already part of a previous life. She was so perfect that he couldn't have made her up – he didn't have the imagination. He was glad that he had never bothered looking for love, because standing in front of him was the proof that he would have had no idea what he really wanted. She was uninterested in the circus or clownish ceremony of a big wedding, and he was interested in sealing the deal as quickly as possible – they didn't marry that afternoon, as it was too late in the day to make the appointment; they didn't marry the next day, as the witnesses they had picked off the street at short notice made an excuse and disappeared as soon as they were paid. So they married the day after that. And ran away to the mountains, like smoke curling into the air, like fugitive scents on the breeze.

He has finished his first circuit of the park, and finds that he's enjoying it enough to do another one; he's sweating a little now, his heart is pumping as much as if he were betting everything on the final roll of the dice, and he is warmed all over by his rushing river-flowing blood, by the kiss of sunshine on a spring morning, by the honeycomb memory – dripping-gold, sticky-sweet – of honeymoon kissing in the mountains in the north of Pakistan. He is warmed all over by Life, London, Love. He finds, to his delight, that he can speed up, as much as slow down, so he begins to sprint faster, and faster. The sedate jog he began with at his front door has become something reckless, and free. But he is already perfectly free, so he has nowhere particular to run. He realises that the only place he ever runs to now is home, which happens to be wherever Samira has chosen to hang her hat.

Samira and her hats. Samira and her vanities, both small and monumental. He didn't know very much about her before he married her, although it didn't matter; he had already been certain that he knew all he needed to know when he first laid eyes on her. And he had been right – every trivial thing he learns about her conspires to make him love her more. Even her flaws, her short sudden temper, her passionate refusal of favours, her occasional cruelty to those who admire her (that poor crew-cut Canadian back in Lahore), her baffling belief that she is nearly always right, seem to him magnificent. It had been her decision to move to London; she dismissed his other suggestions as she didn't want to bump into his former girlfriends. Even her jealousy is touching. And now they are in London, she delights in being different. In Lahore she had achieved this with her daring saris (the blouses strappy or backless for the evenings, sometimes revealing as much as four inches of waist), her modern haircut and her progressive attitude. In London, she exploits her exotic ethnicity; her skinny, childless figure is made for fashion, and she stalks through society perfectly dressed, with the regal insouciance of a jungle cat. She is able to judge the social standing and relative importance of someone at a party within seconds; she herself is universally admired. When Maqil teases her about her love for clothes, the magazines she studies, the boutiques she haunts (where she is greeted by name), the new snappy little hat she has bought, she retorts bluntly, and without a trace of embarrassment, 'It's different for a man. Everyone pretends that they're so modern and liberated, but the truth is that women are still judged by how they look. It's all right for you, Maqil, you can flap around in those old flares without anyone noticing or caring. But the wrong choice of hat could ruin my career.' He likes the fact that she refuses to abbreviate his name; she is the only one who calls him Maqil, his real name; he is surprised by how much he likes her saying it. It feels personal; it feels more intimate than any of his Mike-alike nicknames. Samira is now working in the public-relations department of a glossy magazine, and he has happily delegated the management of his wardrobe to her – after that pointed comment about his outdated white flares from Paris, he made no objection when she chose to retire them.

Samira likes to work, but seems perfectly happy that he does not. She accompanies him to the smart clubs in Mayfair, where he sometimes makes a lot of money at the tables, and sometimes loses so much he can't even cover the cab fare home. She accepts the wins and the losses with indifference – 'If you win, you'll lose it tomorrow; if you lose, you'll win later.' She earns her own money, and pays the rent on the small Belgravia apartment they live in. She describes him jokingly as her kept man; she says this without an edge to her voice. If anything, the words are blurred by affection.

He's running faster now, and faster, and finally starts out of the park towards their flat, stopped only by the occasional traffic light, racing out carelessly in front of a slowly lumbering bus, a big red 74, and more dangerously in front of a beetle-black cab. Some young mother is walking smartly up the road with her offspring held firmly by the hand, the poor lad dressed in the humiliatingly twee uniform of a local private school, in orange knee breeches and matching knitted jumper. It strikes him as odd, now, that Samira and he have never had the children conversation. Perhaps she simply assumes they will. It is just as possible that she assumes they will not. Now in her mid-thirties, she would be considered somewhat elderly for a first-time mother, whereas he is at an age where he could just as easily be a grandfather, back in Lahore. And besides, she likes the freedom of their life as much as he does, the occasional weekends in Rome or Paris, the lingering at hip parties until the early hours; she likes the pertness of her small breasts, and the flatness of her stomach.

He has left the bustle of the traffic behind him now, and slows his pace as he runs into the tree-lined shady square, set around a manicured gated garden for residents, and reaches the chunky stone steps to their building. His heart is still beating wildly, and now he is sweating profusely, steaming with the stuff; he has never felt quite so sticky, quite so soaked through, and it seems obscene for it to be happening here, on a scrubbed London doorstep, rather than in some desert hell-hole. He has something of vital importance to tell Samira, but for some reason he cannot grasp exactly what it is. Samira, in any case, is not at home; she would already have left for work, wearing white sunglasses that form a perfectly round 'O' of appreciation around each of her shaded eyes, with her immaculate handbag and stacked heels. Her perfectly chosen hat. Samira, Samira, singing beside him (off key; she can sing no better than he) in the wilderness. Samira, so furious to find out that she was his second wife: 'What am I then? Your runner-up trophy, your silver medal?' Samira, all angles and sharpness, with nothing soft or sweet to her, like a crisp green apple, a wedge of acid lemon, a slap in the face. He is so full and wet and dripping with this news that he cannot tell, that he bursts with it there on the doorstep, accompanied by the comically small stone lions on each side of him, each no bigger than a large cat on a pedestal, roaring silently on his behalf. He falls sprawled on the steps, twitching slightly, as shooting pains travel up his arm, and the high box hedges of the garden square merge with the luminous, cloudless sky. The world recedes around him, drops down flat like cardboard cutouts once more, and he has the impression that he is looking down at himself from a great height, dripping on the stone steps like a piece of meat on a marble block, a tragic hero on a plinth, spotlit in bleached-white sunshine; there is something carved and satisfying about his pose, something final and unambiguous. Minutes pass and he is unable to say or do anything. So this is it. So here we are. Me and He. Myself and Him. Our doorstep domain, our trembling remains. And this is what remains of all the people we were; this is what remains of Life, London, Love.

London – 1973 – Blackout

'I SWEAR TO GOD, MAQIL, THAT YOU'D BETTER COME through this. You're not leaving me this way. If you dare die on me, I'll kill you. I mean it. And then I'll dig you up and kill you again. I'll make having a heart attack seem like a picnic in the bloody park.'

'A heart attack and a coma. It's punishment, isn't it, pure and simple? You can't lead that sort of life and get away with it. I mean, a coma, that has to be a wake-up call, doesn't it? Hey, did you hear what I just said? Coma, wake-up call? Well I thought it was funny. I bet you Mike would think it was funny; do you reckon he can hear us?'

'Well, this is what your sainted mother has to say: "Samira, please tell Sunny that we forgive him, and that we love him. We pray to God that he recovers. If he does, when he does, please persuade him to return to Lahore, where his family can care for him properly. He will be treated with respect here, as the oldest son deserves. He will be treated like a king. I have lost a husband, I will not lose a son the same way. Allah the All Merciful will not permit it. With kind regards, Maryam Iqbal Khan Karam." The bitch. That manipulative, pious old bitch.'

'You know what I thought when I first heard that Mike had had a heart attack? I was amazed the old bugger had a heart to start with; I thought he had a roulette wheel in there instead, spinning chips and cold hard cash around his arteries. That man bleeds money. He just bleeds it.'

'God, the fortunes that you made in your lifetime, Mike. The fortunes that you lost. Mine included. No hard feelings, though, no point now, is there? And what was the use of earning all that money? What's your legacy, when all's said and done? Nothing. Well, nothing except a good-looking wife. In fact, a *damn* good-looking wife.'

'Damn, good old Mike. We'll miss him, Samira, we really will.'

'There's really no need to miss him, he's not dead yet.'

'What did you say?'

'I said, He's Not Dead Yet (you stupid little man).' This last was said under her breath, and Maqil's visitor didn't hear her. No one heard her, apart from us.

These voices drift up towards him, and recede gently, like waves lapping on a shore. Snatches of conversation briefly illuminate the dark. Different versions of his life play out in his unconscious mind, like dreams: he is in Pakistan, married to the snivelling girl next door. He is in New York and has become an artist, a gangster, an anti-nuclear protester. He is in Cairo, dusting artefacts in the museum by Carine's side. He is in Paris, down and out in a tattered raincoat, taking stolen wildflowers to Oscar Wilde's grave. He is asleep on his back in a white field of snow, on flat, featureless earth in an unnamed country, freezing to death, and as time passes hurriedly, scudding like clouds, he sees the dark red glow of daylight filtering through his shuttered eyelids, deepening to the pitch black of night, and then dissolving back to the colour of his blood with the dawn. Red or Black are the only colours he now sees, in this long, fitful sleep. The colours a baby would see in the womb. Red or Black. Place your bets. The voices of his many visitors and well-wishers seem unsure that he is coming back, but he knows that he is. He knows that he is about to fall back into his world, although he does not know when or where he will land. He knows that the game isn't over, after all. Once again, Samira is right. He's not dead yet.

Maqil finally opens his eyes; he blinks away the luminous red and black shadows, and sees a wall of white and grey. An empty chair beside the hospital bed. A bowl of fresh fruit, including mangos tied in gold ribbons. A pair of sunglasses with round white frames linked by a narrow line on the bedside cabinet. In his blurry vision, they seem to be announcing zero-dash-zero in proud plastic lettering, like a tennis score: Love-All.

Samira walks briskly into the room, nursing a fresh cup of coffee, and stops and stares at him. She is perfectly made up. 'Damn, Maqil,' she tells him crossly. 'I've been lingering by your bedside like a grieving widow for three days and nights, and you have to catch me out the one time I go to get my own coffee. I'd swear you did it on purpose.' He is both touched and impressed by her lack of surprise, by her apparent certainty that he would wake up; her threats aside, it seems that she knew all along that he was coming back – today, tomorrow, or the day after – and was waiting for him. As impatiently as he had once waited for her. As confident in her expectation as a villain stroking a white cat.

'How do you know I didn't?' he croaks, taken aback by how

weedy and rough his voice sounds. Like the voice of an unimportant man. She seems surprised too, and her expression softens, as she sits by his side, and squeezes his hand gently.

'You gave me such a bloody scare. You should have heard the way I've been swearing at you. When they told me what had happened, the first thing I wanted to do was slap you. I mean, what the hell were you doing? Running in the park like some bloody teenager.'

'You're very attractive when you're angry,' says Maqil, admiring the crease in her forehead, the firm line of her jaw. 'If you'd been sat here weeping, I'd have probably gone back into a coma.'

'How do you know I haven't been? Three days, Maqil, three days of you lying here like a lump in the bed. It's like you weren't even you any more. That's a long time not to be crying.'

'Was it really that long?' he says with interest, finally picking up on this. 'I must have lost a bit of weight. My ass is probably better than yours already.'

Samira shakes her head. 'You've been peeing in a bag, and your first concern is the state of your holy butt,' she says, exasperated, almost admiring. 'You know, I talked to the doctors – they said that with your family history and your lifestyle – with our lifestyle, I suppose – this was a car crash waiting to happen.' She inspects the hand that she is holding, the one with the drip needle poked into the back of it, and smooths down the tape that holds it in place. 'Your mother sent a message. She wants you back in Pakistan. She didn't say anything about me – she worded it so carefully I had to read it twice to realise how bloody rude she was being. She thinks I'm not taking "proper care" of you. Apparently, you need to be treated like a king.'

'Kings always have more fun in exile,' he replies dismissively, thinking of the deposed royalty he had rubbed shoulders with in Monaco, when he and the other Parisians went south for the summer. How much they enjoyed being bought champagne, and glumly losing their crested shirts at the gaming tables with beautiful actresses by their sides, and partying on big white yachts. It was so obviously a better life than cutting ribbons in front of hospitals, visiting troops in wartime and factories in peacetime, that he was surprised anyone was taken in by their air of studied gloom and amateurish alcoholism. 'Samira, I have something important to say to you. I was running home because I had something to tell you, and I finally know what it is.'

'Well, what is it?' she asks, impatiently again.

'I've decided that I'm ready to have children,' he says. He watches as her jaw drops and her mouth falls opens, forming an O of astonishment that matches the Love-All of her sunglasses on the cabinet. She realises what she is doing, clamps her lips firmly shut into a hard line, and shakes her head with disbelief. She is saying neither yes nor no, and now it is his turn to become impatient. 'Well?' he asks.

'You will never be ready to have children, Maqil Sunny Karam,' she says. 'I'm telling you this right now for your own good. I thought you knew yourself a little better than this.'

Her unexpected resistance fires him, and he counters petulantly, like a toddler who's been refused a specific toy for Christmas, 'But I want children. We're going to have children.' She lets go of his hand, and gives him a stony look. 'Or just one, maybe,' he adds, in the spirit of compromise. 'A little one. We can fit one little baby into our lives, can't we? They're only so big – it would fit in the spare drawer.'

'Wow,' says Samira, in mocking wonder. 'You'd really give up your spare drawer for a baby? I've heard of the sacrifices that parents make for their kids, but that's just going too far. I mean, where would you put all your mismatched cufflinks and odd socks?' Her sarcasm is so pure that he almost misses it altogether, and for a moment he really does wonder where he would put the mismatched cufflinks and odd socks. Samira seems to think that she's made her point. 'Not one, not ever,' she says firmly, and a little sadly too.

He realises then that she does want children after all – it's just that she doesn't want them with him. He is too old and unreliable, but she has chosen him before motherhood. And so her chance of being a mother is receding gently, just like his hairline, and soon she will be too old as well. His request for children suddenly seems transparent and shallow, a puddle on concrete, reflecting his own rippling face – he thought he might die, that's all, and so he supposed he ought to father a child before he really does die, like any good Pakistani male, to leave another Maqil for his family, to carry on the overbestowed and underused name. He is touched by her selflessness, as it is a gift he lacks – it seems unfair that she should have to make that difficult choice, simply because of the impossible position he has put her in. He sees that she is waiting for something from him, a sign that he agrees with her, and so he nods and replies to her in her native language, 'Yes, yes, fine. You're right.' These are almost the only words he knows in Malaylam. And they are the most useful, as she is right, almost always. So he is not technically lying to her, even as he sees her face flood with relief, and he receives her warm kiss, first on his forehead and then on his lips, before she goes to get the doctor. He has never been more aware of her love, as complicated and compromised as they both were already. But still, love, after all. That men and women should be so comically connected, that their breath and blood should be shared like this, that love should be expressed and reproduced by these trivial physical acts, the softness of a tongue in a mouth, the hardness of a prick seeking its own introduction, seeking to make life, to found a dynasty. That their love might leave an enduring legacy on the earth, or else just a stain on the sheets. Magnificent, ridiculous.

Lying in his bed, he has already started to plot, and feels that frisson of excitement that a new project always gives him. Samira will not make this difficult choice between marriage and motherhood, he thinks, delighted with himself. With possibly the most selfish, arrogant decision he has made in his lifetime, he decides to make the choice for her.

London – 1973 – Entrapment

MAQIL LIKES TO THINK OF HIMSELF AS A MAN OF TRIVIAL concerns, drifting where the wind takes him, but his new lifestyle decision propels him from inaction to ambush. Suddenly he is a man with a plan, a mercenary on a mission. A few days after his return from hospital, he announces a trip to Milan and the Italian lakes, just for fun. Samira is immediately suspicious, and rightly so. He dislikes going to Italy with her; Samira's Italian is obviously much better than his, so people tend to speak to her rather than him; he has the sense of being the funny, stilted foreigner, shown up by his soignée, articulate wife. However, she likes Milan too much to protest, and causes a quiet sensation as she stalks the boutiques by day and the clubs by night. They spend a couple of nights on Lake Garda, and most of it in bed, as neither of them are outdoor types, and it is too hot to do anything outdoors anyway. She sleeps naked at night, and he always finds it amusing that she buys exquisite shift nightdresses, strappy and flowing, specifically so she can put them on in the morning when she gets out of bed, to have breakfast on the terrace. He also sleeps naked, having been broken of his bachelor habit of wearing pyjamas, but refuses to put on pyjamas or even a dressing gown for breakfast. It just seems a waste of time, when he can shower and wear his day clothes straight away. And so this is how they are found at breakfast, sitting at a marble mosaic table overlooking the lake, a pale-gold man in a dark shirt, and a dark polished woman in pale silk, a prosperous-looking gangster and his rumpled, just-out-of-bed moll.

'You're like a machine,' complains Samira. 'We got out of bed at exactly the same time, twenty minutes ago, and in the time it's taken me to go to the loo and drag myself to the terrace for coffee, you're already washed and dressed and look like you've had a couple of meetings and played a round of golf.'

'You know I'm not made for relaxing,' he says, almost apologetically, as he skims last night's *Corriere della Sera* with a pen in hand, marking up the margin of the newspaper with dark blue doodles.

'Why are you reading the obituaries?' she asks, lightly enough to sound suspicious.

'Just an idea I had,' he says.

'Oh for God's sake,' she mutters. Suddenly aware that she is hunching over her coffee like a well-dressed hag with a hangover, she pulls herself up, running her fingers though her untidy hair, and then looks straight at him. 'Give it a rest, Maqil, please. We're having a holiday. I'm not going to spend the next few days watching you grift the bereaved family members of men of influence for their inherited wealth.'

'Now that would just be tasteless,' he chides, delighted at how well she knows him, 'I was just looking at the addresses. I have a feeling that dead people's houses will sell below market price here – they're a superstitious lot, the Roman Catholics.'

She laughs, despite herself. 'Dead People's Houses, Incorporated. As though that's not tasteless.' She sips her coffee, black and unsweetened. 'So you'd buy and sell them on for a profit?' she asks conversationally.

'We don't have to sell them all on; we could pick one and keep it for ourselves for weekends,' he says casually. 'Maybe in Venice, or Rome, or somewhere.'

She glances up at him with surprise. 'A property? Somewhere you own? That's not like you.' She adds with amusement, 'So, are you getting tired of flitting on the breeze, butterfly boy? Are you growing up?'

He shrugs at her gentle digging. 'Well, it's not as though we'd live there.' He adds lightly, 'In fact, you'd better get it in your name. The thought of paying all those Italian taxes makes me itch, not to mention going through the bloody paperwork. You'd get it done faster; your Italian's so much better than mine.' He doesn't look at her as he says this, and seems suddenly a bit too interested in the paper, turning the page with a gentle rustle.

She puts her coffee down and looks at him again. 'Is that your way of saying you're buying me a house?'

He shrugs again, and grins boyishly at her serious expression. 'So call it growing up, if you like,' he says. 'Don't look so cross; most wives like getting stuff – you know, furs, jewels, houses. If we put it in my name, it would get lost at Goodwood before the contracts were signed.' He sips his own coffee, and glances at her with a touch of concern. 'Don't you want to order some breakfast?'

'This is breakfast,' she says, waving her lit cigarette and gesturing towards her coffee.

'You should eat something,' he says.

'Well you never do,' she replies. She is no longer looking at him; she is thinking of an apartment in Venice, or Rome.

'I've got enough duck fat in my arteries to float my boat for a lifetime. You're just running on empty and nicotine fumes.'

'Fine, I'll have some juice,' she says dismissively.

'That's hardly breakfast,' he argues. 'That's just a mixer without the vodka. Have some toast, at least?'

Samira raises her eyebrows at his uncharacteristic insistence; she isn't sure whether she should be irritated or flattered. But she is absolutely sure that she can't be bothered to argue this early in the morning; at least not before she's finished her coffee. 'Maybe I'll have a caffè latte too,' she suggests, by way of compromise. 'Juice and milk, you can't ask more than that.'

'I'll call room service,' he says, jumping to his feet with that easy energy that never escapes him.

'You're weird in Italy,' she calls after him, having finally decided that she isn't entirely displeased. She likes his unpredictability; he never bores her, at least. 'When did you ever care about buying a house, and feeding me up? You've become like an Italian mamma.'

The second part of his project is to announce that he is going for the snip. He does this one evening when they are getting ready to go to his Club. He mentions it casually while he is standing behind Samira, buttoning his jacket as she sits at her dressing table, sliding on her rings and attempting to fasten the tricky clasp of her necklace.

'Good, you need a haircut,' she says, deliberately misunderstanding.

'You know what I mean,' he replies. 'I'll be limping for a week, so you'd better use and abuse me tonight.' She is still fiddling with the delicate chain behind her neck, and so he steps forward, and pushing her hair and her hands aside, does it up for her. She doesn't say thank you, but simply turns back to the mirror and picks up her brush instead; the casual nature of this gesture implies an intimacy beyond good manners. If he pressed her to thank him, she would doubtless point out that she had never asked for his help in the first place; the thought of this makes him smile.

'I'm in Paris for Fashion Week,' she points out to his reflection in her oval mirror, 'so you can do your snippety-snip and limpety-limping without me.' She pauses. 'But of course, you knew that already.'

'Of course I did. I wouldn't schedule surgery with you around; you'd fuss over me and stop me going out.'

Samira turns around and takes his hand in a tight grip, far too tight for comfort. 'You know I don't fuss, and I know you too well, Maqil. I don't know what you're up to, but if I come back from Paris and find that some old girlfriend or your Number One has been sniffing around you with muffin baskets while you're supposedly laid up at home, you better pray that a second heart attack gets to you before I do.'

'Tch, always so suspicious,' he says with delight. 'I love that you get jealous, I really do.'

Executing the third part of his plan is easy; it simply involves switching Samira's pills. She still takes the pill despite his vasectomy, as she doesn't believe, rightly, that he had it at all. There is a doctor, a cardiologist at the private hospital where he had been treated for his heart attack, who owes him a favour. In fact, Maqil had manipulated the unsuspecting specialist into investing in a sure-fire profitable project, which had proceeded to collapse, but he managed to get back most of the doctor's original investment, less of course his own ten per cent commission.

'Remember to tell your wife that these pills are different

from the ones she's been taking. They look the same, and there are fewer side effects, but if she doesn't take them at exactly the same time each day, to the hour, they can't be guaranteed as effective.'

'I'll take care of that,' he promises.

The cardiologist looks warily at him, and asks with a nervous laugh, 'Look, old sport. She does know that she's taking the pill, doesn't she? You're not grinding them up into her morning porridge? If she wants children and you don't, you two had really better talk about it.'

Maqil laughs heartily at the irony of this, practically to tears, before finally admitting, 'Believe me, she's the one who doesn't want children. And as if I'd ever be able to slip pills into her porridge. She doesn't eat porridge in the mornings. She doesn't eat a damn thing.'

And as with every long con, the final stage of his family-planning project is the easiest still, as simple as breathing. He waits until she orders seafood for dinner one evening, and puts a few drops of an unpleasant-tasting medicine, designed to induce nausea, into both their plates. 'God, the crab's off,' mutters Samira. 'Why do I order crab in the summer? What was I thinking?' They both spend an hour throwing up that evening. In an odd way, he quite enjoys the sense of being purged; not while actually vomiting, of course; the streams of acid-soaked fluid shooting out of his throat and nostrils are anything but enjoyable. But the feeling afterwards, the sense of having set a fire down his guts, the acid burning in his damp tissues; he feels clean inside. Hollow and shiny – ringing like a bell. He and Samira sit afterwards wrapped in towelling robes they have stolen from a five-star hotel, sipping iced water with lemon, laughing at the mess they both look. They make love to salvage what is left of the disastrous evening.

And finally, he just has to wait for nature to take its course. Which is hard for him, as he isn't particularly patient. He begins to worry whether his well-laid plan could be scuppered by mere biology. Not his own – he really did visit a clinic during Samira's week in Paris, and verified that all his parts were in good working order, despite his age and lousy diet. All his swimmers were lined up and ready to go. But it only now begins to occur to him that Samira, his slender-hipped, shadow-like Samira, might not be built for motherhood; she is so thin that she barely seems to menstruate. Once again, luck is on his side, and he doesn't have to wait for very long. He watches her body for signs, and in fact he guesses before she knows herself, as he notices her going to pee more often than usual, listens to her complain that her favourite brand of Douwe Egberts coffee had begun to taste metallic, and finally sees her breasts bloom. She is surprised at her weight gain, concerned at her clothes hanging wrong, and eventually goes to see a doctor.

He waits for her at the window, and when he sees her storming back up the road like a scudding thundercloud, he smiles. Showtime, he thinks, and practises his expressions in the mirror. The mirror man gives him a thumbs-up and a wink; he congratulates himself on his cleverness, yet again, and composes his face just in time, as he hears Samira's key in the door.

Samira walks in, slams the door behind her, and thumps her handbag, her favourite Furla in mint green, embossed with delicate calfskin flowers and leaves, on the table.

'Everything OK?' he asks brightly, as it obviously isn't.

She throws him a hard, exasperated look, and pours herself a coffee from the percolator, clanking the spoon against the ceramic cup and banging it down on the counter so that the liquid sloshes over the edges.

'There are some pots and pans you can bang, if you want to make a real noise,' he comments. 'What's up?'

'An idiot would have worked it out before now,' she mutters. 'Why didn't I? Does that make me an idiot, Maqil? Do you think I'm an idiot?'

'What are you talking about?' he asks reasonably.

'No period for weeks on end, getting fat, peeing constantly, and bigger tits than I've had in my life. The wall normally has more boob than me.'

'You're pregnant?' he asks, for confirmation. He keeps his face straight, and tries to look neither triumphant nor annoyed.

'Yes,' she says simply, suddenly not so angry, as though the admission has leached all the brittle energy crackling from her. She sits down, slumps on the white leather armchair, her coffee still in her hand. 'I'm pregnant.'

'God, that's awful,' he starts to say, deliberately unconvincing.

'Don't lie,' she snaps. 'This is what you wanted, isn't it? I knew you never had a vasectomy.'

'Well of course I didn't,' he agrees pleasantly. 'I'm not having anyone mess around with my waterworks. I just hoped you'd believe me and get sloppy with your pills.'

'But I didn't,' she wails. 'I took them every day! If I forgot in the morning, I'd always have one by the afternoon. This baby is some kind of medical miracle. It's the one per cent error rate.'

'So who are we to argue with a medical miracle?' he says, appeasingly.

'You're pleased, aren't you?' she accuses him.

'What do you think? Of course I'm pleased. I'm delighted. You know that I wanted kids.'

'It's too late to terminate – they think I must be seventeen weeks gone already. It's not a little blob of protein there now, it's a baby. With eyes and ears and teeny-tiny toes. It can hear us, for God's sake! It's listening in on us right now!'

'So let's have the baby,' says Maqil, sitting next to her on the

113

winged edge of the impractically pale chair, and putting his arms around her. 'I've been bored lately; it might cheer me up to have a project. It'll be fun.' He nuzzles his face in her neck, kissing just below her hairline, before adding, 'Besides, I think you look quite hot with boobs.'

Despite herself, Samira allows a puff of laughter to escape, before settling back into her gloom. 'I just feel so trapped. And you're going to feel trapped too, Maqil. You may not now, but you will, I promise you that. They call it confinement for a reason. You know I'm right, I almost always am. It's like a curse.'

'Look,' he says, 'I know you think that I'm not reliable-father material, and that I'll lose the school fees every Friday night on the tables. But I'm trying. The kid will inherit the place in Pakistan if I get myself shot by someone who takes a dislike to me. And now you have the apartment in Rome, don't you? Where we can run when everything else falls apart. And I know I lied to you about the vasectomy, but you saw right through me anyway.'

'Of course I did,' says Samira, taking some small consolation from this. 'I always see right through you, Maqil. Like Cellophane. I'm not like everyone else.'

'No, you're not,' he says, pleased with his own cleverness. 'You can read me like a book.' It was a standard play of his, the rueful admission of a small misdemeanour, so that the big one would go unnoticed; it was simple to execute, and always surprisingly effective.

'I just wish I knew how it happened. I really did take the pills, every day.'

'Do you remember the bad crab?' says Maqil. 'Maybe you threw up the pill too.'

'Oh,' says Samira. 'Maybe. You know, I never even thought of that. I suppose I could have thrown it up with the crab.' He wonders whether he should have mentioned it, as he suddenly isn't sure her pregnancy tallies close enough to the crab to make this suggestion believable; he hadn't thought at the time of the mild food poisoning that the dates would be quite as specific as seventeen weeks, but she seems convinced, and even a little guilty. 'Oh, Christ, it's my fault,' she moans. 'How could I have been so goddamned stupid – of course throwing up would affect the pill.' She pushes him away angrily. 'It's your fault too. Irresponsible bastard.'

'Well, you always knew that much about me,' he says, relieved that she hasn't mentioned terminating the pregnancy again, that she doesn't seem to think it is an option. 'One little baby, that's all we're talking about here. Nothing's going to change between us; we can still travel and do everything we want.' He kisses her on her nose, above the flared nostril that still has an inky dot of an old piercing. 'I'll even clear out the spare drawer, if you like?' She lets him hold her, and sighs, but doesn't try to smile. She lights a cigarette, and he says without thinking, 'I guess you're going to have to stop all that now.'

'Oh, here we go,' she says. 'Liar. You say nothing's going to change, and then you're already telling me not to smoke. What's next? Are you going to tell me what to eat for elevenses and start pressing wheatgerm and stinking sardines on me? Are you going to chuck out all the cocktail mixers and tell me to get fresh air and exercise?'

'No,' he lies, as he is already thinking that Samira had better stop drinking and start eating that very day. That she will need to substitute her liquid lunches for wholemeal sandwiches.

Samira glances at him irritably, and says, 'You don't understand, Maqil. It's not just that I don't think you'd be a good father . . .' He shrugs, not taking offence, as anyone would think that. 'It's that I never wanted to be a mother. I look at all those fat old cows shoving their chubby offspring around Hyde Park in their buggies, and I pity them. I just feel so smug that I'm not the one covered in baby sick and simpering over booties and speaking the ga-ga-goo-goo rubbish. And now, look at me. Look at us, Maqil. Knocked up like any stupid free-loving flower child in a field. I just feel so cornered, like someone's played a nasty trick on us. I just feel so, so . . .'

'I know, you said it already . . . trapped,' says Maqil. His reassuring smile falters for a moment, flickers like a shadow passing over his face, and he has to consciously keep it in place, like a politician at a rally. He had been so taken up in his little project that he had left no room for doubt; he is beginning to realise the full cost of his arrogance. Consequences. He would almost feel a bit better if Samira could guess what he has done, so she could yell at him a little or a lot – but she hasn't guessed, and it is possible that she never will. He is too good at this sort of thing; it's what he does for a living. And the beauty of any long con is that no one can see where it first started. At a hospital bed, where he conveniently decided to misinterpret the drifting expression on her face, the subdued tone in her voice as a yearning for motherhood, simply because he thought it was about time he left a mark on the world, instead of a stain on their sheets. A legacy beyond that of his past-its-sell-by-date corpse, a litter of betting slips and a good-looking wife. A child to perpetuate his myth and tell his story to future generations; a dynasty founded with his DNA.

Maqil had assumed that Samira would be pleased with the pregnancy once it was achieved, and take over all the parenting duties, like most women would, and like most women do. This assumption now seems hopelessly naïve; one thing he should have known about Samira is that she isn't like most women, and he has a sudden image of her tripping off to work in her hat and high heels, and leaving him at home with a squalling infant and a bottle of formula. He shudders inwardly at the thought, remembering his brothers' children bickering and tumbling around the Lahore townhouse, littering the floors with their plastic toys and picture books, polluting the air with their indignant animal screeching, their invasive scents of milk and pee and Johnson's baby oil; he had opened the ABC Club at the weekends simply to avoid them. Samira is right, as she almost always is: children are untidy and bothersome. They take up space. They sneak on you. They chain you down. Little manacles. The bells of the ornate church a few streets away start ringing for midday. Just that morning he had heard those same bells, and full of the sense of his achievement, full of Samira's soon-to-be-confirmed pregnancy, they had pealed with celebration, golden rings bursting into the air and scattering like confetti. Now the bells are slow and dull, mocking him too obviously; and with their tolling, he feels once more the sluggish weight of responsibility, family, community, closing around him like iron bands on his wrists, the heavy notes dissolving into the air he breathes, into his damp, living tissues. Heavy metal poisoning.

'So trapped,' repeats Samira unrepentantly, refusing to return the smile that now feels fixed on his face, like melted wax that has set into place and been sealed with a ring.

'Well, at least it's just one little one,' he says at last, still cheerfully, as though determined to be a good sport. He has to get away from her and that baby inside her, the baby that already has ten teeny-tiny toes and is listening in on them, sneaking on their private conversation. He has been far too clever; for the first time in his life, he regrets that there was no one to stop him from doing what he wanted. He springs up, and heads towards their bedroom. 'Maybe I'll go and clear out that spare drawer,' he says.

* * *

Just as they are getting over the shell-shock of sharing their lives with a child, sure in the knowledge that they will never do anything this stupid and irresponsible again, they are given some news. The usually cheerful midwife frowns as she measures the bump, while Samira lies on the sofa, her trousers rolled down to the crotch, her blouse pushed up to just beneath her breasts. Samira has insisted that Maqil leave the flat for the appointment, although he catches a glimpse of her and her exposed abdomen as he walks past the living room towards the front door, her expression fixed rigid with having to put herself through this indignity. He is just about to let the heavy door swing shut behind him when he hears the midwife speak. 'The baby's too big for dates. We'd worked it all out based on when you had your last period, but I think you must be further along than we thought,' she says.

'What?' says Samira.

'What?' says Maqil, walking back into the flat and into the room, ignoring Samira's glare as she sits up and pulls her blouse back down over her stomach. A few weeks further along means that Samira would have got pregnant before he switched her pills or poisoned her food. It means that his clever family planning had nothing to do with the pregnancy, that the baby was the one per cent error rate, or the medical miracle that she had first supposed.

The midwife's expression of cross concentration has cleared altogether, and she smiles serenely once more, enjoying the attention in a gentle way, her round cheeks becoming delicately rosy. 'Well, it's either that, or it's twins,' she says. 'Now wouldn't that be something?'

A couple of appointments later, the midwife is certain, as she presses her practised hands with painfully hard precision down across Samira's abdomen, and listens intently to the grainy whooshing noise from her grey, battery-operated apparatus, like a wartime cryptologist deciphering a tricky code. Two heads and two bottoms. Two subtly distinct heartbeats.

'Just one little one,' says Samira sarcastically to him. The unfairness of twins pinches her face into something approaching misery, and makes her almost unattractive in repose.

'I'm so sorry,' he says at last, finally ready to come clean. This is beyond the worst thing he has ever done; he had never even entertained the possibility of twins, despite having been one himself. He supposes that by the time they are free of the little bloodsuckers, they will both be old and grey and possibly wearing half-moon glasses; they will have become the kind of drearily conventional couple who only converse through their children, dutifully observe anniversaries, and dismiss each other's birthdays with flowers. The kind of couple who look disapprovingly at one another for clattering a silver-plated spoon around the cup as they stir their tea.

'This isn't your fault,' she says. 'Twins run down the female line, apparently, so the two-for-one has got nothing to do with you. Don't think for all your arrogance that I ended up this way because of your super-swimmers. It's just because I produced two eggs; a couple of sitting targets. Unless the babies are identical, in which case it's just a freak of nature.' So he doesn't come clean after all. It seems easier not to; Samira is angry with the babies, angry with herself, and he supposes it wouldn't help any of them if she is angry with him too.

Samira, smoking defiantly throughout her pregnancy. Samira, refusing the proffered glasses of milk or cups of hot chocolate at breakfast, and ignoring the specially ordered croissants from the French boulangerie and the pastries from the Italian bakery that he tries to tempt her with. Samira, stalking off to work without looking him in the face, or kissing him goodbye. Samira, returning and drinking a cocktail, daring him to say something as she lifts her chin and stares him down, looking him full in the face after all. Samira's swelling belly coming between them in bed, until she eventually takes herself off to the spare room, surrounding herself with pillows for support. Samira's face, and arms, and legs and even her ass becoming slimmer than ever, as the infant parasites suck everything from her into her womb; Samira photographed for an article at work, looking like a model with the surly pessimism of her expression, the curl of her lip making her stand apart from the gaggle of ridiculously beaming pregnant colleagues, clutching and caressing their stomachs as though they were in love with themselves. Samira's belly a mass of seething limbs beneath her tailored designer outfits, Samira's swift, graceful movements becoming lumbering and awkward; Samira in hate with herself, uncomfortable and unpleasant to everyone, up to and especially him, her face narrowing like a knife flashing on a dark night.

For the first time in years, he finds himself thinking of Carine, and feels some sympathy for her. So this is what it is like, living with someone who is barely there. When he remembers Carine, he thinks of cool shades of blue and green, whitewashed walls, and the gentle bubbling of water in their courtyard. Of surfaces that were smooth. Polished and dusted daily. He imagines taking a holiday in his old marriage, a weekend break, where he might feel guilty because of his absence rather than his presence, where he might be the one refusing the croissants and stalking off after a bitter breakfast flavoured with bitter coffee. A marriage where he is the one who breaks the cups.

And finally, Samira in hospital, twenty-three hours of labour, one wet baby finally emerging, still in its bag, and the other somehow stuck, offering only a useless hand, and then a foot, however much the doctors try to shift it. They pass the baby girl to him, and wheel Samira into emergency surgery for a Caesarean section, knocking her out in seconds with general anaesthetic and putting the knife to her skin within the minute. As he is ushered into another room by the nurse, it occurs to him that she might not survive, that he could be left alone with a baby girl (a girl! of all things; no son to carry on the name, but a girl!) to bring up on his own. Well, this is his punishment, at last. The heart attack was just a warm-up. He has killed his wife with his own cunning and cleverness.

The little girl in his arms yawns, and then mews a bit, like a kitten. She doesn't seem hungry or cross, and she is surprisingly alert, despite the yawning. Her small eyes are half open, and glittering darkly; it is hard to see what colour they are under the artificial lights. Brown, he supposes, or black. He'd been told in the hospital that babies are meant to have blue eyes, but perhaps that is just Caucasian babies; his cousin in Pakistan has blue eyes, and is considered a great beauty because of it, despite looking – to him, at least – rather soft and pudding faced. The baby is wrapped up closely in white blankets, a red knitted hat on her head. He has no idea where this home-made-looking hat has come from – it certainly isn't one that Samira has brought with her; the baby outfits she has purchased are in tasteful shades of ivory, cream and sand. He can't count the baby's fingers or toes, as he doesn't dare to loosen her wrapping, and so all he can see is a patch of face, a not-quite-real face, unformed and blotchy, a ridiculous little stub of a nose. The baby, so plain and scaly, doesn't look as though she could have come from Samira's sleek, dark body. He imagines Samira's disappointment with it, waking to find that this scrap of humanity is all she has to show for those months of discomfort, for those hours of hard labour, and he suddenly feels protective over the child, because of her ugliness, her scrappiness. His daughter – the result of his plotting, the forest snare he painstakingly set up under a pile of loose leaves, the result of his rather twisted self-love.

The midwife and the doctor approach him, walking quickly and smiling to show that there is no bad news. 'Your wife's fine,' says the doctor, as the midwife takes the baby from his arms. 'She's being stitched up now, and then we'll take her to recovery. She'll come to in an hour or so.'

'That's great news, thank you,' he says. 'Can I wait with her?' Then he realises that both the doctor and the nurse are looking at him curiously. He understands why when the doctor coughs and the midwife speaks up. He has forgotten to ask about the other baby. In fact, he has briefly forgotten that there is another baby.

'You have a son,' says the nurse, kindly. 'A lovely little boy.'

In the early hours of the morning he sits by his wife's bed, and she has both children brought to her, one on each side. A mismatched pair: the scrawny girl, bald and dark and suddenly rather cross, and the chunky-thighed boy, with a good mess of hair stuck down to his scalp with his mother's juices, pale and placid. Samira has already left the pregnancy behind her, and wears a cream silk vest, which ties behind her neck and back, the only thing she could put on with all the tubes running into her after the surgery. She sits up in bed as though the drips to her arms, the blood drain on her stomach wound and the catheter prosaically collecting her pee are all just slightly bothersome accessories that could be shrugged off at any time. She looks like the woman he had breakfast with in Italy, with her just-out-of-bed hair, and just-been-in-bed eyes. She puts the children on a pillow on her lap, looking closely at them, and then she smiles. 'Ugly little things, aren't they?'

'Hideous,' he replies, relieved, and a little jealous that they get the smile rather than he. That he just gets the tail end of it as she glances up at him.

'I guess we'll just have to love them anyway,' she says at last.

He is about to reply, to say something funny or comforting or loving, but sees that she is humming to the babies, and not paying him any attention. He sees with sudden clarity that he is no longer No.1 to his Wife No. 2, the gold to his silver medal. That he is now third on the list, and possibly has already been for months. He sees that Samira's aggression towards the babies during the pregnancy – choking them with her smoke, starving them of nutrients, poisoning them with alcohol, and on one occasion steaming them in an expensive hotel sauna – has all been in vain. She has tried not to love them as much as she loves him and their life together, but she hasn't succeeded. She is a woman like every other after all. And he has made her this way. It is all his fault. Of course, he thinks, looking at his own face reflected in the window beside her curtained bed, the night sky swiftly lifting with light ahead of the dawn, he might just as easily be wrong about this; it might just be another vapid assumption. It occurs to him that this time, he should stop assuming, and simply ask.

'As long as you don't love them more than me,' he says, jokily, coughing to lighten the statement, as Carine used to do. Oh, Carine, if only he could tell her how much he finally understands.

'What a thing to say,' comments Samira mildly.

'Well, that's hardly an answer,' he says.

'It was hardly a question,' she replies neatly, turning her attention back to the babies, to dark and pale, cross and calm, slight and chunky, bald and hairy. He looks at the window again, and watches the reflections of Samira, his anything-but-identical children, and himself; he sees a man with a wife and a conventional family, one boy, one girl, and feels perplexed, and a little disapproving.

London – 1982 – Parenthood

The Karams

THERE IS A PHOTO OF MR AND MRS MAQIL KARAM, TAKEN AT their dining table. We must suppose that one of the children, Mika or Zamir, took the shot, as there is no one else who lives at their smart Belgravia address, a rented apartment with elaborate and expensive furniture that came with the flat, a pair of glossy white bunk beds being the only addition that the couple have purchased, for the twins' room. The photo appears to have been taken some time after breakfast, as most of the breakfast things have been cleared away, but a pot of jam with a sticky teaspoon balanced on the lid remains, as do a couple of coffee cups, which are pushed out of the reach of the couple, and presumably empty. Mr Karam has been caught in the act of leaning back in his chair, of in fact leaning his entire chair back, so it balances on the rear two legs like an obedient dog; he is making an expansive gesture with his arms, which opens his sports jacket and reveals an equally expansive belly, straining the material of a casual shirt in a boisterous shade of green. He must have been telling a story, and we can guess from his attitude that it was something amusing, something profitable in one way or another, as he is smiling widely as he speaks. He is only just made aware of the camera as it clicks, and glances in its direction as he is speaking, his eyes caught on the camera, his mischievous smile facing away towards his audience. He appears to be a jovial, prosperous man, in good health for his fifties, although he no longer looks so young for his age. His hair is cut rather shorter and sharper than he used to keep it back in the seventies, and it suits him, giving him a clean-cut appearance, and making his receding hairline less obvious.

Mrs Karam, the lucky recipient of this amusing tale, is not aware of the camera, and doesn't glance towards it as her husband does. In fact, she isn't looking at her husband either. She is gazing down into the tablecloth as one might look into the bottom of an empty whisky glass, hoping for some sort of answer there, hoping that there might be some kind drop left. The tablecloth is plastic and brightly coloured in broad stripes; it has the practical purpose of protecting the mahogany table below, allowing childish spills to be wiped away without drama or fuss. In sharp contrast to her dressed-for-the-day husband, Mrs Karam still appears to be in her nightclothes, or possibly in some sort of house dress, as the cotton shift she has on isn't the sort of thing she would wear outdoors. Perhaps on the beach, on holiday abroad at a family-friendly resort, but certainly not in Belgravia. Like the tablecloth, the dress is patterned and practical; unlike silks or satins, it can tolerate sticky fingers, smears of hot chocolate or ketchup, and be thrown into a hot wash. Perhaps Mrs Karam is unaware of how closely she resembles the furniture; perhaps she is, given the myopic concentration with which she is studying that cloth. She is thin rather than slim, and the weight of her head seems to be too heavy for her neck; she is letting it droop like a wilting flower, she is letting it hang; in fact, given what we know of her habits, it is absolutely possible that she is hungover. In contrast to the mournful brightness of her dress, Mrs Karam's skin appears almost grey, scraped of its once vibrant polish; it seems somewhat soft, and tender, like something kept buried under wet earth. Her hair is still thick, but she has let it grow too long, splaying on her shoulders, and it is as yet unstyled and unsprayed for the day, and pushed back behind her ears, like a modest nun's, or a schoolteacher's. Her shoulders are hunched, and her back is curved, rather unattractively. The day has just begun, and she already seems to have given up on it.

It is a photo of a happy husband and a haggard housewife. A carefree man with amusing stories, and a woman who no longer cares to be amused. A man who eats for pleasure, and a woman who drinks to forget; a fat man with a skinny wife, and a jam jar with a sticky spoon in the foreground. It is possible that the jam jar is what Mika or Zamir had wanted to take the picture of, as part of some school project to do with breakfasts, or things which begin with J, and that the figures of Mr and Mrs Karam at the end of the table, so obviously unposed and unwarned, are incidental. Collateral damage. It is perhaps surprising that Mrs Karam has propped this photo up on the mantelpiece, as although her husband still looks presentable, his middle-age spread notwithstanding, she looks anything but. She has not gone to the trouble of framing it, as that would seem rather bizarre, as pointless as painting the nails of a pig, but she wants it seen, nonetheless. Perhaps in the way a woman sticks a fat photo of herself on the fridge, as a warning of what she has become, and what she will stay if she carries on as she is. A shrill, scolding voice to match the one in her head, saying, Stop

This to her, and Shut Up to him; telling her to wash her face, rub the grey out of her skin with some Oil of Ulay and a good make-up base in bronze, brush her hair and take off that godawful cotton dress. To raise her head, get up from the table, and walk away. To go back into her real life, one step at a time.

Mika

Mika has two mothers, a forlorn, mourning morning mother, and a rest-of-the-day mother. An inside mother and an outside mother. She feels sorry for Morning Mother, a dreary, unhappy drudge who drags herself heavily from room to room, incompetently tackling basic domestic chores in her nightdress – the dumping of crockery and wine glasses into the sink for the cleaner to sort out, the belated tidying of last night's takeaway containers into the bin or fridge, the collection and opening of the mail – she does the barest minimum about the flat, and does it resentfully, like a Victorian orphan set to work in the scullery. (Mika does not really know what a scullery is, but she imagines that it is hot and uncomfortable and full of complicated labour, like washing clothes by hand, and she has this idea of Victorian orphans, in long tattered nightdresses, from an illustrated copy of *The Water-Babies* that is part of their little library in the bedroom. Her mother doesn't have to wash clothes by hand or even load the washing machine – she has a laundry service that collects them and returns them pressed and folded – but she still manages to make the gathering of grubby clothes from the floor or the basket and squashing them into the cotton bags for whites, coloured and delicates seem an insurmountable task, and often just gives up halfway through.) Mika is tender and helpful to her helpless Morning Mother, and makes her a morning cup of coffee (instant coffee; she is not allowed to touch the percolator, although she wishes she were, as she loves the ceremony of the grinding, the filters, the delightful whooshing of the steam and the bubbling of the water, and the first golden drops that pool in the bottom of the glass jar, the persistent drips that make the shining, bitter-smelling brew). Sometimes they run out of instant coffee, and she gets to open a new jar, to crack the top of the paper seal with the spoon, and breathe in deeply over the top. And sometimes there is no coffee, and no new jar, and on these occasions she makes tea. Her mother doesn't take milk or sugar, and this disappoints her a little, as she feels that she hasn't worked quite hard enough on the coffee (or the tea), and imagines that a generous addition of milk and sugar would make it mean more, somehow. That the lightening and sweetening of the coffee, the pouring of cool milk from the bottle delivered daily on the downstairs step, the measuring of rough crystals and melting them into the drink, would somehow lighten and sweeten her mother's life. Like a sort of magic potion. Black coffee, Mika thinks, is like being given a salad for dinner, or a peanut-butter sandwich for lunch, instead of a hot meal; it is not neglectful, but it requires no care, it is self-limiting, and lacking in the promise of pleasure. Black coffee doesn't seem to show enough love. And this is what she is doing when she makes this drink in the morning: she is showing the haggard Morning Mother that she is still loved. Morning Mother groans when Mika comes into her room with the steaming mug, and gives a muffled 'Hmph' as a thank-you, rather than a kiss or cuddle, as she is still half asleep. But Mika peeks in a few minutes later, and sees her mother sitting up in bed, her mug in hand, and her mother glances back at her, and smiles, a little awkwardly, as though she is aware that she is pitied, and pitiable. Sheepish and harmlessly dismissible. As though she is gratefully aware of a little girl's love.

And then there is the other mother. The post-breakfast

mother, who appears as soon as she needs to be heading out of the flat for the day. Early on weekdays, later on weekends. Mika is proud of this mother, proud to be seen with her and seen by her, and also a little afraid. This mother has a temper, and opinions, and a short, sharp laugh. This mother walks quickly, sometimes too quickly for her to follow, and snaps, 'Keep up, slowcoach,' over her shoulder. This mother paints her fingernails and toenails in dramatic colours (to be fair, the other mother has painted nails too, but they just seem to drain the colour from the rest of her), and paints her face with cosmetics stored in a carved ivory box that is lined with blue velvet. Mika loves watching the transformation between the two mothers, how one goes into the bathroom in her striped house dress or cotton nightie, and the other emerges, damp and shining, wrapped in a thick white towelling robe, her hair slicked back from her forehead and twisted into a towel turban. The wetness seems to lift the grey from her skin, the way that stones always seem jewel-like and polished if they are underwater, and dull and disappointing when they are dry. This mother moisturises her whole lean body with care, starting with a small bottle of pink fluid on her face – she calls it Oil of Ulay, but it isn't oily at all – and then scoops out dollops of cream from an expensive-looking stone jar and rubs it on the rest of her, until she gleams all over, and seems expensive too, but also a little unfamiliar, like a hotel room with squashy carpets, or a newly waxed car. Mika isn't allowed to touch the Oil of Ulay, or the stone jar, but she is allowed to touch the plastic pot of Palmer's cocoa butter, which her mother sometimes rubs on the back of her heels and her toes, on the calluses she gets from fashionable shoes, and on her knees and elbows too. Mika rubs the cocoa butter on her own elbows, and although she has never smelled home-baked cookies, as her mother doesn't bake, or really cook at all, she imagines that this warm, buttery scent is what home-baked cookies would smell like. And then, frequently naked, as she keeps the flat so oppressively warm that she doesn't need her robe, so blandly warm that the flat has no seasons, and Mika wears the same clothes at home all year round, and has to take off her tights and winter uniform the moment she gets back from school, her mother sits at her dressing table and spreads little dabs and dashes of make-up on her face.

She starts with a hazelnut-coloured paste that lights up her skin, smoothing away the pores and lines; Mika knows that her mother is covering up her imperfections, but when the make-up goes on with the triangular foam sponge, it seems to her that in fact her mother is rubbing the imperfect skin away with an eraser, and revealing her real skin, her dewily bridal face beneath. As though she is wiping off a mask, rather than painting one on. Next she carefully applies a puff of powder on her nose and forehead and chin, a brush of blush, and a rainbow of shades for her lids, blues and greens and gold for special occasions, pinks and browns and bronze for everyday. She always paints her lips, once with a pencil, and then twice with a lipstick, kissing a tissue in between layers. Sometimes she kisses Mika instead, a kiss that is sort of a joke rather than a sign of affection, and leaves Mika with perfect lip prints on her cheeks, and a pinky-red clown nose. Next she blow-dries her hair, brushing it back from her face and spraying it into place. Her hair starts out damp and flat against her scalp, and ends up thick and blown up like candy floss. And finally Mika's rest-of-the-day mother steps into her underwear, and puts on her rest-of-the-day clothes, hard clothes with a shape, that look like they're being worn even when they're still on the hanger: smart tailored skirts and stiff blouses with shoulder pads, designer trousers in brown leather with complicated stitching, or twinsets with ornate pearl and bone buttons, all teamed with matching stockings and matching shoes. She looks at Mika once she's dressed, and Mika feels the criticism in her mother's regard, and she is suddenly embarrassed that she is drab and dark and somehow disappointing by comparison, with her one-coloured face (the clown nose notwithstanding), and her flat, one-length hair falling limply down her back. And her mother says cheerily, 'Well, come on, then,' and then she says, 'Where's your brother?' and having dragged him protesting from his room, and gathered them in the hall, after finding shoes and jackets, rest-of-the-day mother buckles up her trench coat and steps out with them into the street.

Zamir

Zamir sees things that he shouldn't, and feels sticky with all the secrets he cannot tell. He feels that he is always behind doors, or hidden under the table; outside, listening in, or else inside and listening out for others. He doesn't mean to be caught in these places, in these awkward situations, but he is so small and furtive that people just don't notice him, or else forget that he is there. He hears his parents arguing as he goes to the living room, and is afraid to push the door open and go in, and so he just stands there, and hears everything. Or else they come into the living room together, in full flood of argument, while he is in the secret world underneath the cheap plastic tablecloth that crackles with life, the world furnished by the dark trees of the mahogany table legs and their little bronze clawed feet. Afraid to go in, and afraid to come out, an accidental spy. His sister, his older-by-one hour, taller-by-two-inches sister, comes into the room as well, and unlike their distracted, bickering parents spots him instantly.

'Amma, Abbu,' she cries out to them, 'Zamir's sneaking again,' and his parents pause, catching their breath, looking down at the extra set of legs in blue shorts among the table legs, feet in cotton socks printed with robots among the metal mouldings of the claw feet, and then carry on where they left off. They're not even going to the trouble of ignoring their children, but just shout as though they weren't there at all. When their parents speak about Zamir and Mika, they don't name them as individuals, but simply call them 'The Kids', as though they were some combined object, some piece of baggage. Something that might be picked up and packed up. 'Just take The Kids and leave,' one voice floats out. 'I'll take The Kids and leave,' another cries back, and the children, now so immune to these arguments that they can listen to them quite sensibly, wonder what it is that they are arguing about, when they seem to be in such obvious agreement.

'Zamir's sneaking, Zamir's sneaking,' trills out his sister, apparently annoyed that his exposure has caused such a small reaction, that he remains hidden in his private place after all.

'Mika's sneaking, Mika's sneaking,' he chants back reactively, far too weakly, not loud enough to be heard over the storm that his parents are making, the thunder and lightning that is rattling the teacups above his head. He sees his sister's bare feet and ankles, dark and scuffed, with coral-pink soles, disappear out of the room, as something clatters, a sound of porcelain on steel or marble, but doesn't break. He feels sick, and as his parents move their argument back into the kitchen, he dashes out from under the table, and to the bathroom, where he locks the door and sits on the cool tiled floor.

And he waits there, with his untold secrets, until the teacup-rattling-clattering storm is over, and his father complains that he needs the bathroom, or else his mother knocks impatiently on the door and asks, 'Are you *all right* in there, Zam-Zam?' but the way she says it doesn't show concern; it seems to indicate more that she doesn't think he is quite all right at all. That he is not quite right instead, one of those creepy not-quite-right children, the quiet, bookish, solitary types who pull the wings off bugs.

He resents this quite a lot, as he isn't all that quiet and he certainly isn't bookish; the atmosphere at home stuns him into silence and stillness, but at school he can be noisy and whining and not very well behaved; he's not clever, and when he can't manage something quickly enough, he will sometimes throw it all to the floor and shriek with frustration as though he has been injured in some specific, blameable way. He saves all his patience for moments like these, waiting in the bathroom.

'Just a bit sicky,' he might reply, or 'Just a bit tummy-achey,' or sometimes simply, 'Just waiting for a poo.'

This last is a feasible excuse, as Zamir is almost always mildly constipated, and spends days waiting for his sluggish system to expel his waste, and then long moments on the toilet trying to push it out, breaking into a sweat with the effort. He once missed an entire episode of *Dogtanian and the Three Muskehounds* trying to go after school. They have taken him to doctors, worked on his diet, dosed him with bran and prune juice and milk of magnesia for emergencies (when he hasn't pooed for over a week, and is clutching at his gut with the unfairness of it, all this baggage that their piece of baggage has to carry), but it seems that that's Just the Way He Is. His mother is fond of telling him that when he was a baby, he didn't open his bowels for the entire first week, and the midwives thought she hadn't been feeding him properly. He has always eaten exactly the same food as his skinnier sister (possibly not the same quantity, as he always scrapes his plate clean, whereas she leaves a judicious amount for scraping into the bin instead), and she passes solids almost every day, effortlessly and without fuss.

When he finally does manage to go, and feels his waste slide from him, sometimes long enough to coil like a dog turd, sometimes compacted enough to block the toilet and need pushing with the toilet brush and reflushing twice, he feels a relief washing over him like no other. It is something like pleasure, the sort of ecstatic pleasure to be got from scratching the severe itch of an insect bite, until the skin breaks and blood is drawn. Sometimes his bottom bleeds a little, in fact, just a drop or two, and when he sees this on the toilet paper, he is full of ambiguous emotion, sweaty with shame, as he makes the unlikely connection between food, and human waste, and harm.

Zamir feels he knows his parents like no one else; listening under the table, behind the door, he cannot help but know what others don't. He knows his father has a peculiar sickness that makes him lie to people so he can earn money from them, so he will claim to be in New York when chatting to a business acquaintance on the phone in their London living room; he will say things like 'The cheque's in the post, I sent it second-class today, it'll be there the day after tomorrow' when he hasn't got the chequebook out of the bureau or visited the post office. His father's peculiar sickness makes him lose all the money he earns, so that on occasion he just doesn't come home, to put off being yelled at by their mother until he has won it back again. He knows that this is a sickness, because that's what his mother says when she thinks Zamir's not there: 'My God, Maqil, this just isn't fun any more. The grifting, the gambling, any of it. It's become an addiction. It's like a disease.' Zamir knows his mother has her own furtive disease: that she goes to the bathroom after dinner, not because she is 'Just a bit sicky' or 'Just a bit tummy-achey', but because she wants to be sick. She eats very little, or so it seems to him, but after dinner she vomits up what she has had, barely digested, as easily as spitting out gum. It is something she has got good at with practice. The first time he witnessed this, standing at the bathroom door, he waited there until she saw him. 'Are you a bit sicky, Amma?' he asked, with genuine concern.

'Some bad crab, at dinner,' she replied, rinsing her mouth briskly. She didn't seem annoyed to be seen, or embarrassed, and so he hadn't realised what he had seen at all. She began to brush her teeth, and during the electric hum she idly ran her hand across the top of his fine, straight hair, and then ushered him out of the bathroom. 'I'll just be a minute,' she said, more kindly than usual. It was her kindness that gave him the uneasy feeling that something might be wrong.

The next morning, at breakfast, Zamir asked, innocently enough, whether his father had had the bad crab as well. 'We had duck, not crab,' said his father distractedly, looking at his newspaper while sitting at the far end of the table, like an impolite guest who had decided to keep his distance until his stay was over. 'Why?' His father had begun to wear glasses for reading, and the light from the long bay window was reflected in them, so you couldn't see his eyes at all.

'I was telling Zamir last night that bad crab could make you ill,' said his mother quickly, with a smile that showed her teeth towards him. 'Never a good idea to eat crab in the summer.'

His father coughed out a short laugh that was meant to sound bitter but somehow seemed embarrassed instead. 'That's right. Never underestimate the consequences of eating bad crab, Zamir. We wouldn't all be here right now if it wasn't for bad crab.' He said it like he really believed it, but it wasn't clear whether it was a good or a bad thing that they *were* all there right now.

His mother laughed too, and glanced at Zamir again, nodding at him to tell him that it was OK that she had lied. She nodded at him as though they had a secret, and it made him feel a little puffed up inside, and important, and a little bit dirty too.

That night, when his mother went to the bathroom after she

came back from dinner, for the first time ever, she locked the door. She did the same every night after that, only opening the door casually as she was brushing her teeth. When Zamir sees her, her white teeth flecked with foam, her mouth minty fresh, all traces of vomit melted away like snow on a damp pavement, he thinks of the spots of blood on the toilet paper, the difficult egress of nourishment, of human waste and harm.

The Twins

Mr and Mrs Karam's children, Mika and Zamir, are often named together as 'The Twins', as all twins are; or else their parents will airily refer to them as 'The Kids' or 'The Children', labelling and dismissing them in the same breath. These combined names imply an affinity that the children simply do not have; their only connection is one of circumstance. They are like roommates brought together by a bulletin board or a newspaper ad, and what they know of each other is forced by proximity; they have had no choice but to share small spaces, their mother's womb for almost nine months, and the spare room for almost nine years. They do not read each other's minds, as some twins are rumoured to do, they do not even read each other's books; their dreams and their opinions are as private as the locked diaries they record them in, and they are surprisingly dissimilar in looks, so much so that people do not automatically assume they are brother and sister at all. Mika is named for and by her father, who controversially decided not to name his firstborn son Maqil as convention dictated, but scandalised the wider family by giving a bastardised, foreign-sounding version of the proud name to his firstborn daughter instead. Mika bears no resemblance to her chimeric name-changing namesake, as she is dark, skinny and so tall that she is already half a head bigger than her brother, and promises to outgrow her father too. In fact, she is the image of her mother, but conspicuously lacking in childish prettiness, a little goofy looking, in fact, with her oversized front teeth. She is disappointed when she studies her reflection, full length, in the mirror in the hall, but she cherishes the thought that one day, when she is big enough to use make-up and wear shoes from Charles Jourdan and clothes from Missoni, she will grow into herself, and her teeth will finally be the right size for her mouth; that even though she may never be pretty, she might have her mother's specific self-assurance that gives her the golden glow of beauty whenever she chooses to switch it on.

Zamir is named for their mother, somewhat illogically, as it was obvious from birth that he would never take after her; he is pale and plump and not-too-tall, with big puppy eyes fringed with fine, straight lashes. The rest of his hair is fine and straight as well, cut long enough to flop to his cheeks; he would be a handsome lad if he didn't always seem so sullen. He is his father, without his famous charm; and while his father is always comfortable wherever he is, sliding like liquid mercury to fill any available space with his shining presence, Zamir is the opposite, always dull and awkward and with a sense of being in the way, even when he is out of the way, curled up under the table with his knees drawn up to his chin, or in his lower bunk bed, cross-legged and playing Donkey Kong. He isn't sociable, and he isn't that bright, and sometimes visitors, relatives and even his mother discuss quietly whether he is quite *all right*; his father doesn't seem to notice him enough to ask even this pointed, pointless question.

Both of The Twins are relieved that their respective unpretty-goofiness and awkward-sullenness do not show in photographs, where they come together with their luminous parents to make an attractive family. Everyone comments admiringly on these professionally taken shots, framed in dark walnut in the living room; they joke that it is as though the Karams had their children in different marriages and brought them together like the Brady Bunch, Samira with her doppelgänger daughter, Maqil with his mini-me son.

Sometimes, despite their differences, the twins have conversations, Mika on her top bunk, and Zamir below; they do not look directly at each other as they speak, as that would be difficult to accomplish (Mika would have to hang upside down, or Zamir would have to half-mount the ladder and hang precariously on to the edge), and so they address the other's reflection in the mirror that is set in the carved armoire opposite the bed, with scrolls and flowers sculpted into the wood, and inlaid with little details in mother-of-pearl and gold leaf. It would be easier if they were to simply sit together on the carpet (they call it The Sea, out of childish habit, as the Axminster that came with the flat is thick and blue-green; when they were younger, toys left on the carpet were described as 'lost at sea', and their round woven rugs were their islands or boats or stepping stones), but they do not; this would involve giving up their own safe property, their terra firma on their bunks, and moving to tricksy, shifting common ground. And so, sitting on their separate bunks, they talk about various things, but almost always come back to the Big Discussion regarding their parents.

'Did you see that the dead blackbird was still there?' asks Mika, as it is usually Mika who starts things off.

Zamir thinks about ignoring her, as he is approaching the top score of almost one thousand on his hand-held Donkey Kong game, pitifully simple and repetitive, each opening sequence always the same, move right four times with a beep-beep-beep-beep and then jump over the barrel where there are no girders overhanging with a perky bounce. Beep-beep-beep-beep bounce! Beep-beep-beep-beep bounce! But he is interested in the bird too, with the same interest that almost every child has in Things-That-Are-Dead. 'The one on the kerb? It's been there three days now,' he replies, climbing up to the crane on the game and doing the final swing to gain his points, rewarded with a little trill of electronic appreciation from the plastic handset, Dum-de-dum-de-DING!

'It wasn't on the kerb, that's the edge of the pavement. It was in the gutter, that's the edge of the road. On the yellow lines,' says Mika, knowing that she is being pedantic without yet knowing what the word itself means, unable to stop herself. When she is older, she will eventually learn to suppress this powerful, burning itch she has to correct people, and smile diplomatically instead; she will only succumb when her closest family are involved, her brother, her mother, her husband.

'Whatever,' says Zamir, dully enough to sound annoyed with her. Beep-beep-beep-beep bounce!

'It was squashed today, the beak was almost broken off. I think someone must have run over it when they were parking.'

'I didn't see that,' says Zamir. 'Gross.' Dum-de-dum-de-DING! He passes 999, and as there are only three digits in the score area, the game has to start again from zero. He sighs with a complicated mix of pride and disappointment, that he has achieved the goal but that he is allowed to go no further. He plays another couple of rounds from habit, and then puts it down. Mika waits a minute before carrying on.

'Amma said she didn't understand why it was still there; she said that she thought a cat or something would have taken it away by now. I thought she meant that a kind cat would come and bury it in the square somewhere. But then she laughed and said it proved that only fat cats live in Belgravia. Not kind ones. Like it was something funny.'

'She meant that the cat would take it away to *eat* it,' says Zamir, pleased to be able to regain some ground after the kerb and gutter confusion, 'Cats don't bury stuff, that's dogs. Cats eat stuff.'

'Cats eat dead birds?' asks Mika, disgusted. 'Gross.' She pauses. 'I thought that was just in cartoons, Sylvester and Tweety-Pie.'

'Cats eat mice, too,' says Zamir, pleased to be showing off this useful nugget of knowledge. 'Tom and Jerry.'

'Maybe a *starving* cat would eat a dead bird, or a mouse. Like I only eat fish if I'm really hungry,' says Mika, still trying to make sense of it all. 'So I guess that the cats around here don't need to, as they all get fed tins of Whiskas and Sheba at home. Fat cats, like Amma said. Like Butter Ball, Mrs Von Schmidt's cat from downstairs.' She pauses, thinking about the overweight orange cat that arches its back and hisses at her in the corridors, and says, 'I still don't get why it was meant to be funny. A poor dead bird becoming cat food.'

'No,' says Zamir, in rare understanding. 'Me neither.'

'I think Amma's a bit mean sometimes,' she adds.

'Yes,' says Zamir. 'Me too.' But then he adds, 'Still, I'd rather go with her when it happens. Even though she slaps and Abbu doesn't.'

Mika nods in assent, her head bobbing solemnly in the smoky stained glass of the old mirror with the bevelled edge. *When* it happens. For her and Zamir, it was never if it might happen. They had none of the naïve certainty that their parents would stay together despite everything, nor that they themselves were the glue that prevented their precarious family from rupturing with the squabbles and squalls of their daily life, punctuated by increasingly long absences from their father, all barely explained, his abrupt departures skimmed over with the briefest acknowledgement. 'I had to buy underwear,' he said after a weekend away. 'I had a meeting,' he said after a week away. 'I had to visit friends abroad,' he said after a month away.

They had heard enough of their parents' heated arguments over the years to know that it would happen, and that then they would have to make a choice, or be chosen. Amma or Abbu. Abbu or Amma. Mika hopes that when the time comes, she will be allowed to choose first, so that she can pick Amma. Otherwise, if Amma is already picked, she will have to go with Abbu – out of a sense of childish democracy, from the playground, where everyone gets chosen for a team, where no one is left out, she would be obliged pick Abbu, to be fair. But she does not love Abbu, although if asked, she would insist with pious insincerity that she does, as she knows it is her duty to love both her parents. She does not love her father, even though he is never mean, and he never slaps; even though he never fails to kiss her when he comes in the door (but not when he leaves; his departures are always unexpected and barely remarkable, a little slice of time when he is there and then he simply is not; he does not bring any attention to these sudden exits, there is no flurry of goodbyes and kisses and the searching for a briefcase or an umbrella, no satisfying little drama for those left behind; he just opens the door and goes). He is not there enough to love – even when he is there, he isn't really; he is at the other end of the table, or in the other room, or charming the constant round of guests he invites to the house. He is there for her in public, out in the restaurant or hotel, playing an affably ordinary dad before the waiters and the liveried staff, but when they get home he checks her and Zamir in the hall cupboard with his jacket, and leaves them there. On balance, Mika, like every child, would rather be shouted at and noticed than ignored altogether. She would even rather be slapped. She hopes she gets to pick Amma first.

The Twins are still children; they can't help but think just of themselves. They do not think of their mother in her bedroom, watching her husband stroll down the smart street, raising a hand as he turns the corner, as though greeting a friend or hailing a cab. They do not think of their mother looking at piles of letters in a drawer, demands from creditors, from the tax office, from the bank, from their private school, the steady stream of letters that start off apologetically long winded and polite, and then inevitably compress over time, becoming curt, cold and brutal. They do not stop to consider whether it is an unfair division of the paperwork in their parents' lives, that their mother has all the bills and printed threats stuffed in a drawer, and that their father has all the bills and printed notes stuffed in his jacket, all the pocket-warmed, pocket-softened cash folded neatly in his money clip to lose one night, and win back another. Their mother is a Grown-Up – she would never skip girlishly out of the house in a borrowed moment of time, the time it takes to yawn or cough or stretch; she would never board a plane and leave them all behind, letting the shredded letters flutter in her wake like confetti on the breeze. As she leafs through the papers, deciding which she must answer, and which she can still ignore, the church bells ring joyously for another morning wedding, and these golden rings spin out like caramel sugar threads into the air; her thick wedding band beaten out to a fine wire, a garrotte. Their mother is a Grown-Up, and for all her domestic incompetence and professed selfishness, for all her generous glasses of wine in the evenings and indulgent hangovers in the morning, for all that she shuffles the household paperwork like a croupier with a deck of marked cards, she knows what a Grown-Up has to do. Their mother has already worked out that the Big Discussion, when the time comes, is not about the choice between Amma and Abbu. It is not about Her and Him. It is about Them and Us. It is the choice between her children and her marriage.

London – 1983 – Prison

MAQIL IS IN JAIL AGAIN, BUT THIS TIME THERE IS NOTHING valiant or brave about it as there was back in the Middle East, where time served was a badge of honour, when he was a soldier in search of truth and against political corruption. Nor is he an honest protester for a worthy cause as he was back in his student days in New York, when he was fashionably anti-war and anti-fur and anti-nuclear and anti-everything-establishment. Now he is just another milk-faced white-collar criminal, doing cowardly white-collar porridge, in the lofty company of crooked account-ants and unethical lawyers. It boils down to the fact that he has lived in the UK for ten years, on and off, off and on, without paying a penny of taxes. He pointed out in court that he spent at least six months of every year abroad, and that his children were privately educated, and used private healthcare, which was taken into account. But his claim to be domiciled in Pakistan was quickly disproved by the fact that he had barely visited his house there in the last several years. And his joke that the proposed jail term would cost the state more than his missing taxes, so that perhaps they should just call it even and let him go, did not go down well. So he went down instead. Six months. Less for good behaviour.

'You shouldn't have worn diamonds at the hearing,' he comments to Samira, who has turned up while the children are at school. 'There's no justice for the wealthy, well dressed and overeducated in this country – we're the forgotten minority.' He is in Wandsworth, awaiting transfer to an open prison, and looking annoyingly at ease; the pale blue outfit suits him, and he picks at the exotic fruit basket Samira has brought him like someone grazing canapés at a charity buffet.

'I didn't wear any real jewellery at all,' retorts Samira, justifiably annoyed, as her fragrant and well-pressed appearance, her articulate performance of a martyred woman tied to a difficult man gained a great deal of sympathy. She had mitigated quite a bit of the damage that his own performance had done. 'You're a very clever man,' the judge had said critically. 'And a persuasive one, too,' he added. He said this with grim finality, and for a moment it seemed to Samira that these were more significant felonies than tax evasion; that her husband wasn't going to jail for the trivial misdemeanour of ignoring letters from the tax office and failing to declare income, but for the venal crimes of being clever and persuasive. It had seemed, at the time between the words were said and the gavel was struck, perfectly sensible and just.

'Just those earrings,' he persists, nodding towards the discreet jewels nestled in pale metal, gleaming against her dark skin.

'These aren't diamonds. They're zircon – one up from glass.' She runs a finger over her left earring, tugging distractedly at her lobe. 'The setting isn't even real gold – this is practically stage jewellery. You think I'm that stupid? That I'd wear diamonds to court? Or across town to this dump?'

'I've stayed in worse hotels than this, in Paris. At least here you can sit to crap,' he says cheerfully, peeling a red-skinned lychee with expert efficiency. 'There was that place in Montmartre where you had to squat. One slip and you'd wreck your Italian uppers.' Samira looks at him with exasperation, and lights yet another cigarette. 'Don't go through that whole pack,' he says suddenly, with a trace of concern in his voice.

'Why, are you worried about my health?' she asks sarcastically. 'A bit late for that, now you're in chokey, and I'm left with the rent to pay and two kids to provide for.'

'No, I'm not worried about your health. I just need the cigarettes for swapsies,' he says. She glances at him, and sees that he isn't joking.

'Bastard,' she comments, almost tenderly. 'You selfish bastard. It's always about you, isn't it? You really don't have to care about me, or the kids. It must be great to be you.'

'Yeah, it's pretty fun,' he agrees, glancing around the grey room full of grey-faced people, at the strip lighting and the narrow barred windows and the cheap vinyl-covered tables. He spreads out his hands, and leans back like a sovereign presiding over a procession. 'Look at me, I'm king of the world.' Samira does not seem amused, and turns her head, blowing smoke rings meditatively in the room. Her bridling energy appears to have drained away, and she is left seeming a little tired, a little bored by his show. She is holding her back straight, but stiffly, as though forcing herself to remember that she is in public, and that she mustn't let herself slump, as she sometimes does over her morning coffee at the breakfast table. Her shoulders are about an inch too high. He feels an urgent need to regain her interest, and asks about the children: 'So, what are you going to tell the kids? Or have you told them already.'

Samira looks at him pityingly. 'Of course I haven't told the kids. Why would I? They're used to you suddenly taking yourself off. They've barely noticed that you've gone.'

'Oh,' he replies, surprised at the little twinge of hurt he feels. He tries to sound careless about the fact that he is cared for less, disguising that it bothers him. 'I always said that constant absenteeism was an underrated parenting tool. Most kids would be bawling into their pillows if their dad suddenly disappeared.'

'Most kids would,' Samira agrees with him pleasantly, but it still sounds like an accusation.

'It's not like I'm the worst dad in the world,' he says abruptly, annoyed by his own urge to defend himself. 'I don't drink, I don't fool around . . .' He suspects that he is whining, and Samira's calm mask goads him into accusation himself. 'It's not like I yell at them, and slap them, and drink like a fish and smoke like a bloody chimney around them.'

'You're right,' says Samira, taking the righteous wind out of his sails. 'You're not. You don't. And sometimes I do.'

He stops talking and looks at her with some admiration; she is the only one who can cut through his bluster with such efficiency, such economy of phrasing. She is the only person he knows who has ever been able to get him to shut up; he has learnt from her that agreeing with someone is the easiest way to end a debate, and get them off their guard.

'You know what my father said to me when I left Kerala,' she says lightly, as though she is just making conversation. 'He told me to avoid men who liked wine, women and song.' He smiles at this, remembering that verse about a jug of wine and his lady love singing in the wilderness; it still makes him think of Samira, shimmering up the stairs of the ABC Club in her saffron-silk sari, even after all these years. 'Basically, to avoid men who enjoyed themselves. But the truth is, Maqil, I would put up with you if you drank or fooled around. I would put up with you if sang your fool head off in public. I would cheerfully swap all our problems for an alcohol addiction, an indiscreet mistress and some eccentric exhibitionism. I could do something about all those things: I could check you into the Priory, I could pay her off, I could call a shrink. But you're the problem here – and I just can't do anything about you.'

They face each other across the plastic-topped table, and he suddenly doesn't know where to look; just like that first time he saw her in the Club, it feels that he can't take her all in at once. He settles his gaze somewhere between her cloud of thick hair and her smooth forehead, delaying the inevitable moment of their eyes meeting. When this happens, it is shifty and uncomfortable, as though each has been caught in an unflattering light, or in the middle of a guilty act. 'You've changed,' he says quietly, unable to keep himself from sounding reproachful.

'And you haven't,' she replies, without sympathy. Her challenge has been laid down, her meaning is clear. She wants him to change. Change, or else. The bell announces the end of the visit, and she leans over and kisses him firmly and finally on the lips, like a mark of ownership, a wax seal on a scroll. She puts her packet of cigarettes in the fruit basket for him, and leaves.

He is suddenly grateful for the prison, for the high walls around, the barbed wire, holding everyone out as much as holding him in. What he fears most, what he has always feared, is a cage, and this is precisely what Samira is proposing. That he leave this temporary cage, which simply restricts his movements, for a more permanent and insidious one: a cage where metal bands will wrap around his chest, constricting his breath and his heart in flight. Samira wants him to change; she wants him to love his cage as much as she has reluctantly learned to love hers, populated by the little parasites he planted in her body, with no choice but to provide them with care – to wipe their noses, pour their milk, hug them when they fall and tell them off when they have been bad. She wants him to be happy with this – a comfortable home and conventional family – to want no more than what he already has. She may as well expect him to drop down dead. He loves Samira, he really does; and he loves his children too, in his own way. He loves the fact of them, that there are two little people like mirrors of Samira and himself, two extra players to dress up like puppets and stroll down the street with, allowing him to play that age-appropriate role of devoted daddy, now that he is too old to play the impulsive lover with any dignity. He loves them when they are out in the world with him, performing their winsome parts in restaurants in Soho, in Alpine ski resorts or the gardens of Versailles, but the truth is that he loves himself more. He has only six months left in which he can be himself, whichever self he chooses to be, and he decides then and there that he does not want time off for good behaviour.

Samira finds that life takes on a different rhythm when Maqil isn't there; she has got used to his prolonged absences in recent years, as he flits off to gamble in other countries, or else to pursue complicated business projects that involve him taking a cut from investors and then running away before he can be held to account for the results. She used to travel with him, before they had the kids, and she found nothing strange or sordid in changing her name along with his, depending on where they were. She thought it was fun. She remembers the first time she signed an assumed name; it was in the Ritz in Rome. Maqil owed them money, and was barred from the hotel in most major cities, and so she had used her grandmother's name, Moona Mishra, a name she had always thought had an old-fashioned movie-star glamour, a name with gold-dusted skin and Vaseline on the eyelids, elaborately coiled and oiled hair and the intricately hennaed hands and feet of a bride. Once they had the children, she tried at first to keep travelling with him, when the babies were tiny and portable, but it soon proved impossible. Her breast milk was slow in coming, as a result of the emergency operation in which Zamir had to be hauled out of her – he had been found stretching out across the top of her womb in the least appropriate of poses, one of those rare babies who simply lacked the instinct to turn down and come out into the air – and she didn't have the patience to breastfeed anyway. But giving the babies formula milk in hotels had its own problems, and despite her fiddling with cold-water sterilisers and kettles, she still didn't manage to keep the bottles and teats clean enough, and the babies soon got ill and fretful. The astonishing egg-yolk yellow of their various discharges – their poos, bogeys and earwax – as bright as the taut spring daffodils in the park, became a murky, leaf-mulch green. She resigned herself to staying at home with the children, and would stare at them with full-blown resentment, while they lay on their backs blowing spit bubbles, staring up at their dangling toys with fierce concentration. 'God, how I hate you,' she would say to them, giving them their bottles and then ignoring them while they wailed in their playpen, as she studied *Cosmo* and *Vanity Fair* and *Marie Claire* and wondered what was happening back at the office. 'God, how I hate you,' she would mutter as the screaming got louder, before finally leaping up from the sofa to go to them. They didn't believe her at all. They were always delighted to see her face hovering above theirs, and would start to chuckle before she even spoke to them, or picked them up – her heart would sink with their open, hopeful smiles, her resolve would weaken. She rocked both of them in her arms, walking around the flat, and stood before the mirror in the hallway, surprised at how attractive the three of them looked, the dark-brown woman with one dark-earthy baby and one pale-sandy baby nuzzling into her skin, like the United Colours of Benetton ads that were all over the underground and bus stops. 'God, how I hate you,' she would murmur to them, and would see in the four liquid mirrors of their eyes that she was smiling back at them as she said it; it turned out that she didn't believe it either. She learned to love her children in the way that a woman in a marriage of convenience learns to love her partner, or an office worker learns to love a thankless job; she found, day after day, waking in the flat with the children, walking out of the flat with the children, feeding the children, changing their nappies and putting them to bed, in the endless unchanging routine, rhythm and toil of their shared lives, in the unavoidable proximity and persistence of their presence, that it was easier to love them than hate them. In the way that it is easier to smile than to frown. To murmur than to shout. In the way that practice makes perfect.

But Maqil's return from wherever he had been, full of the adventures he had had, the money he had made or lost, the people he had befriended or duped, brought an end to the fragile truce with her children, and she found herself resentful once more, of him as much as them, until their shared life re-established itself, and she could go off with him to dinners or parties, leaving the children with an anonymous agency sitter. Whenever he came back, Samira would see herself through his eyes, and dislike what she saw. A housewife. A mother. A morning frump. She disliked the baby weight that she still carried, even though she was relatively slim, and threw up the rich meals that they ate with friends in the expensive Belgravia restaurants; it was something she had done before she got pregnant, on occasion. She was convinced it was what had got her pregnant in the first place. And then she kept throwing up, with determined persistence, as it gave a measure of control in her disordered life, when her husband might or might not be there on a given day, and she might or might not afford the rent, or else receive the bailiffs. Maqil could simply stroll away from all of this, but she could not; if she ever ran away, her children would have to come with her, protesting and dragging their feet. If she tried to run away without them, she knew she wouldn't let herself go any further than the Indian grocery shop on the corner, where they spoke to her in rapid and incomprehensible Hindi, and seemed offended when she replied in English. Even that was too far to go without the children; when they got older, she had started to leave them in the flat when she picked up essentials like loo roll and red wine at the corner shop, just to feel free of them for a few minutes, for the brief walk there and back, until the one time she returned to the building to see them both sitting on the window ledge outside her bedroom, waving to her cheerfully from the fourth floor. There was a double bar around the ledge, which she knew was loose and rusty around the edges; she had mentioned to Maqil once, without any sense of urgency, that they ought to get it fixed and repainted. She dropped her groceries, letting the bottles roll into the gutter, and broke into a sprint. She was surprised at how athletic her running was, the ease with which she ran in heels, and raced up the stairs, faced Mika and Zamir in her room (they had got down from the ledge by then; they had only gone up there in the first place as they had been waiting for her, and wanted to see her return) and gave them both a slapping that they would never forget. Once the danger had passed, the adrenaline in her system made her feel both shaky and cold, and she realised that the chilling numbness in her chest was fear. She was frightened that her children had almost fallen to their deaths. She was frightened that her incompetent and careless supervision had led them to this. And with that fear, with her frightened slapping, her furious screeching, she felt the true measure of her love with all its bewildering ferocity. The animal love that a tiger has for its cubs, a Bengal tiger used to stalking in the forests, tamed and tragic in its rusty double-barred cage.

With this fierce sense of protection, Samira realised that she would have to do something to secure her children's future, and opened a bank account in her maiden name, at a bank that had no dealings with Maqil. She squirrelled away money in her private account like nuts for winter, and kept the chequebook hidden. She asked Maqil for small sums of money, for immediate housekeeping purchases; she was too sensible to ask for a big sum for anything longer-term, as she knew that he'd borrow it back within the week to cover his debts or fund new ones. When they went on a family holiday to Switzerland, she opened a numbered account on the day she was meant to be shopping. She was deliberately vague about household accounts and sold the furs and jewellery he gave her when he was flush, replacing them with fakes or paste; with stage jewellery. She kept these complicated secrets matter-of-factly, and told him bare-faced lies without guilt; there was a certain justice to this, a certain dramatic irony, but justice and irony were not what motivated her. It was done from neither daring nor revenge. It was necessity. And although the various holidays they took together were still fun, she realised that at home, it was easier without Maqil than it was with him. Once more, in the uncomplicated way that it was easier to smile than to frown. To murmur than to shout. When he wasn't there, she wasn't yelling at him angrily about losing another stupid bet, and wasn't yelling at the children afterwards out of frustration. She found herself breathing a sigh of relief when she heard him leave, the door clicking shut discreetly behind him. She began to enjoy his effortless absence more than the ambiguous, controversial nature of his presence.

So now, she is treating these six months without Maqil as a little holiday. For six months she will have the rare pleasure of knowing exactly where he is, and will be certain for once that he is having less fun than her. For six months she will not have to hide her chequebook, her bank statements or her receipts, and will be able to allow herself to think of the future, instead of lurching unsteadily from day to day like a drunk trying to measure her steps down a street. She never considered herself anything more than a social drinker, but with Maqil put away and unable to cause mischief, she finds she is no longer social every evening with a bottle of red to herself on the once-white leather sofa. She is able to wake and face the day a lot more easily as a result. She accepts her morning cup of coffee from Mika, and after a few minutes, wanders to the kitchen, to find that her children, apparently already hungry, are trying to fix their own breakfasts. She struggles to remember what she gave them for dinner, annoyed with herself, as it clearly wasn't enough. Cheese on toast with baked beans, she thinks, possibly. Something hot but without any effort, assembled distractedly during the commercial breaks of *Dynasty*. She watches them for a moment from the door, her beloved brats, with a little pride as they get the orange juice and milk out of the fridge, and shift the kitchen chair so they can climb up on it to get the Weetabix out of the high cupboard. She sees Mika pulling out the good china, and although it wouldn't bother her that much if they break it, the mothering part of her cares that they know how fragile it is, to teach them the valuable lesson that some things can be broken without anyone noticing the consequences (hearts, dreams and ambitions, airy-fairy, flexible, shifting things), and some things can't (the Wedgwood tea service with the pink scalloped edge). 'Morning, Munchkins,' she says casually.

Mika turns around, mortified, caught in the act. 'Go back to bed,' she hisses at her mother.

'I told you so,' says Zamir bafflingly, to no one in particular.

'It's a surprise,' Mika whispers, as though she believes that as long as she whispers, the surprise is still intact. 'Go back to bed.'

'Don't tell me when to go to bed,' says Samira, feeling briefly as she says this that she is the careless, whining child, and Mika the competent mother. She holds the back of a chair, steadying herself back into her proper role, and starts to say, 'And you know you're not meant to touch those cups, they're up there for a reason.'

'She hasn't guessed yet,' says Zamir to Mika, who nods towards him quickly, with a complicit, anxious expression.

'Go back to bed, Amma, ple-ee-ze!' Mika says, offering the *Amma, ple-ee-ze* as a little gift, like a sugary treat. She has stopped saying Amma since she started school, preferring to use Mama or Mummy like her classmates, little Sloaney-pony girls who wear their hair neatly brushed back from their foreheads and fastened with glass bobbles or silver barettes, and who take riding lessons on docile horses in Hyde Park, shuffling a sedate circuit on the sands of Rotten Row, but she knows that her mother would still prefer to be called Amma, and uses it to curry favour with her on occasion. Samira is about to argue, feeling once more that their roles have been reversed (is she really about to start arguing with a child of eight, one third of her weight and one fifth of her years? The alternative seems even less feasible, and deliciously irresponsible – is she really going to let this child of just eight years old send her to bed?). But then she sees the hand-made card on the counter, half hidden under an envelope, and the brightly scrawled writing in bold capitals, HAPPY MOTHER'S DAY, buried beneath fireworks of scribbled hearts and stars and swirls and smiley faces. She is unbearably touched that they have managed to put the apostrophe in the right place.

'I think I will,' she says quickly, and abruptly turns on her heel and goes back to her room. She can hear Mika's voice; she is still whispering, but far too loudly, like a whisper on a stage, as she hasn't yet learned that the point of whispering is to be quiet, to conceal a secret, rather than to show off that she has one.

'She knows, doesn't she?' Mika says.

'I told you so,' Zamir stage-whispers back.

Some ten minutes later, Mika and Zamir come into her room, tiptoeing furtively but without menace, like the helpful little elves who stitch the cobbler's shoes in the night, and then shout, 'Happy Mother's Day' to her. Zamir hands her the card, and Mika, struggling with the weight of a precariously laden tray, puts it down awkwardly beside her mother in the space where their father is meant to sleep. There is a bowl of cereal and a plate with toast, and golden tea in a china cup. There is a tumbler of orange juice and a small pot of marmalade from a hotel, its seal still intact. There is a stolen flower from the downstairs window box, already limp and softer than skin, laid on a lace handkerchief in lieu of a napkin. It is imitation rather than art, as the children have painstakingly re-created the room-service breakfast she ordered for them in Vienna at the Hotel Bristol, and which gave them both such delight. Even so, the tray is beautiful if unoriginal, with all its ceramic and glass circles, the moment is beautiful if unoriginal, and Samira feels ready to surrender to this beauty rather than spoil it with her pedantry. She does not point out that *she* doesn't eat cereal, or toast or marmalade, and that she prefers coffee in the morning, and wouldn't have minded a second cup as her first one is now stone cold. She does not complain about the use of the china cup, with its scalloped edge, and pale roses sprinkled lightly on the rim like a girl's pink lipstick kisses. She realises that her children, in making her breakfast on Mothering Sunday, think that she is a mother like any other, gracious and competent and capable of receiving affection without prejudice or complaint, or else they know that she isn't a mother like any other, and would like to make her one. They look at her expectantly, and it is another performance, another little drama to play out for them, her anything-but-identical poppets in Robots in Disguise pyjamas and a Bahamas Barbie nightshirt with matching leggings in bubblegum pink, dressed for their parts and precisely in position, as surely as she is in her cotton nightie, sitting up in bed and leaning back against the padded headboard. Four brown eyes staring at her, shining and anxious and pleased with themselves all at once. She doesn't disappoint them. 'What a lovely surprise,' she cries out, hoping that she seems as gracious and competent as they require, and genuinely surprised at how sincere her voice sounds. At how well her allocated part fits her, after all. 'Thank you, Munchkins, you've made my day.' She holds out her arms to them, and kisses them, Mika on her nose, and Zamir on the top of his hair as he puts his face down suddenly, as though he is too big for kisses; she beams at them as they smile back, Mika broadly, and Zamir with bashful embarrassment. Zamir goes to pull open the curtains, and a broad ray of sunlight fills the room suddenly, making Mika sneeze with a childish reflex, and lighting the dust suspended in the air. It is a beautiful moment after all; it is a beautiful performance, and everyone, players and participants and audience alike, is happy. Everyone is satisfied with their morning's work.

Later, after breakfast, Mika is unable to let go of the moment, and is already reliving it, carving it into her memory; she chatters with frenzied relief now that the secret is out, as though a gag has just been taken off her, as her mother dresses. 'It was Zamir's idea, the breakfast,' she says generously. 'He remembered we still had marmalade from the hotel in Vienna. But I made it happen. I had to look EVERYWHERE for the marmalade, because it wasn't where you'd have thought it would be, it wasn't with all the other stuff from holiday, and the card was easy, but the envelope was so Almost-Nearly-Impossible to get right because we had to make it ourselves to fit the card, and Zamir never thought we could keep it a surprise . . .' She breaks off, looking at the card up on her mother's beside table, at the tray still on her father's side of the bed, and asks, abruptly, 'Where's Daddy?' as though she has only just noticed his absence.

'Away on business,' says Samira, businesslike herself, snapping on a cream-coloured bra.

'I know that,' says Mika impatiently. 'But *where?*'

'Why?' asks Zamir, and both Samira and Mika look at him in surprise, as though they had forgotten he was there. He has been standing behind the curtains, which had been partly redrawn as Samira returned from her shower and started dressing; he has been looking out of the window. The curtains only fall a few inches below the windowsill, and he was perfectly visible to those in the room, especially as he was leaning forward on the sill, with his rump sticking out comically under the curtain. Even so, he flushes under his pale gold skin, as though he is afraid he's been caught out somehow, spying on them from behind curtains like an inept peeping Tom. He is suddenly embarrassed by his mother's cream underwear. He glances hotly at Mika, afraid that she will start chanting 'Zamir's sneaking' again. Mika, however, is feeling equally embarrassed that she has been talking about Zamir as though he wasn't there, and is trying to remember if she has said anything she shouldn't, whether she has taken too much credit for the breakfast and card, which were his idea after all.

She defends herself hotly: 'Why what?'

'Why do you want to know where?' he asks, sliding out from behind the curtain, careful not to disturb it too much, although

157

his mother has already pulled on a blouse, and doesn't seem concerned about the window any more. 'I didn't think you cared.'

'Of course I care,' says Mika, looking quickly at her mother. 'It's just that I need stamps. Foreign stamps. I'm doing a project. For school.' Samira pretends to ignore the undercurrent of the little exchange, and realises that there must have been private conversations between the children regarding the latest where-abouts of their father, on his current, most elongated absence. She supposes she shouldn't be surprised that Zamir has been missing him more; he lacks Mika's hard edge, he takes every-thing a little too personally. She is glad he hasn't commented on how he has just been ignored by them.

'He won't be able to send you foreign stamps,' says Samira. 'He's still in the UK.'

'But where?' insists Mika. 'They have foreign stamps in Scotland, and Wales.'

'He's just in Sussex,' says Samira unthinkingly, pulling on a pair of royal-blue slacks, with precise lines ironed down the front and back by the dry-cleaners. The colour isn't flattering, but is suddenly ubiquitous, ever since Princess Diana had been photographed in that stiff blue suit with her husband-to-be standing on a box beside her, a nineteen-year-old dressed to look like someone's mother. Zamir collects postcards, even the touristy ones displayed outside the Indian grocers, big red buses and King's Road punks and the Royal Family, including all the Charles and Diana ones in this rigidly unromantic pose. She sometimes buys his Royal Family postcards from him (at a slight profit to her son) to send to her husband; she thinks it only appropriate, given that he is currently a guest of Her Majesty's Pleasure. Distracted by these thoughts of royal blueness and royal postcards, she only just realises what she has given away, but relaxes when she sees that this doesn't mean anything to the children, that they don't know where Sussex is, don't know that it's only a few miles from town and easily commutable, and that for them, saying Sussex is like saying the Outer Hebrides or the Isle of Man. They accept the reality as it is presented to them, and simply assume that Sussex is somewhere far enough to be away on business. She realises with grim amusement that when Zamir and Mika start announcing to their friends, their friends' parents and their teachers that their father is away on business in 'Sussex' for several weeks and months (trying not to giggle at the second syllable, in the way that she, with a notably dirtier mind and a foreigner's objectivity with words, always suppresses a smirk at the first syllable of 'country'), the adults will hide their initial surprise and smirk knowingly too, assuming that Maqil has simply left her, or has a mistress in the Home Counties, as predictable as any other extravagant man approaching a mid-life crisis. She almost wishes he had. She almost wishes she had a simple, predictable life, and a simple, predictable husband. It occurs to her that it wouldn't be so hard to achieve this wish, if this is what she really wants; she couldn't leave him, not with the children, not without them either, but he could leave her. If she prompted him to do so, he could leave her in a heartbeat. It would be easy. Worryingly easy. As easy as letting her children surprise her with breakfast; as easy as going back to bed when she is told.

London – 1982 – Family

DESPITE HIS BEST EFFORTS, MAQIL GETS TIME OFF FOR good behaviour. As his first serious girlfriend had astutely pointed out, he just couldn't switch off his ever-loving charm. He disliked being bored, and so he ran chess tournaments and reorganised the library. He improved his golf handicap on the mini course attached to the open prison, playing alongside staff and even the governor in friendly competition. He told clean jokes to the guards, and dirty ones to his fellow inmates, and networked effortlessly, making useful contacts among the disgraced but wealthy captains of industry caught pocketing their pension funds, inside traders, tax evaders like himself. Diary dates were made for when their time was repaid, appointments were scheduled on yachts in Marbella, at the George V in Paris, in the casinos of Monte Carlo. He learned to cook on kitchen duty, following recipes to the letter, and was surprised at how straightforward it was; Samira had never even tried to cook, and he told her during one of her weekly visits that it was just a matter of adding, mixing and heating, and said that he would teach her how to make Beef Bourguignon and Shepherd's Pie and Apple Crumble with Custard. 'Hah!' replied Samira with her customary bluntness. 'As though you'll be making Apple Crumble with Custard once you're out of here. Hah!' Which was true, of course. And he even began writing again; not a novel, which still seemed too much of a long-term project, even with six months at his disposal, but plays, which he had performed in the prison, with all-male casts. The most successful play involved three characters waiting in a café for a mysterious woman to arrive – a speaker, a subject and a listener – as one man irreverently narrated the other man's history with the absent woman, and the third was their sceptical audience; he told Samira that the woman in the play was her, but again, she said, 'Hah! As if I'd ever be like that. As if I'd moon around with magic in my eyes and secrets in my shadows. You must have been thinking about one of your soppy French girlfriends.' And again, she was right. He had tried to write it about her, but it hadn't worked out; Samira was rather too brutal, too angular for romantic fiction.

And so, with just over four months served, the prison governor thanks him for the success of his latest chess tournament and the book club he has established in the prison library, offers his praise for the enjoyable production of *Wait for Her*, and wishes him well on the outside. In his turn, Maqil wishes the governor well on the inside, with a little sly humour given the man's reputed problems with his digestion, and takes a cab to the station. He could have taken the cab all the way back to Belgravia, but he is annoyed that Samira said she couldn't meet him when he came out, and he thinks that arriving back on the discomfort of public transport will make him seem suitably martyred. It turns out that the performance is unnecessary, as

Samira isn't at the flat to greet him either; nor are the children, although of course they'd be at school. He paces around the flat, feeling suddenly as caged by the extravagantly papered walls and the plaster cornicing and ceiling roses as he did by the locked doors and barred windows of his cell. He changes out of his smart suit, the silk blend that he wore to court and went down in, which remained miraculously presentable even after prison storage, showers efficiently, and pulls new clothes out of his wardrobe, all scented by lavender sachets and mothballs, which Samira must have efficiently put in when he started his sentence. Samira didn't know how to cook, or clean, or do laundry, having grown up in India and having had servants all her life, but one thing she knew about was looking after clothes. Pushing his arms through the sleeves of his weekend tweed jacket, the lining rustles expensively, and he is gratified at how well it hangs on him now that he has lost a little weight; the lavender scent bothers him, though, he smells like a delicate old lady. It is becoming less and less likely that Samira and the children will leap out from behind the curtains with a cake that says *Welcome Home*, and he decides that it will serve Samira right if he's not there when she comes back. He goes out for lunch at his club, where the staff and management annoy him by making no mention of his prison stay, having clearly been instructed to ignore it discreetly, rendering useless his store of amusing prison stories and acquired gaolbird humour; they ask after his wife and children instead, and he has to lie, rather than admit that he hasn't even seen them yet.

He returns to the flat in the later afternoon, confidently assuming everyone will be home, as the school day should be over, but no one arrives back until well after five p.m. He hears the lift mechanism grinding, and the rustle of bags on the landing, and then finally the turn of the key in the lock. 'Your Abbu's home,' he hears Samira call out to the children, as she realises that the door is no longer double-locked, and then she walks in. 'Hey there,' she says, casually kissing him as though she had only seen him last week, which she had. 'Hello, Daddy,' says Mika, pleased enough to see him, but not particularly surprised or delighted. She goes up to him for a kiss, and seems a bit nonplussed when he swings her up in his arms, and so he puts her back down again, a bit too quickly. Zamir hangs back, trembling and almost upset-looking; he does not smile or speak, but when his father opens his arms to him, he runs to him and holds him silently, his own arms wrapped fiercely around him. The intensity of his son's emotion slightly embarrasses Maqil, who has to ease himself out of the embrace, and sees from Zamir's crumpled face that he has been holding back tears. 'Well, son, there's no need for that,' he says, having no idea what a father should say at this moment, how a father should behave. What he really wants to say is 'Please, please stop all this bullshit boo-hooing, you're making me uncomfortable,' but he knows that he can't. He is grateful to Samira and Mika for their dignified indifference, their nonchalant acceptance of his presence and absence, and looks helplessly at his wife for guidance. She shrugs, as though to say 'Kids,' and finishes unpacking the small bag of groceries she has with her. She then goes up to Zamir and gives him a hug, a sensible hug that has no neediness to it, and brushes the damp from his eyes with the flat of her hand with a practical, efficient gesture.

'Let's have some tea, now that your Abbu's back. He can tell us all about his adventures in Sussex.'

'Was Sussex a Success, Daddy?' asks Mika, with a grin, as though she has both planned and practised this little tongue-teaser, this sensible question. She seems delighted with it: Success, Sussex (that forbidden second syllable!).

'It was,' he says, as Samira brings out the good china in

163

recognition of his return, and lays out a selection of delicate pastries from Patisserie Valerie.

'They didn't have Apple Crumble with Custard,' she says, as a private joke, 'so we went for Tarte aux Pommes.'

He tells the children his prison stories as they drink warm milk, tinged tan with a touch of tea, and lick sticky fingers studded with flecks of flaky pastry; he replaces the word prison with hotel or office, depending on which is more appropriate.

The next morning, he is surprised to see that Samira has already dressed for breakfast, and that she is sitting at the table with her coffee while the children work their way through cereal and juice. 'There you are,' she says with artificial brightness, as though he has kept her waiting in some way but she is determined not to criticise. 'Well, seeing as you're up, I'm off. The kids need to be standing outside in ten minutes. Their satchels are by the door.'

'Where are you going?' he asks reasonably. It seems a bit early for the hairdresser, or to get her nails done, and both seem perfectly done anyway. It seems even a bit early for teeth-cleaning at the dentist, or the dry-cleaners.

'Work,' she says, with the same artificial brightness. 'The kids are in the after-school club until five p.m. I'll pick them up then, unless you want to get them earlier.'

'You're working again?' he asks for confirmation, but she is already kissing him impudently on the cheek and walking out of the door. 'How are the kids getting to school?' he calls down the stairwell after her, as she hasn't bothered to wait for the lift. It occurs to him that he has no idea where their school is; he cannot even remember what it is called, although he supposes that the children would know.

'The school bus picks them up. In ten minutes, like I said,' she calls back impatiently, and he hears the heavy front door to the building creak open, and then swing shut with a dull thud.

He looks at the children, who are looking back at him a bit curiously, like visitors to the zoo watching unusual animal behaviour, and he feels oddly exposed. He isn't used to being alone with them, especially not in the flat. He knows what he would need to do with them in a restaurant, or at a social gathering (he would order them food, he would make conversation with others about them), but in an empty room, with ten minutes stretching out before him, he feels dumb and helpless, like an actor who has lost his script; once more, he doesn't know how a father should really behave. He goes to the percolator and pours a cup of coffee. He considers pretending that he already knew their mother was working, but he knows he cannot pull this off with confidence, as he has stupidly given it away by showing his surprise. Children are generally good at detecting bullshit, anyway. 'So, how long has your Amma been working?' he asks companionably as he sits with them, not at his usual faraway place at the other end of the table, but in the seat Samira has just vacated. Mika simply smiles and shrugs, concentrating on her cereal, and Zamir mutters, 'I dunno. A while.' He realises that they don't want to answer him, from some unspecific loyalty to their mother; because she hasn't told, instinctively they feel they shouldn't either. He waits a few minutes, pretending to read the paper, doodling down the edges with a Biro.

'So, how long have you been going to the after-school club?' he asks instead, as though it is a completely unrelated question. 'Is it fun?'

'About three weeks,' says Mika, easily disarmed by his apparent show of polite interest. 'It's OK. We get fruit and milk, and do our homework, and can play in the school garden if it's not raining. And we have music on Thursdays. I'm doing the piano, and Zamir's doing the guitar.' Zamir grunts in acknowledgement, and goes to the hall to start buckling up his satchel. The boy has left over half of his cereal, and he supposes that he should tell him to finish it, but it seems a step too far into parenting. Mika does it for him. 'Zam-ir,' she calls out after him. 'You're wasting food. There are people starving in Africa.' Zamir does not appear to question the direct link between his porridge and Africa, and returns to eat a few more spoonfuls, chewing mechanically and without interest. He does not look at his father, and is possibly embarrassed himself now by his display yesterday. He goes back to the hall, and shouts for Mika from there.

'If you're not ready, slowcoach, I'll go without you.'

'I *am* ready,' Mika protests, sliding down from her chair. She kisses her father on the cheek, diplomatically, with politeness rather than real affection. Anybody could be her father, he thinks, and she would still kiss them with the same pious sense of duty; the mere fact that he is her father, regardless of his behaviour or absence, compels this show of love. He supposes he should approve of her good manners, but something in him is dismayed by the hypocrisy of her kiss; he would rather she threw an honest tantrum and kicked him in the shins; he would rather she ignored him pointedly and refused to look in his direction. He knows that none of this is her fault; she is simply doing what is expected, just as he once did. Sincerity, he thinks again, would be too much to hope for.

He gets up from his chair himself, and follows his children to the hall, where they are fiddling with the buttons on their coats, and heaving on their satchels. 'See you tonight,' he says, as Zamir opens the front door.

'Does that mean you'll be here when we get back tonight?' asks Zamir suddenly, over his shoulder, not quite turning around to meet his father's eyes.

Maqil shrugs. 'Maybe. I haven't decided what I'm doing today yet.'

'So why did you say "See you tonight"?' asks Zamir, turning around properly to look at him. He looks as though this brief conversation is suddenly painful to him, as though he might cry again. Maqil feels himself beginning to panic, and he knows he should reassure his son that he will be there, that it is the least he can do after a four-month absence, but he just can't. He can't make the simple promise to be there that evening, or any evening; it feels too much like a trap. He is trying to think of an answer to this perfectly logical question when Mika replies on his behalf, as though she can see that he is struggling and has decided to help out, as one might a confused foreigner on the underground.

'It's just an expression, stupid,' she says impatiently to Zamir. ' "See you tonight" or "Call you later" are just expressions, like writing "Wish you were here" or "Lots of love" on a postcard.' She walks out of the door that Zamir has been holding open with his shoulder, and says, 'Let's go,' as he drifts after her. She calls back into the flat, 'See you tonight, Daddy,' as though to prove her point.

'Stupid isn't a nice word to say to people,' says Zamir as they walk down to the front door, his voice echoing up the stairwell. 'I'm telling Mum you said that.'

'Don't be such a sneak,' replies Mika.

'And that isn't a nice word either,' he says, finally, as though the conversation is over.

Maqil goes back to the table, drinks his coffee, and shakes his head. He hasn't a clue how to parent. He knows it and the kids know it too. It suddenly occurs to him that a proper father would have walked down the stairs and waited with them, or at least have checked that the bus had arrived, that the children had got on safely. He walks hurriedly to the window, but he is too late. The children are no longer there, but he thinks he can just see the back of a bright blue school bus turning the corner. He supposes that it is more likely that they are on the bus than that they have been kidnapped, but makes a mental note to call the school at nine a.m. to double-check. He feels proud of this decision; he isn't quite so irresponsible after all. He is in a Belgravia flat on his first morning back from prison; his wife is working, his kids are at school, and he is . . . free. He is surrounded by Life and London, and he suddenly has the urge to be out of the flat and in the open air, to drive an open-topped car all the way up Highgate Hill, and look over the city and beyond. He has already forgotten about the chess tournaments, the prison book club and the nascent emerging of his literary talent with a set of not-too-indulgent plays. He has already forgotten that he knows how to make Beef Bourguignon and Apple Crumble with Custard. But he decides to show off his new golf handicap, and calls up an old crony, a minor politician whom he has yet to bankrupt, laughing as they agree to play, and asking if he cares to make it interesting.

In fact he forgets to call the school, but he at least makes sure that he is back before five p.m. If he is honest with himself, he is not fully motivated by not wanting to disappoint Zamir (although this is what he tells the politician, who had wanted a rematch to try to gain back what he had lost on their gentleman's agreement); rather he is curious about Samira's work. She has installed a new filing cabinet in his absence, replacing the drawer that used to be stuffed with the domestic paperwork – the drawer now contains the children's school projects instead. The filing cabinet has a lock, just to keep the children out he assumes, as the key is unimaginatively taped to the underside; he flicks through the folders while he waits, seeing nothing more exciting than household accounts and various threats from old creditors. It occurs to him that she has hidden the key in too obvious a place, that perhaps she is humouring him, hoping that he will feel satisfied that he has cracked the feeble code, and not bother looking further. He starts to conduct a search for further paperwork hidden in less obvious places, but soon loses patience, and is pleased when he hears the noisy mechanism of the lift, and the children's chatter, and her waspish tone as she berates Zamir: 'When I say hold hands crossing the street, I mean it.'

'It's what babies do. I'm not a baby. It's embarrassing. People might stare.'

'Babies don't hold hands, babies are carried or pushed. And I don't care about you being embarrassed, I care about you being squashed into a big red stain by the number 74 bus. That's when people are really going to stare.'

Maqil waits in the hall, and looking at Samira's face, tight and thin lipped, and Zamir's sullen expression, can't stop himself from interfering. 'Well, that's a bit dark, isn't it?' he says to Samira, stepping forward to help her off with her coat. 'You know, he's eight now, I was running all round Lahore when I was eight.'

'He's nine, Maqil,' Samira snaps at him. 'And you can keep your opinions to yourself. I'm not going to wait until he's road pizza just so that I can say "I told you so", to the two of you.' During this exchange, Zamir and Mika have slipped past their parents to their bedroom, Zamir looking humiliated and Mika determinedly straight-faced, although she gives a brief, embarrassed smile to her father on passing him. Maqil decides that the ship has probably sailed on him being an involved parent, and doesn't bother arguing. 'So, would you like a drink?'

'Yes, I bloody well would,' says Samira, still crossly, and

then smiles despite herself, as she realises how comically bad tempered she sounds. 'I mean, yes please, darling,' she corrects herself, with humour and obvious sarcasm. She goes to their bedroom, shrugging off her pink and gold Chanel jacket as she walks, and hangs it back up in her wardrobe.

The kids are watching TV and Samira is on her second gin and tonic when Maqil finally asks, 'So, how's work? It's been a few weeks now, hasn't it? Are you back at the magazine?'

'No,' says Samira. 'Of course not. I couldn't work those hours with the kids. It would be impossible with school pick-ups.'

'So what are you doing?' he persists.

'Odds and sods, research and admin mainly. I met Percival for tea at the House of Lords, and he offered me a job.'

'You're working for Percival?' he says in disbelief. Percival was one of his less lucky investment clients, who had lost his shirt on an inventive Cayman Islands deal that had gone bad. Despite this, he had been one of Maqil's most frequent visitors in hospital during his heart attack, mainly because he had always had a massive crush on Samira. 'You're working for another man?'

'You say "another man" as though he's attractive,' she replies with amusement.

'I'm not sure I like you working for someone else,' he says.

'And you say that as though I've been working for you,' she says. 'You're not my boss, Maqil, and I haven't worked for you for years. I'm not one of those Pakistani hostesses whose whole job is bolstering up their husband's career with their home-made samosas and judicious flirting with men of influence.' She nods towards the golf clubs, propped up by the wall. 'Speaking of which, you didn't waste much time getting back to work. Who was the chump?'

'Just Hugo,' he shrugs. 'Don't worry, you won't have to

avoid him socially, I never take him for too much. He's one of my "cut and cut again" clients; I just clip a bit from him now and again, and let him grow some more. And sometimes I even let him win, just to keep him coming back.'

'Never underestimate repeat business,' says Samira drily.

'Exactly,' replies Maqil. He has just been drinking soda water with lemon, and puts his glass down. He looks at Samira, her thin legs stretched out on the leather sofa, her feet bare, with slightly callused toes from wearing high heels, her nails painted and gleaming like candied fruit. His long-suffering spouse, so lovely and brittle. 'Do you want to get a sitter tonight when the kids go to bed? We could go out for dinner, and then to Claridges for the night.' He waves his money clip, grinning mischievously. 'Hugo's paying.'

'Sounds wonderful,' she says, but then shakes her head, smiling ruefully. 'But not tonight. I've got work tomorrow.' She gets up from the sofa, draining her drink with a brisk efficiency that seems to be more about avoiding waste than enjoyment, just as their son ate his morning cereal, and goes to the kitchen. 'I'd better put something together for the kids' dinner. Do you want anything?'

When she asks this apparently innocuous question, it seems like a challenge. A dare to see if he will treat her like a housewife and expect her to prepare him something. A dare to see if he will step up and offer to help, to make that Beef Bourguignon as he once promised, or even a token effort of beans on toast. He remembers what she said, or rather what she failed to say at that first prison visit. Change, or else. Change, like me. But he is unwilling to change, to step up. Or else he is unable. For the last few months, his wife and his children have been withdrawing from him, as he has withdrawn from so many others; they have been preparing to let him go. He is just another house guest who has outstayed his welcome, a hospital visitor whom they

171

are too polite to ask to leave. His wife will not make love to him in Claridges, his daughter displays diplomatic affection as a matter of courtesy, and his son is mortified to the point of silent tears by the fact that he still cares.

London – 1984 – Theft

HE TRAVELS MORE THAN EVER, MAKING LUCRATIVE DEALS
with his new network of prison cronies. He sometimes suggests
that Samira go with him, but she won't leave the children; he
sometimes suggests that the children go with them too, but she
won't take them out of school. She feigns indifference to her
job, describes it as something trivial she could leave on a whim,
but he sees the renewed pride in herself that paid employment
gives her, the smart click of heels as she leaves the apartment,
the shrugging on of a smart jacket, the efficiency of her goodbye
kisses to the children. Now she is working again, she no longer
asks him for money for household costs, the rent or uniforms;
much like before, she no longer mentions money at all. Unlike
before, if he tries to boast or complain about his big wins
and bigger losses, she seems so uninterested as to be bored,
as though it is a dull hobby he has recently picked up, like
stamp collecting or trainspotting; sometimes she even walks

distractedly out of the room while he is still talking. She shouts less at the children, and has stopped arguing with him altogether. He watches his family at breakfast, from the other end of the table, from behind his newspaper, and feels utterly excluded, as though he wasn't the one who had chosen his other-end-of-the-table seat and ignored them all first. The lack of drama at home causes him to seek drama elsewhere; he tracks down and harasses famous authors and literary editors into looking at his prison plays, he begins to behave with reckless daring in his business dealings, he makes promises he knows he cannot deliver, and takes too much money from those who are neither gentlemen nor men of their word.

His second heart attack takes place while he is away on business in Rome, and this time when he wakes, Samira is seated in the chair by the bed, with the children by her side; it seems that she has been able to take them out of school after all. He wonders if she would have come if it had happened in any other town; she is fond of Rome, and they have the holiday apartment here. Perhaps if it had happened in Stuttgart or Warsaw she would have left him to his own devices. She has a magazine on her lap but is not reading it, just tapping the perfumed pages with her oval manicured nails in this season's frosted fuchsia pink. Mika is on another chair, imitating her mother unconsciously with her neatly crossed ankles, still in uniform, as she goes through a stack of *Archie* comics that are sliding across her lap. And Zamir is cross-legged on the floor, still in uniform as well, but now that his tie and jumper have been removed, with his white shirt and black trousers and golden skin and dark hair, his unsmiling expression as he plays another beeping game with his thumbs, he looks like a miniature Mafia man.

'My God, Maqil,' Samira says quietly to him, when she sees him stir and look at her, 'you'd really do anything to get attention.' She smiles after she says this, and her eyes are brighter than usual; it takes him a little while to realise that this is because there are tears in them. He realises that she thought he was about to die, and wonders whether, as she pulled the children out of their classes, and hailed a cab to Heathrow, and argued with Alitalia to get the first standby seats available, she had felt relieved.

The family have a brief Roman Holiday, and Samira cuts her hair smart and short, just like Audrey Hepburn in the movie, until he is deemed well enough to travel. He returns to London to have the bypass operation; his recovery room features an over-the-top bouquet of flowers that makes his own eyes water, and provokes sneezing that rips through his sliced and zippered chest. Samira collects the flowers and takes them back to the flat, filling three vases with them. When he is sufficiently recovered, he starts to take the children on occasional weekend strolls through Hyde Park, as some light exercise is prescribed. They seem a bit bemused regarding the circular nature of these walks; there appears little point to walking when there is no particular destination except where they have first come from; in fact, he finds it strange too. Still, they don't want to disappoint him, and so they all vocally admire the spring daffodils and narcissi, the narrow waterfall trickling down into the Dell, that enclosed garden with the occasional winsome rabbit scampering about like some animated illustration from a children's book, their special weeping willow tree for secret picnics. He wonders if they are as bored with him as he is with them. He irresponsibly buys them cake in the café, even though they are due to have lunch at home, to keep them occupied while he reads the paper. He knows that somewhere along the way, sometime between his children's birth and his prison vacation, he crossed the line into useless, to his presence not having any more value than his absence. He realised this at the hospital, when he saw Samira and Mika and Zamir all waiting calmly to see if he would survive, because they knew that their lives would carry on exactly as they had been, with or without him. That it did not really matter whether he was alive or dead. It was a blow to his natural vanity, but hardly a surprise – he could not claim to have protected his family, or to have provided for them; he can barely claim to have parented his children, and he struggles even now to show commitment and concern. He is the one who buys the extravagant holidays in five-star hotels, but not the one who puts the food on the table; he still doesn't know exactly where the children's school is. He is still unwilling or unable to change. He supposes that he should leave them all to get on with their own lives, but he has always thought he was a moral man, in his own particular way. He isn't sure that he is strong enough to abandon his family. He isn't physically strong enough, even.

It turns out that Samira is strong enough for the both of them. The final straw comes when she returns home from work one Friday afternoon with the children to find the police in the flat, called by the neighbours after a break-in. The place has been ransacked, money and jewellery has been stolen and her filing cabinet has been shot open. No one was physically threatened or came to any harm; Maqil was in the flat at the time and displayed admirably sensible cowardice by hiding under the bed. The intruders have left a note on the mirror in the hall, in smeared red writing; not written in blood, but rather comically with Samira's Yves Saint Laurent lipstick in Cherry Crush. The note simply says, *Payment in kind*.

'What does that mean, Mrs Karam?' ask the police, having already asked her husband and learned nothing useful.

'It's Ms Rai,' she snaps. 'I use my maiden name.' She gathers the children to her, and adds, more politely, 'I really have no idea. May I take the children to a hotel? I don't think they should see all this. You can get in touch with us at the Cadogan, on Sloane Street.'

'They were just trying to scare me,' Maqil shrugs, sipping a soda water in the hotel lobby. 'And it worked, I almost peed my pants when I heard them shoot the cabinet.' He mentions this cheerfully, as though he is almost pleased that someone considered him important enough to behave so dramatically. He has never been afraid to admit that he is a physical coward, a man of words rather than of action.

'Who was it?' asks Samira.

'Oh, take your pick,' he says airily. 'Anyone who wants their money back. And they've taken it now. So we're good – there's no need to worry.'

'We're good?' she says in disbelief. 'Men with guns have opened fire in our home, the home where your children sleep at night. We're not good. What if this isn't the end? What if someone else wants their money back?' She shakes her head. 'You know, I used to worry about how we were going to cover the rent. Wouldn't that be great, now, just to have the rent to worry about?'

'It's me they want,' he says reassuringly. 'I'll just skip town for a bit. You should come with me, you and the kids. It'll be like Rome without the hospital food. It'll be like the old days.'

'It's not a bad idea, you leaving town for a day or so,' she says. 'You know, you should really get going before the officers find the expired visa in your passport and call Immigration.' She leans over and gives him a kiss, a warm and almost passionate kiss. It takes him completely by surprise, and he realises while he returns the kiss that it is a valediction. She is not saying goodbye out loud, but then, when he thinks about it, she never said hello either; love is leaving him as suddenly as it arrived. 'It was never a bore with you, Butterfly Boy,' she says suddenly, as she breaks off the kiss. 'You know, if it wasn't for the kids, I'd come with you, I really would.' Perhaps she realises that this sounds like goodbye after all, because she hastily qualifies what she has said: 'For a day or so, I mean, in Paris or New York or wherever you decide to head off to for the weekend.' She gets up, straightening her skirt, and speaks quickly, as though she might otherwise not be able to get all the words out. 'You see, the kids can't do without me, like you can. I know I'm a horrible mother and probably always will be, but I think they'll let that go one day. I think they might even forgive me, because I've been here for them. Because they need me. They *need* me, Maqil. But you don't.'

'I'm amazed you know me that well, to be able to tell me what I can or can't do without. To tell me what I need. I haven't even worked that out myself yet,' he says.

'You know I'm almost always right,' she says. 'It's like a curse.'

He nods, beginning to grin. 'You almost always are,' he says, before adding casually, 'I guess I could go tonight, stay away tomorrow, and come back the day after?'

'So, the day after,' she repeats, like a promise, swollen with the damp, empty air it contains. 'I'd better check on the kids; are you going to finish that off before you come up?' She gestures towards his soda water. He nods again, and so she walks away from him to go up to their hotel room, where the children are watching TV with the hotel sitter, a plump, doll-like woman from the Philippines with a wide smile and flamboyant scarves, who looks like a fairy godmother from bedtime stories, as though she has pockets full of sweets and small knitted gifts. He watches Samira stroll towards the lifts, intending to raise his glass to acknowledge her, but she doesn't look back; even when she goes into the lift and has to turn back to push the button, she doesn't move around quite sufficiently to meet his eye, and he sees her profile instead, illuminated by electric light, as the sliding doors close. He waits a moment, and then goes out to the street to hail a cab. His exit is barely remarkable, a little bite of time in the life of the lobby, just about captured by the security cameras; one moment he is there with his soda water, and then he is not. Now you see him, now you don't. A man who lies, and flies away. In the cab, his pockets are heavy with the jewellery that the paid goons didn't get their hands on, and he has the chequebook to his wife's account, and the deeds to their place in Rome. The flat really was robbed, he had arranged it, and in the gap between the robbers leaving and the police arriving, he had made preparations. He had made good his escape plan. He is not leaving Samira, not really; she is the one woman he would never leave, as long as she wanted him to stay. But the fact of the matter is that she wants him to go; she has finally admitted it out loud, even. Like his shadow twin, she is fond of his company, but is better off without him. Unlike his shadow twin, she refuses to put up with his parasitical nature, refuses to be squeezed into the corner, refuses to sustain him any longer to her own disadvantage. She said that he doesn't need her; but they both know the truth is that she doesn't need him, that she hasn't needed him in a long while. He supposes that it's fair to say that this knowledge had begun to eat at him a little; to upset him, even. He was the one who had written on the mirror.

Samira knows him, after all. She has always known him. Three days later, he receives a delivery at the George V in Paris: it is his valise, packed with his most desirable suits, his favourite blue cashmere pullover, and the small metal box with his cufflinks. There is an attractive photo of them as a family, professionally taken before his stay in prison. There is also, rather bewilderingly, a photo of a jam jar with a spoon on the lid, with the two of them in the background at the breakfast table. There is a note in the case that says, *Payment in kind*. He only realises the true import of this when he goes to pawn the jewellery on Monday morning, and discovers that it is all paste, and worthless. Stage jewellery, just for show. When he goes to cash the cheques, after practising forging his wife's signature to perfection, and discovers that the account is empty and the overdraft has been cancelled. When he makes enquiries regarding borrowing against the place in Rome, or even selling it, and receives a telex in the hotel informing him that the property has already been sold, and the funds transferred to a private account in Switzerland.

With this elegant *coup de grâce*, he sits back in his room and orders champagne. He is not really a drinking man, and unlike his wife he almost never drinks alone, but this night he makes an exception. He tips the waiter generously with one of his few remaining notes, and raises a glass to the mirror man, who shares his stunned admiration. 'To Samira,' they say together, in chorus. He obviously should never have got her pregnant; he could live happily without the kids, despicable and cowardly though it might seem, the fact is that he has moved on from them already, but he is suffering now at the prospect of living without her. He still wants her to be by his side, singing off key with him in the wilderness. It is unfair, he thinks, that he and she should be bound together in this way, that love should be soaked so deep into their flesh that it seeps into their fossil bones, their airy souls, but that somehow, despite all this, it should still not be enough. His love is sincere, but insufficient. He is insufficient. Cowardly. Despicable. Himself. He sends a telegram to her office, which offers no confession or apology, but which reads simply, *Well played*. He goes out into the twinkling lights of the Parisian night, reminding himself that the game doesn't end with losing; the game doesn't end until it has been won.

Madrid – 1988 – Art

HE'S BEEN LIVING IN SPAIN, AND DESPITE BEING MORE THAN middle aged, has been having something of a second youth. His sartorial elegance has suffered without Samira's influence, and there is no muted grey or navy in his wardrobe; instead he wears shining white and black against his tanned-toffee skin, and has been guilty of sporting gold jewellery – a 24-carat chain, chunky and mannish enough to match his money clip and newly acquired Rolex. He even wore a medallion once, but decided against it; his chest seemed too narrow and hairless to carry it off. He has grown a moustache, like Magnum PI, and when he wears a dinner jacket he thinks he looks every bit as good as the current James Bond. He likes the fact that he looks like what he is – brash and golden, style over substance. He calls himself Miguel, and struts like a peacock, like a powerful criminal with an entourage packing guns, girls, drugs and cash. In fact, he has no entourage, and although he has started associating openly with the sun-seeking criminals on their gleaming white yachts, he is just a minor offender, and the rainbow of small, clever crimes that he commits are still just as much for fun as for money.

'There is of course the matter of the charge . . . the handling charge,' says the young official delicately in Spanish.

He raises his eyebrows, but then realises that the gesture is too subtle to be noticed, particularly behind his glaring mirrored shades, and so he lifts them up, looking the official in the eyes. He is a little jealous of this man's effortless olive-oiled youth; he is more than a little jealous of the thickness of his hair, so springy that he has an absurd urge to reach out and touch it, to push it down gently with the flat of his palm, to see if it might bounce back to the same height. 'So,' he asks pleasantly, 'are you asking for a bribe?'

The official is surprised by the lack of subtlety, and responds tersely, 'Of course not, *señor*. It is the handling charge.' He shrugs and starts to get up, and the official's delicacy vanishes. 'Doubtless you are above making bribes, *señor*?'

'Oh God, no,' he laughs, pulling his money clip out of his trousers once he is on his feet; it seems that they are too fitted for him to get his hand in his pocket while he is seated. 'Making them, taking them, it's all the same to me. The only thing I'm above is six feet of earth, and I intend to stay that way.'

'As do I, *señor*,' smiles the official, and writes a number on a piece of paper, sliding it across the desk. The man known as Miguel glances down, and pulling notes from his money clip, reaches over to shake the enterprising young man's hand, with his own hand damp and soft with paper.

As he walks from the shade of the air-conditioned offices into the blazing Malaga sunshine, bone-white and blinding, he replaces his mirrored shades and puts on his hat. He is overcome with the sensuality of life, in these places of heat and humidity through which he travels; he thinks of Samira, often, and of how much she would have enjoyed it, how she would have worn a bikini on a wealthy man's yacht with the same indifferent elegance with which she wore a ballgown. He does not think of his children; he struggles to remember what they look like even, as the stylised, posed photo that Samira sent him, and which he has kept, does not resemble his recollection of them. He does not think he has ever seen Zamir looking as handsome and toothy as he does in that photo – he struggles to remember any specific occasion when he might have seen Zamir smile. His abiding memory of his son is of the top of his head, his body crouched around a bright plastic hand-held game. And Mika never wrinkled her nose in that winsome fashion, and when did she ever wear her hair in a ponytail, drawn back from her forehead and fastened with iridescent glass bobbles? It must have been done especially for the photo session. Only he and Samira look like themselves, irreverent and mildly glamorous, and if they hadn't had the children between them, he would possibly have torn the kids out of the shot altogether.

It has been a few years since he left, and it does not occur to him that his children have grown, that Zamir is finally taller than his mother, and has lost any appealing childish solemnity for adolescent gawkiness, with hands and feet too big for his body, a neck too thin for his head, and a wobbling voice; that he has taken the desertion personally, and his core of embarrassed unhappiness sometimes sinks into depression or explodes into anger. It does not occur to him that his daughter has acquired braces, and nipples (although, like her mother, almost no boob), and is distressed by a scattering of pimples on her chin and forehead, which are barely visible to anyone but her – she locks herself in the bathroom, squeezing them painfully until they become red and weeping, and her mother, no stranger to locking herself in the bathroom, starts banging on the door, and scolds her with 'For God's sake, what have you been doing?' when she sees her daughter's damp eyes and blotchy face. For him, the children are frozen in time and have remained just that, children. If they went on holiday to Marbella, he would walk past these two awkward teenagers in the street without a backward glance; and they, on seeing the tight-white-suited, toffee-tanned, mustachioed not-quite medallion man flashing with gold and with mirrors for eyes, would probably do the same.

He has never been particularly artistic, although, like almost everything, drawing is something he can do quite well without trying. Sometimes, when he is waiting for someone in a restaurant, or is early for an appointment, he might put aside the crossword and doodle instead on whatever is to hand. A coaster, a napkin, the feathered margin of the newspaper. His doodles are quite engaging, with their energy and cartoon simplicity; he can capture the profile of a teenage waitress with a single fluid line, and the way her hair is tucked back behind her ear with another. He can pick out the features that matter, and ignore those that don't, scribbling the form of an elderly man with a stick, his face almost blank but instantly recognisable by the straight line of a nose, the gash for a mouth, and the two deep grooves across the forehead, a face drawn in four dashes. He does not pick these particular subjects from yearning for his lost youth, or from fear of the future; there is no Sphinx riddle on the passing of time in his scribbling. He gets bored, that's all, he likes to keep his hands busy, and so he draws what he sees. And when his guest turns up, or his name is finally called, he scrunches up the coaster, the napkin, the newspaper, and leaves it there or throws it away. It never occurs to him that anyone would want to see what he has drawn – for him, art has no value as a spectator sport, the fun is all in the doing; looking at art usually bores him to bad behaviour.

Which is why it is odd to find him in the Prado in Madrid. He has been twice before, once with Samira, and once with Samira and the twins when they were babies. Both times he had followed her briefly, and then made an excuse and left while she walked briskly through the rooms, looking at every painting and studying the associated translated blurb, giving equal or more time to the small squares of printed information in serif fonts as to the huge, varnished canvases. He sometimes wondered if Samira felt obliged to like galleries, simply because her degree had been in art history. Her consumption of the art, the thoroughness with which she worked through each piece, reminded him of the trudging way his son ate his porridge – it had little to do with appetite, and everything to do with duty. It was as though Samira liked a clean plate in this instance too, and felt compelled not to waste the art put out for her. But it wasn't as though she looked at the actual paintings on sufferance; she seemed to like them in the way that she liked most beautiful things, her appreciation of the aesthetic that diplomatically encompassed designer clothes and tea cups, sunsets and cathedrals; it was just that she liked the stories behind the art a little more. She would go to the gift shop after visiting a gallery, and skim through books with exactly the same pictures she had just seen, buying those that offered the most gossip on the painters and their works; she was, after all, a woman who read magazines. Privately he thought that art galleries were just places to have a stroll, and go for a coffee afterwards, like a village square or a well-tended urban park. He would normally be at the gallery coffee shop within fifteen minutes of walking in, and read the paper or do the crossword, or doodle on the borders if he'd done both of these already. But this time he is walking carefully through the rooms, and paying attention to all the paintings on exhibit; he is staring at the smallest frame with rapt interest, dawdling rather than doodling. And when he reaches the last hanging space, the last mounted piece, followed by the signs to the gift shop and the café and the restrooms, he walks back around, swiftly, and starts again.

He is looking at the Velázquez when a voice speaks up behind him: 'They are *magníficas*, no? But Goya is my favourite.'

'Really? Which one was Goya? Do you mean that moody saint, stuck with arrows and tied to a tree in the moonlight?' he asks, turning around. He sees an elderly, insignificant-looking man with round spectacles, who had dressed that morning to seem less significant still, in shades of greyish tan and dull taupe; an altogether beige man who most people would have trouble remembering. If Maqil had to draw his face, he would do nothing more than a couple of circles for the glasses, a lower-case L for a nose, and a Morse dot-dash-dot for his mouth. A Charlie Brown face without the childish roundness or appealing concern around the eyes. It occurred to him that if this man committed a crime, he would only have to remove the round glasses, his only distinguishing feature, and he would practically be invisible.

'That is Saint Sebastian,' says the man, disappointed by his response. 'Goya is one of the great artists, he is not a subject.' He adds reproachfully, 'They told me you had an eye for art.'

'I don't,' says Maqil cheerfully, 'but I have an eye for detail.' Of course he knows who Goya is, but he cannot keep himself from telling small lies; it is an automatic instinct, and the lie itself always makes him feel as though he has the upper hand: he knows something that the other doesn't, the other thinks he is man who has never heard of Goya, and he has the deep satisfaction of knowing that he does. He begins to stroll away, and the little man scurries after him.

'All the same, it seems that you didn't find it, *señor*. I have been watching you, I saw that you have started again. I wouldn't feel bad. You are clearly no professional, and even for someone who knows, it is like a drop of water in the ocean.'

'Now where the hell . . .' mutters Maqil to himself, still walking through the rooms. 'You know,' he says over his shoulder to his shadowy companion, 'galleries should be better organised. Like libraries and bookshops. Gauguin next to Goya. Mondrian next to Modigliani. They just bung anyone next to anything – it's impossible to find what . . . Ah, here it is.' He stops finally, in front of a small painting set in a cluster with other similar pieces, a delicate collection of landscapes, precisely brushed studies of changing light. 'The best place to hide is in a crowd. Isn't that so?'

'I'm impressed,' says the man. 'How did you know?'

'The dust,' says Maqil. 'The dust is different on this one. Differently distributed. This one looks like it was cleaned with care, since all the fingerprints are gone, and then redusted; but the dust looks like it was put on when it was flat on a table. There's not enough between the frame and the glass at the bottom, if you look at the others.'

'*Mein Gott in Himmel*,' says the man, lapsing into his native German with astonishment as he peers at the painting. 'You're right.'

'Next time you're prepping a forgery, dust it upright on the wall, not on the table, little tip for next time,' says Maqil cheerfully. 'If God's in our machine, the devil's in the detail. As to the art, like you said, I'm no expert, but everyone seems to think you'll do for the job, so here I am.'

'And what machine are you talking about, *señor*?' asks the man, rather coyly, like a young girl who has been suddenly won over with a bunch of flowers and an outrageous compliment. Or else one who has scorned these trivial gifts, but has just discovered that her suitor has hidden depths, that he writes poetry and is kind to animals.

'We'll deliver it when we get the negative. How long do you need to work on it?'

'You can't rush art, *señor*,' says the man. 'And counterfeiting is as much an art as any forgery.'

'Well don't take too long,' says Maqil pleasantly. 'Probably best that we don't annoy Don Raõul, or it'll be back to forging cheques from the Social Security office to scrape out a living.'

'I have never done that, *señor*,' says the man, rather sniffily.

'Good for you,' says Maqil. 'I was talking about me.' He strolls off to the café, cheerfully, as he has won the bet he made with Don Raõul, who didn't think he would find the forgery in the Prado. The devil was in the detail. He is looking forward to the counterfeiting operation with an almost childish delight; he couldn't believe he hadn't thought of it before. All the money he has made and lost at casinos, the money that he treated as casually as play money after all, with the same gleeful ignorance of a toddler who knows the value of nothing, while still being convinced of the worth of everything, who would throw out an expensively engineered toy in order to play with the box it came in. Why had he never got round to making money for real? Using the Costa del Sol contacts he first made in prison, with backing from a local businessman who calls himself Don Raõul but is really Ralph from the Wirral (tattooed with the chorus of 'Ferry Cross the Mersey' across his back and Liverpool FC on his forearm), he is bringing together a team of skilled craftsmen. The forger he is commissioning to create the negative is an elderly Jewish printer who once bought his life in a Nazi camp by producing over a million counterfeit pounds sterling, which he churned out expertly with hand-cranked machinery and substandard gelatine. His work is highly regarded, his craft as pure as a master baker creating artisanal bread by hand, mixing flour, yeast and salt with water, and nothing more, stoking the furnace to 300 degrees with foraged forest wood, and sliding damp loaves from willow proving baskets into the oven. The bread will only last the morning rush, that's the thing: all that care and sweat and hard labour in basement rooms heated like Hades, and the stuff has a shorter shelf life than milk; if not eaten in the day, it will be hard and jaw-breaking by night. His play money won't last much longer – it will be consumed with delight, with real appetite. He promises himself this; he has always been a man with little baggage, and his shiny new money won't weigh him down either.

He takes a seat in the café and orders a dark, bitter coffee, and a small pastry sweetened with intensely yellow custard and sprinkled with rough sugar crystals. He stiffens for a moment as he sees that the forger has wandered into the café too. The forger notices him sitting there, and sensibly decides not to stay; it is probably best they aren't seen together again, for the moment at least. The forger is careful not to exit so abruptly that it might seem unusual enough to be remarked upon; he dithers for a moment by the drinks, selects a bottle of water as though considering a purchase, but then replaces it and leaves. Maqil reads the paper, doodles in the margin, and realises that he is being watched. There is a woman in the café who is openly staring at him. Not a particularly attractive woman, and much too old, that is to say almost his own age, but still he puffs his chest out a little, and feels pleased that he has been noticed. Feels pleased with his white suit and toffee tan and gold chain and shades. Feels pleased that he's still got it, whatever it is.

He takes a sip of his coffee, puts it down on the saucer with a slight clatter, and the discordant note it strikes, thick white ceramic on ceramic, suddenly prompts his silent admirer to speech: 'My God, Mehmet, it is you, isn't it!' she says in Arabic, repeating in astonished French, *'Mais c'est bien toi!'* He thinks about denying it, but it's too late, as he has already met her eyes. Carine, his No. 1, with the soft brown waves of jasmine-scented hair, his old wife, is fast on her way to becoming old herself. Her hair is now cut short in a sensible and matronly style, and is coarser, with a harsh shine from the dye she uses to cover the grey. Her thick eyebrows, once like birds in flight, are finer, as is the fashion, and make her seem more surprised than she already is. She is no longer slim, but she is elegantly dressed in a light linen suit that helps disguise this fact; her calves are still presentable, and she is wearing leather shoes with a low heel, comfortable for walking. His gentle Carine, a still pool of forbearance, is now a middle-aged woman in comfortable shoes. He tries to remember the shoes she used to wear in Cairo, stitched hide sandals in the dusty street, sequinned and embroidered slippers for home, and yes, leather shoes with a low heel for work. He never thought of Carine as a woman who wore comfortable shoes, but it seems that she always was, and he never noticed. She is wearing just enough make-up not to look like someone who doesn't care about her appearance, but not enough to look like she cares too much. She has clearly decided to grow old gracefully, and she is graceful now as she smiles at him, and says, 'It's so good to see you.' He cannot help himself smiling back; she always had beautiful manners, as well as beautiful Arabic.

'You too,' he says, and indicates the spare chair at his table. 'Would you care to join me?'

She nods, and lifts up her own coffee cup, and her large handbag, and a small pile of paperwork from her table, and walks over. She starts to speak before he does, her words bubbling up and spilling over, like water in a fountain, like soup in a pan. 'I looked right past you at first. And then I saw the newspaper, and the way you were scribbling, and then I thought it might be you, but you seemed so different. I didn't know if you were in fancy dress or in hiding or in some government protection scheme. And you didn't seem to know me. So I thought it probably wasn't you, but I thought, my God, I know that one forgets people, but people one has been married to, those people you really ought to remember. And then you clumped your coffee cup down, and I knew. I knew.' While she is talking, she isn't able to look straight at him, and starts fussing with her papers, straightening them on the table to neat edges. She glances up, and sees herself in his mirrored shades, sees her distorted reflection, and looks briefly dismayed, before laughing: 'My God, look at me. I'm babbling. And I'm tidying the table like a housewife.'

'You look very well,' he says, as he has been thinking the same thing and doesn't want to sound unkind. He takes off his glasses, realising that it is inconsiderate to keep them on, as they oblige her to look at herself when she looks at him.

'Well, thank you,' she says. 'You look very well too.' She adds, with a touch of mature mischief, 'And full of yourself, as always.'

He laughs. 'Oh Carine, it is good to see you. Really. The things I've wanted to tell you over the years.'

'It's rather too late to apologise, Mehmet,' she says, without malice.

'I didn't mean that,' he says, suddenly feeling rather guilty, as although he is fully aware of how unfairly he behaved towards Carine, it has never, had never, occurred to him to apologise. 'I just meant that I know what it's like now, to be married to someone who isn't there. Who won't eat the damn stuff you order from the bakery.' He gestures to his pastry, and then breaks it in two, and putting half on the edge of his saucer, pushes the plate over to her. 'For old times.'

'For old times,' agrees Carine, and accepts the broken pastry. She dips it in her coffee, and eats it with a sigh of pleasure, with the harmless greed of the slightly bigger woman she has become. 'Well, we've broken bread together. Who'd have thought it?' She brushes the crumbs from her fingers with a napkin, and says, 'I married again, as well. I have two children. They're grown-up; they're in college abroad and speak English with American accents. When we used to have breakfast, they barely noticed me either. When I travelled for work, as I am doing now, I'm sure they barely noticed I was gone. Being married to you prepared me for having adolescents.' She says this with generous humour, but he frowns as something occurs to him.

'How did you marry again? Legally, I mean. We never got divorced.'

'You're dead to me,' she replies flatly. 'Legally, just as you say. I had you declared dead. It was easier than abandonment.'

'Ah,' he breathes with comprehension. 'Of course.' He grins. 'I never had to go to that trouble. I'm Muslim, I could have four wives if I wanted.'

'Well, God help your other wives,' says Carine. She is looking at him closely again, and he is a little bit afraid that she is going to ask him to dinner. That she will expect him to sleep with her once more in her hotel room with the same politeness with which he first married her. He is afraid of seeing what is under her clothes, of seeing how the presentable calves might lead to plump or fissured thighs with blue veins snaking up from behind her knees; he is afraid of white belly fat, crêpe wings of flesh on her upper arms and the low, heavy weight of her motherly breasts. Of her respectable mother's haircut beside him on a pillow. Her eyes are still pure and untouched by age, and he remembers that she is younger than him, albeit just slightly. Part of the subtle disgust he feels at the thought of her body beneath the linen suit is the disgust he feels for his own; seeing her would mean revealing himself. His greying chest hair, his less than perfect ass; he is aware that his unnaturally elongated prime is coming to an end.

'You're working, you said? Are you still in Cairo, still working for the museum?' he asks suddenly, trying to cover up his discomfort.

She smiles slightly at the flurry of questions, and shakes her head. 'Are we really going to make small talk? Well, why not? Talking about anything bigger would just be awkward.' She sips her coffee, and says, 'Yes, we're in Cairo, and no, I'm no longer at the museum, although my husband still works there. You may even remember him, Kamel Mahfouz? He's part of the management team now. I work at the university. I'm just here in Madrid to give a few lectures.' She finishes her coffee, and begins to gather her paperwork again, this time tidying it into her handbag, square and functional to match her comfortable shoes. He realises that she is not going to ask him to dinner after all, that she is preparing to take leave of him, with as little ceremony but rather more politeness than he did all those years ago. She has asked him nothing about himself, and he feels a little annoyed about this; he didn't expect her to have been pining for him all these years, and he would probably have lied if she had asked anything, but he would have liked to be asked all the same. He would have liked to be asked to dinner and to bed, even; he would have liked the opportunity to make up an excuse.

'I've got two kids too, you know,' he says. She smiles and nods, but does not ask their ages or their names. Her silence makes him want to speak even more, to blabber like she did. He is aware that he is losing control of their interview, and wants to gain it back somehow. 'I haven't seen them for a while,' he says finally. She nods again, as though this is what she expected, and he realises that she is looking at him with something like pity, or possibly relief. She thinks that she had a narrow escape.

She is grateful to him for leaving when he did, and not giving her children that he would run away from and not be bothered to see. She is grateful to him for leaving when he was still handsome.

'I would say keep in touch,' she says delicately, 'but it's never been something you've been good at. It would just be an expression. But you do know how to get in touch with me, if you want to. You've always known.' Her handbag is packed, and she picks it up and arranges the strap neatly over her shoulder. He stands up with instinctive politeness and goes to kiss her cheeks, which are very soft, and delicately powdered with a floral scent that isn't quite jasmine but some more insipid family member; a mild maiden aunt in prim hose and buckled shoes. 'It was good to see you,' she says sincerely. 'And I'm glad that you still wear those cufflinks,' she adds, before walking briskly away. Her shoulders are hunched, a little higher than they should be, and he wonders whether she cares more than she has let on; whether she is trying to control herself and keep herself from crying; he knows it is unlikely, and he knows that it is unkind to think this, but he almost wishes she would. He would rather think he'd broken her heart, once upon a time, than failed to make any impression whatsoever.

He sighs, and finishes his own coffee, tapping his pen on the newspaper thoughtfully where he has started doodling again. He picks up his sunglasses, and winces at the sight of himself in the mirrored lenses. At how she has seen him. He looks away into the window of the café, but can now see his ghostly reflection on the glass instead, as though it is following him about. What was it she had said? Fancy Dress? In Hiding? He is suddenly aware that he looks ridiculous, with the same instant clarity that a fat father of four on a Harley Davidson might have on catching his own eye in a shop window while waiting for the lights to change. Or a woman in hooker heels and clinging animal print who sees a sad old tart on a security camera as she enters a department store, and is torn between pity and laughter in the split second before she realises that she's looking at herself. He is finally seeing what other people see. He goes to the cloakroom, takes off the white jacket, the shades, the gold jewellery, and is left a tanned man with too much facial hair, wearing an open black shirt linked with discreet sapphires. He shaves with the razor he keeps in his inside pocket for tidying his moustache, tucked next to a folding toothbrush kit taken from a plane journey, and buttons up his shirt. He is still dissatisfied with the trousers, and so he pays the attendant to give him spare uniform trousers in plain grey; a synthetic mix, but perfectly respectable looking. When he walks out of the gallery, his damp hair smoothed back from his forehead, darkly dressed in a good shirt and cheap trousers, he is respectable, smooth faced and unremarkable. The forger has been waiting for him outside, intending to follow him discreetly; not from any sinister motive, but from an inappropriate fascination, like a schoolboy with a crush. He is looking out for an overconfident clown blazing in white and gold, with a movie-star moustache, and so misses him completely.

After a while, the forger returns to the café, to the corner spot where he had seen him sitting, and notices that a woman who had left the café some time ago has returned, and is standing at the corner table, leafing through the abandoned newspaper. There is nothing unusual about this, not even when she rips out a page, and puts it in her pocket; it could be anything, after all, an interesting article, a tempting personal ad. The unusual thing happens next: she takes the page out of her pocket, as though finally deciding against it, scrunches it up and leaves it on the table; and then she turns on her heel, and walks away with her eyes shining with tears, her mouth trembling, her face threatening to crumple like the paper. Once she is gone, the forger sits at the table himself, and picking up the scrunched-up ball, smooths it out. The article on the page about Basque separatists isn't particularly interesting, and nor is the advertisement offering reduced-price Beta max videos, but down the border of the page there is a drawing. It is a doodle of a man with round circles for eyes, an insignificant lower-case L for a nose, and a dash for a mouth. He recognises it as himself, with a little shame that he has been so easily reduced and reproduced; he feels a complicated pride, that he has finally, in his old age, succeeded in becoming insignificant, a long-term ambition since he left the Nazi camp, but also that he has been noticed, captured in ink on a page rather than in a filthy room with a cement floor for hosing out excrement and blood. He looks at himself for so long that he almost doesn't notice the other scribbled drawing, further down the margin. It is of a young woman, her profile drawn in a single fluid line, her ear represented with a simple C; there is a small five-pointed flower set within her waves of doodled hair, like a periwinkle or a jasmine.

Marbella, Spain – 1991 – Money

YOU'D THINK THAT MAQIL WOULD FINALLY BE IN HIS element – gold so pure that he could sink his teeth into it. In fact, it turns out that the success of the counterfeiting operation leaves him with a profound depression – I suppose because it leaves him with nothing to do. In the past, he was always able to bounce back after failure, but now that he has succeeded, now that he has won the game, it seems that it really has ended. He has almost no satisfaction from playing with his play money; he treats winning and losing even more indifferently than he did before, as it really doesn't matter if he chooses red or black, or loses the count or misreads the deck. It has become as pointless as playing a one-armed bandit fixed to give a jackpot every time; he just gets tired of pushing in his coins and pulling the lever. It's boring. He's become a bore to himself. He finally under-stands the melancholy of the exiled royalty in the casinos; he sits glumly with them in bars, sipping champagne with a sour expression on his face, as though it is cod liver oil or something equally distasteful and medicinal. He has plenty of money, and it has paralysed him. He no longer grifts for a living, he doesn't plot any more long cons or organise inappropriate investment projects, but for the first time in his life, he feels like a fraud. He even doubts the integrity of his despair; in the mornings he drags himself from his soft hotel bed to sit and stare on the balcony, no longer dressed for the day, but slumped in a towelling robe with the hotel logo embroidered on the chest; he waits for the night, and wonders whether this is just another part he is playing, and playing badly, without sufficient feeling. He suspects this most strongly when he is listlessly flicking though the television channels in his room; his misery seems too made-for-TV, too obvious to be real, it seems that this misanthropic figure in a robe is just another clichéd character in a sitcom. Sometimes, when he switches on the TV, he doesn't even have the energy to flick through the channels; he just stares at the screen, which welcomes him by his current name, typed out white on black and correctly spelt; at his reflection flickering indecisively in the box. He misses Samira, horribly, and is sure that she would know what to do. He considers going back to London to see her; but he remembers the subtle humiliation of his interview with Carine, and doesn't think he could bear to see Samira living a happy life without him, walking with that firm step to her apartment, and not missing him at all. He even considers going back to Pakistan, in his darkest moments, but he is too afraid of the cage of his elderly mother's sympathy, of her gently offered 'What will you do now, Sunny?' and his brothers' smug I-told-you-so attitudes, with their respectable jobs, wives and lives, their little places marked out on the planet.

'Go and see your wife,' says the forger, who does not frequent the casinos, but has taken to spending his weekends on the Costa del Sol, not on an obvious shiny yacht, but at a little studio near the beach, where he paints enormous seascapes that he embellishes with metallic detail using real gold and silver, hammered to foil confetti. This is his only extravagance, despite now being wealthy beyond most people's wildest dreams, and he otherwise lives a quiet, invisible life in Madrid, in an apartment building where all the doors look the same, left and right, above and below. When the forger is in town, Maqil drags himself out to join him for coffee on the shady terrace of a local café, a place the forger frequents once the best early-morning light has gone. The forger invites him gently, as though he would take flight like a jittery wild animal if pressed, and he never formally promises to come, but they are often found together there, surrounded by lush greenery planted in extravagantly sized pots, with mercifully few flowers, as they both suffer from allergies. The forger's Spanish is perfect and almost accentless after forty years in the country, but when he speaks English, he gives away his past, and sounds Jewish and German all at once. 'Go and see your children,' he continues, as Maqil simply shrugs and answers through his nose with a dismissive exhalation. 'You're lucky to have a wife, to have children. My wife and I never had any; we never had the chance. She was just twenty-four years old when she died in the camp; she was shot. Not because she was infectious or too ill to work, not because she had been caught trying to escape, or even for speaking out of turn; she was shot because someone beside her in the line had spoken out of turn. A pointless death, like so many others. And if I could have just one more day with my Hannah, do you think I'd waste it sitting here with you, watching you snort into your coffee?'

'My first wife had me killed off to make the paperwork easier. My second wife has probably done the same by now,' he finally says. 'She doesn't want to see me. I'm dead to her.'

'To be honest, Miguel, you might as well be,' says the forger, brutally. 'When I first met you, I thought, My God, What a Man! You were so rude, so full of life, so full of yourself. And now, you're nothing. You've given up on being who you are, whoever that is.'

'What is this? A criminal intervention? Tough love? A bloody motivational seminar?' he mutters.

'It's just advice from a friend,' says the forger. 'Go and see your wife and children, and get out of Malaga.' He lowers his voice, so that only Maqil can hear him. 'The business cannot afford for you to be so dejected,' he says seriously. 'Don Raõul is worried that you'll give us away, the way you're spending money, throwing it around, throwing it away like paper. My negative is as perfect as it can be, but someone will work it out one day, and when they do, our associates will blame you.'

'I've always thrown money around; I did that even when it wasn't just paper,' he replies tersely.

'I say this as a friend,' repeats the forger. 'Stay and enjoy your success, discreetly. Or take your money and run.' He leans back, and smiles just slightly. 'You know, it's been forty-seven years since Hannah died. It happened in Auschwitz.' He pulls back his limp cotton sleeve, and shows him the numbered tattoo on his forearm. 'Before we were sent there, I had morals, I had courage, even. I printed political pieces, anti-Nazi propaganda. When she was gone, I printed money for the Nazis so that I would survive the camp. I have done many things in my life that I'm not proud of, I have kept my head down and my mouth shut, but I think that Hannah would be proud of me, after all, because at least I have survived. I have lived and outlived. And you, my friend, are a survivor too.'

Maqil gets up from the table, and meets the forger's eye. 'Goodbye, my friend,' he says, repeating in German, '*Auf wiedersehen, mein Freund.*'

'*Mein Gott,* Miguel,' complains the forger, 'you should never speak German to a German, with that Swiss accent of yours. You sound like a dairy farmer.'

Maqil grins for the first time in a long while, and walks off across the street, but when he turns around to wave, he sees that the forger has gone too, and has already blended into the street furniture, into the crowd of brightly dressed locals and flashy tourists strutting and posing in the sun. He looks for his friend, but the forger keeps his head down, just as he said. Maqil cannot be sure, but he thinks he catches a glimpse of beige or brown moving through the parade, a muted shade like that of a thrush hopping nimbly through a flower bed.

London – 1992 – Reunion

HE NEEDS A FORGED PASSPORT TO FLY TO LONDON (HIS earlier incarceration for tax evasion makes obtaining a visa difficult), and has to pick out a nationality and name. But for some reason he struggles with this simple task, and decides he doesn't have the patience to wait for the paperwork anyway, so he leaves Spain with his real passport instead. This means that he has to travel to the UK across the Irish border, betting correctly that the authorities there won't bother to check his passport at the fluid grass-soaked frontier between the Republic of Ireland and the British territory in the North. He enjoys the convoluted odyssey through Ireland, and makes it more complicated still by hiring a car, rather than taking a train or a bus, for the journey from Dublin to Belfast, getting lost on the small roads and avoiding the motorway. Alone on the road, well dressed, more than middle aged, with neatly cut hair, he feels like one of those oddly respectable people who inhabit the borders of their own lives, like a travelling salesman, or an elderly butler serving someone else's family in a stately manor, whose real life, hearth and home is happening somewhere else. Pale, freckled children from the damp villages ride their bicycles alongside him and bang on his windows, sometimes mischievously, sometimes with menace; the youngest ones ride high on the handlebars, or sit awkwardly on the frame behind their brothers or sisters, dragging their feet in the dirt; sometimes he sees three to a bike, all at the same time. He keeps his windows wound tightly shut, he offers them nothing. He is aware of a hopeless nostalgia for his youth, for that endless journey from Paris to Pakistan, with the wind in his hair, a song in his heart, a tenacious spider hanging from his wing mirror, gloriously unaware of the fragility of its fate. Then, he had been going home, and he had dreaded and delayed his arrival. He is unsure whose home he is going to this time, and when he finally arrives in London, he still feels lost and indecisive. He doesn't feel he can walk up to the old flat and ring the bell; he doesn't know if Samira even lives there any more. He takes the tube to South Kensington, and on strolling past the Rembrandt Hotel opposite the V&A Museum, decides to check in. He had been to a wedding at the hotel once, an old-fashioned Hindu wedding with a fire for the bride and groom to walk around, and an extravagant buffet of both Indian and Western food; he remembers that the king prawn biryani had been rather better than the seafood risotto, which had been too dry, with overcooked prawns, and undercooked rice.

He showers in his tasteful room, with pale narcissi printed on the heavy curtains, shaves and wears his flattering blue cashmere sweater; but after all of this, he is still disappointed by his appearance. He is no longer handsome, in the way that a woman of a certain age is no longer beautiful; the final stage of his transformation seems to have happened too suddenly, as swiftly and irreversibly as one of his famous exits, a blink-and-you-miss-it magic trick: now you see him and now you don't. Without ceremony, he has been replaced by his painting in the attic. He stares at himself, critically and unhappily. His hair is still dark, but thinner than before, and higher on the forehead. The wide-open puppy-dog eyes of his youth have become hooded, as though the weight of his eyelids is more than the delicate facial muscles can support, the skin puckering and creasing around them. When he tries a smile, the creasing is even worse; the effect of his crinkled eyes now seems demonic rather than charming. And most distressing of all, the pores on his nose have expanded; he can see them now, standing a whole foot away in the mirror. He cannot imagine that anyone who looks at his face would be able to avoid staring at these holes, with the same unflattering fascination one would give a prominent port-stain birthmark or a glass eye. He had laughed at Samira once, when she had complained about a couple of almost invisible pores in the dip of her chin, barely pinprick sized; she had gone to an exclusive women's beauty salon in Knightsbridge, and asked about treating them, and was told there was very little that could be done beyond her usual regime of cleanse, tone and moisturise; it seems that pores are genetic. That they will out with age as inevitably as wisdom teeth and nasal hair. Like the joke he used to tell at parties – What's the second sign of getting old? Hairs in your nose. What's the first sign? Looking out for them. He remembers his Uncle Zafri's bulbous, pitted nose – when he was young, he had joked to his parents that it should be honked like a horn, and they had laughed first, and looked dutifully disapproving afterwards. He never watched his father become truly old, and shudders to imagine the face of his future, a crumpled map of lines and pits and broken veins, paper skin on his skull like frayed tissue on a lantern. He has not celebrated his birthday since he left Samira, but looking at himself now, in his elegant room with a view, he is suddenly aware that he is older than his father was when he died. He is the age at which it is acceptable to die in Third World countries; the age at which loyal servants in the big houses of Pakistan become hunched over and sentimental about their wives and children and grandchildren in the villages, and demand more than the customary two weeks' leave to visit them; the age at which prosperous Punjabi landowners panic about their mortality, and jeopardise their social standing by taking attractive mistresses or youthful second wives. The age for death, nostalgia and folly. He did not think he would live this long; he thought that by now, by this foolishly ripe age, he would have killed himself with his careless insouciance, or else been killed by his enemies.

He glances out of his window to the lavish stone arches of the entrance to the museum, at the statue of Prince Albert, youthful and dapper, welcoming his guests, and above him, an aged Queen Victoria, as round and sober as a Victoria plum, stiff with the rustling of stone silk. The one who died young seems to have had a better time of it than the one who was left behind. To kill or be killed suddenly seems a more attractive proposition than the one ahead of him, which is, rather blandly, to live and let live.

He is not brave enough to go and see Samira, and so he stalks her instead. He lingers behind newspapers in cafés, and watches for her when she comes out of the manicured square and walks briskly along the main road. She is still at the old flat after all. On weekdays she comes out before nine, and goes straight to the tube station, so he supposes that she is still working. At the weekend, she emerges later, and he follows her at a safe distance, sporting a hat and dark glasses like an old-fashioned spy, as she works her way along the smart shops of Sloane Street and

Brompton Road. She stops for a coffee at Gloriette, the old-fashioned patisserie with a cosy tea room upstairs with red velvet banquettes, where she used to order birthday cakes for the children: Thomas the Tank Engine for Zamir, with a smiling blue-grey face that seemed an odd colour for something you were meant to eat, and Barbie with swirling skirts of pink iced sponge, buttercream and jam for Mika. And once Samira had ordered a cake for her own birthday, a simple lemon cake with rolled white icing and pale sugar-crafted yellow roses, the closed petals so perfectly sinister that they looked real, her name extravagantly looped across the cake at a jaunty angle. She had served it at a dinner party she was having for her birthday, and with the way her name was written, confidently swirled from corner to corner with the conspicuous absence of a 'Happy Birthday' message, it looked like her signature, her stamp of ownership on the cake. Something she had made, rather than something being offered to her. The guests all assumed this, and she didn't correct them, and he realised that this may have been her intention all along, when she carefully explained to the patisserie precisely how they should put the inscription, 'Not "Happy Birthday Samira", just "Samira", in script as big as you can make it, corner to corner not side to side.' She generously admitted to her guests that the sugar roses came from the patisserie; there was, after all, a limit to credulity, which is why she had also requested the white icing to be plain, and not bordered or corniced with flourishes; no one would be able to imagine Samira filling an icing bag, fitting a shaped nozzle and patiently squeezing a series of perfectly uniform shells or stars.

Samira sits outside the café, and does not look back at the window of glossy and frilled cakes with wistful nostalgia or admiration or even greed; she just sips quickly and then calls for the bill before she has even finished, with her characteristic impatience. When it arrives, she doesn't wait for the waitress, but leaves her change on the table and walks off, as though she is in Paris rather than London. He is briefly tempted by the idea of sitting in the seat she has just vacated, of holding the change that might still be warm from her hand. He isn't able to, as the waitress hurries out anxiously to collect the payment from the table, and then seems relieved as she counts her tip; she looks up to wave her thanks to Samira. But both he and the waitress realise that in the flurry of change-counting, Samira has disappeared altogether; she could be in any shop, or have slipped down any street. He tries the narrow entrance to the nearby mews, hears the clicking of high heels on cobbles, and almost runs after her, forgetting to be discreet. He supposes he is lucky that it isn't her after all, as the middle-aged woman in the Chanel suit he has been mistakenly chasing sees him, and gives him a questioning look, edged with disapproval, before she too disappears. He realises that the woman has walked through what the locals used to call the Hole in the Wall, the insignificant door-shaped entrance in the ancient wall that closes off one exclusive little street from another, and he hangs back before going through himself. He passes the local pub, and is aware of his breath, of the thudding of his heart, as he sees Samira in the distance, walking towards Hyde Park. He keeps her in view, staying close to the painted pillars of the grand houses that line the street, the broad stone steps to the front doors softened around the edge, like used soap; he intends to hide behind the pillars in case she turns around, but she is completely unaware of him. She crosses into the park, picking her way carefully across the sandy horse track of Rotten Row, and then carries on. He is confused as to why she is walking in the park, as Samira was never the kind of woman to stop and smell the flowers, and she isn't dressed for exercise, especially with those high-heeled, high-fashion boots. Her boots are black and white ponyskin, like the Eames lounger she used to admire in the Conran Shop but which he never took the hint and bought for her; just like the lounger, the shoes look expensive and uncomfortable.

With these thoughts of shoes and shops, he finally realises that she is walking to Oxford Street; of course, with the London traffic, cutting through the park would be quicker than a cab or bus, and the tube involves a torturous change. He follows her along the line of plane trees, the acid-fed leaves spread out like open hands, forced to keep his distance as the park offers less cover than the street, and he begins to feel rather foolish, dashing from tree to tree like an inept flat-footed detective or comic-book villain, with his dime-store disguise; it is impossible to be discreet, and the scattering of tourists and mothers with buggies are beginning to look at him curiously. He takes off his hat and sunglasses, and wonders what he'll do when she reaches the long straight path that leads to Marble Arch, once she crosses over the little bridge on the Serpentine, where there are no trees to hide behind, however foolishly. He knows where she's going, so he decides that he may as well run ahead there and wait for her, rather than follow. He jogs swiftly the long way around the Dell, but once he is on the other side, he can't resist looking back at the little bridge. He once took a photo of Samira there, casually dressed in a floppy silk shirt and leather slacks, holding the babies as neatly as though they were accessories, a pair of matching boy and girl handbags from the Harrods sale. She had stood with her back to the bridge, the green of the tree-fringed lake misting behind her, and had glowed, briefly, like a woman from another, more perfect, world. A woman untouched by the troubles of engorged leaking breasts and baby sick and bright yellow poo and fearful shrieking in the early hours of the morning; a woman untouched by fits of wicked temper and resentment, bouts of baby blues and mild alcohol dependence. She had looked like the woman who had swept up the stairs towards him that first day, with her firm step under the regal silk of her sari, and the confident exposure of inches of smooth brown skin at the waist. A woman who had not only come from a more perfect world, but around whom this more perfect world had formed. He finds that he has walked right up to the bridge, looking out over the same view as in his photograph, standing where Samira once stood, but then stiffens as he hears the clicking of high heels behind him. He doesn't panic, as it might not be Samira; Knightsbridge is full of high-heeled women, after all. But when the clicking stops and he turns around, he sees Samira looking at him, an amused expression on her face. He wonders if she remembers the photograph, if she is looking at him standing on the bridge, an ageing man in blue cashmere, a man without a wife or children, without anything but the misting of green water behind him, and sees him as what he is, an imperfect speck drifting in an imperfect world.

'Well,' says Samira. She says it slowly, with the beginning of a broad smile. 'Well, well. Mr Karam.' If she is surprised to see him, it barely shows; only the sound of her careful breathing as she looks him up and down indicates some attempt to master herself. When she speaks again, her tone is assured and teasing. 'I won't say hello, as we never got around to saying goodbye.' Her smile is infectious, and he returns it, and steps towards her. She stretches out her manicured hand, and for a moment, an awful moment, he thinks that she is going to reach for his own hand and shake it politely, as one might with a casual acquaintance or colleague. Instead, she touches his face, just lightly with her fingertips. His suddenly aged, lined face, with pores on the nose, and heavy hooded lids. He shuts his eyes, and feels her cool palm against his cheek. With her touch, the cool dryness of her hand resting on his skin, he has a rushing, molten feeling that flushes through his body, through his damp flesh and knotted joints and connective tissues; a feeling more extraordinary than relief or hope. More than happiness, even. He feels like he has been touched by Midas, and turned to living, liquid gold.

Later, he watches Samira as she rolls out of bed, and pulls on an exquisite satin shift, something between day- and nightwear, too flimsy to wear out, but too detailed for bed; she then shrugs on a heavy silk dressing gown, letting the sleeves slide down her arms and making a casual knot at the waist. After she had the twins, Samira had complained that her body from boobs to knees was wrecked and that she'd never wear a bikini, a sari blouse or a tennis skirt ever again; she had pointed out her heavy, too-low breasts, the wrinkled stomach, the stretch marks and fat deposits and veins on her thighs. In fact, with the sort of rubber-band resilience normally reserved for teenagers, her flesh snapped back into place after the pregnancy, and within six months the only hints that she had had children were an over-bearing softness to her flat stomach, which gave when pressed like meat that has been tenderised, and the silvery, rapidly fading stretch marks and Caesarean scar, which caught the light and still gave her lean body a solemn sort of expression in repose, like a soldier with long-healed battle wounds, who refuses to speak of the war. She is wearing her hair longer than before, a slightly messy cut that frames her face like a young actress, and tumbles towards her shoulders. There is something gloriously irresponsible and vaguely dissolute about her, like the publicly acknowledged mistress of a powerful man, a prince or politician, or else a wealthy woman who has openly taken lovers young enough to be her children. 'What?' she asks, turning towards him; she still seems fairly amused by the turn of events.

'It's unfair,' he complains. 'I mean, just look at you! I've aged exponentially, and you haven't at all. You've got younger, if anything. People would think you're my daughter, not my wife.'

'Flatterer,' says Samira, glancing at herself over her shoulder in the mirror that hangs on the wall, and smoothing the dressing gown over her hips. She stretches out her arms with a contented, cat-like gesture, the wide sleeves falling back to her shoulders, and then turns to study herself properly. She seems pleased by what she sees. 'You're right. Living without you seems to have agreed with me. Think of the wrinkles I'd have had with all the stress.'

'I've got wrinkles, and I haven't had any stress,' he argues. 'It's genetic. That's what so unfair. You've got good genes. And I've got lousy ones. I've got the genes of a fat-assed, wrinkly, pock-nosed Punjabi. I'm turning into every ugly uncle I ever had.'

'My God, all this time and you're still going on about your ass,' says Samira. She tosses a striped flannel bathrobe over to him, and going to the dressing table, begins to brush her hair. 'You know,' she says conversationally, 'I know how vain you are, and I had planned exactly what to say when I saw you again. *If* I saw you again. Assuming you weren't in some box on the way to a crematorium oven. I rehearsed it even. I was going to say, with a rueful expression, "Maqil, my God, you've got fat. And old." I thought it would be fun, my little bit of revenge after all these years. I thought of watching you deflate like a punctured balloon.'

'Well, why didn't you?' he asks crossly, and he gets out of bed himself, a little stiffly. He considers dressing, but his clothes are on the floor, and his back hurts too much to stoop; to put it bluntly, he isn't used to the exercise he's just had; making love has put a physical stress on some little-used muscles and joints, and he'd prefer not to demonstrate his stiffness, his weakness to

Samira. She has always had a caricaturist's talent for pouncing on flaws. So he pulls on the bathrobe instead; he notices that it is from Marks & Spencer. He wonders when Samira started buying bathrobes from respectable, middle-class shops, instead of stealing them from wildly expensive hotels. He supposes everyone has to grow up sometime, unlike himself, who is growing old instead.

'Well, it didn't seem so funny, once I saw you. Besides, you're not fat, you're thinner than ever, so that wouldn't have worked. And I couldn't call you old, because you have got old, after all. It would be like saying "Hey, Limpy" to a cripple. Insults don't work if they're true. It would just have been cruel.' She says this casually, still brushing her hair, and doesn't notice that he really does deflate; he would have preferred her to lie with something romantic, to say that for her, he hadn't changed a bit. But Samira was never the type of woman to go in for that gooey sort of nonsense. Rather insensitively, she carries on: 'I mean, there was a kid at one of the charity events we organise who told another kid, a massive south London lad he was competing with, that his mother was a prostitute. "Your mum's a junkie whore" was how he put it. Trash talk, is what they call it, I think, a colourful exchange of insults designed to unnerve an opponent; it's all a bit American, they must get it from the TV. Anyway, the big kid didn't trash-talk back, like he was meant to, didn't call the other one a butt-munching faggot, didn't even punch him. Instead he just burst into tears and had to be looked after by the nurse all afternoon. Turns out his mother *had* been a junkie, and arrested for soliciting; he and his sister had to be taken into care and adopted by their uncle. So like I said, not funny if it's true.'

'Now that's a touching story,' he says. 'I get it, I'm old. You're hot and I'm not. You're Beauty, I'm the Beast. You win and I lose. So what was this?' He gestures towards the bed, the rumpled linen in tasteful shades of off-white and ivory, the sheets and covers whipped and rumpled like a meringue mess with cream. 'Was it just . . . pity?' He can't bring himself to say 'pity sex'; the term feels too flimsy and modern to describe the ancient, inglorious thing they have done. Bodies, tongues, heated skin, weight supporting elbows digging into the sheets, the silver sliver of a stretch mark, a thin and wrinkled ass. And the act itself, the brutally practical mechanics of it, the sucking and sliding organs, first dry and then damp, no different in the essentials than that performed by animals, than that of the creatures that hauled themselves out of the primordial ooze, here in these elegant, edible cream sheets. That he and Samira, evolved intelligences illuminated by emotion, should be brought to this. The pity of it, after all.

'Oh Maqil,' she says with sympathy, suddenly meeting his eyes. 'Maybe it was. You know I've always been fond of you.' He feels dismayed by her concern, the same dismay he had felt when he thought she was going to shake his hand politely in the park. He would rather, like his children years before, be yelled at and noticed than kindly dismissed. She maintains her poised, gentle expression for a moment, but then suddenly breaks character and bursts out laughing, her compassionate mask evaporating as she cackles helplessly. 'God, I'm good! I was right, that *was* fun!'

He catches up with her, and starts to laugh himself, putting his arms around her and dropping a kiss on her shoulder. 'You bitch,' he says affectionately.

'Oh, I couldn't help myself. I had to say something to get my own back. I forgot to do it in the park – I was just too pleased to see you,' she says, finally calming down. She looks at him critically in the bathrobe. 'Well, at least it fits. Although it would be quite hard for a bathrobe not to fit. Julian's a bit taller than you.'

'Who's Julian?' he asks, rather stupidly, as it is already obvious. Julian is a man who keeps his Marks & Spencer bathrobe in Samira's wardrobe. 'Your boyfriend?' Samira raises a mocking eyebrow at the childish word. 'Your partner?' he suggests instead. She shakes her head, smiling. 'Your husband,' he says finally, not bothering to conceal his disappointment.

'Ex-husband. My Number Two.' She grins, and adds, 'My silver medal.'

'I didn't know you'd remarried,' he says, wondering why he is so surprised. The truth is that since he'd left Samira, he had been entirely uninterested in other women, and an absurdly romantic, albeit vain part of him had hoped that she had been the same: a fairy-tale princess, waiting faithfully in her tower for her prince to return. Which was ridiculous, given how impatient she had always been.

'I remarried twice,' says Samira. 'You know how quickly I get bored.' He doesn't say anything to this, and so she brightly suggests, 'Coffee?'

'Please,' he replies. They are both getting up from the dressing table when a young woman comes rushing into the bedroom, still in her outside jacket, an oversized garment in brown cord, with a delicate diamanté 'M' pinned on the lapel. He recognises his old jacket and the pin before he recognises the girl, who has unstyled hair of indeterminate length, neither long nor short, and glasses with sensible black frames; he had bought himself the pin (that is to say, Samira had chosen it and he had paid for it) in Vienna. He wonders whether the coat and pin had been given to her by her mother, or whether she herself had dug them out of his mothball-scented wardrobe.

'Mummy, I need you to—' She stops and takes in the scene. 'Oh, I'm so sorry, I should have called. I'll come back later.'

'No need, darling,' says Samira mildly. 'I'm putting on some coffee if you want it.' She gets up and straightens her dressing gown again, before wafting out of the bedroom, leaving Mika standing there awkwardly with the elderly stranger in the bathrobe.

'Hello, I'm Mika, Samira's daughter,' says Mika, determined to make the best out of an embarrassing situation and salvage it with good manners.

'I know,' he says, standing up, unsure how to greet her. He forces himself to resist the cowardly urge to say 'Pleased to meet you,' or some other appropriate formula, to shake her hand like a stranger and hope she won't notice who he is. His unexpected response causes Mika to look at him curiously, and then she says, 'Oh my God. Daddy? Daddy!' She claps her hand over her mouth, and then suddenly composes herself and falls back into politeness for refuge. 'How nice to see you. I hope you had a pleasant . . .' she looks at the room, takes in the rumpled bed, and finishes weakly, '. . . journey. Are you staying long?' And then, not waiting for the reply to any of these questions, she says, 'If you'll excuse me, I think I'll help my mother with the coffee. Do make yourself comfortable.' And she all but runs out of the room.

Well, it seems that people don't really change. It would be more surprising if they did. Mika still has her knack for diplomacy and a reputation for propriety; she smiles insincerely so frequently, nodding enthusiastically at a tutor's dull exposition or a fellow student's shaky hypothesis, that at the age of eighteen, she already has laugh lines etched on her face, a pair of brackets around her mouth giving her a permanently pleasant expression that is a little too matronly, a little too old for her. Her boyfriend, Gregory, a long-haired, long-legged biochemist at college, listens indulgently when she complains about the lines, which she will one day learn to tone down with make-up but never disguise altogether. 'You shouldn't smile so much,' he says fondly; he thinks she smiles simply because she is a sweet-natured person, and sees nothing duplicitous or sinister in her habit. When he says this, she throws him a look he can't quite read, an opaque, clouded expression, before her face settles into its habitually agreeable resting position. Gregory appreciates her commitment to courtesy, her smiling politeness, her mother-friendly manners; he's from Glasgow, from an outspoken, critical family, and he himself describes his father as a 'dour Scot', as though his dourness and Scottishness were somehow inextricably linked. He likes the fact that he is able to say this, as if anyone else did, it would be considered inappropriate and even a little racist, in the way that only Mika might get away with labelling her wealthy compatriots at Imperial College, the ones who walk around campus branded with shiny labels from head to toe, from Gucci shades to Prada heels, as 'Paki Princesses', although she wouldn't, of course, as she is far too nice to name-call; he thinks that she is the nicest girl he knows.

This illusion is something that Mika has deliberately cultivated; she knew she would never be pretty or cool enough to join the catty crowd of the most popular girls at school, and so she opted for being nice instead. It was a smart decision, and it helped her become popular herself, getting her through the humiliation of braces at school (sometimes she looks in the mirror and still sees her teenage face with goofy teeth leering back at her, even though her teeth have been straight for two years now), and the indignity of glasses at college. Even without her glasses, she despairs of her looks – the hair that won't lie straight, her boyish straight-up-and-down figure – and so she tries very hard to make it seem that appearances aren't important to her. She dresses blandly, avoiding make-up and accessories and anything that smacks of effort; this casual insouciance, the air of not-caring, gives her a certain status, at least among the bookish, geekier crowd. Whereas the flippy-haired girls with mascara and hot pants are derided and only distantly, guiltily admired; those girls sit in covens at the college bar, in an impenetrable circle, approached only by the sportier boys when they are drunk and brave enough, and don't get asked out as much as they think they ought. Mika is asked out rather more, by perfectly pleasant boys who aren't the most attractive, who like Mika just as she is, and would be uncomfortable if she made herself better looking. Gregory, whom she has dated for almost six months, can see the latent prettiness in Mika that a little grooming would coax out (he has met her mother, after all), and panics slightly if she displays it in public. In the library, the other day, the central heating had been on too high, and she had pulled off her jumper, and her glasses with it, leaving her looking exposed and vulnerable for a moment, especially as she yawned and rubbed her eyes. The narrowness of her torso rising from her baggy jeans, the soft undersides of her arms exposed as she raised them behind her head, in her brother's old Malcolm X T-shirt bearing the legend *By any means necessary* underlined by a gun (did she ever buy her own clothes?), the bluish shadows under the damply bright eyes; all of this was suddenly, disturbingly appealing, and Gregory was transfixed for a moment, and then worried as he saw a shifting around the library table as other people noticed her too. It seemed a transformation as obvious as a stern secretary shaking the pins out of her hair, whipping off her glasses and pouting to burlesque music. 'What?' asked Mika, as she replaced her glasses and pulled her jumper across her shoulders, tying the sleeves at her neck with an ungainly, bulky knot. 'Nothing,' he replied, grinning with relief that she was already back to being her; the others at the table seemed relieved too, and settled back to their books, the ripples of guilty interest caused by her exposed arms, her exposed eyes, calming to still water. Her mother is frustrated by Mika's refusal to engage with fashion, and comments frequently that she is wasting her youth (and her more than acceptable figure) dressing in a uniform of jeans and jumpers in the winter, leggings and shirts in the summer, and tattered trainers all year round. Mika's entire wardrobe would fit in a suitcase or a drawer, and she only has one pair of jeans. Samira is uncertain whether she has ever washed them; what would she do, after all, in winter, when she has nothing else to wear? Samira jokes cattily to Mika that she should wash them one leg at a time, like the women in Kerala who lived in the slums by the river, and would wash their single sari by wrapping half around them, and scrubbing the other half, and leaving it out on the flat rocks to dry.

The truth is that Mika does care about appearance, but intimidated by her mother's grasp of fashion, by her magazine pedigree, doesn't want to compete, and so withdraws altogether. She tells herself that she would rather be respected than pretty, and liked rather than admired, although part of her already knows that in the real world, it is both possible and desirable to be all of these, and that one does not preclude the others. The truth is that Mika's ubiquitous niceness disguises a harder edge, like that of a politician kissing babies on the campaign trail, that her friends only glimpse from time to time (those unreadable looks, quickly dismissed, that shift so quickly they wonder if they imagined them), but her family, that is to say her brother and mother, are fully aware of her true nature. They would not be surprised to know (although she has not yet told them) of the time she was coming back from school on the bus when she was twelve years old – riding the number 74 alone as Zamir had stayed back for football practice – and a fattish, oldish man in a raincoat, a trilby, with a brown leather briefcase sat beside her. The man placed his briefcase on his lap, and she was aware of his hand moving underneath it, adjusting his trousers perhaps, or looking for something in his pocket. Then, some minutes later, she was aware of a feather-light touch on the tops of her thighs, so light that she thought she might be imagining it. She looked down, but the large man took up a lot of the space of the double seat, and his briefcase was partly covering her legs too. She was almost sure that her skirt was shifting, and her skin was being touched; she glanced at the man, who was looking in the opposite direction, but his breathing was getting heavy and his face was becoming red. A more timid child than Mika would have borne it, and sat silently cringing next to a masturbating stranger who may or may not have been touching her; a less composed child than Mika might have panicked and screamed. Mika made no accusation, but instead said in a bright voice that rang through the bus, in the direction of the man's left ear and his fat red jowl, 'Excuse me, sir. Would you mind moving up a bit, please, you're crowding me.' Every eye on the bus snapped towards the man, who got up immediately and wordlessly, with just a strained grunt of acknowledgement or discomfort, and stood until the next stop, at which point he hurried off, his briefcase still held firmly in front of his raincoat. 'Thank you,' Mika trilled after him, certain now that his behaviour implied guilt, and feeling justified in twisting the knife a little, and she beamed beatifically at the conductor, who beamed back at this preternaturally gracious little girl who said 'Excuse me' and 'Sir' and 'Please' and 'Thank you' without being prompted. Mika liked the fact that the people on the bus didn't know that she was more than just a gracious little girl; she was a little girl who didn't put up with disgusting adults who behaved badly. She liked knowing more than they did – she was more of her father's daughter than she realised.

Mika is even less inclined to put up with adult bad behaviour at eighteen than she was at twelve; she goes into the kitchen after her mother, who is spooning coffee into the percolator filter and humming tunelessly. Her mother smiles vaguely in her direction but avoids catching her eye, and doesn't seem about to offer any excuse or information about why Mika's father has suddenly turned up in her bedroom. 'Do you need a hand with the coffee?' Mika asks.

'No thanks, sweetie, it's all done,' says her mother, flicking the switch. The whooshing sound of the percolator starts immediately, and hot amber drips begin pooling at the bottom of the glass jug. 'But if you like, you could put out the coffee cups, and milk and sugar.'

'Does Daddy take milk and sugar?' Mika asks, carefully keeping her face neutral as she says this, as she introduces the explosive word Daddy into the air between them. She half expects her mother to deny it's him altogether; it hadn't escaped her that her father hadn't replied to her when she called him by name, as though he would have denied who he was too.

'What a question,' says her mother mildly, as though the answer should be obvious.

'How long is he staying?' persists Mika, still with a neutral, disinterested voice. She realises that she has implied he might be staying at the flat, which she doesn't want to acknowledge; it seems absolutely wrong that someone could just walk back in where they left off eight years ago. Like having your cake and eating it too. 'Staying in London, I mean,' she corrects herself quickly.

'I really don't know, sweetheart,' replies her mother, busying herself with inspecting the coffee, lifting the lid and letting the steam escape. She says the 'sweetheart' with a rather hard tone, as though Mika has just crossed the line into being annoying. 'It's not as though we've talked.'

Mika puts out the coffee cups, pointedly using the good ones from Geneviève Lethu that her mother keeps for company, rather than the cracked oversized ones in stripes and spots that are used for family. She pours the milk into the matching jug, and spoons brown sugar into the matching bowl. She even goes to the biscuit tin and puts a selection out on a quarter-plate. 'Pretty,' comments her mother on the arrangement of the cups and the biscuits, possibly wishing once again that Mika would transfer some of this care into her own appearance. Mika resembles her mother a great deal, and it pains Samira to see her girlhood looks so deliberately mismanaged; it seems closer to sabotage than neglect. As though Mika has gone through a photo album of memories with a marker pen, making Samira's hair bushy rather than thick, drawing over her fluid clothes with comically boxy replacements, a square for a T-shirt, two rectangles for jeans, and replacing her eyes with circles for spectacles. It would take so little, thinks Samira, looking critically at the top of Mika's head as she fusses with the arrangement like an old lady: just a decent haircut, jeans that actually fitted, a top made for a girl rather than a boy (why did she insist on wearing Zamir's old T-shirts, especially that grubby-looking Malcolm X one; was she being *political*, in some way?). It would just take glasses that framed her eyes instead of making fun of them, or better still, no glasses at all. Mika is only slightly short sighted, she doesn't really need to wear glasses all the time, mainly for lectures or driving. Some-times Samira is vain enough to wonder if she wears them expressly to annoy her, a belated attempt at teenage rebellion that her daughter had never indulged in, with her straight As and perfect school attendance. And as for make-up, well, Samira doesn't think that young girls *have* to wear make-up – youth is the one time a woman can get away without wearing make-up and not look either washed out or like a washerwoman, but for the evenings, or occasions, a little bit of lip gloss wouldn't be so hard, would it? It took all of four seconds to put on, and how many times had she told Mika that a slick of beige lipstick made someone look instantly groomed. She had bought her several, expensive ones with gold dust from Yves Saint Laurent, cheap ones from Boots that she thought Mika might be more likely to use. Why wouldn't a young girl want to have soft and appealing lips, instead of a fine line of a mouth so similar to her skin colour as to be barely visible? She is briefly so annoyed at Mika's appearance that she wishes she hadn't shown up; it feels that she is letting the side down. She is annoyed that Maqil will see that she has let their daughter grow into a middle-aged, well-behaved frump, well before her time.

Mika, meanwhile, has finished fussing with the biscuits and gone to the bathroom, and has decided to avoid messy confrontation altogether. She won't ask her mother the obvious questions – why is Daddy here, and have you just been shagging him? Using the tact and gift for self-preservation that will later help her to dizzy heights in her future career, she decides to delegate. She'll get someone else to deal with the mess, someone else to do the wet work; she calls Zamir, who is at a weekend training session with his work colleagues, and leaves a baffling message with the receptionist. 'Could you tell him that he has to come home right now – it's an emergency. Tell him our father is at home, having coffee with our mother. And that they're wearing dressing gowns.'

Mika's parents might be wearing dressing gowns and drinking coffee, but they do not refer to their inappropriate situation, and are instead talking about perfectly normal things. Mika's father asks her about college, and seems surprised that she has chosen to go to one in London, minutes away from the family home. 'Mathematics at Imperial,' he murmurs, and she can see that he is wondering how to work this into a story, a story that somehow involves a bigger, braver and more impressive daughter than the one he has.

'Imperial College is one of the best in the country for sciences,' says Mika defensively. 'Everyone knows that. It has a better reputation than Oxford, even. For sciences, it's Impbridge, not Oxbridge.'

'You didn't think of trying for Cambridge?' her father asks, not meaning to sound critical, but Samira takes it as criticism anyway.

'She didn't get in,' interrupts Samira. 'God knows why, she had four As at A level. And an S-level distinction.' She looks a little too hard at Mika; it is clearly a touchy subject between them. Samira still thinks that if Mika had dressed better, she would have done better at the interview.

'And right round the corner from home?' he says, adding mischievously, 'Well, it must be a great comfort to your mother to have you so near.'

'It's where I wanted to go,' shrugs Mika. 'I didn't want to have to schlep all the way to Bristol or Durham or Edinburgh. I *like* being near home.' She smiles pleasantly as she says this, as though she's not trying to sound critical either, but her mother recognises the dig, and smiles.

'And you can have all your little friends around for tea,' says Maqil unthinkingly, realising that he has just spoken as though Mika is eight rather than eighteen. He has given away that he still thinks of her as the girl he left behind, who had play dates and tea parties and Barbie pyjamas. The girl he walked with in the park, who pointed out the daffodils and ate cake with her brother while he read the paper; he doesn't mention this – it is still too soon for this sort of nostalgia. Fortunately, Mika takes his comment as a joke.

'Mummy says that my friends are too big and hairy and smelly to mess up her nice living room,' she says.

'That's right,' says her mother blithely. 'That's exactly what I say.'

'Big and Hairy and Smelly?' asks her father. 'What, are your friends Yetis? Gorillas?'

'I wish,' Samira replies for her. 'They're Science Geeks. Mumblers and Shufflers. All of them dripping with teenage awkwardness. Her boyfriend is the worst.'

'Maybe we should go to the club tonight,' says her father, generously adding, 'You can bring your boyfriend.' It turns out that the thought of his daughter with a boyfriend is so bizarre that he can't bring himself to be disapproving.

'I don't think he could come,' says Mika. 'The club still has a dress code, doesn't it? He doesn't have anything he could wear. I mean, he doesn't even own a tie.'

'Doesn't own a tie?' sputters her father. 'What sort of bullshit bastard doesn't own a tie?' He surprises himself with his own prejudice; he surprises himself by how much he suddenly sounds like his elderly uncle, the sort of traditional father who would bicker over the pots and pans he is expected to include in his daughter's dowry, as he mutters, 'A Cambridge man would have owned a tie.'

'What are you doing?' asks her mother, as Mika checks her watch surreptitiously for the tenth time.

'Nothing,' says Mika. 'I just remembered that Zamir said he might pop back a bit earlier than usual.'

'Ah, Zamir,' says her father. In the flurry of coffee and small talk and avoiding anything worth avoiding, he had briefly forgotten that he had a son, just as he did when the child was born. 'What's he up to?'

'He was at the LSE,' says Mika. Her father sighs: the London School of Economics, yet another local college. What had he done to his children, for them to have so little sense of adventure? He had crossed continents when he was sixteen, and they at eighteen are sticking stubbornly within shouting distance of their mother's skirts, as though still in need of cuddles and nose-wiping and bo-bo fixing. He had thought that once they were grown, he and Samira would be free of them. If he is honest with himself, he was waiting for them to be grown before he came back to see Samira, and yet here she is, and here they are, sitting at the table or on their way over. He realises, looking at Samira looking at him, to see how he is taking the news of their children's unadventurous forays in higher education, that she will never be free of them. That she will never stop being a mother, never try to shrug off parenthood as easily as he did.

'But he dropped out,' Mika adds. 'He didn't see the point of finishing the degree.' Her father nods encouragingly to hear more; at least dropping out promises something more interesting than staying in. He remembers that his son looks like him, and wonders whether he has become a chip off the old block after all, the mini-me to carry on his drifting, unfettered legacy. He thinks suddenly of all the lives that Zamir might possibly have – he could be a teenage rock star, on the road with his band. One of those edgy performance poets, braving ridicule and shouting over the drunken conversations and boorish laughter at difficult venues, or speaking from the spotlight into a hushed, dark room as solemn as a church. He could be backpacking around gritty jungle hell-holes, or building hospitals in the African desert. He could even be back in the Punjab, staying in his father's old house, appalling his grandmother with his pious liberalism as he volunteers for an NGO and administers polio drops to grubby-faced grinning children in the villages. 'He's gone straight into a bank training scheme instead.'

'A bank?' repeats her father in disbelief. His son is a banker; worse, his son wants to be a banker. His disappointment is so palpable that Samira starts to laugh.

'Yes, a bank,' she confirms. 'The Midland Bank, that big one up on Poultry in the City.' She adds, 'And he still lives at home. Mika has her own place now, for termtime at least. She lives in the Imperial halls up in Prince's Gardens—'

'I live in a *box*,' interrupts Mika. 'A twelve-by-twelve-foot cell, between two other cells, above one and below another. There's barely room for the bed. I'd rather be at home . . .'

'So I've got rid of her, but I can't get rid of Zamir,' continues Samira, ignoring Mika cheerfully. 'I tried charging him rent. I tried raising the rent to higher than market rates. He just won't go. I think he's trying to take *care* of me.' She says this lightly enough, as though she is joking, but there is an edge to her voice, followed by a dismissive shrug. He wonders if this little transition is what happens to all relationships, between parents and children, husbands and wives: indulgent tenderness, followed by impatient exasperation, eventually followed by flat contempt. He wonders if this is how she would have felt about him, if he'd stuck around long enough; he wonders if this is what was happening to his parents before his father died. (His father, attacked by his own modest heart in middle age – so quiet, so ineffectual, so easy to love and dismiss – how could an extraordinary woman like his mother, a woman who stood in the shadows and bolstered him up, speaking on his behalf like a ventriloquist with a dummy, how could such a woman not eventually begin to despise him?)

Mika pours them more coffee; but something in the way she doesn't ask them first smacks of authority rather than deference. She gives her mother a warning look, as though she has been caught speaking out of turn, and begins to rearrange the plate of biscuits and fold the serviettes. It reminds him of Carine fussing with her papers in the art gallery café; he suddenly sees his daughter as the courteous, middle-aged housewife she will one day become, married to either this college boyfriend or the next, with teenage children of her own. In fact, for a moment, an illusion shifts into place, establishes itself with quiet confidence, that she is this competent mother already, catching their eyes, tacitly warning them to mind their manners. And right on cue, another responsible grown-up arrives, in a blustering fury of old-fashioned fatherhood and righteous pronouncements.

'You!' storms Zamir, bowling in from the hall, dressed in a dark suit, wearing a tie with some repeating pattern of beer-filled pint glasses and footballs. 'You!' he yells, his uncharacteristic rage rendering his face briefly unrecognisable to those who know him. 'What the hell are you doing here?' he manages to choke out, saliva sputtering from his lips with the forced conviction of someone who knows they have to hold on to their fury at all costs, or else they will give way to tears. 'What are you doing here with my mother?' Zamir's still adolescent beard has been shaved inexpertly, and there is a scratch on his chin in which the white dust of dried toilet tissue lingers. He would look like his father, albeit taller, were it not for the contorted expression. Watching him with fascination, Maqil thinks of a pale, gentle beast in a field, that has been nipped and bitten to madness by a cloud of buzzing insects; he thinks of an elastic band stretched tight to the point of fraying, humming with stored energy, ready to twang back into place or else snap apart with a whip crack. He is trying to remember when he last felt as gloriously angry as that, an anger that frees movement and justifies the petulant punching of soft furnishings and the breaking of crockery – he's not sure he ever has; he's just not made for emotion in this way. He is always, wholly, untouched. Other people's anguish and tears slip off him like river water off his sleek feathers, like dew off the daisies in the park. He can blank out Zamir's incoherent accusations to flat white noise, mute him like a TV screen, and just see his mouth opening and closing, guppy-like; the effect is almost comical. Maqil has the impression, as he reaches for Samira's hand under the table, feels the warmth of her calf against his, that they are not sitting with their children after all (although Zamir is not sitting, but is grasping the back of the chair, his knuckles white and proud, as though he would like to pick it up and smash it to pieces on the floor, or on his father's head), but have become the rebellious children themselves; as though his daughter and son have put themselves in fancy dress, in costume, just so they can play the parental parts in this family pantomime. Mother-Mika's glasses sit on her nose like a prop, the bland dryness of her lips is too deliberate, and Father-Zamir in his suit, his Adam's apple bobbing angrily above his collar, his neck thin and exposed by the short City haircut, is like a caricature of himself, a cartoonist's impression of a banker. He imagines a director calling Cut, and telling Zamir, 'You're trying too hard, too much volume, too much with the hands. Let's try it again, and this time don't just tell us how you feel, show us.'

In a way, he finds it extraordinarily touching that their children have chosen to take over these roles from them, to play at being the traditional, proper parents that they might always have wanted for themselves, Zamir blustering like a Punjabi patriarch about the return of the unsuitable boy who has breached Samira's honour, Mika sitting with her hands folded at the table, as though her Malcolm X T-shirt was saying *Keep calm and carry on* instead of *By any means necessary*, with quiet dignity behind the shield of her spectacles, waiting for the storm to pass so she can offer appropriate comfort (a handkerchief, a hug) and clear the table. There is an illogical sense of completing a Donneian circle on a map, one leg of the compass firm, the other rotating around; he finds he ends where he once began. In its way, the moment is perfect; like the circle, it is complete. He feels briefly, as the blizzard of upset tips about him, that he is young again, a young lover, his lover's hand in his.

* * *

The next day, Samira visits him at the Rembrandt. 'The reason Zamir's so angry is because he cares,' she says. 'He missed you when you went; it would have been easier for him if he could have just forgotten you, or hated you, but he couldn't. He can't. It's going to get him in all sorts of trouble, his propensity to care. Mika was OK; she's more like you, she doesn't let things touch her.'

'You make it sound like I'm dead inside,' he says. Samira gives him a sharp look, and he realises that with everything she has just said about Zamir, he had only really listened to what she had said about him. His selfishness no longer seems quite so impressive. He wonders what kind of monster he is, to be really so indifferent to his children.

'Not dead,' she says. 'Just dying.' She manages a small smile. 'Well, we all are, aren't we?'

'Suppose we all have dinner at the club,' he suggests again, with the vague idea of making amends. 'A family thing.' Dinner seems a bit banal, but he has no idea what else they could do; Mika and Zamir are too old for trips to the Zoo, too young for the Opera (which bored him and Samira to tears; they had only ever gone for the interval snacks, and spent the rest of the time surreptitiously doing crossword puzzles), and he supposes it would be inappropriate to take them to the races. Besides, it would be nice for the kids to see him in his element; he had gone to the club last night for dinner after his unceremonious exit from the flat, and been welcomed like a returning hero; he'd shared a cigar with a famous Pakistani cricketer, who had invited him to his home in Islamabad, and champagne with a famous Jewish tycoon, who was on suspiciously good terms with his Spanish associates, and even asked after them with a wink.

'Mika would come, but Zamir wouldn't,' Samira says. 'But organise it, by all means, before you go.'

'Before I go?' he repeats, asking a question. She nods in reply, her bright eyes becoming even brighter; she is careful not to blink too quickly, as though she wants to avoid tears falling, and she smiles at him with surprising tenderness. He doesn't say it, but he thinks it again and again, Oh Samira. Come live with me and be my love. Come sing with me in the wilderness. It would be useless to say anything out loud, as she has already decided not to elope with him again, just as firmly as she decided not to have his children, all those years ago; she is probably right, she almost always is. He had both ruined and redeemed her with motherhood, whereas he hadn't even been touched; perhaps he really was dead inside; dead people didn't bruise, or scar, or bleed. He could cope with her tenderness, with her exasperation even; but he doubts he could cope with her eventual contempt, to be dismissed as he has dismissed so many others. He feels a pang of remorse for Carine all over again.

'The thing is, Zamir will come round. I know that he's sitting at home right now doubting the sincerity of his anger; we both know that he yelled at you and kicked you out because he was afraid that otherwise he'd sob and throw himself into your arms. He wants to come round. He wants to have a father in his life, he wants to have a father to love, who'll love him back. That what I'm worried about. That Zamir will come round, sooner than you think, but you won't. You'll be embarrassed by his affection, and head off again when you get bored, because that's who you are, and I'll be left picking up the pieces, clearing up the mess. And I've done that once before.' She adds, smiling again, almost mischievously, 'I guess once was enough for me.' Her tone makes him think that she's not just talking about Zamir, or even their afternoon fling together the day before. She's talking about their whole marriage. He's the sort of man of whom a wife will say, 'Once was enough.'

'It wasn't altogether my fault that I left, you know,' he

230

says eventually, although even as he says it, he knows that this is a lie.

'I never said it was,' agrees Samira pleasantly, so pleasantly that he knows that she knows it is a lie as well. Her diplomacy is admirable; yet again she has shown him that the quickest way to end a conversation is simply to concur.

'So, what is this? Goodbye?' he asks a little petulantly.

'Of course not,' says Samira, picking up her handbag and going to kiss him on the lips, her mouth warm but the gesture and movement somewhat curt. 'We'll have that dinner, with Mika and her boyfriend. You can grill him about his intentions, play at being an old-fashioned paterfamilias – we can have some fun with him. I'll lend him one of your old jackets and ties, if there are any left. Mika keeps stealing your stuff.' At the door, she turns around and looks at him. 'And you know that with you, I'd never say goodbye. Although I will say this . . . good luck.' She grins and adds, 'I even mean it.'

When she is gone, he sits in his hotel room alone. His lavishly furnished room. Approximately eight minutes' walk away, up Exhibition Road and to the right, Mika has her twelve-foot-square cell, between two others, with identical rooms above and below. And not much further in the other direction is the flat that he once called home, which his son had righteously thrown him out of, flinging his clothes after him from the fourth-floor balcony, like a wronged mistress. There was something wonderful about the drama that fury had unleashed in the boy, this otherwise passionless boy who works in a bank from Monday to Friday, from nine to five, and lives at home with his mother. Perhaps there are hidden depths there after all; perhaps Zamir had only become a banker in order to avoid becoming his father. But the life Maqil has chosen for himself suddenly seems just as unadventurous and small, a slipping-away, sliding-around life, a touching-no-one life that has occurred in a series of rented rooms. He wonders whether in making and losing money, moving around, marrying, breeding, surviving, he has somehow, unfailingly, missed the point of it all. It feels possible that a more wonderful life, a luminous life has been happening somewhere else, somewhere near but just out of reach, like a party he is anxious to join, a magical place where he is neither alone or unowned; as though charging through all of these neutral rooms, leading down the long corridors of his life, rooms below and above, left and right, he might finally find the one he's been seeking, and stumble through the door with his name on it, painted in gold like a star's dressing room, where the party has been waiting for him. Like a child pushing aside fur coats in a wardrobe and tumbling into Narnia.

He looks at his reflection critically, his ageing face, his tired-looking lids; he is becoming less and less fond of the man in the mirror. He avoids catching his eye, he suddenly has no desire to hear his advice. He imagines smashing the mirror into pieces, as he once smashed a coffee cup on his terrace in Cairo, but like Samira, he can no longer be bothered with cleaning up the mess. He walks to the window, and heaves it up, too late to be able to see Samira clicking away in her heels. He looks instead at the museum opposite, the young prince and the elderly queen who was left behind, the dark elegance of the soot-stained stone, blackened by years of London's grime. His room with a view, on to the achievements of greater men than he. It's too early for nostalgia, he tells himself, again. It's too early for regrets. I'm dying, but I'm not dead yet. He remembers something that Samira had told him in the past, while he sat nonchalantly in a prison, coveting her cigarettes, and he reaches out for this memory, for the smoky softness of her breath as she spoke, for the words like streamers on a fan, fluttering gaily and brightly on the breeze towards him. He reaches out for comfort, for the bird-in-flight moment of joy her words had held, for the belief that she had spoken the truth, as she was almost always right. Her casual judgement on the life he had chosen. She had said, 'It must be great to be you.'

Hong Kong – 1997 – Medicine

HE'S BEEN LIVING IN HONG KONG, BUT UNLIKE MOST OF the well-heeled expats, the usual Filth (Failed in London, Try Hong Kong) with whom he occasionally associates, he never made a decision to move there. He simply began drifting east, and eventually out of Europe altogether. He passed through Pakistan, passed through his home town even – he turned up at his mother's front door as casually as a neighbour popping over for pooris – but conspicuously failed to stop there. It would have been too much like ending the game with an unlucky card – Go Home to Pakistan, Go Directly to Pakistan, Do Not Pass Go, Do Not Collect £200. He left the Lahore household just as abruptly, somewhere between breakfast and mid-morning tea – and kept on drifting. When he got to Hong Kong, he thought he'd take a chance – it was typically bloody minded of him; the British were leaving, so it seemed more interesting to stay. A new name, and a new country – a blank canvas in a city where he couldn't speak the language, and where there would be no doubt that he was a foreigner, but just another foreigner of indeterminate origin, jostling for position in the crowd. Perhaps he hoped that this would be the beginning of the luminous other life that he had been seeking, waiting behind an unopened door, and that he was beginning to think he had strolled by altogether.

He admires the modernity of the Hong Kong architecture; he has always embraced change, perhaps rather too freely, and he likes seeing the skyline shift daily, the cranes swinging over and picking at the landscape like insects. A thoroughly modern man, he is quick to exploit the commercial potential of the internet; not as a new way to communicate – as he is unashamedly poor at keeping in touch with his ex-wives and children, family and friends – but as a new way to play. It is what he does best. He makes a great deal of money establishing a site that conceals an illegal online gambling ring – like printing money without the effort of actually having to produce it in hard copies; it just ticks electronically into an account in one of his names, just numbers on a statement accumulating extra zeros – and he is now making a great deal more money by selling the concern to Mr Wu and his familial associates, during a dinner at Felix in Kowloon. He is rather good at doing business with the crusty Chinese businessmen in Hong Kong, elderly patriarchs like Mr Wu who call him 'young man' despite his advanced age, as they are still old enough to be his father. He likes their endless ceremonies of drinking and gambling and cigars, the superstitious avoidance of the number 4, the uproar when a spouse or daughter is caught in public wearing an apparently inauspicious colour on a day of commercial importance (he will charmingly smooth away familial dishonour, insisting that the gown must have been a different colour altogether, that the camera recording the offending outfit had somehow distorted it). His business at Felix has been concluded successfully, and as Mr Wu orders more imported whisky at astonishingly high prices, our modern man in Hong Kong excuses himself to go to the gents'.

The broad window overlooking the lights of Hong Kong in the gents' loo is astonishingly elevated too, and as he relieves himself, gazing out into the night of diamond dust, across the fairy glimmering of the city, he feels something shift in a subtle way, as though he has finally managed to fall in step with himself, instead of dropping behind or hurrying ahead. He guesses that this is what satisfaction feels like, and he is always satisfied when he manages to offload some piece of baggage, especially a tricksy and illegal business, with competitors threatening to close him down, 'by any means necessary' and with a loaded gun, as Mika's T-shirt had once prophesied. And if he is honest with himself, now that he has lost most of his interest in food, and he was never that interested in sex or sport, peeing is the closest to heaven he can come these days. The flushing relief as the fluid streams from his straining bladder, a golden ammonia-scented rain as he enjoys the architecture. The morning piss is the best one, and he can hardly wait to get out of bed to have it. Although now, as he is shaking the final drops, he feels a burning sensation. This used to be the sort of thing he would ignore, with the casual lack of interest in his health that contributed to his third heart attack, but he has been forced to change his ways since his last stay in hospital; he is now on constant medication for his blood pressure. His mother is on constant medication as well, back in Pakistan; she is a diabetic: a lifetime of sweetness, of managing household affairs and people of influence with sticky syrup and lighter-than-air pastry delights has finally caught up with her. On his brief visit, he saw the depressing ceremony of her treatment, the pointed instruments on a sterile tray, rendered banal by the everyday consistency of it, the pricked thumb dripping blood to test the glucose, the preparation of the insulin jab. When he looked at her, he thought that she could as easily have been his older sister, with just the seventeen years that separated them; and she treated him less like a son, and more like a long-lost love, with the curious intensity that his absence has brought to their relationship; she forgot to maintain maternal distance and dignity, to establish her authority, and instead confided her regrets, her weaknesses. She showed him the patch of irritable eczema on her inside arm, which she hid from the rest of the family with sari blouses cut long to the elbow. He sympathised, and showed her his own light rash of eczema, on his chest and throat and the backs of his hands, pulling across his shirt as she slid up her sleeve, like warriors removing their armour after the battle, realising that their scars could finally be displayed, and stories told of past glory around a camp fire. He has more scars than he realised. His eczema barely used to bother him – he hadn't even realised it was eczema before, and had been rather proud of his slightly dry skin, his hands soft and womanish rather than greasy and oafish like most men – but now the rash is deeper in his skin, and makes him scratch blood into his sheets at night, exacerbated by the city-state smog. He washes his hands, noticing how the backs are even redder than usual and a little scaly across the knuckles, and goes back to the table.

He returns to the city on the Star Ferry, with a few others in evening dress like himself, and some drunk-looking tourists in flip-flops and tie-dyed trousers, and gets a cab back to the apartment. The pool in the complex should be closed for the night, but there is still someone swimming, and from the little puffs of effort he realises who it is, and goes and sits on a sunlounger at the end of the pool, waiting for his wife to finish the length. She harrumphs to the end like a graceless hippo, splashing too much, and then squeaks with sputtered surprise when she sees him. She pulls off her goggles instantly, with the endearing hasty vanity with which a woman would whip off her glasses or let down her hair when running into an old boyfriend at the supermarket. 'Jay-sus, Mikey, you scared the living daylights out of me,' she says. He grins; she normally sounds rather proper, but her Dublin accent emerges when she is surprised or irritated. It makes him think of her as a girl in a bonnet, scurrying down narrow cobbled streets with field-fresh flowers in her arms, for all that she is a woman approaching middle age, with dimpled white flesh straining against a sensible black swimming costume.

'Swimming after midnight – you're breaking the building code,' he says with mock severity. 'They could chuck us out of here. How did you get past the night security guard?'

'I didn't – I just flashed him some boob,' she says cheerfully, passing a hand to him. He starts to help her out, wondering for a brief moment if their intended action will have the opposite effect, and whether she will haul him into the pool instead with her weight advantage. He smiles to think of it, of himself sputtering and wallowing in the shallow end in his suit, and her flapping around him with concern, and suddenly feels affectionate and protective towards his prettily plump, too-white wife. He picks up a towel, and wraps it around her, giving her a hug through the flannel. 'Thanks,' she says, going to pat her hair, and realising that she still has her unflattering swimming cap on. She yanks it off with a painful snap, pulling her eyebrows up with surprise, and then starts working through the damp auburn mess of her hair with her fingers, pulling out the sodden band that had tied it up, and rubbing briskly with the towel. He waits, watching her movements, assured and practical, rather than graceful; the Irish freckles on her nose and broad shoulders, on her otherwise very pale skin, which is shining with luminous blue in the light of the pool. She notices that he is looking at her, and is worried that she is keeping him waiting; she stands up abruptly, and pushes her feet into her flat flip-flops, 'Come on,' she says warmly. 'Let's go up.'

In the lift to the fourteenth floor (populated by foreigners like themselves, who don't care about the inauspicious number 4), she pulls at her hair thoughtfully. 'I keep thinking I should cut it. Then I think that short hair on a fat chick isn't a good look for me. I'm not sure it's a good look for anybody.' She sighs. 'I'm fat, frumpy and in my forties. I never thought it would happen.'

'It's OK to be fat in Hong Kong,' he comments. 'Everybody else is so skinny. Being fat is a sign of prosperity.'

She looks at him a bit crossly. 'I wasn't asking for you to agree with me.'

He thinks for a moment, and says, 'Well, I'll disagree then. You're not fat, you're not frumpy, and you might be past forty, but you've still got a cleavage that stops the downtown traffic.'

'Still offensive, but better,' she says, leaning against him slightly. The lift arrives, and he walks ahead of her to open up the apartment. 'I went swimming because I couldn't sleep. I was worried about you, with those thugs over at Helix. I thought you'd get sent back beaten up in a cab if you didn't agree to their terms.'

He frowns, as she has an annoying habit of renaming places with what she thinks they should be called, rather than what they are. She knows that he was at Felix, but she mistakenly called it Helix the first time they went there, and persists with it. Just as she calls the Zinc Bar (where the bar is round and wooden, and not made of zinc) the Rink Bar, and Mr Sen's Hairdressing, Massage and Beauty Emporium, a busy and bustling place full of scurrying therapists and shouted orders in harsh Cantonese, ironically Mr Zen's. He reacts to her error as one would with a child who is learning to speak; he repeats it back to her correctly, but doesn't make a fuss that might show he finds it irritating, or make her self-conscious. 'It was fine at

Felix,' he says, pausing after Felix, emphasising the 'F' as though he was breathing on a candle flame, making it flicker. 'You know I'm a coward, I hate to get beaten up, especially over something as stupid and replaceable as money. And I'm a great negotiator; I always make sure the other person gets a good deal, so they think they owe me. Favours in this town are worth a hell of a lot more than haggling over the last ten per cent.'

Bernadette smiles with relief, showing her small white teeth, little pearls against the natural pinkness of her lips; she had once cut her lip with his razor (embarrassedly admitting that she had seen a stray hair on the corner of her mouth and had tried to shave it off, as she couldn't find her tweezers to pluck it), and rivers of blood had spurted out, and didn't stop for thirty minutes. It was as though all the blood under her skin congregated at just these pouting, sensitive areas on her body, these pink sugar peaks, her lips, her nipples, her labia. 'So it went well?' she asks, already knowing the answer. She looks at him with adoring fascination, as though she were some student ingénue with a crush on her lecturer; she seems to think that he is the most interesting man in the world, and is amazed at her good luck in having caught him, at having been plucked from the crowd to stand by his side. She makes him feel as though, in some complicated and illogical way, he is famous; that he is some world-renowned star, and she his number-one fan.

'Of course it did,' he replies, pulling off his tie, and unbuttoning his shirt. 'Coming to bed?'

'Of course I am,' she replies flirtatiously. They have only been married a short time, and she still seems to expect romance, something that he finds it hard to provide. He supposes that it is the disadvantage of being married to a much younger woman, although otherwise he feels little guilt or sense of the age difference being inappropriate; she is over twenty years younger than him, so it is true that she is young enough to be his daughter

240

(say if he and Susie Santini, back in New York college days, had tied the knot), but it is also true that she is still old enough to be the mother of his actual daughter, and so he would have no qualms introducing them, although he supposes the necessity and opportunity will never arise. It is probably a good thing, as he suspects that Samira, Mika and even Zamir would be mercilessly kind and sympathetic to Bernadette, the type of derisive sympathy one gives to the disadvantaged, firstly because she is stuck with him, and secondly because she is, in truth, a little fat and frumpy. She wages a constant, comedic battle against the fourteen pounds she has gained since turning forty (perhaps these numbers are inauspicious for a reason . . .) and never manages to pick out clothes that flatter her figure; she looks best in her work uniform. Their friends say she has such a pretty face, such pretty eyes and hair, and leave the rest of the sentence obviously unfinished – such a pretty-pity about the rest. He doesn't mind these flaws on her part; in fact, he is relieved that she isn't slim or fashionable, as he would hate to be that cliché, an ageing man with a beautiful young wife, with people whispering behind his back that he must have money. He even tries to be supportive of Bernadette's various diets, but privately maintains, in weight as much as in business, that the last ten per cent is hardly worth fighting over.

Bernadette sees his expression, although he is careful not to look dismayed, not to let his face fall, not to let on his weariness that she might expect more from him this evening than a good night's sleep. With the shrewd observation and instinctive kindness of a career care-giver, she smiles more gently, and gives an unconvincing yawn. 'Of course I am,' she repeats in a different tone. 'I'm beat after all that swimming. I'm all in.'

He gets into their bed, so wide as to be square, and settles on the arrangement of firm pillows that Bernadette plumps into place every morning. A few moments later, she pads into the room on her bare feet, wearing a cotton nightdress printed with clouds, and snuggles next to him. He had always valued thinness in the past, a lean hunger to his lovers, but now that he is almost-old (he may as well admit it, finally), he finds he can appreciate the comfort of her heavy breasts against him, the abundance of her flesh, as though having starved himself of flesh for so long, he can no longer get enough; he values the quantity of her, of having more wife in his bed; he feels as cosy as a child in the circle of her arms. Perhaps it is precisely because his mother no longer plays her mother's role that he suddenly welcomes the attentions of a woman like Bernadette. She is a midwife by profession, but had treated him in hospital; the maternity ward tended to be less busy than the rest of the hospital, and on quiet night shifts she often helped out her colleagues on the main ward. She had brought his pain medication in the early hours, and checked his drip, and taped back the needles that slid into his veins; and he had enjoyed being looked after by her; so much so that he brought her home with him. There is a frisson of letting go, of falling away, as she kisses him chastely on his dry cheek, and smooths his hair back from his forehead. Bernadette never had any children; her first marriage, which had taken her briefly back to the Ireland of her early childhood, had been short lived and unsuccessful. She has a vast capacity to care, to mother, that she had first exercised with her dying father, then in her chosen profession, and now is exercising with him. She likes being a wife again; she loves being a younger wife to an older man, and feels girlish and desirable because of this. She fiddles with her hair in his presence, she holds herself straight and pulls in her stomach; she cares how she appears to him. He thinks that she might even love him; he realises that he doesn't deserve this, that he barely deserves to be liked, let alone loved. He worries that with age he will become less likeable altogether, a belligerent old man who will rely on his wife to smooth things over for him, to apologise tacitly for his behaviour. An old man who bores people with his symptoms; he remembers the burning pee, and sighs, deliberately enough for her to notice it.

'Are you all right?' she asks with concern. He almost smiles, remembering how that sort of question used to irritate the hell out of him, how his younger self had bitten off poor Carine's head for daring to express concern. And now he is courting it greedily, like a vain girlfriend at a dinner party patting her hair to draw attention to it, inviting a compliment on her new cut.

'It's embarrassing,' he says with mock humility, and then explains, 'It's started to burn when I pee. I noticed it in Felix.'

'Oh poor darling,' says Bernadette. He can see in the shadows how relieved she seems; she has taken this as an apology for his rejection of her this evening, as an explanation that he would if he could, but that right now he simply isn't capable. 'It might be a urinary tract infection. Annoying, but no big deal. I'll make an appointment with Dr Gao for tomorrow.'

'Thank you, sweetheart,' he says gratefully. He is suddenly unsure if the gratitude is genuine, or whether he is play-acting for effect, performing to his audience of one. Like a spoilt American teenager who can no longer tell whether or not he is being sarcastic when complimenting his mother on her baking skills or efforts with the PTA and Little League. What is genuine is this, the slight dampness of her skin, the warmth of her body against the sheets, her own gratitude to him. He thinks, disloyally for a moment, of that poem about a large white woman, wearing gloves, wandering through a field. There seems a solitary dignity in the image, that of an ocean liner in stark white and royal blue, parting water in the silent distance; or else a snow-pawed wolf stalking a mountain terrain. More dignity than being rejected by a wizened old gnome like himself. He feels the need to be kind to her, and wearing this charitable notion lightly, like a mask or an assumed identity, something shrug-offable, he presses his face against the softness of her neck, and whispers, because he knows how much she likes it, 'Good night, Mrs Lee.'

'Good night, Mr Lee,' she replies, appreciating his need, his kindness.

In Hong Kong, the name he goes by is Mikhail Lee. A new name for a new life. But he can't help abbreviating it to Mike out of habit.

There is a day in every life when you realise that you're closer to the end than the beginning – when you finally notice that you've gone over the hill, and that the road up has become the road down. So I can tell you now, with the dreary precision of hindsight, that the next day was to be the beginning of his decline, physical and then moral. One following the other, like dominos toppling. As his body begins to give up, in small ways, he finds he doubts the likelihood of anything beyond the grave, and feels like calling out to a crowd, like a croupier in a casino, 'Place your bets,' as he sets the wheel spinning, seeing what will come up when the game is finally played. Black or Red, Shadow or Light, Death or Life. You take a chance, as you really have no other choice. And if there is only darkness, on the other side of the grave, beyond the looking glass, what does it matter anyway? If anything he was or is, anything he does or did, will simply be extinguished like a flame; his luminous self turned to ash, his misdeeds washed away like writing in the sand. It turns out that this monumental day begins in a deceptively ordinary way, with a medical appointment made by his wife. He goes to Dr Gao, who has an expensive practice near the Peak, and an expatriate client list of ruddy-faced long-termers and pallid newcomers. She has a British nurse to help with all these foreigners, who maintains a cheerful efficiency as she bustles about. She weighs him and takes his blood pressure and temperature before his appointment. Dr Gao is brisk and efficient; it seems likely that it is just a urinary tract infection after all, but she takes a sample to be on the safe side; she sends him out with a prescription for fifteen days' worth of antibiotics, and paracetamol for a fever he has started to develop. She points to the rash on his hands, the dryness of his cheeks, and recommends he returns for another appointment to discuss his eczema.

The fever is meant to abate within a few hours, and the burning pee in a few days; even so, Bernadette calls him from the private hospital where she works, and tells him she thinks he ought to stay in bed. Her gentle bossiness when it comes to his health ought to irritate him, but doesn't; Growth, he thinks, perhaps he is finally Growing Up. But of course he doesn't stay in bed; he takes up an invitation for a dim-sum lunch near the harbour with Richie, one of the less savoury pieces of Filth, who complains about how difficult it is to travel and get business done, when all the authorities know who he is and where he's been; he whines that the US Embassy have refused his visa for the third time. Maqil chews on his bok choy; he ordered it specifically so that he could tell Bernadette that he ate vegetables at lunch; he enjoys meriting her approval, basks in it like a baby being praised for its bowel movements, and spends much of his day performing for her imaginary applause and hushed admiration. He assumes that his companion is just making conversation, and nods sympathetically, wondering why Richie, who is really Richard, has never changed his name. The poor man is already disadvantaged by his greasy appearance, the thick texture of his hair and skin, scarred with join-the-dot pockmarks, like old-fashioned smallpox on an ancient farm labourer back in the Punjab. He knows for a fact that Richie dislikes his first name being shortened so winsomely, but he has let it happen, encouraged it even, as the name Richard Richards is too much of a burden to carry, too much like a practical joke; and the alternative nickname of Dick or Dickie is even harder to carry off with dignity. There should be a club for people saddled with thoughtless names such as these, for the Richie Richards, Bob Roberts, Gerry Geralds to console one another. As Richie drones on, he thinks of more exotic equivalents: Abdul Abdullah, Momo Mohamed, Jak Jakubek, Soren Sorenson. His mind starts ticking over with examples of funnier names that he might weave into conversation, not today at lunch with Richie, but at the races or the golf with cronies less likely to take personal offence. Who's that woman fluttering by the window? Annette Kertan. Who's that woman who just fell out of the window? Eileen Dover. Who's that man with the shovel digging her grave? That's Doug Nicely. Who's the gravedigger who forgot his shovel? That's Douglas Nicely. He suppresses a puff of laughter at his own silly wit, and finds that Richie is looking at him, and not seeming that amused. 'It's easy for you to laugh,' says Richie. 'You've beaten the system. You know, I looked you up when we first met, and couldn't find you. You're off the grid, not domiciled anywhere, no taxes paid, no embassy is owning you. You're like a ghost. You may as well not have existed until three years ago.' Maqil shrugs and smiles, as though he's just been paid a compliment; he has kept up his usual policy of not telling people where he's from, simply by never volunteering the information; he has a politician's gift for swerving around a direct question. His old age has made his ethnicity even more ambiguous; most people in Hong Kong assume from his name that he is of Russian-Chinese parentage, and guess from his accent that he was brought up and educated in the West. Richie does not seem satisfied by his slight gesture, and leans over to him. 'Seriously, how do you do it?'

'I've not done anything,' replies Maqil lightly, trying not to show that he is taken aback by Richie's casual assumption that he is some kind of career criminal. It has honestly never occurred to him before that perhaps he might be; he had always thought of himself as maverick, free spirited, delightfully quixotic. Nothing as bland as a fugitive, on the run from the law. In fact, the law has never been that interested in him, his UK tax skirmish notwithstanding, and that was simply because he had made the mistake of spending too long in the same country and legally raising a family there. He does not think that he has ever done anything significantly illicit: he has never imported or exported those profitable poppy powders and chemical pastes, or distributed them to dealers and addicts and socialites; he has never sold big guns to bad boys. He had frequently grifted from and occasionally bankrupted his associates, but he did not think of them as victims, as they were intelligent, healthy and well-connected businessmen like himself, and like himself were just as capable of rebuilding their wealth; and sometimes his reckless decisions had paid off, and he had made them money instead. The main victims of his Spanish counterfeiting operation had been the local casinos and betting concerns; otherwise he was sure that the cash injection had boosted the local economy. If he thinks about it, he is a latter-day Robin Hood, with all the cash he has taken from the rich and spread around for the littler people: florists, cab drivers and extravagant tips for people who worked in restaurants. He is no criminal, he is practically a philanthropist. 'I've nothing particular to hide. I just get bored easily, that's all. I move around.'

Richie seems unconvinced. 'There's money in it, you know,' he says. 'In cleaning up people's pasts. Or creating new ones. For other people who get . . . bored easily, and want to move around.' He looks straight at him. 'I know I'd pay for it.'

'Oh for God's sake, Richie,' says Maqil impatiently. 'If you want me to sort something out for you, just say so.'

'I'm not saying anything of the sort,' replies Richie with irritating coyness; he winks at Maqil, and then stops a waitress wheeling past a trolley of fresh duck dumplings. He tries to flirt with the woman, who is wearing a crisp white shirt, fitted to her flat chest and narrow waist, and a black tie; a smattering of acne makes her seem both very young and slightly streetwise. She barely responds to his banter, stone faced to the point of insolence, and barks out something in Chinese to another passing waitress, before giving him a mocking look along with a basket of dumplings, and departing. 'She's a spunky one,' says Richie, apparently attracted by her obvious disdain.

'You're older than her father,' says Maqil, trying one of the dumplings. It isn't bad, but he decides not to have another. In fact, he doesn't even finish the one he has taken; the fever has affected his appetite. Once more he imagines Bernadette's approval, that he had put aside the fatty duck.

'A bit hypocritical coming from you, you dirty old sod, with the bit of stuff you've got at home,' comments Richie. 'I bet naughty Nurse Bernadette comes home in her uniform and puts you right in your place.'

'She's a midwife, not a nurse,' says Maqil flatly. He is neither flattered nor offended, but simply bored of Richie's company, the adolescent humour, and decides to leave. 'But I meant it when I said you're older than her father. Her dad's Jimmy Lee. No relation to me, I'm afraid. He runs this place. He runs lots of places. So it would probably be wise not to drool over his little girl, or you might get your past cleaned up quicker than you expected. Your present and future, too. Without a fee.' He gets up to go, throwing down more than enough dollars to cover the meal and the tip, even though Richie was the one who had invited him, and adds almost kindly, 'You know, Richie, a word of advice. Most women hate being called spunky. Or feisty. Or sassy, even. It's pejorative. Which means it's a little bit insulting.'

He allows himself to indulge in being a little bit insulting himself, explaining the word, but his paternal air is disarming, and Richie doesn't take offence, and holds out his hand. He shakes Richie's proffered hand vigorously, taking it in both of his, and holding it a bit too long and tenderly, making a point of skin contact, his dry palms enclosing Richie's greasy paws altogether. He stops the handshake just at the point when it seems inappropriate, when it seems as though they are simply holding hands. 'So long, old chap,' he says, finally turning to leave. 'But just another word of advice,' he adds, turning back again with perfect comic timing. 'Take napkins when you go to the gents'. They're out of paper. I had to use my hands.' He laughs as though he's made a joke, holds up his palms with a rueful shrug of surrender, and Richie laughs too, uncomfortably. At the door, he turns back and sees Richie looking at his own hands, turning them over front and back, and then dabbing a napkin in his whisky and water to wipe them over, like an inexpert husband trying to clean streaks off a wine glass.

He doesn't bother with the medication for the fever that he barely felt, and it comes back, worse than before, enough for him and more significantly for his wife to notice once she gets home. This time he does stay in bed, as Bernadette wants to fuss over him. He lies there and sleeps on and off, with cold shivers, complaining when Bernadette boosts the aircon and replaces their duvet with a light sheet. 'I'm freezing,' he mutters rebelliously.

'You're on fire,' responds Bernadette flatly, suddenly more medical professional than wife. 'You're almost forty degrees. It's this or a cold bath. You decide.' He likes it when she speaks to him in this practical way, with prim and starched efficiency. It is how she had dealt with him in the hospital, her very pink and unmade-up lips held in a firm line, a telltale trace of concern around her eyes, in the crease of her otherwise smooth forehead.

She had worn her hair pulled back and neatly twisted into a bun at the base of her neck, but when she came off her shift, she made an excuse to come back to his ward in her day clothes, her hair loose over her shoulders, a too-bright lipstick applied that made her mouth appear like a wound, and her normally translucent redhead's skin wan and sore looking by comparison; dressed up for his benefit if not to her advantage, she had stopped by his room to say goodbye. That's how he realised that she had noticed him, too.

He is pleased that Bernadette doesn't wear too much make-up, generally. She never wears it at home or at work or for casual outings to the 7–11 grocery shop on the corner, or the fruit market down the steps towards the town, or even for lunches of noodles and fish-ball soup in the open kitchen diners that spill into the street, sitting on folding chairs at Formica tables, with salt cellars plugged with damp rice. She just wears it for what she calls 'Going Out': a designated trip to a proper hotel or restaurant, where there might be a sniffy maître d' and a choice of cutlery. The truth is that she doesn't know how to put make-up on, and her attempts make him think of a child playing dress-up, painting on a wide clown mouth and surprised circles around the eyes. She doesn't seem to know that the purpose of make-up is to conceal imperfections, to define and improve without really being seen itself, the way that a disciplined pinch of salt is meant to bring out the flavour of food, and not be a flavour itself (except in England, where his children were encouraged by clever marketing to eat 'Salt and Vinegar'-flavoured crisps, which he found curiously addictive, like anchovies and olives). Bernadette cooks with almost no salt at all, because of his blood pressure, but lacks discipline when it comes to self-decoration; she piles green shadow on her lids until her lids look green themselves, as though the colouring was the whole point. She would spot her error if she ever looked at a fashion magazine, but she is not one of those women who reads magazines, and he quite admires this. She is, however, a woman who reads romantic fiction, from Jane Austen to Mills and Boon, and he admires this rather less. Especially the ones in the Doctor-Nurse romance category. He harrumphs with disdain, thinking about the covers of these cheap paperbacks, saccharine blondes in perky hats peering up through their eyelashes at the chiselled jaw in the white coat. Bernadette hears him grunt, and comes through. 'Aren't you comfortable?' she asks, and begins re-plumping the pillows behind him.

'Oh for God's sake,' he says. 'I'm really not that ill. I can walk, and talk, and pee. I think I'm just pretending to be ill to indulge you.' He tries to sit up, but he suddenly feels dizzy, and briefly disoriented with the abrupt movement, and his eyes do feel hot in his head, or possibly it is his eyelids that are feeling hot over his eyes.

Bernadette laughs, a little charming yelp, oddly musical in its way. 'Yes, you're the one that's indulging me. That's exactly what's going on here.' She puts an arm around him, and helps him sit up comfortably, rearranging the pillows yet again, and passes him the TV remote. 'I'll get you something to eat. I don't think you've eaten all day.'

'I'm not hungry,' he says, flipping through to the news channels. Recently, he has found all the news to be depressing, to be personally depressing, as though world events have conspired against him. He really is that vain, he supposes, to think that it's all about him. He has watched the Hong Kong handover to China reported on the international networks. Islamic fundamentalists bus-bombing tourists in Cairo. Rioting from Dumcree to Belfast, after the Orangemen parade. An Indian woman winning the Booker with the great Indian novel, reminding him of the great Pakistani novel that he could have written during his ABC Club days, a story of witty young men educated abroad, and corruption and cleansing revolution, if only he could have been bothered with the typing. He has watched the chaotic election of a well-connected man in Pakistan, beating both Mrs Bhutto (her husband nicknamed Mr Ten Per Cent by the hostile press, claiming that was his cut on any state project) and that famously handsome cricketer he'd had drinks with in London. The sort of thing that made Punjabi landowners, fifty years after bitterly won independence, claim to be nostalgic for the British. He has watched the landslide victory in the UK for Blair's Labour Party. Princess Diana on holiday on a yacht with a shopkeeper's son, and tabloid wits commenting cruelly on the size of her ass, a bag of spanners in a bikini, as though a once-presentable divorcée, a single parent of two, didn't have the right to date someone unremarkable who'd take care of her, didn't have the right to breathe out in swimwear, didn't have the right to age at all. (It is a mark of his astonishing egotism that he takes such personal exception to this. Does he really think that he is on a par with the most photographed person on the planet?) Everything falling apart without him in all the corners of the world he has frequented, or worse, everything just carrying on. With him. Without him. As though the two were interchangeable.

'Of course you're not hungry, you've got a fever. But you still need to eat and keep fluids up. I'll get you some chicken noodle broth. It's Mum's special recipe; it did my dad no end of good,' says Bernadette. She has the disconcerting habit of describing her stepmother, her father's second wife whom he met in Hong Kong, as her mum, as though she was the one who gave birth to her, as opposed to the unfortunate Irish lady who was carried away by breast cancer in her early thirties, whom Bernadette refers to as 'Mammy', like a little girl, on the rare occasions she mentions her; or more accurately 'Poor Mammy', with the shaking head and tolerant expression reserved for the terminally ill. Her clearest memories of her real mother are of a bald and bad-tempered woman, suffering on medication, and finally dosed to calmness on morphine; she has an album of photos of a laughing, plumply pretty redhead spooning apple sauce into a baby girl, pushing a pink-clad toddler on a swing, building sandcastles with the same puffy-faced infant on a gritty Dublin beach, and she wouldn't know this woman or this child at all if they both didn't so closely resemble herself. Whereas Betsy Kwok Finnegan, her father's No. 2, is the one who drove her to school from the age of twelve, and picked her up again; the one who warned her against tampons and boys and rock music; the one whom she rebelled against, argued with viciously ('Ungrateful girl! I have raised a viper in my bosom,' Betsy once shouted back with endearing illogic) and had tearful, laughing rapprochements with, to the bewilderment of her mild-mannered father. It confuses people at social events when Bernadette introduces Betsy as her mum; they are increasingly used to Westerners adopting winsome little girls from China as their daughters, not bossy old harridans as their mothers. Betsy made a half-hearted attempt to be Catholic and adopt Western habits for the duration of her marriage to a Westerner, but after her husband's death reverted instantly to the old ways; Bernadette was in her twenties by then, training to be a midwife but still living at home, and with a foreigner's sensitivity made no comment when decorative shrines and scented incense appeared in her father's house. Even now, she fails to be embarrassed by Betsy's ubiquitous comments regarding good and bad luck, and the superstitions that she states as fact, as Betsy is family. Her only family, in fact. When Betsy's cousin died, Bernadette even cooked a dish of scallops with ginger for Betsy to place beside the corpse, and purchased exquisitely made paper replica bottles of champagne and brandy, adding to the fancy feast provided by other relatives to help him into the next world. An apparently rather dressy next world that the elderly gentleman would be entering with mirror-shined shoes, the smooth soles without a single telltale scuff to show they had ever touched the ground.

Maqil had gone to the funeral with his wife and mother-in-law, and had been discomfited by the realisation that he had reached his sixties and never seen a dead body before. His own father had been buried weeks before he had arrived home; Muslim burials were traditionally rather quick. And the few funerals he had attended in England had involved a firmly closed casket. Working at the hospital, Bernadette saw dead bodies all the time, and was surprised by his squeamishness. He thinks he would have been all right if the body had been covered soberly to the face, in a hushed room, perhaps with the odd gothic candle for atmosphere. But there was something almost more ghoulish about the celebratory nature of this funeral, the glistening food next to the body like a misplaced family picnic, the heady scent of flowers and burning incense, the posters hung from the walls wishing the deceased a joyous next life, blazing with bold characters for Fortune and Happiness and Prosperity. And that nicely dressed old man napping calmly in his casket at the centre of all this commotion, like an overtired babysitter. In fact, Maqil had been to more restrained children's parties. Every time he looked at the body, there seemed to be more food on the table there, as though it was reproducing itself next to him, like bacteria. He had begun to feel dizzy with nausea, with the food fucking next to the corpse, and the posters shouting to outdo each other with their aggressively upbeat labels, like perfume bottles in a brash boutique display. He couldn't engage with death in this way, he couldn't be near it, and when the service began, with respectfully enthusiastic grief from the mourners, he made an excuse and left so hurriedly that it was verging on the rude, as abruptly as hanging up a phone. He heard his mother-in-law sniff loudly in disapproval. 'That man,' she said to her stepdaughter. 'That man has no respect.' And then she added, as though it was connected, as though it were in some way a personal insult to him rather than to her stepdaughter's cooking, 'And the scallops are overcooked. Too dry. Chewy looking.'

'This would be the father that's been dead for twenty years?' he calls out to the kitchen. 'How do you know that Betsy's soup didn't help him on his way?'

Bernadette ignores him. 'And in fact, Mum got the recipe from her mother, so it's really Grandma's soup. And it's mine as well, as I make a few adjustments for health. No salt or soy or MSG. Three generations have worked on this soup for you, you should appreciate the effort.' She begins clattering in the kitchen.

'Just open a damn can if you want to bring me soup; don't be such a bloody martyr,' he calls out again.

'No need,' she replies, wafting out of the kitchen with a porcelain bowl printed with dragons, and a matching soup spoon. 'I made it while you were sleeping. The trick is to use water you've cooked rice in. Adds extra starch. It's really easy to digest.'

'Baby food,' he mutters in disgust, looking at the cloudy soup and the dry rice cakes placed next to it. 'Just get me a Farley's rusk, why don't you?' But the tray is placed carefully on his lap, like a gift, and because she expects him to eat it, he decides he will. He finds it oddly pleasant to give in and be told what to do. Besides, he half expects that if he doesn't eat it himself, she might start to feed him, which would be a step too far into indulging both him and her. He lifts a cautious spoon to his lips, blows across the wide bowl, and tips a little into his mouth. It is light, fragrant with spring onions and chicken, and almost sweet-tasting. The soup equivalent of expensive green tea, the stuff that Bernadette buys for several hundred Hong

Kong dollars a pound to serve to company, and then uses and reuses in her white stone teapot for herself, adding hot water until the tea is practically clear, and the pure notes of scent are like a memory. 'It's good,' he admits.

'I know,' says Bernadette, but she seems pleased all the same.

He dozes off that night with CNN still droning on in the background. He is unsure what Bernadette is doing, although he can hear her bustling about in a housewifely manner, humming happily to herself. She seems delighted to have him at home, taking up the bed, requiring her attention, even though it is something of a busman's holiday for her. At some point in the early hours he wakes, covered in sweat, and feels much clearer and better. The magic soup, and the paracetamol served with it, has worked – the fever has broken. He falls back into a fitful sleep, until he is woken early the next morning by the urgent need to pee. He sighs with pleasure when he does so, sitting on the toilet like a child on the potty, rather than standing up. He imagines his bladder deflating like a wrinkled balloon. Dry and chewy scallops; he was sure it was some coded comment on his looks, or else his virility. He knows that Betsy dislikes him. She probably disliked Bernadette's first husband too; she is the sort of woman who expects her child, even a foreign stepchild, to be at her constant beck and call. She dislikes the fact that Bernadette is caring for him now, rather than caring for her; she probably resents most the fact that she has to call before she visits (something Bernadette, rather than he, has insisted upon, as though they might otherwise be caught frolicking naked in the living room like newly-weds), and that she can no longer rearrange the furniture and the cutlery drawer in her daughter's home. And what she dislikes most, what she complains about most frequently and vociferously, is the lack of respect. It is true that he speaks to her as a contemporary, but she is barely ten years his senior. She views all his attempts to charm her with suspicion. He stands in front of the mirror, and as he washes his hands he notices that the eczema rash that runs over the back of them has small pustules across the surface, like heat bumps but more prominent, as though they are filling with air. The bathroom is dimly lit, with no outdoor window, and so he leans forward and looks closely at his face. The eczema there is bumpy there too; it feels itchier than usual, and oddly plastic. It is as though his skin is simmering underneath, boiling up into bubble wrap. He leans forward, and experimentally squeezes one of the bumps near his ear; the skin pops with a surprising definition, clear fluid released rather than air. He washes his hands again, and calls for Bernadette.

'I think I've got chickenpox,' he says to her, indicating his face and hands. 'Can grown men get chickenpox, even if they've already had it?'

'It's not chickenpox,' says Bernadette, looking at him closely. 'The rash is appearing just in the places where you've had eczema. It must be some kind of secondary infection. I suppose being run-down would make you susceptible, but God knows where you caught it, you haven't been out anywhere.' She is already calling Dr Gao for another appointment. 'I don't like the look of it,' she tells the receptionist on the phone. 'It wasn't there last night, and now it's spreading like wildfire. We need to see her as soon as possible . . .'

He lets Bernadette disinfect his skin, cautiously, wearing gloves herself as a precaution; he is beginning to feel an almost electric tingling in his face and hands, an oddly pure feeling that is strongest when he presses his lips together, like a spark struck from a flint. He finds out at the doctor's that he has eczema herpeticum, a strain of the herpes virus that attacks skin with eczema, especially when the patient is unwell, as he has been. He is given a course of medication, and spends five days hiding his ravaged, bubbling face in the apartment, until scabs rise up through the thick, plastic skin, and spread over the clusters, before finally popping off like dark, shiny counters, leaving pocked scars behind. Bernadette tells him reassuringly that the scars aren't so bad, that they'll fade; she still has no idea how he got the virus, but said it could have come from anywhere, from casual contact with anyone who had it. He doesn't bother to tell her about the dim-sum lunch with Richie, about the joke he had played on him, holding his hands. He thinks of Richie dabbing his hands with whisky to disinfect them, and the irony that Richie was the one who infected him, rather than the other way around; that Richie has had the last laugh, although he won't give him the satisfaction of knowing this.

He has something of an epiphany during these five days, his self-imposed quarantine. (The doctor hasn't told him to stay in, but she has told him to stay away from pregnant women and children. He supposes he is probably infectious until the scabs fall off.) It is different from his last stay in hospital, when he had been seriously ill. He can cope with the thought of death, a quick and clean death: a heart attack, a guillotine, a bullet. What he finds difficult is the idea of living in constant, niggling, itching discomfort, living as an old man. How much of his life will be spent being old? Here he is, with these slightest of maladies, and yet he needs medication to hold him together, he is wrapped up in prescriptions like a mummy in linen bandages. He counts the meds off on his fingers: antibiotics so he can pee freely (Who's that man with the bladder problem? I. P. Freely), plain paracetamol to keep down the fever, antivirals for the herpes simplex clustering on his skin, antihistamines to stop him clawing away at the itching on his face and hands, the omnipresent blood-pressure medication, and the vitamin supplements that Bernadette insists he take to make up for his chaotic eating habits. What next? Insulin jabbed in like his mother's solemn daily ritual? Calcium for his breakable, bird-like bones? Other men who have enjoyed successful youths fight old age with virile tans from outdoor tennis and entertaining on their yachts, they have new children in their sixties with their second wives; but he has already become too old for the fight. His carefree life has caught up with him, and his long-neglected body, barely or badly fed, barely exercised, genetically disadvantaged with heart disease and diabetes, has turned around and bitten him on the butt. He is so much of an old man that he is practically an old woman; they may as well throw some HRT into his medication cocktail and be done with it. And what has he done with this life? What is his legacy, besides the two uninspiring children whom he never sees, whose joint birthday he fails to remember? His life has shrunk to this: a high-rise flat, a wife, and a disapproving mother-in-law. He has never done anything of note, never even tried to write the great Pakistani novel – he is hardly Pakistani himself, any more. He is hardly anything; his only great achievement, his only great work of art, has been himself. He had intended to create a new man for a new life, but has instead succeeding in effacing himself, and created a nowhere man in his place, with no baggage, no history. It is a sort of gift he has; it occurs to him that it is something achievable for anyone, if they are willing to pay the price.

When he is better, he looks himself in his ravaged face, and calls up Richie. For an immodest fee, he offers to give him a new identity, to erase his past, his status as Filth, to allow him to take on his new business opportunity in the States. He begins to offer other people new lives, new histories, new passports and paperwork. He is like God, without the judgement. He is unashamedly corrupt. He makes new friends, and avoids his enemies. It is oddly compelling, and something of a relief, giving in to crime like this, losing his grip on morality just as he has lost his grip on his own mortality; it feels like the logical consequence of having allowed Bernadette to take over his care, to give him Three Generations soup. Letting go of the ledge he has been hanging on to by his fingertips, and falling towards his end. Perhaps this is who he always was. Perhaps he always knew this, but was too embarrassed to admit it to anyone, even himself. A man of caricature rather than character. Say it out loud, say it proud: I am Cowardly, Despicable, Myself. The only small revenge he decides to take on Richie Richards, for unwittingly passing him his skin infection, is to make sure he has an equally stupid name on his new passport. To be honest, I can't remember what he picked out for him. This is one small detail from the story of his fall, from the road down, that escapes me. It wasn't a terribly important detail, after all. It could have been anything. I. P. Freely. Douglas Nicely. Holden Hands.

Hong Kong – 2002 – Identity

IT SEEMS THAT THE TROUBLE WITH A STARRY NEW LIFE, OR even a star-struck new wife, is that neither stays new for long. It seems to Maqil that the trouble with success is just as obvious: the higher he flies, the more likely he is to get his wingtips scorched, and the further he has to fall. Flying high, falling free. Icarus with his wings of wax. For a start, his profitable new business is doing rather too well – he is in danger of being noticed and exposed – and his selfless spouse is ageing before his eyes, her concern for his own well-being now irritating rather than engaging. He doesn't want to upset Bernadette, and so he grins and bears it, but the truth is that she has become something of a nag on the matters of his medication and family, areas she feels in which she should have jurisdiction.

Her latest affectionate nagging is about a trip to Pakistan – she thinks they should go together on a holiday. She points out that he travels all the time, but never takes her with him. He points out that the places he travels to, Afghanistan, the Middle East, are places that she doesn't seem that keen to travel to anyway. She points out that they never had a proper honeymoon, the long weekend in Macau notwithstanding. He replies that if she wants a honeymoon, he'd be happy to go somewhere traditional, Paris, or London, or somewhere fun and kitsch like Monte Carlo or Las Vegas. She retorts, shrewdly, that it would hardly be a honeymoon if he spent the whole time gambling in windowless casinos, and telling her to run on and see the sights herself. She points out, finally, that he is not getting any younger, and that his mother certainly isn't; she thinks he ought to visit before she dies. 'So we go and have some tearful valedictory moment. And if she doesn't die this year, then what?' he asks, rather meanly.

'Then you go back next year, and the year after that. You go back every year until either you or she is dead,' says Bernadette practically, without a trace of sentiment. She has a strong sense of family duty, having so little family of her own. 'An annual visit for your elderly mother. It's the least you can do. You know you mean the world to her.'

'Because I'm the one who got away,' he replies mutinously. 'You don't think she'd be that fond of me if I was constantly under her feet, taking up space in the house, do you?'

Bernadette throws him an exasperated look, and starts putting together some things for her stepmother into a carrier bag. Her movements are as fussy as those of his first wife in the art gallery all those years ago; just as Carine was then, Bernadette is now in her fifties. She wears her hair differently from when they first met; she had been persuaded to get it cut as short as Princess Di's had been, but it hadn't suited her, emphasising her round cheeks and the folds in the back of her neck that were particularly pronounced when she looked up. She had grown it back until it was just long enough to tie back

262

for work. Most of the glossy auburn shade now comes from a bottle, applied monthly at Mr Sen's; her eyebrows are finer than they used to be, as she plucks out the grey. Her cleavage is still impressive, but her stomach bulges, soft and doughy, over her waistband, and for 'Going Out' she now favours underwear that is big enough to contain it altogether, pushing her belly into a round, hard mound. It feels as though she is somehow catching up with him, faster than either of them thought she would; like a flower caught on time-lapse camera for a nature show, bursting into bloom with animated vigour, and then fading, flopping, dropping petals and shrivelling back to the ground. Instead of keeping him young, he has made her old, as though it was just another of his recurrent contagious infections. Sometimes it feels that she might be too old for him already. He has started to avoid her at night, moving right to the edge of the bed, turning deliberately on his side with an action that is daring for someone of his age, as he is balancing just on his hollow hip, his elbow, his shoulder, his heel. Those fragile bird bones that might crack and shatter like china if he fell off the edge of the bed and on to the smooth marble of the floor. Bernadette doesn't comment on his nightly distance, so perhaps she hasn't noticed. No, of course she must have noticed. Perhaps, then, she doesn't mind, or else hopes that it is just a phase that will pass, and will pass more quickly if attention isn't drawn to it. Like a patient being fussy with the hospital food, or a toddler playing up in a supermarket. He wonders why he tortures her in these subtle ways, plays these silly games; he suspects that if one night he decided to roll across the chasm of their bed to her side, and hold her in his arms, if he showed her the same voluptuous, unconditional affection she tried to show him, she would stop fading, and bloom once again, unfurling petals and springing back up towards the sun. 'The one who got away,' she repeats at the door, picking up the packed carrier bag and hoisting her handbag over her shoulder. 'Past tense. That's the point. You're not going to keep getting away with it for ever.'

Her observation seems curiously apt, and for a moment he thinks that she is going to teach him a lesson and walk out on these final words of warning. He would admire her if she did. Instead, she sighs; it is the sigh of a long-suffering spouse putting up with a cantankerous husband, one she must steer through the perplexing business of life, guiding him gently through endless and ordinary days of grocery-store purchases and bill payments and small social duties. Their life together is thoroughly unremarkable, untouched by drama or tragedy; she is no Cleopatra to his Caesar, no Eleanor to his Henri. She is Bernadette Finnegan Lee, conspicuously lacking in the lively aggression, in even the spunky-feisty-sassiness, that people like Richie claim to admire in romantic heroines, and she is trying not to show her impatience as she says to her much older husband, 'So, are you ready, then?' He starts inwardly, as he had forgotten briefly that he was meant to be going with her; Bernadette visits her stepmother every week, and asks that once a month he accompany her. A show of support for her, and of respect for his mother-in-law. Another small social duty; dull but perfectly painless, for him at least.

'Of course I am, I'm always ready,' he says good-naturedly. 'I was just waiting for you,' he adds infuriatingly. In fact, he is ready, as he is always dressed for the day, and he carries everything he needs in his jacket pocket, up to and including his passport for impromptu overseas trips. His small suitcase is always packed, as he gets calls at short notice for his services. He is able to help most people, those seeking entry to western Europe and the States, cleaning up past paperwork and setting up new passports. He likes the puzzling and research it involves; the delicate nature of forgery is less banal and more varied than in his counterfeiting days. He tells Bernadette that he is helping

264

old friends and clients discover distant family members, and gather missing papers for administrative purposes, which is not so far from the truth. The way he describes it to her, it sounds as if he is simply dusting off and filling in family trees, which seems an appropriate hobby and occupation for someone of his age, and it keeps him busy, which Bernadette approves of. Like most people, she thinks that old age is better spent being busy than bored. She frequently cites the example of her father's oldest friend, who died a few weeks after he retired, giving up his life for lack of occupation, due to too much time on his hands. The way she goes on about it, you'd think that time itself is something you could overdose on, and is best restricted, like salt, sugar and fat.

When she talks about this sort of thing, he is always careful to look as though he is listening with interest to her opinion, as he has always been fond of Bernadette even though he doesn't think that she is right. The truth is that people don't die of boredom, not really, they just fade away gracelessly and die of something else: heart attacks, strokes, cancer of the bowel, the bladder, the testes, the cervix; they die of flu or Aids, they break their knees falling downstairs or their hips in the shower, and pick up fatal secondary infections in the hospital. The prognosis of old age is terminal, the same for everyone, the destination predetermined, whether you are bored or not. He is in his seventies now, and is older than almost everyone he knows, his mother and his mother-in-law notwithstanding; his peers are dropping dead around him like flies, and Bernadette no longer expects him to go to funerals. She avoids them herself, and sends extravagant flowers instead. They never discuss death between them, the intricacies of provision or burial preferences, even though many others in the congested city have already reserved their highly exclusive plots and chosen their granite and even the font for their carved epitaphs; perhaps she thinks that it is something else that will pass, if she politely ignores it. He has told her once before that he thought he would be dead before he was old, like that song by the British rock band; he remembers once how the band performed at the Brit Awards when the kids were young, and how Mika and Zamir laughed and laughed at the forty-something men bravely singing their hymn to youth with an apparent lack of irony. 'The Who?' Mika had joked. 'More like The Whoever! They're singing about being young, and they're practically dead already.' Maqil had been recovering from his heart operation, watching TV in the sitting room with them, taking up the whole couch with his legs, and he would have laughed too if he'd had the chance, except that Zamir suddenly glanced at him, and nudged Mika to silence with a hissed 'Shut up, shut up!' that was too obvious to be missed. Zamir had realised that his father was older than the men they were laughing at, and had only narrowly missed death himself, and then Mika did too, and stopped laughing abruptly. He hated the sympathy on Zamir's part, and the diplomacy on Mika's; he had hated being thought of as old even then, and that was twenty years ago.

They take a cab to a quiet residential area near the beaches, where Bernadette's stepmother is spending her days, in a confused fog as thick and grey as the smog-filled sky above the city, as thick and greasy as the waves that lick the shore. They sign the visitors' book, and Bernadette chats easily with the starched nurse, mainly in English, but throwing in a few casual phrases in Chinese. He recognises *ni-hao* for hello, and he thinks he recognises the word for snow. They go to Betsy's room, where the nurse introduces them with exaggerated formality, as though it is their first visit, and Betsy is an honoured guest rather than a patient. Betsy's Alzheimer's came on more quickly than might be expected; it had started with her forgetting her keys, but then she started to forget what keys were in the first place.

She had refused to move in with Bernadette, and had stayed with her widowed sister-in-law until it became too difficult for the equally elderly lady to care for her, even with the day nurse that Bernadette organised and paid for. Betsy is sitting up straight in her room, facing in the direction of the television, but not looking at it. 'Hello, Mum,' says Bernadette, as brightly as she would to a child she was trying to charm. 'Have you had a nice morning? And what a nice shirt, you look so pretty today.' To be honest, Betsy isn't looking her best; although her clothes are neatly pressed, there is something slightly askew about them, and he knows that Bernadette is itching to stand her stepmother up, straighten her collar and smooth out her skirt. Betsy's dyed black hair has a centimetre of grey at the roots, and dandruff gleams in the rest like crystals set in tar; the effect is oddly similar to that of the stars at night, and he remembers the view from Felix, a night of diamond dust. Betsy scratches the back of her head with a casual, instinctive gesture, and a small shower of flakes scatter and settle on her shoulders like snow; he wonders if this was what Bernadette had been talking about with the nurse, discussing the merits of medicated shampoos. It seems absurdly trivial, now that Betsy is in need of round-the-clock care, with her memory shredded to lace, to be worrying about dandruff.

Betsy smiles vaguely, and blankly. 'Hello, little person,' she replies. She does not recognise Bernadette, and she does not know or care if Bernadette is someone she should recognise. Her dementia is advanced enough that she no longer finds the loss distressing. She speaks with the same tone to everyone, politeness edged with sarcasm; if she feels sadness, she disguises it behind condescension. She is looking with interest at the bag that Bernadette has brought, and has placed carefully on the side table.

'They tell me you ate a good breakfast today, Mum,' says Bernadette encouragingly. 'That's nice to hear.'

At the mention of food, Betsy suddenly looks a little crafty. 'Breakfast was not so good today. Too dry. Too chewy.' She adds, 'I'm still hungry,' glaring accusingly towards the open door, where the nurse is talking to someone in the corridor, before giving a meaningful glance at Bernadette's bag.

'I brought you a present, Mum,' says Bernadette. 'I mean, we did, Mike and me,' she adds hurriedly, generously including him, even though he is now pacing around the room with apparent disinterest, just looking for something to do. He finally sits down with the newspaper that Bernadette has brought with her, and looks at the crossword. 'Your favourite, Danish Butter Cookies.' She opens the box, and carries it over to her mother, sitting beside her. As she takes a cookie out of a crinkled paper case, Betsy opens her mouth immediately, with obedient trust, just as she would for her daily medication, or for her temperature to be taken. He thinks of a baby bird waiting to be fed, and watches Bernadette as she resists the instinctive response to pop the cookie into the expectant mouth, and instead presses it into Betsy's dry and brown-spotted hand, so that she can eat it herself, with dignity. 'Try one, Mum, they're nice.'

Betsy looks at the cookie in her hand, and places it in her mouth, beginning to chew thoughtfully. 'Soft and sweet. Not too dry,' she concedes, nodding her head. Bernadette beams at the praise. She pulls out the travel backgammon from her bag, and sets out the counters. It is one of the games that Betsy still enjoys playing. Bernadette has told him how Betsy and her father used to play chess, and how if he won, he'd propose a few games of backgammon as well, to give her a chance to beat him back.

When it is time to go, Betsy puts her fragile bird claw on Bernadette's plump, freckled fingers, and says, as a warning, 'Little one, that man.' She indicates Maqil. 'That man, he has no respect.'

Bernadette feels the visit has gone well, and is cheerful when they walk outside and get into their waiting cab; he is cheerful simply because they are leaving. 'I don't know why you want me to come down with you,' he says. 'I can't talk to her, or do anything helpful. I haven't a clue what to say to her. If I do say something she looks at me like the furniture's just spoken. That's what I am in Betsy's room. I'm just added furniture. Something to walk around or bump into.'

'She remembers you, that's why I want you to come,' says Bernadette. 'She's forgotten me, but she remembers you. She remembers that she never liked you. That little moment of lucidity, I need it, more than her. I need to know that she's still Betsy, inside.'

She leans back against the sticky seat of the taxi, and feeling it suck against the damp of her neck, reconsiders, and sits up straight again. 'Poor Mum,' she murmurs, just as she used to say 'Poor Mammy' when talking about her real mother. 'You have no idea how much I used to hate her, when I was younger. I was always forcing my dad to take sides. If I wore something in cashmere, she'd accuse me of wearing acrylic. In public, just to embarrass me, I swear. When I bought groceries for the house, she always told me I'd spent too much on stuff, or too little; she'd make me return the canned beansprouts if she could save ten cents a can on a different brand. She'd ask me to taste her soup, and if I said it was fine, she'd always add more salt. If I said it needed more salt, she wouldn't. I know how petty this sounds now, but at the time I thought she was a complete pain in the ass. I married Seamus and moved back to Ireland just to get away from her; I hated it all the time I was there, stuck away from my friends in this wet, grey town, with an eejit who drank too much and flirted with his secretaries. I only stuck it out so long because I didn't want to have to come back and listen to her saying, 'I told you so.' But when I finally did come back, she didn't say a word. She was looking after my dad, then, when he was dying. I remember thinking that my dad was lucky to have her; I wondered whether he took as good care of my poor mammy when she was dying. I hoped he did, but I wasn't sure. I think that's why I started the medical training.' She turns towards him. 'You've still got a mother, you know. You're lucky. I've had two, and I've managed to lose them both, one way or another.'

'Careless of you,' he comments, but he says it kindly, with humour.

He finally agrees to the trip to Pakistan some months later, when Mika emails with surprising news. Mika is keen on electronic mail, and has set up addresses for all the family who don't already have one through work; it allows her to keep in touch the way she prefers, with polite regularity and without the risk of intimacy; she doesn't solicit replies to her quarterly status updates, which she diplomatically copies to everyone, even her elderly paternal grandmother, who has never approached a computer screen in her life; he imagines that the messages are printed off for his mother by the valet, and given to her at breakfast with the post. The email that she set up for him is pleasingly anonymous: addresseeunknownXXIX@mail. com; he likes the comic wink in her choice, although he doesn't know what the XXIX means, as 29 has no particular significance to either himself or her. Perhaps he was simply the twenty-ninth addressee unknown to be registered on the system. Mika's news is this: Zamir, after years of apparently dating a variety of interchangeable brunettes from his bank, is finally getting married, to an American girl whose parents are from Pakistan. The wedding will be in London, but they are having an engagement party in Islamabad. In a postscript to the email, she asks for his current address – it strikes neither of them as odd that his daughter doesn't know where he lives – and tells him that an invitation to the party will be on its way. He tells Bernadette about the engagement party casually some time later, when she is already organising the dates and the tickets for the trip to Lahore, as though the party has just come up as some irrelevant side bar, a tiresome coincidence.

'Well, do you want to go to it?' asks Bernadette.

'Hmm, it's all the same to me, one way or the other. You decide, sweetheart,' he says, shrugging his shoulders. 'It's an extra flight to book, isn't it?'

'Well of course you're going. He's your son,' she says, matter-of-factly. 'You really ought to start appreciating that you have these things, mothers, sons. Family. Lots of people don't.' She looks wistful for a moment. When they first met and married, Bernadette was in her forties, and it would have still been possible for her to have a child; she knew he would never have agreed to try, and didn't ask him. Like everyone, she regrets what she hasn't done, more than anything she has. Bernadette shakes her head, as though shaking away disquieting thoughts, and makes a note for the travel agent. 'I guess we allow three more days then, for the Islamabad trip. It won't be a problem with work, they owe me so much holiday this year.' She puts down her pen, and pushes up the glasses that she has recently started to wear, before deciding to prop them up on the top of her head. 'I suppose that your son's mum will be there too.'

'I suppose,' he says. His silence is eloquent, and he realises belatedly that it would have been much less suspicious and much more reassuring to say something; to point out that Samira never had any boobs to speak of, and that Bernadette is years younger than her. Bernadette purses her lips just briefly, at the prospect of reuniting her husband with the love of his life, before giving a sweet professional care-giver's smile.

'Well, won't this be fun? I'll look forward to meeting them all.'

For all of Bernadette's organisation, he is still unsure whether he will go to Pakistan after all, or whether he will make an excuse at the last moment. Something to do with his health, something credible but obviously untrue. He isn't that excited about seeing Zamir or Mika or his ageing mother; he wants to see Samira very much, so much so that he is worried he will make a fool of himself. And he is too old to make a fool of himself and still look charming; at his age, he will seem either pathetic or senile. What does he think will happen when he sees her? That they will run away like teenage lovers, and hold hands under the ancient tamarind trees of the hotel's landscaped gardens? The more he dwells on it, as he goes about his business in Hong Kong, the more he thinks it better that he doesn't go. Nobody is really expecting him to turn up; he was weeks late for his own father's funeral, why would he be on time for something as inconsequential as an engagement party? His family are more used to his absence than his presence; turning up would just be out of character. He feels for the first time a slight weight of expectation; it is a novel experience, the sort that he supposes society hostesses feel, that they must conform to type, display charming manners and provide appropriate refreshments. That they must make enthusiastic conversation with bores at charitable functions. That they must go through the motions of being themselves. This is something that he feels he needs to do as well; to keep the role of outcast, of black sheep, of free spirit, he has to inhabit the self that he has made and nurtured all these years. People rely on him to behave in this way, to feature in the stories that are circulated about him, that have achieved the glow of legend in the telling, like an ancient stone carving that shines where the hands of awestruck visitors have passed over it. It is more than expectation. It is obligation.

He occupies himself with his latest enterprise, and makes a point of meeting the individuals he is helping; he isn't stupid enough to trust go-betweens. Face to face, he thinks he can tell the difference between someone covering up minor crimes from their past, and someone plotting more serious crimes in the future. He was in London during the IRA terrorist attacks, he was in Spain when the Basque separatists caused trouble, and he was in the Middle East during all manner of bitter conflicts. He is just a white-collar criminal, a procurer of paperwork, an intellectual, in a way; if he suspects a political rather than a commercial purpose, a plot of any sort, he turns down the commission, charmingly, as being beyond his skills. One particular party, represented in an initial meeting by a polite Muslim in Western dress with a smooth face that he keeps touching, as though his beard is still there, in the way that soldiers in bomb blasts still feel their missing limbs, is particularly insistent. Not threatening, but the way he keeps saying 'my friend' and 'my brother' seems to imply that he is anything but. The potential client tries addressing him in Arabic, and Urdu, and Hindi, as though trying to work out where he is from; Maqil keeps a blank enquiring face, as though he doesn't understand, and speaks only in English. He advises with great regret that he will not be able to help.

On his return to the flat, later that evening, he feels a sort of disquiet that he knows isn't justifiable by any specific menace; he keeps thinking of the man's index finger tracing his tender philtrum, his thumb brushing his naked chin, the gesture repeated again and again, as though calming a cat on the brink of agitation. He supposes that he is just beginning to become a panicky old man, with a quavering voice. Still, he feels reassured by the security guard at the entrance to his building, at the code he needs to punch into the lift to reach his floor. He feels reassured, like his friend the forger back in his Madrid apartment building, that all the doors along the long corridor are identical. That no door has his name on it. He lets himself into the flat, and sees Bernadette fiddling with the plastic wrapping on a box of chocolates. 'Hello,' she says, going up to him coquettishly and giving him a kiss on the mouth; she is always pleased to see him, but this time she seems positively delighted.

'Hello, sweetheart,' he says cautiously. 'Chocolates, eh?' he adds with a conspiratorial grin, as Bernadette is still always on a declared diet, which she never tires of breaking.

'So sweet of you to send them, although I've no idea why you did,' she says, scrunching up the Cellophane and tossing it away. 'I've been staring at them all afternoon, and decided I couldn't resist.' She adds, flirtatiously, 'I keep saying you shouldn't undermine my diet . . .' She pulls a chocolate from the box, and is about to pop it into her mouth when he steps forward and takes it from her, with a gentle movement, so as not to startle her. She looks at him in surprise, nonetheless.

'They're not from me,' he says, by way of explanation. Her eyes widen, and he explains, reassuringly, 'They're *for* me. They're medicated. They have my blood-pressure meds in them. They were a gift from some pharmacist I helped out.' He empties them into the bin.

'Aren't you going to have them?' asks Bernadette faintly, looking sadly at all the chocolate thrown away.

'God no,' he says. 'They're diabetic chocolates. Disgusting. Diabetic chocolate isn't chocolate. Like frozen yoghurt isn't ice cream.' He looks at the chocolate in the bin, and thinks of the stray animals he has seen around the garbage area recently, of a couple of street people who sometimes shelter near there, who go through the rubbish bags for half-smoked cigarettes and the leftover booze in the bottom of the bottles.

'Could you go downstairs and get a cab, sweetheart?' he asks. 'Mum's not well, we have to go and see her. I'm sorry I didn't call to tell you first; the battery's low on my phone.'

'Oh Christ,' says Bernadette. 'What's wrong? Why didn't they call here?'

'It's not so bad, but I think we should go,' he says. 'I'll just be a minute. Call of nature.'

'Of course,' she says, gathering her handbag, her wrap. She glances at herself in the mirror distractedly as she leaves, pushing at her hair, and then shaking her head at her silly vanity at such an inappropriate time, goes out into the corridor.

As soon as the door clicks shut, he picks up his always-ready suitcase and puts it by the door. He opens up an empty case, and taking a supermarket bag from the kitchen, sweeps all of Bernadette's toiletries from the bathroom shelf, her face cream, her tweezers, her lipstick, her soap, into the plastic bag, knots it, and throws it in the case. He takes her passport from the bureau, puts it in his breast pocket with his own (one of several), and adds a few handfuls of her clothes to the case too, underwear and pantyhose from her top drawer, the trousers she usually wears, the silky loose tops she has begun to favour. It takes him about three minutes. Finally he squirts kerosene in the bin, and drops in a lighted match. The fire alarm goes off with the smoke, and he shuts the lid of the bin, satisfied that not even the dogs or the hobos will try to eat the chocolates now. He picks up the cases, takes the lift downstairs, and finds Bernadette waiting agitatedly in a cab, as the fire alarm from upstairs trips off a warning bell in the lobby that drifts out of the main doors.

'What are they for?' asks Bernadette, looking at the small cases by their feet as the cab moves off.

'The airport, please,' he asks the cab driver. He turns towards Bernadette. 'What do you think they're for?' he says a little belligerently. 'We're going to see my mum. We can't go with nothing. I packed some stuff for you, but your case is pretty empty. I figured you'd want to do some shopping. Get some stuff made. Amma will load you with clothes as soon as we get there, anyhow.'

'Your mum?' asks Bernadette. 'You mean *your* mum, not mine? You mean we're going to Pakistan? Right now?' she asks.

'Of course we are,' he says, unfolding his newspaper and hiding behind it.

Bernadette looks cross, and then starts to laugh, at the adventure and daring of it. She has always admired his irresponsibility, as she is so responsible herself. It seems absolutely right to her that he would impulsively whisk her off early on the exact same trip that she has been organising for months, his now-or-never attitude. 'I'll call work from the airport,' she says. 'I don't know if you're romantic, or just completely mad.'

'Just a fond and foolish old man,' he replies calmly. 'Fond of you, mainly. There's no fool like an old one.' He has the chocolate that Bernadette had picked out, wrapped in plastic in his pocket. When he gets it tested in Pakistan, he will discover that it is laced with a common, unsophisticated toxin, the type most gardeners would keep in their sheds; not enough to kill someone healthy, but enough to make them sick for days. He has already decided that it might be time to walk out on his little business, at least for a while; he leaves Mikhail Lee, that successful businessman of indeterminate background, back in Hong Kong.

Lahore, Pakistan – 2002 – Engagement

THEY ARE IN PAKISTAN WEEKS BEFORE HIS MOTHER IS expecting them, and so he takes Bernadette to Islamabad and Karachi, staying in the expensive hotels that pride themselves on Western cuisine produced in polished steel kitchens, but where she insists on trying local specialities in the streets. She gets a moderate case of food poisoning, from eating fried fish at a stall, and throws up for days; for the first time in her life she is laid up and helpless in bed, but he has learnt from her example exactly how a spouse is meant to behave in these circumstances, and imitates what she did for him when he was ill, so closely that it might be considered mocking. He plumps her pillows, insists she keep up her fluids, and gets the hotel kitchen to make a passable imitation of the Three Generations soup, with chicken broth, spring onions and the water that rice has been boiled in. She loses eight pounds, and although she will gain it back over the next month or so, she is delighted, and keeps walking in front of the mirror in her underwear. While she is recovering, he sends word to his mother that he is in the country, and finds out that she already knows, that the jungle telegraph has been humming ever since he signed a hotel register with his real name. It seems that everyone has heard the news that he's on his way back, and he imagines a chorus of birds and beasts, a steady, rhythmic noise like the chuffing of a homeward-bound train, 'Sunny's coming, Sunny's coming, Sunny's coming', the chanting that bursts into a roar of applause and celebration, of tears and fireworks, as he finally pulls up in a rented car on the wide driveway of the Gulberg townhouse in Lahore like a returning hero from a just war: 'Come Out! Come Cheer! Sunny's Here!'

On their arrival, Bernadette is looking unusually charming in an overpriced and somewhat overembroidered shalwar kameez that she saw in a boutique in the Karachi hotel, displayed on a mannequin alongside the Armani dresses, with a matching wrap designed for chilly air-conditioned interiors. The older servants have been gossiping about his previous wife, who in repeated mythology was skinny, black and opinionated; they nod with approval at Bernadette's curves, her pale Irish skin, her dyed auburn hair. And most of all, her geisha-like deference to her husband, which is matched by her respectful bearing towards her mother-in-law, who is myopic behind thick bifocals, but whose elaborately drawn-up hair still gives her the appearance of elegance, even in her late eighties. Bernadette seems delighted to be visiting her husband's childhood home, and the obvious pleasure in her flushed face gleams as warmly as the copper threads in the complicated front panel of her outfit. 'So pretty,' says her mother-in-law, gesturing vaguely towards Bernadette's face and figure, so that it is unclear whether she is talking about Bernadette herself, or simply her choice of clothes. 'I dreamed of you, my dear,' his mother says. 'I dreamed and prayed that my Sunny would find someone like you, to care for him in his old age.'

'Oh, he'll never be old,' says Bernadette. 'I'm rather counting on him looking after me.' He smiles, but then looks at Bernadette questioningly; it is unlike her to try to be charming, so it is possible that she actually means it. Looking after people is not his strong point; four days in a five-star hotel with Bernadette, the easiest patient one might ever expect to have, was frankly enough. He watches as she fusses over his mother, and feels relieved, as he decides that she was joking. Bernadette is the one who does the looking after, the caring; it is her self-appointed role. The women are soon sitting having tea with fried pastries and salted fruit, and he drifts after them, surprised not to be the centre of attention. The relatives and servants are milling around Bernadette like a new bride, or, less flatteringly but more accurately, like a complicated new appliance to be unwrapped slowly and admired from all angles, a freezer that spits out ice cubes, a washing machine that also tumble-dries. White goods – large, foreign and superior. What will she do now, what will she say? He sees his mother smiling with pleasure as Bernadette eats the pastries, drinks the tea sweetened with condensed milk, generously forgetting her diet in order to accept the hospitality pressed upon her, and it occurs to him that timing is everything. Perhaps both Bernadette and his mother know that if they had met thirty years ago, his mother would have snubbed her just as ruthlessly as she had Samira, and dismissed the red-headed twenty-something Bernadette as a fat Western whore; that Bernadette would have described his mother, just as she once described Betsy, as a pain in the ass, and would have run to the next continent to get away from her. He supposes he should be pleased that they seem to be getting on, and sipping his own tea, makes conversation with his younger brothers and his waspish sister; but he keeps glancing at his wife and mother with a fascination that is almost anthropological, the meeting of two opposing tribes over a territorial dispute. The territory, of course, is him; he is egotistical enough to admit that. But he is disappointed at how quickly the territory seems conceded; he is finally, for the first time in his life, making an effort to belong, but it feels that he belongs to neither of them after all, and that they belong only to each other. They are talking about girlish things on which he has little opinion, hair and jewellery and shoes and clothes, that bizarre feminine complicity brought about by shopping. He competitively starts talking about sport with his youngest brother, even though he doesn't care about the national cricket team at all. He nods distractedly during his brother's cheerful exposition of their fortunes, still looking over to his large white wife and his desiccated nut-brown mother.

'So pretty,' repeats his mother, fingering the peaches-and-cream material of Bernadette's wrap. 'Tell me, is it cashmere?'

Bernadette smiles, widely and sincerely. Her cheeks become round and plump with pleasure. 'Yes,' she replies happily, casting a glowing look towards her husband. 'Yes, it is.'

He is sitting on the veranda to the guest suite with Bernadette, looking out over the garden. She is wearing yet another shalwar kameez; it is an outfit that suits her larger frame, and which she finds as comfortable as pyjamas. He is dressed in a plain white kameez as well; he likes the anonymity, blending in with everyone else on the street. He thinks he would stand out too much in his Hong Kong tailored suits. He is still troubled by the thought of the young Muslim man he had met; when he sees someone stroking a freshly shaved chin in the street, or the bazaar, or a restaurant, he can't stop himself looking at them sharply, as though they might be warning him in some subtle way. 'I'm so glad we came,' says Bernadette. 'It reminds me of Ireland, being here.'

The comparison is so inappropriate that he can't help but be a bit sarcastic. 'What does, exactly? The heat, the coconut trees, the dust?' he hazards.

She doesn't take offence. 'Oh, just having a garden, having space. My grandmother had a house with a big rambling garden outside Dublin. I stayed there for a while when poor Mammy was in hospital. There were big thorny bushes of brambles that covered the back wall; I used to prick my fingers picking the blackberries. My granny made a pudding called junket with them; or sometimes we just had them with cream and sugar. Or as jam on soda bread.' She looks dreamy, and wistful, and for some reason this troubles him a little.

'Not like you to get nostalgic for the old country,' he comments. 'I thought you hated Ireland.'

'It's the weather I hated most, when I went back,' she replies. 'The weather here is pretty good, it's hot, but it's dry. Not as stifling as Hong Kong. And you have room to breathe here; we're lucky to have a patio in Hong Kong. Most people don't even have that. Here you've got guavas and mangos and chickens in the garden. It's amazing.'

'It's not amazing,' he contradicts firmly. 'It's just a nice house in a nice street with a garden, in a medium-sized town where the electricity isn't reliable and so everyone keeps a generator for blackouts. You're beginning to sound like the tourist office. Picturesque Pakistan.'

'You say that like it's an insult,' she comments, still gazing out over the garden. She stands and waves to a heavily pregnant servant walking below with a basket of fruit, who waves back awkwardly as she balances the weight of her load. 'Hello, Anita,' she calls cheerfully, as though she is already more than a guest. 'Sweet girl,' she says, turning back to sit beside him on the cane chair. 'I wonder how she'll manage when the baby comes.' He grunts with indifference; he thinks he'd rather indulge her nostalgia and her annoying Western interest in exotic garden produce than talk about babies and how to manage them.

He finds himself disengaging more and more from Bernadette as the days and weeks go by, as Zamir's engagement party approaches. Perhaps because she is disengaging from him. She becomes part of his mother's household seamlessly, whereas he remains the grumpy guest, an annoying visitor. He feels like a child who is shown up by a better-behaved friend he has brought round for tea, and who sulks and pouts afterwards: 'You'd rather have her than me!' She begins spending evenings with his mother, in the beginning because she offered to do her blood tests and insulin jabs, but then he saw that she spent longer and longer in his mother's rooms, trying on outfits, having her hair oiled and plaited. His sister turns up sometimes, and they get pedicures and manicures together, and go out to the bazaars and the shops. He wonders what they could possibly be talking about, and begins to feel a little jealous; he has got used to Bernadette caring just for him. Back in Hong Kong, he liked to think that she passed her days imagining his wry responses to her everyday battles; that like him, she played out her small victories to his imagined applause. He doesn't suppose that she is spending all this time with his mother just to please him, or even to be polite. He wonders whether she suffers from the same disease as every orphan, even at her advanced age: that in her fifties she is still seeking a mother, and having all but lost Betsy has decided to adopt his. That she is still searching for home, for that elusive room marked with her name, and that she has finally found it.

'Have you ever thought about moving back here?' she asks, innocently enough, one evening before getting into bed. He shifts over to the edge, as far as he can possibly go, to show his lack of interest in the matter; he realises belatedly that the gesture has lost all effect, as he has been sleeping on the far side of the bed for months. 'My dad always intended to go back to Ireland before he died. Never made it, of course. He got too sick too fast, and then he couldn't travel,' she adds. He still says nothing, and so she prompts him. 'Well,' she asks, 'have you?'

'No,' he replies shortly. 'Never.' He is tempted to roll over grumpily, but he already has his back to her, and turning once more would land him on the floor. Instead he punctuates his statement with a short, disbelieving snort.

'Hmm,' she murmurs thoughtfully, not put off by his bad humour, and he feels compelled to make his point more forcefully.

'Besides, I don't believe it matters where you die. Why should it?'

Bernadette moves towards him, addressing his back, his quarter-profile. He listens to her, watching the moonlight shadows from the window, the pattern of the tree leaves pressed against the glass. 'What about where you were born, doesn't that matter either?' she asks gently.

'Of course not,' he replies. 'Anyone can be born anywhere. If it's not where they belong, not where they want to be, they can just move. Actors move to LA, opera singers to Milan, chefs to Paris, nerds to Silicon Valley, bankers to London, nuns to Rome, hookers to Amsterdam—'

'So the places in between,' interrupts Bernadette, 'are they the places that really matter?'

'Don't be daft, sweetheart,' he replies indulgently. 'In-between places matter the least.'

About ten days before Zamir's engagement party, the pregnant servant goes into unexpected labour a few weeks early, her waters breaking while the family are dining on the terrace. They hear her cry of shock as the amniotic fluid gushes out over the stone steps that lead to the garden, and watch as she tries helplessly to staunch the continuing flow with the end of her sari and return to the servant quarters, but each step brings a fresh seepage, and she is in tears with the public indignity of it, as she hobbles with the material stuffed between her legs. Bernadette runs downstairs to help, while the rest of the family carry on eating. She makes Anita comfortable, and returns to speak to her mother-in-law, surprised that Anita has apparently made no arrangements with the local hospital, and seems entirely unprepared for a home confinement. The family look on as though mystified by Bernadette's concern, as she urgently lists the items that are needed for the birth – plastic sheeting, portable gas and air, latex gloves – as though they should all leap up and start organising this themselves. This is Pakistan, after all, and that is a serving woman from a village, with no money or family connections; in this country, women of that background have been known to give birth on long train journeys, and carry on to their destination, their other children clinging to their skirts. The guard might not even stop the train, unless the newborn fell through the toilet chute the mother was squatting over, as had happened once across the border – the baby had been swiftly recovered, wailing and comically unharmed rather than tragically maimed. The family assume that women like Anita have the same rubber-ball resilience; they bounce from home to home, touching no one, untouched themselves if they are fortunate enough to be plain; they are common, in the blandest sense that they are ubiquitous, replaceable, just another small bird pecking out an existence in the city, sending money back to aged parents and children in their village. They find Bernadette's bleeding-heart liberalism disturbingly exotic and rather inappropriate, like that of a daughter of good family returning from a Western education with modern cropped hair, an

284

unbecoming summer tan, an offensive upper-arm tattoo and worst of all, modern, unbecoming, offensive *ideas*. 'I told the silly girl to go home to her village two weeks ago,' complains his mother, discomfited by Bernadette's baffling implication that they are somehow responsible for providing Anita with a safe and comfortable birth. 'Girls should go home to have their babies. Her husband's there, her mother, all her family. I told her I could spare her.' She huffs, and finally concedes, with a long-suffering sigh: 'I'll send Munjo to fetch Dr Kharnum.' Dr Sherifa Kharnum is reluctantly respected in the neighbourhood for setting up a local clinic for family planning and women's problems; she is rather glamorous for a working doctor in her late forties, and is always impeccably made up, with her hair swept up as if she is about to attend a garden party; her glamour ends at her slender neck, where she wears a gold chain with a tiny replica Koran in gold and green enamel, which nestles in the hollow of her throat. From collarbones down, she dresses drably for her work, in plain cotton saris or shalwar kameez in muted shades, clothes that can be boil-washed for the purposes of hygiene. His mother mutters to the rest of the family in Punjabi, as she doesn't want to seem ungracious in front of Bernadette: 'Always costing us money, these silly young girls. Dr Kharnum will charge extra for coming out of the clinic today.'

'I'll look after Anita until the doctor arrives,' says Bernadette soothingly, seeing her mother-in-law's irritation, and generously attributing it to concern. She seems remarkably calm about this sudden responsibility, considering she hasn't worked on the maternity wards for a few years now – she took a promotion that involved her working in the office instead. He guesses that she stopped because she found it too hard to deliver other people's babies, or simply because every mother she helped assumed that she had to be a mother herself. No one expects Bernadette, the wife of the eldest son, to handle the delivery on her own – it would be as inappropriate as a Dauphin's consort waiting on her handmaid – but as it turns out, Dr Kharnum is attending to an emergency, and doesn't arrive for two hours. To pass the time while they wait for her, Bernadette mops Anita's brow, helps her breathe through the contractions, measures increasing and rapid dilation to ten centimetres, and finally helps Anita on to all fours on a clean sheet and delivers a healthy baby girl. She ties the umbilical cord with cotton ribbons from the mending basket that she has boiled in soapy water, and cuts it with similarly sterilised scissors from the kitchen; she then hands the damp and slightly bloody infant to her mother to nurse, while she waits to deliver the placenta. Bernadette keeps her composure in front of Anita, but she is sweating profusely with the effort of it all – Maqil is summoned to hover outside, pacing in a comical imitation of an expectant father himself, so that he can interpret her requests for the servants.

'A very good job,' says Dr Kharnum approvingly to both Bernadette and Anita once she has finally turned up, as she checks the baby's responses and the mother's blood pressure. 'So, you couldn't wait for the doctor?' she asks the infant in a normal voice, rather than the cooing tones that most people use for babies; neither Bernadette nor Anita realises at first that she is talking to the child, rather than them.

'Baby came out so fast that I barely had a chance to get the rubber gloves on to catch her,' replies Bernadette, with a ghost of a laugh. Now that her job is done, she has become pale and uncomfortable, and avoids looking at the baby as she suckles on Anita's brown-nippled breast. Dr Kharnum doesn't notice her discomfort, and jabs Anita in the thigh with an oxytocin injection to hurry up the third stage, as Bernadette prepares to leave her with Anita and the baby. 'Thank you, thank you, madam,' calls out Anita as Bernadette goes, adding in heavily accented English, 'Baby thanks you too.'

A few days after the birth, when the postnatal bleeding has begun to subside, and she has recovered sufficiently to put up with the discomfort of a twelve-hour train journey, Anita does go home to her village after all, but she leaves the baby behind. When the child is discovered, crying lustily in plain view in the servant's quarters, it is thought to be some sort of hormonally prompted forgetfulness; a messenger is rushed to the station, but Anita's train has already left. His mother wonders out loud whether Anita has gone mad with postnatal depression, while Bernadette walks the baby around the garden to calm it down. No one else wants to touch the screaming little scrap. The elderly valet, Fayaz, eventually admits the truth, as he was responsible for hiring Anita, his cousin's granddaughter, in the first place. It turns out that the baby is not Anita's husband's child; in fact he is unsure whose child it is, and supposes that the father, whoever he is, must be married. He is careful not to cast slurs on Anita's character, as she is after all his own flesh and blood, albeit distantly, but there is the definite implication in the 'whoever he is' that even Anita might be uncertain as to her child's paternity. 'These girls,' he shrugs, 'they come to the city, they watch romantic movies, they lose their heads.' He makes it sound both regrettable and inevitable; it seems that Anita's husband is willing to take her back – they have a son together, she is a hard worker and reliable earner – but not with the baby, whom she has left in Lahore to be adopted. 'Silly girl,' says his mother mildly, keeping her temper for Bernadette's sake, disguising the fact that she is apoplectic with outrage at being left a baby to manage like a stray kitten in a box under the stairs. She looks suspiciously at every male in the household, every regular visitor, from the elderly valet to the cook to the driver to her own nephews and grandsons. Anyone could be the father of the girl's child; she does not dare to send the baby to the orphanage, in case it is her own flesh and blood.

Bernadette is as practical and caring as ever. 'The poor little mite. We'll send word to Anita's parents; maybe they'll take the baby on. And if they won't, we can get her adopted. I'll look after her in the meantime; she's only tiny, she's no trouble at all.' The baby, as though determined to prove her wrong, starts squalling again, her eyes squeezed shut like a kitten's and her mouth a red rectangle of distress. Bernadette seems unperturbed, and begins jigging her up and down. 'Don't cry, don't cry, little girl,' she coos. She asks Fayaz, 'Do you know what Anita called her? I can't keep calling her little girl.'

'She called her Baby,' he replies. 'Baby in English. She said she liked the sound of it. That is her name.'

Bernadette looks questioningly at him, and then to her husband. 'Really? Just Baby? Isn't that a bit unusual?'

'Not that unusual,' shrugs Maqil. 'For a pet name. A family name. You're asking the man who was called Sonny.' He'd intended to say this with rueful irony, but the effect is spoiled by having to shout over the wailing.

'So I guess it's Baby, then,' Bernadette says, crooking her forefinger and offering the pale knuckle to the infant to suck. She would never give a finger; too many germs could gather under the nails. Baby calms immediately, and sucks rhythmically, with fierce concentration. 'Baby, Baby,' Bernadette murmurs to her, and then switches to Chinese: 'Baobao, Baobao.' The baby seems to like this. The cross look on her forehead smooths over, and Bernadette creates a little sing-song chant of 'Baobao, Baby,' which reminds him of a seventies hit. Bernadette has a pleasant singing voice; she had been part of the church choir in Dublin before she moved to Hong Kong, white robed, red haired and freckle faced, singing first for Poor Mammy's life, and then for her eternal soul. She doesn't care that she seems a bit ridiculous, cooing nonsense in front of everyone. The pale discomfort she had on delivering the baby has disappeared; she is glowing like an expectant mother herself.

Both he and his mother look helplessly on, as they lose Bernadette to a routine of three-hourly feeds. She doesn't trust the other servants to take care of Anita's cast-off child, rightly assuming that they would just leave her screaming and get on with their own duties. Bernadette meanwhile becomes even softer around the edges, less defined, as she is occupied by sudden motherhood; or rather, sudden motherhood occupies her instead, fills her with an imperial expansion to the tips of her fingers and the ends of her toes. Even her hair seems to spring out with new life, and she tames it with a sensible plait at the back of her neck. The blue eyes that used to be clouded with crystallised concern are now dewy and clear as rainwater. She hums tunelessly to the infant, rearranges the sparse brown curls, strokes the unformed nose, listens to the shallow breath from the open kitten mouth, and lets the tiny hand grip her finger, poke at her eyes and pull her hair. Bernadette smells permanently sweet now, like the Nestlé formula she feeds the baby, a milk-and-cookies scent. He stops bothering to teeter at the edge of the bed at night, and takes up his full pillow width, lying flat on his back; Bernadette is too occupied by the baby in the top drawer of their bureau to notice him anyway. It annoys him that he can't remember when they last made love, and he doesn't know whether to be relieved or cross with her when she says that she won't go to Zamir's engagement party, as she shouldn't leave the baby, and she certainly couldn't travel with her. She promises to get the baby adopted as soon as she hears back from Anita and her parents.

He travels to Islamabad a day ahead of the rest of his family, as he can't bear the thought of having to travel with them, and checks into the hotel where the reception is being held. He is walking to his room when he passes a woman in brown leather slacks and a sleeveless linen top, stepping out of a hotel boutique with a label-emblazoned bag in each hand. The labels shout for attention, Gucci, Dior, and he sees these first before he sees the woman's face. 'God, you've got old,' says the woman, stepping back from him, her thick hair bobbed at her jaw and fashionably dyed several subtly different shades of espresso.

'God, you've got fat,' he replies, although it's not true. Samira is probably a couple of dress sizes bigger than she used to be, but she used to be on the verge of skinny. She looks annoyingly good for a woman in her sixties. In fact, she looks better than Bernadette despite being ten years older than her, and he thinks it is probably a good thing that Bernadette won't meet her.

'At a certain age, you have to pick your face or your figure,' she replies, grinning. She kisses him very properly on each cheek. 'I didn't think you'd be coming to this shindig.'

'I said I would,' he replies.

'Well, that doesn't mean a thing, does it?' she says sensibly. She looks over his shoulder for a younger woman laden down with luggage. 'Isn't your wife with you?'

'No, she's back in Lahore. It's a long story,' he replies. 'She's looking after a maidservant's abandoned newborn illegitimate love child.' He sees Samira stifle a laugh, and he lets himself laugh with her. 'In fact, that's pretty much it. It wasn't such a long story after all.'

'Ouch,' she replies. 'Ditched for a baby. That's got to hurt.' She adds mischievously, 'Most men get dumped for other men, or at least for a really good career opportunity abroad.'

'So where's your husband?' he asks, looking over her shoulder much as she did, for a younger, handsome man laden down with even more expensive-looking bags. He knows from Mika's emails that Samira had remarried some years ago.

'Which one?' she replies pertly. 'There are so many now that I give them numbers instead of names. Like in *The Prisoner*.

Number Four is back in London consulting divorce lawyers and splitting our photo albums. Number Three has found someone who is far less trouble and is living in Rome. Number Two has been widely discredited by a parliamentary scandal and is enjoying gardening leave at taxpayers' expense. And Number One is right here.' For a moment there is silence, and she is looking at him, looking at her. For a moment he really thinks that she will let her designer purchases slide to the floor, that he will drop his suitcase, the same suitcase that she sent to the George V all those years ago, and they will take each other in their arms, and that nothing will ever come between them again. The moment passes: he is an elderly man in a suit crumpled by travel, and she is an ageing socialite who has chosen her face over her figure. She looks at her watch, a slim Rolex in platinum. It is the only jewellery she is wearing; she no longer wears a wedding band. 'I've got some time before dinner with Zamir's in-laws. Do you want to have a drink?'

'Sure, I could spare a bit of time before my very busy evening of watching CNN with a room-service club sandwich.'

'Is that a hint?' she asks, as they walk towards the bar. 'I guess you could come to the dinner, if you like. Zamir would have asked you if he'd known you were here already.' She pauses. 'You know, he'll be really pleased to see you. He didn't actually think you'd show up.' She says it as a warning, to prepare him for outrageous demonstrations of affection.

'The last time he saw me, he threw me out onto the street in your ex's dressing gown. I guess absence really does make the heart grow fonder.'

'Well, he's proud of you, I think. He talks about you at dinner parties, now that you're this big-deal Hong Kong businessman. He thinks you're legitimate, at long last.' She sits at the bar, and orders a gin and tonic. He hesitates and orders the same; he would actually prefer a cup of Earl Grey, but there is something too elderly about ordering tea at a chic hotel bar, something too pipe-and-slippers and bedjacket about it. He is aware that people are looking at Samira with interest; she seems to have chosen Western clothes to stand out in Islamabad, just as she chose saris to stand out in London at black-tie events. He has always quite liked her vanity. 'I heard you sold that website you started,' she says. 'So what sort of business are you into these days?'

'What a question,' he replies mildly. Samira laughs, as though he has said something hilarious.

'My God, Maqil,' she cackles. 'Or whatever you're calling yourself at the moment. You never change, do you?' She seems pleased by this. And at first he is pleased too, but then the pleasure sinks suddenly, replaced by a cold flash of irritation he is unable to hide, as his face narrows and his mouth hardens to a line; his older face is more transparent than the opaque, smooth face of his youth, the muscles lax and less obedient. 'What's up?' asks Samira, seeing his unease and lacking the manners to ignore it. His saintly Bernadette would have noted his expression, and said nothing; she would bear and forbear, refrain and abstain. He is surprised to be thinking of Bernadette when he is sitting at a bar with Samira, whom all men of a certain age are guiltily admiring; he is thinking of how she looked when he took leave of her earlier that day, in a pale blue silk shalwar kameez that suited her creamy, freckled complexion, with Baby lodged comfortably in the crook of her arm. Not so much Saint Bernadette as an old-fashioned Madonna and child; like an unimaginative Christmas card, traditional and well meaning. He had mentioned casually after lunch that he'd decided to take an earlier flight, that the car was already waiting to take him to the airport, and she had given him a seraphic smile, and waved him off without a trace of disquiet or passion. And now he thinks about it, Samira has greeted him with neither as well. His sudden departures and sudden appearances are no longer the stuff of legend, are no longer worth remarking upon. It is just Sunny being Sunny. Maqil being Maqil. He has become predictable.

'It's just the way that everyone expects me to be irresponsible the whole time. It's beginning to feel like a burden. Just another sort of familial commitment. A duty.' He says these words, Burden, Commitment, Duty, with heavy distaste, as though they are swear words or insults; he imagines shouting them out loud, as stridently as street vendors selling their wares, as furiously as housewives driving fruit-thieving urchins from their gardens, as ripely as the servants swearing at a visiting foreign cricket team while they watch a match on the black-and-white television in their quarters. He downs the gin and tonic, and defiantly orders Earl Grey tea after all. Samira watches him, with apparent sympathy.

'Well, Maqil. I guess that's just the bed you made for yourself,' she says eventually. 'It's who you are.' She smiles slightly, and adds, 'Do you remember that fable I used to tell the children? I can't remember if it was Aesop or La Fontaine, but it was about a scorpion who asked a turtle for a ride across the river. The turtle refused to risk being stung, but the scorpion pointed out that it would make no sense for him to sting the turtle, as then they'd both sink. So the turtle gave the scorpion a lift, and just when they were almost at the opposite bank, the scorpion stung her anyway, and they both started to drown. "Why did you do that?" asked the turtle, before they went under. And the scorpion said, "I can't help myself. It's what I am. It's in my nature." ' She puts her hand on his, and he looks down at her dark fingers on his pale, liver-spotted skin. The delicate blue vein that curls across her tendons towards her wrist bone, the oval nails professionally polished to dark bronze. He feels suddenly unable to look her in the eyes, and she removes her hand as easily as she offered it, and calls out to the bartender, 'Make that tea for two.' She turns towards him and says, 'Well, Zamir's in-laws are far too proper. We can't turn up for dinner with them stinking of gin, can we?' He feels unbearably touched by her solidarity, by this slightest of concessions; it feels briefly as though they are standing shoulder to shoulder against the world. She knows exactly who he is, and she is sitting beside him all the same. Me and you. Tea for two.

At the engagement party the next day, an intimate gathering by Pakistani standards, of just a hundred and fifty people, he still feels unable to live up to his reputation. In the years he spent away, his myth has overtaken him, the international man of mystery with a career in every country, the winner and loser of legendary fortunes, the dilettante gambler, the internet entrepreneur. His absence has been more powerful than his presence, and those who are meeting him for the first time say things like 'So this is the famous Maqil Karam', and look him up and down with obvious disappointment, the elderly father of the groom stitched into an appropriate suit with the white rose buttonhole pressed upon all family members. Looking at himself in the mirrored wall of the grand reception room, he sees exactly what they see; like them, he is once more surprised at how small he is in real life, and how much smaller he is becoming, as shrunken and shrivelled as rotting fruit in a bowl. His laugh sounds hollow, as though coming from an empty space in his belly, when he tells his usual repertoire of jokes and amusing stories. He has the sense of parodying himself and not doing a particularly good job, as though some distant country cousin is gussied up to play his part, while the real Maqil Karam has run away to Monte Carlo with a suitcase of fake money, his pockets stuffed with the wedding jewellery. He shouldn't have come. He should have remained absent and extraordinary, not present and correct. He drifts from group to group at the party, occasionally joined by Mika and her current boyfriend, a milky-looking English accountant called Dan, or by Samira and her hangers-on, or by Zamir and his fiancée Jilania, or by his mother and his brothers and his sister, and feels curiously disconnected. He feels as though he isn't there after all, that his true self might really be in Monte Carlo, throwing it all away on red, or black. That his true place on the planet is alone by the gaming tables, and not in a room surrounded by family and friends. His unconventional, carefree life has led to this banal conclusion, greeting guests at his son's engagement party like any other proud father; he has been forgiven, he has been forgotten. He may as well have become a banker like his son. He may as well be dead.

'Well, doesn't Jilli look lovely,' Mika says, linking her arm with his, another show of solidarity, more public and less sincere than her mother's. She would never do that if they were in private; she is showing the guests that they are a normal family. It makes him think of those long-married couples who only demonstrate affection in front of an audience, waiting for a door to shut behind them so that they can break apart and bicker. He plays along.

'She does,' he says, following Mika's gaze to the bride-to-be. 'But it's looking at Zamir in a dinner jacket that made me double-take. It was like looking at myself when I was young. I could have cried.'

'With pride?' asks Mika, with interest.

'With horror, I thought I was so much better looking than that . . .'

Mika laughs politely, and Samira hears the strained note, and floats over, in a burnt-orange-gold sari that complements her bronze manicure, and makes her look almost bridal herself.

'Hey, Mum, we were just saying how lovely Jilli looks,' says Mika. She links her other arm with her mother, and then smiles in a sudden pose, holding her head still and showing her teeth, as the photographer's flash goes off. Her hair is loose, slightly damp from the hotel pool, and looks a little sloppy compared to everyone else's; he can see Samira glancing at it with disapproval, wondering why Mika didn't blow-dry it, or at least put it up. Mika's frames are now designer, and less heavy than the ones she used to favour, but she is resolutely un-made-up, although she has conceded to the occasion by dressing in a shalwar kameez in pale green; she looks elegant from the neck down, even with the flat, plain sandals she is wearing, and she tells everyone who admires her that the outfit is her mother's, as though it is her mother's responsibility and nothing to do with her.

'Jilli does look pretty,' agrees Samira. 'She's a real little doll. Like Barbie in Brown,' she adds waspishly, before smiling again for the camera.

'Mu-um! Please don't be so bitchy,' hisses Mika.

'Well, there's something so unimaginative about it, darling,' says Samira, removing her arm from Mika's and redraping her sari, letting the silk flow like liquid over her shoulder. 'All those interesting girls he brought home from the bank, and then he's up and marrying the only Punjabi he stumbled across on a dark night. A Paki Princess whose Dadi makes samosas. We may as well have stayed in Lahore and got him to marry the girl next door. And I know she's perfectly nice; she's girl-next-adorable. But it's like the mother ship called him home.'

'I thought you'd be pleased that he's marrying someone from Pakistan,' comments Mika's boyfriend, Dan, who has returned with a ruby-red glass of pomegranate juice, as he doesn't drink.

'Why would I? It's not as though *I'm* from Pakistan,' replies

Samira. She turns towards him. 'Maqil, have you met Dan, the man who can? Apparently no one can like a man called Dan.'

'Mum,' says Mika warningly.

'I don't think so,' he replies. 'The one I met was called Dan the flying man. He's quite the catch. Rather like I was, once upon a time.'

'Are your parents making fun of me?' Dan asks in bewilderment.

'Of course not, they're talking about someone else,' Mika improvises smoothly. 'My cousin's husband Daniyaal.' She adds brightly, 'Let's get some nibbles.'

'Is he a pilot, your cousin's husband?' asks Dan, as she steers him away towards the tables, around the waiters bearing trays of fried finger food, and drinks decorated with fruit and flowers on cocktail sticks.

'More of a frequent flyer,' they hear her say.

'Have you embarrassed Dan again?' Zamir asks, appearing by his mother's side.

'He makes it so easy, darling,' says Samira, without a shred of remorse, adding confidentially to Maqil, 'Dan's so painfully dull, when Mika first introduced us, he lost me at hello. No matter what he says, all I hear is blah-blah-blah. At least I took the time to speak to him just now; I usually just nod and smile vaguely at appropriate intervals.'

'And you wonder why it took me so long to bring Jilli home,' says Zamir.

'I don't wonder about that at all,' she starts to say, obviously intending to add something witty and effortlessly offensive, when Zamir interrupts her and says, 'Dad,' as though he has been calling him that all his life. In fact, the first time he ever called him Dad was the night before, at dinner in front of his future in-laws. 'Dad, I've got a friend who wants to meet you, he's a bit of a fan of yours.'

'Mr Karam,' says a smooth-faced young man in a tux, with an American accent, replacing Zamir at his side, 'I'm a real admirer of your work.'

He feels a cold chill, thinking of the young man in Hong Kong. 'What work would that be exactly?' he asks politely. He is looking for the exit doors, he is looking at the trays of food being circulated, wondering who prepared them.

'Your plays, of course,' says the young man. He repeats in a hushed, conspiratorial voice, 'Your prison plays.'

'Oh, those,' he replies with relief. 'How did you get hold of them? I thought they must have been thrown out or lost.' In fact he is lying; the truth is that he hasn't thought about them at all. Not since he left London.

'Zamir came across them in the household filing. I met him at a party in London, and when he heard that I had contacts at a publishing house here in Islamabad, he sent them to me. I'm putting together an anthology of Pakistani writing in extreme circumstances; during war, natural disasters, by prisoners of conscience, wrongfully accused terror suspects.' Maqil has to suppress a laugh at his dilettante efforts being associated with such heavy, worthy material, which gives him a brief look of discomfort; the young man interprets it as criticism or modesty, as he carries on almost apologetically: 'Of course, it's mostly poetry, rather dark in places, but your plays create a balance in tone, and they're the perfect length to include. And of course, I admire the plays greatly; the bittersweet comedy is deceptively poignant. The reviews they've got speak for themselves.' He sips his drink; Maqil has noticed from his breath that it is plain tonic with lemon, the sort of drink you order if you want to give the impression that you are drinking when you are not. He's not a big drinker himself, and does the same thing at weddings, after the first cocktail and before the champagne toast; he has seen card counters in the big casinos do it too. 'I've got to ask,' says the young man, 'how did you manage to get such amazing reviews for unpublished works? When I saw the review sheet to the plays, I couldn't quite believe it. I had to verify the sources. Such famous writers, the literary editors of *The Times* and the *Telegraph*; the ones I could get hold of all confirmed the reviews they had given.'

'Oh, those,' he repeats, aware that he is mocking himself a little. He allows himself a smile as he remembers the London days after prison, when he created drama simply because he was bored, and had given himself a mischievous little vanity project. 'That was easy. I looked them up, and drove around to all their houses, and told them that the plays were the work of my dying father, and it was his dream that his writing be read by them. Then I went around the next week, and told them that he was dead, and asked what they thought of his work. They obviously hadn't read the stuff, and if they had, they weren't going to say anything pejorative to a grieving son. I got some great reviews.' He grins, remembering the little play he had put on at all the doorsteps of these famous men and women, in their sitting rooms sobbing over English breakfast tea. 'Harold Pinter was the most difficult one. All he could come up with was "Your father's plays are a work of talent." Just that, "a work of talent". I put his review last.'

The young man looks uncomfortable for a moment, and then laughs. 'Zamir told me to watch out for you. He said that you were full of it.' He realises how impolite this sounds, and adds hastily, 'Full of funny stories, I mean.'

'I would think he meant bullshit,' Maqil corrects him pleasantly, not taking offence. 'And he'd usually be right. But honestly, that's how I got the reviews. I frankly think that getting them was as much a "work of talent" as the plays. Took me longer than writing them, anyway.' He adds, 'You do know, by the way, that in the UK I was just in prison for tax evasion.

Not for exposing government corruption or anything – that sort of thing happened years before, when I was a journalist back in the Middle East.'

'That sounds fascinating,' says the young man. 'You must tell me about it. Corruption. Terror. False Identities. Means to an End. It all makes for great reading.' This is the second time that the young man has needlessly included the word 'terror' in his conversation, and he has had no reason to include 'false identities' at all. Maqil looks at him rather sharply, more sharply than he intended, as the young man apologises: 'I'm sorry if I'm being indiscreet, or making assumptions, Mr Karam,' he says. 'Perhaps I've had a few too many,' and he drains his glass, and waves it ruefully.

'Not at all,' he says smoothly. 'You know, I'm not sure I caught your name.'

'Nasser Sulaiman Khalil,' he says. 'My friends call me NSK for short, but only in New York; I studied there.' He looks straight at Maqil now, and adds, 'When I was younger, I preferred just being called Khalil, or rather, Kal-El. Superman's real name. I liked the idea of being a superhero undercover.'

'I'm sure that Islamabad is the perfect place to be an undercover hero, Nasser,' he says, 'fighting crime while you play at being a mild-mannered publisher.' He gestures towards Nasser's empty glass of lemon and tonic. 'Would you like another?' he asks politely.

'I will if you'll join me,' replies Nasser, a bit too eagerly, in response.

'Oh, I'm too old to drink much these days,' he replies, waving to the waiter to come over. 'They say that the second sign of old age is getting hairs in your nostrils. The first sign is looking for them to begin with.' He takes a gin and tonic from the waiter's tray, and passes it to Nasser, adding conversationally, 'Did you know that the second sign of a cheat is someone keeping a clear head while pretending he's not? That's the second sign of someone not to trust.'

'What's the first sign?' asks Nasser, despite himself.

'It's obvious, isn't it? Looking out for the second sign to begin with . . .' he says, laughing. He moves away from the young man, towards his mother and brothers. 'Will you excuse me?' he says, with old-fashioned charm. As he turns around, he thinks he hears a surreptitious click behind him, part muffled by a dinner jacket, like a gun being taken off safety; he is almost certain now that the man who calls himself Nasser is working with the local police, that he has contacts in New York and London who are searching for the same suspicious group who contacted him about the passports to travel to the West. That he introduced himself to Zamir in order to get in touch with him. Maqil is glad that his head is still clear; if he was to collude with terrorists, however unwittingly, the very worst that would happen to him is that he would be put in jail until he died. But if terrorists thought he was giving information regarding them to the police, the consequences would be further reaching. More than old fashioned. Medieval, as they say in the movies. He remembers the story of a family from the north, back in the forties, who had defied the local landowner regarding their property boundaries; the men had been found bleeding to death in the fields with their genitals stuffed into their mouths, the women had been tied up with their children in their own saris, their house set on fire, and left to burn.

He carries on a conversation with his mother, his brothers, his sister, with his daughter and son and their partners. He talks to family and friends. He sees Samira's burnt-gold sari flashing as she works the room with the skill of a professional PR. He no longer feels that he is drifting around the crowd, but that he is standing quite still, and everyone and everything is circulating about him, like planets spinning around the sun. At the still centre of it all, he recognises that he does not belong here, or with anyone. His real self is already in Monte Carlo with the fake money at the tables, and he feels the impatient need to catch up with him. He notices Nasser, the undercover fan of his work, approaching him again, and he moves off quickly, disappearing into the milling guests and towards the kitchen exit.

'Well, you don't *know* they won't be happy. You're hardly an expert on marriage, Mum,' he hears Mika saying. 'You've had four of them.'

'I rather think it makes me more of an expert than someone who's never married at all,' replies Samira drily. 'And I hope it does work out for Zamir. I don't want to go through another one of these parties for him. Marriage is like pregnancy; once, quite frankly, is enough.' She spots Maqil as he moves past them through the crowd, and raises a hand, waving him over. He gives her a stricken, yearning look, but carries on to the door. She sees him at the exit, sees his face, and understands. He is unreliable, untrustworthy and irresponsible. He is going through the motions of being himself. I can't help it, he cries out to her silently, he calls to her with the thudding of his weak and congested heart, it's who I am. You of all people know this. It's in my nature. Mika is still talking to her mother; he sees the glint of her glasses and her surprisingly delicate profile, and Samira looks over her daughter's shoulder and raises her hand once more. 'Good luck,' she mouths. She is letting him go, but of course, she is used to it. He thinks of Bernadette, just briefly; she has got more from her trip to Pakistan than she ever dared to dream; she has got what she has been seeking all her life, a mother, a baby. He sees her being comforted by one, and comforting the other; she no longer needs him. The decision is made. The croupier in Monte Carlo calls out *Les Jeux Sont Faits*; the final bets have been placed and the ball is dancing around the roulette wheel with a silver flash. A pistol gleaming in a dark hand on a dark night. The crash of the moonlit waves, washing away the letters scraped into the sand. He nods at Samira, and slips through the door.

Paris – 2008 – Music

MAQIL IS AT THE OPERA IN PARIS, WATCHING *The Magic Flute*. Opera normally bores him to tears, but he was invited by an acquaintance, and decided he had better turn up for the snacks. He has stuffed his sagging hollow cheeks, his loose-skinned belly, and finally the crisply stitched pockets of his good suit with the careless, shameless greed of a roadie at a film shoot; '*Mais comme il est gourmand,*' say the other guests indulgently, the women sequinned and bejewelled, glittering by the private buffet like Christmas baubles. He likes the fact that in French, the word for greedy isn't the slightest bit pejorative, that you can praise a child who finishes off his *tarte aux pommes* for his *goûter* with exactly the same indulgent phrase, while cutting him another slice. In fact, he isn't greedy. He is hungry. He hasn't eaten properly for almost three days. Money no longer weighs him down, but now that he is approaching eighty, he notices the inconveniences of its absence. He is struggling to survive on the overpriced coffee of the capital; he has lost weight dramatically, and had his belt re-punched twice over to hold his trousers up. He is wearing his cashmere sweater under his suit jacket to fill it out properly. He is certain that he has shrunk in height even, that he can feel bones rather than soft padding on the soles of his feet, that the world seems somehow higher and bigger than it used to; he has to reassess his place in it, revise his judgement of distance and reach, like someone wearing their first pair of glasses. His face is becoming bony, bird-like and predatory, with a beak of a nose suddenly prominent in his sunken face; his hands look like his mother's spotted claws without the French manicure. It feels a hundred years since he was handsome; he had come to terms with spending much of his life as old, and ill; he is finding it harder to spend so much of his life as ugly. Young men look at him with curiosity, like some-thing ancient and undistinguished in a museum, surprised that such a thing still walks and talks and shits, that the decaying machine of his body still works, that the feeble heart still pumps blood adequately around his strangled arteries rather than letting it surrender to gravity and pool in his boots. Young women look at him with sympathy, and speak to him loudly and distinctly, as one might to a child, as Bernadette used to speak to Betsy in the care home; he once offered his seat to young ladies, but now they offer their seats to him, and stand up promptly when he shambles his way along the Métro carriage or bus aisle with his cane. He didn't seek out the cane himself – it was issued to him during his last stay in hospital. He was sent into the emergency ward when he collapsed on the street, and had the humiliation of being carried to the ambulance in a wheeled stretcher that looked like a baby's buggy. The ward was white and cheerless, but he surprised even himself by staying for the indifferent food that was carted to him by a hard-faced woman from Guadeloupe, resolutely un-made-up, but with elaborate cornrows and beaded braids that implied a hidden vanity – eating three meals a day suddenly seemed a pleasure rather than a chore, even though the vegetables were either canned or boiled to death, and he suffered from constipation for a week afterwards. He kept the cane when he discharged himself; it is white plastic with an ergonomic handle, and looks medical and temporary, a cane for someone who has suffered a minor setback. But in fact he has secretly started looking in the windows of an old-fashioned cane shop, with lovingly carved and waxed and varnished and polished examples, canes that might be for life rather than a Parisian Christmas. He obviously cannot afford any of them, and is considering the mechanics of shoplifting something so long and thin; he thinks that if he practises a straight-legged limp, he might be able to hide it down his trouser leg.

The Queen of the Night's aria begins, her notes shrill and as crisply cut as the glass diamond tiara she wears over her wig of tumbling gypsy tresses. She screeches melodically about sundering the ties of blood and kin; he has lost the baggage of his family as well, but he has noticed that this also has its inconveniences. He rather misses being looked after by Bernadette; when he had soup in a cheap Chinese restaurant the other day, he was almost in tears thinking about her, not so much as his wife, but as his nurse. His fragrant healer. It seems to him that no dish will ever be as fragrant and healing again as her Three Generations soup; he knows that she now prepares it for her new family in Lahore, for his mother, who treats her like a daughter, and for her three adopted children. Baby is still called Baby by everyone, but her official name, chosen by Bernadette, is Elizabeth Anne. After poor Betsy and her poor Mammy. She has taken on two others, from girls in trouble who sought help from Dr Kharnum's womens' clinic, where Bernadette now volunteers: a boy named Finnegan after her father, and another girl whom she has named Maryam for his own mother, and who is the darling of the family. Bernadette emails him with photos and updates him on their progress; she seems sad rather than angry about his absence, and still appears to be waiting for him. She would be shocked if she knew how he was living. The last thing he ate was a rotisserie chicken bought from an early-morning market; he had forgone his usual coffee at the George V, where he went daily, and spent the seven euros on food instead. He had felt his mouth fill with saliva on the walk back to his basement room (he would have preferred an attic room, but can't afford that either), and could barely wait until he was through the door before he tore apart the greasy paper, shiny and transparent with the rich oils oozing from the chicken's skin; he pulled the flesh from the bird and stuffed a first heavenly morsel into his mouth. He was so desperate for it he could barely stand up; his hands felt clumsy and in the way, and he had to resist the urge to fall on all fours on the floor and rip directly into the meat with his jaws like a slavering dog, as though it was prey. The full circle of the Sphinx riddle, the four legs of infancy and advanced senility. A civilised man who has regressed millennia, turned animal with age, barking madly at the moon. The aria ends, and the soprano playing the Queen of the Night stops howling herself, and sails off on her paper moon into the ocean of the velvet-draped night sky, backlit and pocked with stars; he reaches into his pocket, and pulls out a dainty savoury pastry from a serviette, filled with *rillettes de canard* and caramelised shallots, and munches on it. '*Je suis gourmand*,' he admits ruefully to those who share his box. '*Le canard, c'est ma faiblesse.*' It is embarrassing for him to admit that his body has needs, the basic need for food. He feels let down, unevolved; he has pills for everything but this. But they nod with approval. They see his suit and sapphire cufflinks, and assume he is a wealthy eccentric – the greed of a rich man at the opera is more socially acceptable than the hunger of a poor man in the street. Everyone trusts a man who eats.

He returns to his basement flat after midnight, and has difficulty opening the door; the mail that he hasn't answered all week is piled up on the mat, and making it stick. He bends with difficulty to pick it up; every time he bends over in this way, he wonders whether he will ever be able to get up again. It is like a daring little game of chance he plays several times a day. This time, he wins again, as he straightens his creaking back and spills the mail across the little table in the living room, which also contains the corner kitchen, and his folding metal bed dragged from the innards of the Clic-Clac sofa. He drops the invoices from the hospital in the bin, along with the bills for the water and electricity and gas. He glances with amusement at the threatening solicitor's letter from the phone company, imagining the wan face of the secretary who typed it out, who rubber-stamped the signature and sent it down for franking; he can see her lank hair and bitten nails, worn down by her quiet, disquieting job of threatening the impoverished or careless; then he drops that in the bin as well. He had been fond of quoting Oscar Wilde in his youth, albeit not quite brave enough to declare his genius at national borders; now he quotes him out loud to acquaintances he is not intending to trim or grift: 'I shall have to die beyond my means.' He finds a certain childish glee in leaving debts unpaid; he owes over a hundred thousand euros to the Ritz Hotels alone. He has got away with it all his life, and he is still getting away with it. He isn't dead yet.

He hangs his jacket up, and takes off his cashmere sweater, which he puts back in the small suitcase he keeps packed by the door. He goes to the bathroom to relieve his bladder, washes his hands scrupulously, and walks back in to find a young man sitting at the table looking at his remaining mail. The young man glances up at him and nods casually, as though he has been there the whole time. An appearance as sudden and flawlessly executed as a magic trick: now you see me, now you don't. He might have simply risen up through the floorboards. Materialised. Maqil looks at the front door, the case standing by it, and at the young man who is sitting in the way, nonchalantly blocking the exit. There is a window, but it is covered with ornate bars to discourage burglars, and to protect the glass from the cans and rubbish that adolescents throw down the stairwell. There is another small window in the bathroom that he is not nimble enough to climb through. There is no way out, and so he offers his unexpected visitor a drink.

'That's very kind of you,' says Nasser. 'What do you have?'

'Tea, or coffee. Or tonic water, if you like,' he replies, moving to the cupboard above the kitchen area, which is just a sink, a hotplate and a small fridge, with a plug-in oven on top. He sees that his guest is armed by the way his jacket his hanging; he is surprised that he has the authority to bear arms in France.

'Just tonic water will be fine,' says Nasser. 'I don't want to put you to any trouble.'

'I've moved addresses every other month for the last six years because of you, and now you don't want to put me to any trouble?' he replies, pulling the bottle of tonic out of the low fridge, wincing as he rises with it, and taking two tumblers of thick green glass from the cupboard.

'To any *more* trouble, then,' says Nasser, showing his surprisingly white teeth with a grin. He looks terribly pleased with himself, and can't stop chatting when his tonic is brought over, expansively indicating the other seat for his host. 'I almost can't believe we've finally got you. We just missed you in Monte Carlo. We thought we had you in Madrid, but we were too late. And it turned out you were never in Prague – you wouldn't believe the paperwork you have to go through to hunt down someone in Prague.' He raises his glass to Maqil, who just looks at him impatiently, and sips his own drink.

'You say that like I'm a fugitive, but I'm not. I keep telling you people that I know nothing. I never did. I just pushed around a little paper, that's all. It was more of a hobby than anything else.'

'I never said you were a fugitive. But it seems that you're protesting a little too much, given that you live on the run, and keep a packed bag by the door and a passport in your jacket.'

'I'm running because of you. And I've always kept a packed bag by the door and a passport in my jacket,' he replies crossly. 'Ask any of my wives.' He drains his tonic water, and thumps the glass on the table, finally feeling free to act like what he has become, a belligerent old man. 'It's *Foucault's Pendulum*, that's what this has become. You should read it sometime, seeing how fond you are of fiction. It's smoke without fire. You're convinced I know something, so THEY'RE convinced I know something, and everyone's after me and baying for my blood, and it's just a French farce because I haven't any blood left, and what I know is precisely nothing at all.'

'Given all that, you'll be safer in custody. And seeing as you've avoided all our legitimate attempts to contact you, I have no idea what you do or don't know. I'm only here to protect you, after all. We'll have you extradited to Pakistan – your family can visit.'

'They'll get to me in custody. Here, there or anywhere. In Pakistan it'll be so easy, there's hardly any sport to it. A sitting target in a cell. You may as well paint a bull's-eye on my forehead.' He gestures towards the weapon in his guest's jacket. 'Why don't you just do it now, and save everyone the trouble?'

'That's rather dark, for someone like you. You know, Mr Karam, this is a good day for me. Finally. My career's been a study in failure since the first time I laid eyes on you and lost you in a crowd. My colleagues make jokes about me. And you're making this a lot less enjoyable for me than it could be,' replies Nasser. He drinks his own tonic, and stands up. 'So, are you ready?'

Maqil feels an overwhelming panic, and looks around the room for a mirror, somewhere he can catch his own eye and seek reassurance in reflection. He may as well face it: this is the beginning of his end. Well overdue, but he was never one to pay his debts on time, hardly one to pay his debts at all. He is as disappointed in his fear as he is by his hunger; he feels let down by himself, diminished and unoriginal. He had believed he was someone extraordinary, and now it seems, all these long years that he has been sought by others, that he has simply been an ordinary man seeking himself. Navel-gazing, looking dewily into his own eyes, looking again and again, and yet seeing nothing. He thinks of all the languages he does not speak and will never understand. He thinks of the gifts he has squandered; perhaps he was not so gifted, after all. 'No, I'm not ready,' he says. 'Could we talk, just for a moment?'

'You're not going to talk your way out of this one,' his guest replies bluntly. 'So put your charm back in its box and let's go.'

'I don't need charm any more,' he says. 'I've got something much more powerful. Pity. People see me doddering around on my own and pity me. I pity myself, even.' He sighs. 'I really just want to talk. If it wasn't you here, but one of them, sitting with that gun pointed to my head, I'd still want to talk. I need a confessor, and I've no one here but you.'

'What do you want to confess?' asks the young man, interested despite himself, leaning over the table. He clearly expects some secrets to be spilled, red and bubbling like blood; he thinks he is due some luck, and that his good day is about to get better. A hero's return. A prisoner. A confession. A closed case.

'That I've been bad,' he says simply, like a child. 'I've been a bad son, a bad husband, a bad father. That I've been shallow and selfish. I've let down those who relied upon me, I've deceived people who liked and trusted me. And the real pity of it, even now that it's all coming to an end, is that I don't even feel sorry. I don't feel remorse. I have to confess that I've enjoyed my life. My bad life. It's given me an indecent amount of pleasure.'

'Are you confessing, or boasting?' interrupts Nasser, but he sits back down in his chair.

'I'm not boasting,' he protests. 'I'm just trying to explain that I don't think it's my fault. The way I am. I wasn't lucky enough to be good, and so I turned out to be bad. It's . . . in my nature. I don't know what other way to be. I'm always the man just about to walk out of the door, with my suitcase packed. I'm the man who is good value at parties, and remembers to tip the staff, even if it's with my last dollar. I don't know how to be an ordinary man, with a house and a job and a family. I don't know how to be a man; how to protect, and provide.' He shrugs helplessly. 'Maybe I was just wired wrong.' He gets up and takes their glasses to the sink, and neatly putting on rubber gloves, he washes them with cheap lemon-scented washing-up liquid, and then dries and replaces them in the cupboard. He wears the gloves to wash up because of his eczema, a raw red river bubbling over the backs of his hands, like a living parasite sinking into his skin; the gloves are an absurd pink that seems somehow clinical rather than feminine, and as he pulls them off with an elastic twang and smack, he notices that his guest is still wearing his outdoor gloves. It is cold outside, and it is cold inside, so the gloves are not unusual, but with this banal observation he feels a flicker of disquiet. He wonders if the young man has been advised not to contaminate the scene, so they can seek evidence of his supposed criminal associates; the explanation seems

312

plausible, and he wonders what he is trying to persuade himself of, what he is deliberately failing to acknowledge.

The young man watches him wash up, and his eyes brighten briefly as the glasses are put away, as though he has had an idea, something that has occurred to him for the first time. It is the idea that he was never here; that the best day of his career is still before him. He isn't enjoying this as much as he thinks he deserves; anticipation is almost always greater than the act. After a moment, he says, 'Perhaps you didn't try. To be a man. To protect and provide.'

'Oh, I tried,' he replies. 'Perhaps not hard enough. And now it's too late, of course. Because here you are. And here I am. And this is what's become of all the people I ever was.' He looks around the desolate apartment, at the young man facing him, and remembers once upon a time, a long time ago, when he had been the young man sitting on a bed in a desolate apartment, and his uncle had appeared to send him back to Pakistan. And now the roles are reversed, but he is still being sent back to where he belongs. A Pakistani home. A Pakistani jail. To eventual death. The difference doesn't seem so significant any more. 'And you know what I'd really like to say? To all of them. To the ones I let down. To the ones who are missing. I'd like to say Forgive Me. I'd like to say it again and again, I'd like to hear it echo around the walls. I'd like it to ring like church bells across Paris, London, Lahore and the whole wide world. Forgive Me. Forgive Me.' He remembers running in a park, and falling down at his front door, the first time he died, though it was just for a few seconds. Life, London, Love. His life isn't flashing before his eyes; instead the memories stream around him, like fish raising their heads to the surface before sinking back into the depths and swimming away. Death, Paris, Despised. There is something complete about it, after all. Somewhere, far away, a bell is ringing, as lonely as a dog barking at the headlights of a lorry passing in the night, wishing he were something more ancient and extraordinary, a wolf howling at a full moon. 'And I wouldn't want a dramatic scene. Some huge party where they all welcome me back with open arms. A crowd with balloons and banners at the airport. I just want to sit across a table like this from my daughter, and ask her how she's doing. Whether she's really planning on marrying that dull young man. I want to ask my son how it feels now that he's going to be a father himself; whether he feels what I never could. Whether they worry about their futures, and how to live their lives. I never really spoke to them. I never really spoke to anyone, when I come to think of it. Not like I'm speaking to you. I just entertained them, and then withdrew when they bored me.' He sighs, finally. 'And now it's too late. I was never a whole man. I was an almost-man, and I'm almost dead.' He stands and picks up his jacket from the chair, and starts shrugging it on. 'Don't worry. I'm not expecting you to forgive me on their behalf. I think I'm ready now.'

'An almost-man, almost dead,' repeats his guest thoughtfully, as he stands himself and removes his firearm from his own jacket. 'But you know, Mr Karam, you're not dead yet.' He places his standard-government-issue weapon on the table between them, and sits back down. He confides with careless intimacy, 'I took the tip myself; the team don't know I'm here. It's within my powers to deal with this myself, tidily. To save everyone the trouble, as you said.' He studies his gun gleaming in the dull light, as though he doesn't like what he sees, as though he is a photographer who has composed an ineffective shot. His seated pose now seems awkward rather than casual, and then there is a clicking under the table, muffled by his jacket. It is the same clicking noise that Maqil remembers hearing at the engagement party all those years ago, like a gun being taken off safety. It occurs to him that his well-connected guest might have another weapon concealed on his person, one that is non-standard issue, untraceable.

'Oh,' Maqil replies blandly, with comprehension. 'I see. You're not just on the side of the law. You work for them as well.' It seems it will be his final night after all. It seems his confession was better timed than he thought. He feels a physical weight fall from him, and he stands straighter, knowing that he is soon to be unburdened more fully. His shoulders drop an inch. He doesn't feel slightly afraid any more. He feels like a rich boy who's finally been let out to play in the street; to roll in the mud and run with ragamuffins, and play at cowboys and Indians. It is an adventure. He is Peter Pan, and he hasn't grown up after all. Death is just another adventure. He does not know if there will be darkness or light on the other side. Black or red. Place your bets.

'You don't sound that surprised,' comments his guest, obviously ill at ease; he is sweating slightly despite the cold air of the apartment. Maqil, finally so comfortable in his skin, feels sorry for his guest, and wonders if it is Nasser's first blood. He cannot imagine what it would be like to squeeze the life from someone with a trigger, or slice it out with a knife. He has never raised his hand in anger, although when he was a child he was instructed to slap his younger brothers if they were bothering little sister Uma. Even this he did with uninterested obedience, a slap-flap of a hand that he didn't really mean: '*É!* Stop tormenting her. Go play in the garden,' he would say in a bored voice, barely raising his eyes from his comics, as his baby sister rolled on the mat in front of him, and her ayah fussed with preparing mashed red lentils and rice for her lunch. He glances at his guest, his aggressor, and is suddenly irritated by his unease; he isn't playing his role properly. Maqil hopes he isn't incompetent, and that he is capable of making a clean shot. He doesn't want to have to drag himself around the basement flat like a wounded stag.

315

'It's not that surprising,' he snaps. 'Another corrupt police-man. Another politician on the take. Another writer in a café. Another woman on a diet. Big deal. I guessed anyway; I was wondering why you still had your gloves on. Wet work, is that what they call it, in your profession?'

'I said, the team don't know I'm here,' Nasser repeats deliberately, as though he's been misunderstood. 'Don't you see, no one else is coming for you. I didn't tell the local police I'd found you. And I didn't tell Them anything, seeing as I have no idea who They might be. I'm not terribly flattered by your opinion that I'm colluding with terrorists, but from what you've said, it sounds like it's all been in your head. *Foucault's Pendulum*. It was my instruction to take you into protective custody, but it seems you mainly need protecting from yourself. You'd be able to refuse our protection, like any free citizen, but it could be a long legal process. I think it's tidier this way, like I said.' He steps back, and allows Maqil a clear path to the door, his suitcase beside it.

'You're letting me go?' he asks for confirmation, finally understanding, almost disappointed. The game isn't about to end after all. And he feels tired once more.

'I'm beginning to wonder whether I could be less predictable myself. I've spent years looking for you, and I've always done things by the book. Never broken the rules. And now I've found you, I suppose I can afford to bend the rules a little after all. I can do something extraordinary. I can let you go. I can let you try, really try, before you die.'

Maqil has underestimated the power of sincerity, his powers of persuasion. His charm. His famous bloody charm. It isn't to be the death of him, after all. He walks swiftly to the door, and picks up his case. 'So, what will happen to you?' He supposes he should feign concern, just to be polite.

'Do you really care?' his guest replies with interest. 'You see, you're trying already.' He picks up the firearm he left on the table, and replacing it in his jacket, begins to fasten his buttons. 'The team will believe me when I say I lost you again; it's the great thing about having established a reputation for ineptitude over the last few years. Another near miss won't surprise anyone. Perhaps I'll quit and do something different with my life. I might run the family farm. Or start a small publishing house.' He adds, with a smile, 'I might even publish those plays of yours. They're a work of talent, after all.' He puts his hand in his pocket, and Maqil hears that clicking sound, and freezes; his discomfort shows enough for Nasser to notice it, and he pulls out a silver lighter apologetically, clicking it once more. 'Sorry, a nervous habit. And a disgusting one, I know. Don't worry, I'll wait until I'm outside before I smoke.'

'Goodbye, then,' Maqil says at the door. '*Khuda hafiz*,' he adds in Punjabi, before he pulls it shut behind him. The young man was right: it was just in his head, after all. There is something both tragic and comical about it, that all this time he has been running away from a plot of mainly his own making. All the same, he walks out into the dark Parisian night, astonished that he is still free. Astonished that he has talked his way out of it, without even trying that hard. He has refused safe passage home in protective custody; he has refused to be saved, even from himself. Saying goodbye to the young man who has been chasing him feels like saying goodbye to his younger self. Is it possible that all either of them were ever seeking was simply a better man than the one he has become? He imagines, as he drags his case through the streets with his cane tapping in time to a barking hound, to the intermittent stringed screeching of a cat fight and the low drone of late-night traffic, what it would have felt like to have cold metal pressed to his temple. To hear the shot. To leave the brittle prison of his skeleton, to break out of the slack, papery walls of flesh and skin. Blown to the stars

317

he has been staring at from the gutter, a firework made from funeral ash. He thinks it would have felt like becoming music, something ephemeral set free from the cage of the dotted-dashed page, from the black-and-white bars of notation, bursting with a joyous explosion; a melody released to fly into the night air, higher and higher in increasing echoing circles, like the golden, celebratory pealing of church bells, touching those they pass with the intimacy of warm breath. With Happiness. Is he happy? He must be. He's a man with a song in his heart.

Biarritz, France – 2012 – Reflection

TODAY HAS BEEN A DAY LIKE MANY OTHERS. I HAVE A routine of sorts here, haunting the hotels and bars of Biarritz like a daylight ghost, disappearing from one place and appearing in another, now you see me, now you don't, just waiting for the night, to put on the show of being Magnificent Me at the gaming tables. I make my own company more bearable by telling stories – I once had a reputation for being quite talented at this, for being good value at parties. It passes the time, and it's eminently affordable, given my straitened circumstances. Talk is cheap, as I've said before. You'll forgive me for repeating myself, for telling the same stories, day after day; it's what old men do, after all. Just like all those dull old duffers who drone on about the war, as though there hasn't been a war since, as though we're not at war right now, all the time, inside and out. I'm no war hero, or casualty of conflict; I'm not pretending that there's any meaning behind my chatter – there is no searing truth, no great tragedy to be sought, no historic misdeed to be exposed. It's just entertainment, that's all. Every day is as dismissible and delightful as entertainment. My son is concerned by my conspicuous lack of occupation and so he asks me across café tables, down twanging copper lines, through wireless connections that break down and reassemble his heavy sigh for my benefit, 'What do you *do*, Abbu?' He and his sister asked me the same question when they were children, as they had no idea what I did for a living, and didn't know what to tell their friends or teachers when it came up. Well, this is my Final Answer, as they say on that quiz show; I watch the French version here before dinner, *Qui Veut Gagner Des Millions?*. I like the host – I used to watch him presenting game shows in the eighties when I gambled in Monte Carlo; he's been around for years, just like me. I was once a journalist, a literary club director, an investment rainmaker, a prisoner, a counterfeiter, an internet entrepreneur. I was once a son, a husband, a father. And now I'm a Storyteller. Final Answer. Much like that play I wrote years ago, there are just three of us in this story – the one who sits patiently and listens, the one doing the telling, and the one who is talked about – we're all here, in this poorly stuffed chair, in this poorly filled suit. You and Me and He. Magnificent Me has become Magnificent We. There's a term for this demented psychological condition of mine – this habit of talking to myself and hearing voices – but I'm not sure it's anything as clever and complicated as that. I think it's as simple and straightforward as Loneliness. Old and Alone, Dying and Done For. But Not Dead Yet. It is difficult to admit, even now, that perhaps I didn't get it right, after all. That my own company wasn't always the best, and that there might have been a better life carrying on somewhere else; that it is carrying on right now, waiting for me to join it. I've known this for a long time, and never tried hard enough to do anything about it. I should, perhaps, try, just as I promised that young man. Some small part of me should try.

The truth is that I am too old to try. The truth is that I would rather speak than act. The words are prettier than the deed, just as the lilting lyrics of love songs are prettier than the music of making love itself, with the associated grunt and squash of fleshy organs. I know that the sporadic contact I now keep with my family is as much of an inconvenience to them as it is to me. I know that I'm an embarrassment, because I'm still living on my wits and on occasional good luck in France, running up sky-high hospital bills that I will never pay, and refusing to go home to my constant wife in Pakistan; refusing to go home and die. My mother passed away in the Lahore townhouse earlier in the year, with Bernadette sponging her brow and holding her hand until the end, her midwife's role reversed: she no longer helped people come into the world, but instead helped them to take leave of it. I heard that Bernadette was given the household keys, one by one, during my mother's fortunately brief illness, and that after the funeral, she wore them all at her waist as my mother had once done, to honour her, like an old-fashioned Punjabi matriarch. No one in the family had objected; they were grateful to have Bernadette take over the running of the house; they were even more grateful to have had a full-time carer, free of charge. They treated her with all the respect that the wife of the firstborn son was due. They have even become unreasonably fond of her adopted ragbag of children, whose skinny calves and dark skin must give away their roots, but whose carefully chosen names and good manners reveal the quality of their care. The family know that I occasionally look at my anonymous email, and urge me again and again to come home. My son seeks me out, meets me for coffee, and even sends me money on the sly, without telling his mother or sister or wife, and I'm so embarrassed at being dependent on these occasional payouts, and the affectionate nagging that goes with them – 'What do you *do*, Abbu? All day, out there on your own' – that sometimes I'll hang up on him before the money transfer is made. I make excuse after excuse to avoid meeting my grandson (they have called him Boo, a ridiculous name, and I can't remember what it might be short for; he was Baby Boo when he was born, and now that he can totter, he is called Little Boo instead). I'm worried that the long-awaited interview would disappoint both Zamir and the child, or else that I would be disappointed myself. I say that I'm too unwell, that the flu might well finish me off, and that I can't risk catching nursery germs from the toddler; this seems plausible, as everyone appears to think I should take better care of my health, and from all reports the child has a constant sniffle and streaming nose. But even if I wasn't old and ill, and the infant wasn't suspiciously snivelling, there would still be disappointment, because what Zamir so desperately wants from this meeting could never happen: my grandson will never leap joyously into my arms, and I will never swing him in the air with the bluff jolliness of Santa Claus, and we will never laugh together in a flower-filled meadow with a happiness as pure and redeeming as holy water flowing through a holy land. All that would happen is that we would meet, in a hotel, or bar, or café, and the child might or might not cry when presented to an elderly, ugly stranger, and there would be some stilted conversation; the waiter would take the shot of when Little Boo met Grandpa, and we would tick that box, say goodbye, and get on with our lives. The truth is that they do not need me. They just need the idea of me, and that is enough. The idea of a grandfather, a father, a husband. They want no more from me than a photo in the family album with a caption underneath. They are waiting for me to die, as though my life has been a nasty illness, and death is the only relief to be offered.

I pity them as much as they pity me; we are bound together, and they will not be relieved until I die either; and at my death, I will finally stop being an embarrassment, and evolve into the subject of an amusing cautionary tale, delivered with an indulgent, rueful shaking of the head. A caricature as much as a character. An anecdote. A story.

Unfortunately, I am unable to oblige them. I'm still capable of enjoying life on occasion, and sometimes I enjoy it indecently. I gamble with the merry recklessness of someone who has nothing left to lose; I lift money from those soft or stupid enough to let me; I am capable of being as corrupt and furtive as a painting in an attic. The truth is, I don't know any other way to be – I can't help myself. I can't stop living. I know how to die, but I simply cannot. I suspect now that I will end with a whimper, rather than a bang; that I will never feel that cold finality of a firearm pressed to my temple. I will not burst into flames like a firework, or pop like a confetti-filled balloon. I will keep walking, talking and occasionally shitting. I will keep my heart tick-tocking, my organs functioning and my tissues moist with appropriate medications. And in the midst of this business of living I will simply recede, the party balloon shrinking and shrivelling into a damp rag; I will be gradually rubbed away like a bloodstain on a carpet, trod over and trodden in, until as faint as memory, but never completely erased. I could carry on like this for years. I might carry on for ever.

'Why did you pick that address?' I ask my daughter, over coffee, during an awkward lull in the conversation. She has recently started seeking me out as well – rather less often than Zamir, and only because she doesn't want to appear lacking by comparison; she is normally the one who performs the small social duties, who sends the birthday greetings to elderly aunts, who puts spare presents of liqueur chocolates and bath crystals under the Christmas tree in case visitors surprise them with unbidden gifts that courtesy requires they reciprocate. When she emails me about a possible meeting, she makes the point that she isn't going out of her way for me, that she happens to be in Paris for business and has an hour to kill; that although she feels obliged to let me know she is there, I shouldn't feel obliged to turn up. Her carefully worded combination of duty and dignified detachment annoys me so much that I usually do turn up; besides, I like the train journey into Paris, the break to my routine. I notice the curious looks she gives me, at the hair dividing over my collar, the missing button on my shirt; she is still unfailingly polite and refuses to comment on any of these lapses. She sits across the table from me, her hair shining and neat, her suit pale grey, her glasses light and fashionable. She wears a modest amount of make-up: some powder on her nose, lipstick in a muted shade of beige. She is suddenly a stranger to me, except for the polite smile lines etched faintly from nose to chin like brackets, even when she isn't politely smiling. She has grown up. I only knew her as a child, I spent almost ten years living in the same apartment with her as Samira raised her, and I find it hard to find traces of the child I knew in the composed woman before me. This is just another brief meeting in Paris, not the first, not the last, but it seems to me that they all blend together into the same grey afternoon. She doesn't appear to care, not in the way Zamir obviously does; I really am just another small social duty to be crossed off her list. Still, I find it much less uncomfortable to meet with her than Zamir – her coldness is reassuring, and she does not try to hug me, or offer me money – but I cannot have the thrilling conversations with her that I once imagined; I never do ask her why she married that dull young man, the milk-faced accountant, although I look at the photographs from the wedding with interest, posted online for friends and family to order. Samira is with another gentleman companion in a tailored suit; her latest escort is younger than me, but who isn't these days? He could even be younger than her; it is hard to tell, when she continues to look so good for her age. I talk with my daughter about small things: the weather, my health, suddenly remembered fragments from our briefly shared past that illuminate this inanimate present, another stilted rendezvous at a café, on stiff wooden chairs. I imagine that she has a list she goes through; notes for our conversation that she has prepared alongside the notes for her Parisian meetings in the industrial suburbs. I feel myself fading away before her eyes – a ghost of my previous self. I would rather be truculent than translucent, and so I try to shock her, or embarrass her; sometimes I'm downright rude, and play the part of my Chacha Zafri, an elderly Punjabi dangerously teetering on the edge of bigotry. I dare her to storm off in a temper and abandon me. But she is impossible to offend – she refuses to engage with me, to play the game; like Samira, she frustratingly ends the possibility of any dispute with feigned agreement, cheating me of the fun that might be had from a quarrel.

'What address?' she asks. Her face is perfectly blank, and I realise that she has misunderstood my question. She thinks I am asking for information about her home address, which she hasn't given me since she moved following her marriage. I haven't asked for it, and I wonder if her withholding it is some passive-aggressive punishment for all the years that I withheld my address from her. I owe my children years of past addresses. In fact, she hasn't asked for my current address either. Zamir asks me all the time, and so I come prepared with an excuse, that I have to move out the next day because of the heating or rats, and haven't decided where I'm going next, that the hotel name is something complicated in Basque and I haven't got the right spelling – but I never need these excuses for Mika. I'm fully aware that it is childish of me to keep this Post-it-note speck of information to myself; after all, both she and Zamir know I'm in Biarritz – I've always liked the faded glamour of the resort, and now the slightly warmer weather in the south makes me feel less stiff when I move, and it is not so expensive out of season – and they could probably guess that wherever I am living, it is within walking distance of the casino. Mika has a more practical reason to keep her address to herself – she probably suspects that I will use the information in some subversive way: borrow against her assets, or sell her house from under her. She thinks the worst of me, although she would never say this to my face. I know for a fact that she once cancelled a credit card after one of our meetings, when she saw me glance at it on the table; she assumed I was memorising her number. I know that she disapproves of Zamir giving me money; I suppose she thinks pragmatically that if they can starve me out of France, I'll go back to Pakistan, and be less of an embarrassment. And of course, once I'm back in Pakistan, these small social visits on her part would no longer be feasible or required.

'Not *your* address,' I say impatiently, as though she is being precious or unreasonable in some way. 'That email address you picked out for me. AddresseeunknownXXIX, et cetera et cetera.'

'Oh that,' she says. 'It was so long ago, I can hardly remember.' She stirs her coffee slowly, and finally lets the spoon clatter on the saucer. 'Sonnet Twenty-Nine,' she replies eventually. 'Shakespeare's Sonnet Twenty-Nine. I came across it one day, and thought of you and Mum.'

'Sonnet Twenty-Nine,' I repeat with interest. 'Do you remember how it goes?'

'No,' she says briefly, and as though worried that she might have been rude, softens her reply immediately. 'I'm afraid I don't.'

'Perhaps I'll look it up. In a library. Or online,' I say, just making conversation, without any intention of really doing so.

'As you wish,' says Mika. She rummages in her handbag, and finds a tissue, to blow her nose daintily; she rubs off a little of her powder, and I see that her nose has been reddening with the icy air. Her mobile beeps, reminding her that her next meeting will be starting shortly, and she gathers her things. I stand up with old-fashioned courtesy when she does, and she gives me a quick look that seems to be neither curiosity nor concern. She can see how shabby I look today, and she is taking the measure of my mortality. It is obvious that I'm not looking after myself any more, not the way that Bernadette did. Perhaps she thinks, perhaps she hopes, that every meeting she has with me will be the last. 'Do you have any regrets?' she asks suddenly, breaking role, breaking our rules of engagement. It is a question I would expect at a deathbed, not in a stale suburban café, where everything somehow smells of fag ash even though cigarettes have been banned from cafés for years.

'What?' I say, buying time before I need to answer. 'Sorry, I didn't hear that?'

'Oh, no, nothing,' she says, perhaps relieved by my transparent evasiveness. 'I'd better get going.' She puts her mobile away, and turns to face me. 'Regarding the sonnet,' she says cautiously, as she pecks me politely on the cheek, her lips barely touching me, the tip of her nose cold against my skin. 'A warning. A spoiler alert. I don't really remember it, but I suspect that it may not be too flattering. I think I thought I was being clever when I picked it.'

After that promising little review, I decide to look it up anyway. I find it in both French and the original English in a nearby web café, while I wait for my train. I laugh out loud, a little bitterly, at the opening, and find myself a little weepy at the end, like a teenage girl at a romantic movie. I never thought I would live long enough to get sentimental over poetry. On my train back to Biarritz, I lean against the cold glass of the window, and watch the grey suburbs and weedy greenery beside the railway line move by in a blur, exposed in the harsh white light. Fragments of the sonnet ripple back to me in wide circles, stones thrown into a pond. *In Disgrace with Fortune*, I think, my temple damp with the condensation against the window. *My Outcast State*, I repeat silently as I accept a cup of indifferent coffee from the beverage cart that rolls heavily down the aisle. *My Bootless Cries*, I mouth to myself, as I study the slack pudding faces of the middle-aged couple sitting opposite. I blow across the top of my coffee, a gesture that is prompted by habit rather than necessity, as the coffee is already lukewarm, and sip it. *Myself Almost Despising.* The brutal frankness of these cold-tipped, pointed words; Mika has always had this hard quality to her, a brittle nut hidden behind her chocolate-smooth veneer. It is probably my fault, the result of my wayward genes, if not the straightforward consequence of my abandonment. She never got to be Daddy's girl. I begin doodling down the side of a newspaper, first drawing the sad couple across the table, but then find myself writing out the last two lines of the sonnet, and staring at what I have written, as though it is something I have just composed myself, and am dissatisfied with: . . . *For thy sweet love remember'd such wealth brings, That then I scorn to change my state with kings.* Once upon a time, He loved Her. And She loved Him back. It is something I have never forgotten; even though I now know that love isn't enough. I used to assume that my daughter never knew me at all. But now, and in the routine days that follow, I wonder whether she perhaps knew me better than either of us thought, but just didn't like what she saw.

It has been a day like many others, just as I said, and tonight has been a night like many others, too. I went out to gamble in

328

my glad rags, and now I have finally returned to the hotel through the darkly shimmering rain-softened streets. The road up and the road down are the same. The defiant vigour I felt on leaving this evening, tapping my cane flamboyantly, has been wrung, dripping, out of me. I have lost almost everything, and only have about three hundred euros left, enough to cover me for a couple of days. Tonight. Tomorrow. The Day After. I have until the day after tomorrow to work out how to get more. Mika would refuse to give me any money; she would offer a flight to Pakistan instead. Payment in kind. Zamir will give me money if I ask him, followed by his plaintive questioning, his echoing plea, eerily reminiscent of my mother: 'What do you *do*, Abbu? All day, out there on your own? Why are you doing this to yourself? You've got to look after yourself. You've got to go home and let us look after you.' Zamir's wife keeps a holiday home in Pakistan, and they are thinking of moving there permanently; she has never liked London, and both her parents are ill. Zamir has never lived in Pakistan, but has started referring to it as home, a habit that must irritate Samira beyond words. But he can't help it – he is who he is. He was always more of a Punjabi than I was – wherever we brought him up, he would always have been a good Asian boy, a boy who loves his parents and works in a bank. I open my valise, always packed in case someone decides to come after me, although I am sure that I am no longer a priority for my creditors or any ongoing investigations following that Hong Kong business; perhaps they assume I must already be dead. About one third of my case is now dedicated to various medicines; in the end, it all comes down to this. The bits and pieces that urge my heart to keep beating, my kidneys to keep filtering, my digestive system to gather energy from my erratic diet, my bowel to push out the waste with more or less success. Sleeping and eating are no longer enough to keep me alive. Without the pills and powders and jabs, administered in a timely fashion and appropriate order, I would simply stop working; I would simply drop down dead. I have never been tempted to miss a pill or a powder; I have never been tempted to take more than I need. Not once.

I look at the letter I started this evening, before I went out. Our story, his and mine. My debt, in the simplest sense – as it is what I owe. I'm not tired, and so I begin writing again. It is no longer such a struggle; it feels almost a relief. I'm close to finishing when I'm distracted by what I see in the mirror. It is as though my own reflection is trying to catch my eye. I am hearing a voice again, a low, irritating voice, and eventually I decide that the best way to dismiss it is to acknowledge it out loud; after all, I'm alone in a room, so there's no one around who'll think I've gone mad. 'Yes, yes, what is it?' I ask testily, like an impatient headmaster interrupted by an idiot child during assembly. I'm satisfied by the surprised silence that follows, and carry on writing. But a few minutes later, the voice begins again, whining in the background. After a while I realise what it is saying. The voice is calling my name. One of them. All of them. The voice is multiplying, and my various names are echoing around me, like the ringing of church bells. I try to finish off what I'm doing, but I'm thinking of Mika now, of her unnaturally smooth hair and our wasted conversations; I think about the time, just a few days ago, when I failed to answer the only honest question she had ever asked me. 'So, *do* you have any regrets?' I ask out loud, to the man in the mirror, my most constant and sympathetic listener over the years. I feel that I'm no longer in my chair at the desk, or pinned behind the glass with my reflection, but somehow filling the space between us, like dust suspended in the air. Me, He, We. That I am the delirious music of my name pealing and leaping around the room, everywhere and nowhere all at once. That I am as insubstantial as the dancing, glancing fairy lights that I suddenly see spinning around the room, as though thrown from a mirror ball.

'Just one,' the reflection replies. 'I shouldn't have had the children.' I stop to see if this statement will shock any of my fragmented selves that are in the room, but it doesn't. Perhaps it is for the best that Mika never heard the answer to her question. 'We'd have carried on together if it wasn't for the children. And the fact is that I could have lived without them. I did live without them; quite easily as it happened. But I found it hard to live without her.'

The voices are converging, becoming louder and insistent, shouting my names less melodically and more urgently. All my names, all at once, a deep, compelling chant, like a cry for help from the bottom of a well. I am being called, and called, and called again. It is irresistible. It does not feel that I am being called to account; it feels rather that I am being called to another place, to that magical room with my name marked on it under a gold-leaf star, to the party in my honour. To the more wonderful life I have missed out on. The others are scratching on the window in frustration, outside and looking in, unable to join the celebration. I cannot hold out any longer; at last I reply, and shout back, 'All right, all right. I'm coming.' As firmly as though I were mountain rescue, with a rope and foil blankets and hydration sachets, as though I have someone to save. And with these words, my body crackles and fizzes with electricity. With fireworks. My face falls slack and lopsided, the arm holding the pen drops limply to the table, and when I repeat, 'I'm coming,' my voice is slow and slurred and blurred, as though I am shouting underwater. I can hear the cheap clock on the dresser, tick-tocking. The voices are still murmuring around me, saying their thoughts out loud, as though there might be a ventriloquist with a puppet body slumped at the desk of this rented room. He loved Her, the voices say, He must have. It matters that He loved Her. It matters that She loved Him back. My muscles loosen, my clenched hand opens as gently as a flower; the pen I have been holding falls, and rolls across the letter. I am no longer able to smile, not even with the half of my face that remains in place, but something in me is smiling, something deep down and unharmed, a chip of bone, an ooze of marrow, as I watch the man in the mirror dissolve to grey shadow, in the world beyond the glass. I'm a child in the womb, once more, buried in ink and blood, waiting to see if there might be darkness, or light, on the other side. Black or Red. I've waited too long for this; this time, I'll take a chance. I'm coming, says the chip of bone, the ooze of marrow, those bits of us that persist stubbornly, for a few minutes, when everything else is broken. I'm here.

Lahore, Pakistan – 2012 – Funeral

THE FUNERAL LOOKS LIKE IT WILL BE SURPRISINGLY WELL attended. Zamir sits in the Lahore house, struggling with the speech he has to give. Mika cannot attend at short notice, and she points out that she saw their father just a few days before, when he was still alive; she does not think he would be that concerned whether she turns up now he is dead. She will not, she says, go out of her way for him. He supposes that she has made a private vow not to let her father's wayward actions disrupt her life, not to let him get away with it, whatever it is, even on this day of all days, the day that he will be wrapped and scented and go into the ground.

'Say he died in Paris,' Mika tells him on the phone. 'He'd have preferred to have died in Paris.'

'But that's not what happened,' protests Zamir. 'It's not the truth. And what I really wanted to say was—'

'No one cares about the truth,' interrupts Mika, with the

directness reserved for siblings and spouses. Her voice echoes oddly over the long-distance line, so it seems as though she is interrupting herself as well as him, and she pauses between sentences, allowing herself to finish, before she carries on. 'He certainly didn't. He cared about telling a good story. A ripping yarn.' And then she adds, 'And say it was a heart attack. It's more romantic, isn't it? A heart breaking in Paris. A bit more poetic than a stroke in a budget hotel on the south-west coast.'

'Any other tips?' he asks, with heavy sarcasm. He is beginning to think that Mika is feeling guilty for her absence. Why else would she bother him so much on the actual day, interfering with the arrangements, nagging him about his speech; perhaps by making him busy at the funeral, she feels busy and involved herself, privately, if not publicly. When she first called him that morning, he was sure she had been crying; her voice had sounded hoarse, and she had defensively blamed it on a cold before he had even thought to comment on it.

'Just one more,' says Mika promptly, as though she had been waiting to be asked. 'Shakespeare's Sonnet Twenty-Nine. If you can't think of anything else. I think it might have amused him, a little.'

When she finally hangs up, he looks at the blank page in front of him, and the pen in his hand. He hears his toddler, Boo, playing in the next room. The children's DVD he picked out for Boo to watch has an irritating, high-pitched arrangement of classical music; it sounds electronic and plucked on gut, all at once. He has no idea what he is meant to write. Just write the truth, he tells himself. Just write anything. He makes a hesitant start. My father's name was . . . my father's name was . . . Well, the truth is that he had many names. He made his home in many places. He casually abandoned careers, families, wives. He made and lost fortunes carelessly. He was charming, and he was liked, but he wasn't always admired, or envied. His decline was frightening. He never raised his hand in anger, never felt grief, never told us that he loved us. He got away with it all, right until the end. And he is remembered, with anger, and grief. And love. Always love. It turns out that he is still getting away with it, even now.

'Abbu, can you fix it?' calls Boo from the doorway in his mother's Punjabi, his chunky legs very brown against white linen shorts. Zamir doesn't register what has been said at first – his own Punjabi isn't very good, he is still learning – and so his son repeats himself impatiently in English, adding pointedly, 'Look, it's broked.'

Zamir looks at the Stickle Brick car pulled in two in his son's hands, and corrects him automatically: 'You mean, it's broken, Munchkin.'

'I said that,' insists his son. 'It's broked.' Zamir takes the car, and slots the bricks back together. He is about to reach for his handkerchief, to wipe away the snot that seems to be permanently smeared on his son's upper lip, when Boo snatches the car back from him and stalks off stockily into the next room, without a thank-you or a goodbye, letting the door swing shut behind him. It reminds Zamir eerily of the times he was transferring money to his father, and how he too would hang up without a thank-you or a goodbye, sometimes when he was still mid-sentence. He feels guiltily relieved that his son shares no other traits with his paternal grandfather – that the child has neither charm nor appealing good looks. Zamir suddenly feels like a child himself, just as he did when he first heard the news of his father's death, broken to him with bumbling uncertainty by Mika, who had been called by the staff of the cheap hotel where his father had been staying. 'They say that he's gone, disappeared. They kept saying "*Il est disparu*",' she had reported. 'Dan says that could mean he's passed away, but I think it's more likely that he's just done a runner.' Her French

had not been good enough to fully comprehend the circumstances, and a nervous laugh had been threaded inappropriately
through her voice, as though she refused to believe the worst
could have happened, and was certain that their father was
simply up to his usual tricks. Even when Mika's husband had
called the hotel manager back, and cleared up the ambiguity of
the kindly meant euphemism, Zamir hadn't believed it either;
right up until the body arrived, and then he looked his father in
the face and realised that it was him after all. That there was no
last joke to be played on them, that he really hadn't burdened a
corpse with all his debts and gone skipping off into the
wilderness. At the sight of his father's slack face, the muscles
pulled to the side, his pitifully thin body, Zamir did something
he hadn't done since he was very young. He had dropped to his
knees, and prayed. And then he had buried his head in the
pillow of his arms on the floor of the mosque that had received
the casket, and cried out loud.

'Abbu,' trills Boo from the next room. 'It's broked again.'

Zamir sighs. 'I'll come in a minute, Munchkin,' he calls back.
Jilli is still out, spending the morning with her own ailing
parents; she has more pressing concerns. She seems to be in
agreement with Mika; to her mind, the living outrank the dead.
He knows that she is probably right, but still his head sinks to
the desk, his back hunched in defeat. He wishes he could hide
somewhere, under the table, behind the curtain. He wants to cry
again, to shout out loud, *My Daddy's Dead, don't you
understand, my Daddy's Dead*. He wants to blame his briefly
absent wife and all-too-present son for not understanding this,
but at the same time he doubts the sincerity of his sorrow, just
as all those years ago, as his mother had perceptively pointed
out, he had doubted the sincerity of his anger. He suspects that
he is simply feeling sorry for himself.

'Abbu! Ab-bu!' shouts Boo, practically howling now. 'I said

it's broked again. You need to fix it! Now! Now! Now!' He sounds more distressed over his Stickle Brick toy than anyone else seems to be over his recently deceased grandfather. A man he never met. A man who died writing a letter, which covered three pages of hotel stationery, in which he had minutely listed all his names and addresses for the last eighty-one years, all the homes, hotels and rented rooms, all the characters he had created, moved about like pawns on a chessboard, and somehow outlived. *Sunny Karam, 18 Garden Walk, Gulberg, Lahore, Pakistan, 1931.* The map of his life laid out for someone else to plot on a chart, a story for someone else to write. *Mike Cram, Carlton-Rose Hotel, Sahara Road, Las Vegas, USA, 1956.* Zamir has kept the letter in a clean transparent file; he has studied it, again and again, for some sort of clue, for inspiration, a hidden code in these waves of changing names, the dates set against exotic addresses. *Mehmet Khan, 5 Hamad El Sheikh, Cairo, Egypt, 1965.* As though it is a puzzle, a treasure hunt, and that it might somehow lead him to the real letter, buried in a steel box under an X, a last will and testament, the proper story, completed with a final declaration of love. *Miguel Caram, Hotel Costas, 21 Avenida Del Agua, Marbella, Spain, 1989.* Isn't there anything else you had to say to me? Isn't there anything else, thinks Zamir, that you had to say at all? *Mikhail Lee, Flat 147, The Highview, Victoria Avenue, Hong Kong, 2001.* The letter is unfinished, but Zamir has written his father's last address on a Post-it note, and stuck it to the plastic sleeve of the file. His father had made a habit of never telling his children his current address. *Maqil Karam, Hotel Leval, 92 Rue du Charpentier, Biarritz, France, 2012.*

'I'm coming,' Zamir calls out wearily to Boo. He and Jilli spoil their son. They try not to, but they can't help it. They reward his frequent tantrums with cuddles and treats, they instinctively say yes rather than no to anything he asks.

They want this boy to be happy, to give him the golden childhood that Zamir once imagined, and Jilli once had, but the more they give him, they more they give in to him, the less happy he seems to be. This is the only truth that is left. Zamir is a grown man, with a child of his own, and his father has gone and left him again, without saying goodbye. The funeral will just be a funeral, and everyone will play their expected parts. And then there will be another evening and another morning. There will be today, tomorrow and the day after that. His valediction will just be words, and will be forgotten as soon as they are said. Perhaps Mika is right; perhaps he should just say that his father died of a heart attack in Paris; perhaps he should read out a sonnet.

His name is being called again, plaintively, almost angrily by his son. He is an ordinary man, but at least he is needed. To protect and provide. To mend broken things. He has a wife and a child to do this for; he has an identity, he has a place on this planet. He should be happy with what he already has, and let this be enough. 'I'm coming,' he calls out once more, dropping his pen and letting it roll across the paper. He goes to the door, which gleams briefly around the edges, as if illuminated. He knows that there is light on the other side.

Acknowledgements

With thanks to:
My husband, Phil Richards; our boys, Jaan and Zaki; and our girls, Zarena and Alia.

My mother, Niluffer Farooki, and my sisters, Preeti Farooki and Kiron Farooki.

My editor, Imogen Taylor, and my agents, Clare Alexander and Ayesha Karim.

And with thanks to my father, Nasir Farooki (1929–2002), who intended to write a book called *All Gamblers Great and Small*, but never did; for all the strange and various journeys he took in life that helped inspire this novel, and for always being compelled to make things interesting, as gamblers do. Without him, I would have been a different sort of writer, and this would have been a different sort of book.

Roopa Farooki is the Ambassador for Relate's Family Counselling Service, a registered charity that provides advice, counselling and workshops to children, parents and families in need of support.

www.relate.org.uk